RELEASE ME

THE NEW HAVEN SERIES
BOOK 3

J.L. SEEGARS

※ Created with Vellum

For the hard hearts in search of a tender love. May it find you in time.

"The scar meant that I was stronger than what had tried to hurt me."

— JEANNETTE WALLS

AUTHOR NOTE

Please be aware that this story involves sensitive topics such as sexual assault (off page and not between the couple), domestic violence (not between the couple, in a brief flashback), passive suicidal ideation, sex work, sex trafficking, exploitation, homicide and drug abuse that, in one instance, is fatal.

While it is always my intention to provide a comprehensive list of potential triggers, you might find while reading that this list is incomplete. I urge you to consider your own health and well-being before diving into Nadia and Sebastian's story.

THE PLAYLIST

01./ shelter by Tori Kelly
02./ To Die For by Sam Smith
03./ Run Through Fire by Pink Sweat$
04./ You & I (Nobody in the world) by John Legend
05./ Proud by JoJo
06./ breathin by Ariana Grande
07./ After Tonight by Justin Nozuka
08./ The Few Things (with Charlotte Lawrence) by JP Saxe
09./ Kiss It Better by Rihanna
10./ Belong to You (feat. 6LACK) by Sabrina Claudio
11./ Partition by Beyoncé
12./ Snooze by SZA
13./ I Was Made for Loving You (feat. Ed Sheeran) by Tori Kelly

1

NADIA

God stopped answering my prayers years ago.

It took me too long to notice it—the way every hopeful utterance was met with silent indifference from an empty sky mocking me for daring to look up, for thinking there was anything waiting for me in the clouds besides raindrops that fell for the sole purpose of washing away my tears, invalidating their existence, and disappearing my pain.

But once I noticed, I stopped praying altogether.

Until tonight.

Tonight, the sky is clear. Dark and starless with not even a moon in sight, and I hope the absence of distractions will make it easier for me to be heard.

Tonight, I'm trapped in a car with a man who is under the influence of every illegal substance known to man, traveling almost a hundred miles per hour, headed straight for a tree that was standing long before God and I became estranged.

Tonight, I'm thinking of my mother and how she used to say everyone prays in the end, and I'm wondering if she prayed when she knew death was imminent.

I bet she did.

She probably prayed for me. That I would have a good life even though the only family I'd ever known was trapped on a doomed tube of metal falling from the sky.

Maybe she prayed for herself. Maybe she held my father's hand and prayed to live.

I don't know what that's like. Wanting life. Craving survival.

We take the curve, and the car spins out. He presses the brake and curses. Wild blue eyes with blown pupils swing in my direction, begging me for something. Reassurance. Direction. I don't know. Whatever it is he wants, I can't give because I'm preoccupied with the foreign flavor of hope on my tongue.

The tree is a hairsbreadth away. Burnt rubber scents the air, and the quiet prayer becomes a chant that bursts out of me.

Fierce.

Desperate.

Final.

"God, please just let me die."

2

NADIA

The aching in my shoulder indicated the arrival of a June thunderstorm hours before a raindrop fell from the sky. When the clouds decide to open up, I'm a full city block away from where I need to be, and I sprint—with the only copy of my resume I could afford to print over my head—down the sidewalk to try and make it to the doors of the grandiose building housing Cerros Hotel before the white blouse and black pencil skirt I splurged on for this job interview are soaked through.

Splurge.

If I wasn't so busy dodging rain drops the size of my fist, I'd laugh at the word. At the way it suggests that I, a desperate girl in a strange city running from more than the inconvenience of mercurial clouds, have two red cents to rub together let alone use to indulge in fashion-based luxury.

In truth, these clothes aren't worth the money I paid for them or the energy I expended haggling with the sales clerk in the thrift store around the corner from the roach motel I'm staying at to get the price down. I'd used the five bucks I saved to buy the first set of heels I've worn since I climbed out of the wreckage of an accident that should have claimed my life and ran like I wanted to live.

Now I'm running again, but it's not for my life. Well, at least not directly. I won't die if I don't make it to Cerros in time to interview for the waitress position I saw advertised online when I was browsing the job boards in the library. Not today at least. Maybe in a few weeks when the money I stole off of the dead man whose unseeing eyes still appear in my dreams runs out. I've been careful with it. As careful as I can be when the motel I'm staying in doesn't have a working fridge or a stove, and I have to eat out for every meal. As careful as I can be when I had to set half of the scarce amount aside, so I can buy a bus ticket to somewhere far away if *he* ever finds me. As careful as a person can be when what you have wasn't enough to begin with and you've spent months without a job because being anywhere that isn't your crappy motel room feels unsafe and you have no valuable skills outside of years of trading your body for money that never, ever touched your hands.

My chest burns, and there's acid churning in my stomach. Lazy waves made of toxic waste lap at my ribs, caressing the shame that carved itself into my bones the first time I was sold to a stranger to pay for someone else's debts. It cuts right through the meager meal I had for breakfast—two saltines and the watered down remnants of a cup of sweet tea I had with dinner the night before—and unleashes every anxious thought wrapped around my gut.

I can't do this.

I don't belong here.

I'm a joke. A whore. A walking, talking waste of space.

Those words aren't mine. They didn't originate in my mind, and they've never crossed my lips, but they belong to me in a way that nothing else has since my parents died. More than the clothes on my back or the soaked and slippery patent leather pumps on my feet that make my entrance into the nicest building I've walked into since I made New Haven my home more of a sliding stumble than the graceful, confident stride I'd pictured in my head.

I'm all flailing arms and quiet curses as I gain my footing under the watchful and curious gazes of the crowd of hotel guests and the staff members gathered in the lobby. By default, a wobbly smile curves my lips as I straighten my blouse and pull my rapidly disintegrating resume to my chest. The ink is starting to run, and I hold it gingerly as I make my way up to the concierge's desk where the woman behind it looks like she's already done with the conversation we have yet to have.

"Interviews for the Cerros rooftop are happening in the conference room down the hall to your left," she says, tilting her head to the right to indicate the hallway just over her shoulder. Her eyes never leave her computer screen.

I wish it stung that she is being so dismissive, but I prefer it this way. When people look through you, they don't take the time to look *at* you, to mistreat you, to abuse you. I've spent more of my life than I care to admit on the other end of callous glares and angry hands. So long that parts of my body still grind and creak to tell the tales.

Invisible wounds.

Hidden bruises.

Fractured bones that never healed correctly and ache whenever it's going to rain.

"Thank you." She's still not looking at me, so I don't bother smiling before turning away from the desk. I do wince though when I realize I have to turn back around to ask for information she didn't give me. "Can you point me to the nearest bathroom?"

Now she is looking at me, and although her facial expression remains neutral, I can tell by the way her eyes trail up and down my body, she doesn't approve of my being here in this immaculate building where the floors are gold veined marble and the fragrance being pumped through the vents is one of a kind, custom tailored to this space and the luxurious aesthetic my appearance is a direct affront to. After what feels like a long silence, but is really only a few seconds, she responds.

"There's a restroom back near the entrance, Miss…" she trails off, brows lifting in a silent order for me to fill in the gap she's left.

"Hendrix," I provide, rolling my shoulders back and tipping my chin up so the name doesn't sound as weird as it feels on my tongue.

"Right, well, good luck, Miss Hendrix."

"Uh, thanks."

It doesn't take me long to find the bathroom, which is overflowing with women who are here for the same reason I am. They stand in clusters of expensive clothing and cloying scents, crowding each other out, competing for space in front of the mirror to fix their makeup and hair. I don't bother looking at my reflection because I know that whatever I see there is a problem I don't have the tools or patience to fix.

Instead, I head over to the furthest wall where there's an unoccupied hand dryer and start it up, holding my resume underneath the rush of hot air and trying not to think about how my mother spent my entire childhood forbidding me from using one because of how unsanitary they are.

Once certain the paper won't disintegrate the moment it leaves my hands, I leave the bathroom on the hunt for the conference room. I'm in the middle of the lobby when I see the rip. Staring at me. Mocking me. Laughing at me for thinking the sparse lines on the crumbling page would be enough to make me belong in a place like this. Tears born of doubt blur my vision, but for some reason my feet start to move again. A wisp of determination my father used to say I got from my mother carrying me forward without my permission, with no thought or care for the people moving through the lobby around me, only stopping when they have no choice but to because my body has collided with an unmovable force.

"Shit." I stumble back. "Sorry."

"Don't be sorry, be attentive."

The voice—dark, sensual with a hint of reproach weaved between the threads of a gravelly timbre—cut through the trance of self-doubt pooling in my gut and demand I turn my attention to the large man looming over me. Somewhere in the depths of my mind I find myself appreciating the subtle notes of what I'm sure is an expensive cologne. Only men with more money than morals spend thousands of dollars on scents you can barely smell.

The notes I do pick up are like his voice. Dark and elegant, spiced with hints of rum and coffee. Burnt barrels of cedar wood steeped in sugar cane and decadence. And now that I'm looking at his face—the two thick slashes of dark brows over turbulent champagne pools, a broad nose leading to full lips turned down in an angry, bewildered line that require retribution for my lack of attention—I've decided the scent fits him.

My head snaps back as if I've been struck, and my hands turn into fists. *"Excuse me?"*

"Alert. Awake. Watchful. Observant. Perceptive. Vigilant. *Focused.*" He crosses long, muscled arms across his broad chest, and I watch the seams holding the expensive graphite gray fabric of his suit together stretch. They're stressed like I am, bewildered by the audacity of the man demanding more from us when we've already given all we can. "Be any of those things, but don't be sorry. I have no use for apologies."

"You have no—" I can't even bring myself to repeat his obnoxious words, and his lips quirk at my hesitance. "Who talks like that? Never mind, I have to go. Once again, *sorry* for bumping into you."

I step around the imposing lines of his frame, moving carefully to avoid bumping into anyone else. The swarm of women who were occupying the bathroom earlier have emerged looking, I'm sure, the same as they did when they entered it, so the lobby has gotten busier and louder.

So loud I don't hear him call out to me the first time, or the second. It's his hand wrapping around my arm that forces my gaze from the hall leading to the conference room and back to his face. He rounds me, releasing my arm when my features telegraph my desire to not be manhandled on my way to a job interview.

"You dropped this."

He extends his hand, and in it is the piece of paper I'm hinging my whole future on. The piece of paper I didn't even realize I'd dropped. There are shoe prints on it, and the small rip I convinced myself no one would notice is a full blown tear now. Horror splashes across my features in that way it tends to do when you refuse to truly accept its presence. In repeated splatters, in rude and intrusive increments you tell yourself mean nothing until the splatters turn into torrents and you have no choice but to accept that you're no longer looking at the rain because you're in the middle of the storm.

I attempt to take it from him, but my fingers stall mid-air, unable to fully commit to holding destruction in my hand. He reaches for me again, wrapping thick fingers around my wrist and forcing the tattered page into my palm.

Our eyes meet, and his gaze rests somewhere between impatience and pity.

"It's probably for the best."

I blink rapidly to dispel the tears of frustration trying to pool in the corners of my eyes. "What?"

"You don't have any experience as a waitress."

At no point during this exchange did I see him look at my resume, but his comment—which just so happens to touch on another one of my insecurities surrounding this damn job—suggests that he's read it in its entirety. I mean, that wouldn't be hard considering how fucking short it is. I'd been too scared to go into detail about anything for fear that someone would look too closely.

"I don't need experience to serve rich assholes expensive food or wine they don't appreciate and can't even pronounce."

What I don't say is that I've been serving rich assholes for years now. On my back. On my knees. On their laps while their friends watch. Taking orders and handing out plates won't be hard, compli-cated or demeaning, and that's enough for me.

The corner of his mouth twitches, and I can't tell if it's some kind of nervous tick or the start of a condescending smile meant for me.

"Guess we'll find out, won't we, Miss. Hendrix?"

He sticks around long enough to soak up my shocked expression and leave me with the distinct impression of his superiority. Then he's gone, walking back towards the entrance where he was heading before my apparent lack of attentiveness interrupted his day. I watch him go, noting the luscious sweep of locs fashioned into a ponytail at the nape of his neck. They hang past his shoulders, landing somewhere along the broad span of the top of his back. He doesn't turn back to look at me, which makes me feel like he found me as unremarkable as my resume. It stings even though it shouldn't, even though since the day of the accident I've relished in the absence of the male gaze.

"Interviews have already started," the woman from the front desk calls out to me. Her tone is flat, censorious, and exactly what I need to get moving again.

The hallway outside of the conference room is packed and buzzing with energy. I find an empty seat that keeps me on the edge of everything, far from the women who are here because they believe a job at a high-end restaurant will lead to them marrying one of the wealthy men who frequent it and further still from the men who think this job will put them in a position to sleep with their female co-workers. While everyone talks, trading stories about the places they've worked before and what it would mean for them to get to work for some guy named Sebastian Adler—I remain quiet, channeling all my energy into staying in my seat. Into pushing down the words of the man in the lobby that told me something I already knew to be true: I'm being stupid.

This plan to run and hide and try to carve out a new life somewhere in between is stupid. Trying to get a job as a waitress when all I am, all I have been since the day of my college graduation, is what the monster I'm running from made me.

Worthless fucking whore.

That was his favorite line. His go-to. The one he reached for when he wrapped his fingers around my throat or stole my breath with kicks to my ribs. When I was with him, in the grips of his unending terror and threats, I managed to convince myself his words weren't true, but here, in the real world, they are my gospel. A toxic deluge that has marked me, stained me, made it so nothing—the clothes, the freedom, the luck the women I met at the shelter in Florida told me I have—is enough to make me into something different, something better.

Even the man in the lobby knew it. He sniffed me out, marked me as ignominious within seconds of knowing me. And it's the recollection of the pity in his eyes when he looked down at me that pushes me to my feet, convincing me to go home and save myself the embarrassment of walking into this interview with a torn resume and broken pride.

Everyone in the hall turns to look at me, but only the woman at the open door of the conference room addresses me directly. "Nadia Hendrix?"

"Yes, but I'm—" I pause, unsure of what I'm about to say because I don't know whether I'm going or coming.

The woman looks down at the clipboard in her hand and then back up to me. She's got a kind face, but her eyes are flared with panic and annoyance. "I have at least thirty other interviews to get through today, Miss. Hendrix, let's move it along."

She coaxes me forward with a sweep of her hand that makes someone behind me snicker, and then I have no choice but to move towards her, stepping into the room where it feels like more than my immediate financial security will be decided.

3

SEBASTIAN

She was surprised I knew her name.

I was surprised I could make it out underneath the ragged, torn edges of the cheap paper it was printed on. Even more surprising is the way my brain has chosen to hold on to it. To her wide, soulful eyes with sadness shuddered behind the puddles of whiskey that are her irises. To the way her lip curled with disdain when she called my future customers rich assholes and, in the same breath and with no additional words, suggested I was one of them.

She was right about that.

Growing up as an Adler, a family known for having its hand in everything from shipping to entertainment and media, means I grew up rich, but it was building my own business and constantly having to prove I was more than Everett Adler's rebellious older son that made me an asshole. My brothers would probably say I was one long before I started Adler Holdings, Inc. That might be true but I'm certain walking into meetings regarding the purchase of multi-million dollar buildings and seeing faces fall because I was there to represent my own interests and not that of my father made it worse.

Back then, everyone wanted to be associated with the institution that is Adleron Enterprises—our family business—but not the burgeoning empire I was building brick by brick. While they'd kill for the chance to point to a building housing a new media imprint and brag about personally negotiating the terms with a titan in multiple industries, they didn't want anything to do with the man who studied at the titan's feet. Every purchase, every negotiation, every contract was a fight. A fight to demonstrate my competency and skill. A fight to step outside of my father's large and looming shadow. A fight to prove I wasn't just some trust fund kid blowing his money on a feckless plan that would never be successful.

Now that I have proven myself, to my father—who has always been supportive despite being disappointed in not being able to pass the mantle on to me—and everyone else, I'm comfortable admitting that I'm rich all the time and only an asshole when I need to be. And today in the lobby with a stranger named Nadia Hendrix wasn't one of them. In fact, I'd venture to say I was doing Nadia a kindness—something the wariness sprinkled across her features told me she hasn't had a lot of in her life. Something any one who works for me will tell you I don't usually have the time or inclination to extend. Truthfully, I don't do kindness in my professional life. I do respect and clear expectations. I do wages and benefits well above the industry standard, but I don't do kindness.

Except for Nadia, I had.

As I walk into my parent's home, late for our weekly lunch because of the train wreck of a conversation in the lobby, I tell myself it doesn't matter if I behaved abnormally with her because the instructions I left with the hiring team not to make an offer to anyone without serving experience mean I'll probably never see her again.

"You're late." The words come from the end of the long hallway that leads into the large, open concept kitchen and living room my parents always host us in. I'm in the middle of toeing off my shoes when they find me, and I look up to see my youngest brother, Luca, walking towards me. Even though I'm the oldest, Luca is the one who looks the part. He's taller and more dense than I am with a bald head and a thick, black beard that stands out against his chestnut skin and makes him look much older than his twenty-eight years of age.

"Kiss my ass." I pass by him, shoulder checking him just to remind him he's *my* little brother not the other way around.

"Swearing in your mother's house," he tisks playfully, dogging my steps the way he always did when we were kids. He thought being the same size as me meant he could go everywhere I went. When he surpassed me in height and weight, it wasn't a thought anymore, it was a hard truth only he abided by. "Thought you knew better than that."

I roll my eyes. "Grow up, Luca."

"Is that all we're gonna get from you today? Three word sentences and a permanent scowl?"

"You can have my foot up your ass too, if you'd like."

"Sebastian Adler! Watch your mouth." My mother's admonishment reaches my ears before my feet carry me into the kitchen where she's mixing a vinaigrette to dress the salad in the bowl in front of her and wearing an apron that says 'Kiss the Cook.' Her umber skin is covered in a fine sheen of sweat that tells me the meal she's made is as extravagant as she is beautiful. I round the counter while Luca drops down in a seat on the other side of the island and wrap my arms around my mother, not caring about the way the wild cloud of salt and pepper curls on her head tickle my face. She hums softly but continues her work, pouring the dressing over the greens while offering her cheek up for me to kiss.

"Sorry for cursing, Mom," I murmur against the side of her face, breathing in her scent. She smells like she always smell, like home and this kitchen she insists on cooking every meal in even though she could easily afford to hire a full time chef and kitchen staff.

"No, you're not. You're just sorry I heard you."

"Yeah, you're right."

She shoos me away with a laugh, urging me to take a seat at the counter next to Luca's annoying ass. He's on his phone now, scrolling through social media. It takes me a second to realize that all the photos on the feed he's looking through belong to the same woman.

"New girlfriend?" I ask, making a show of appearing interested.

I'm really not. Luca is always on the hunt for someone new. He goes through women faster than my rooftop restaurant goes through servers. In the year since I hired my cousin Vince to manage the restaurant, our turnover rate has more than doubled. Usually, I don't work with family, but I hired him because my aunt Adrienne—Mom's twin sister—asked me to help Vince out after he moved back home from California. Since he had experience managing restaurants, at least according to his resume, I took him on, hoping him running the rooftop would create less problems for me, not more.

Since I brought him on, there have been a slew of server resignations leading to repeated searches to replace the people we lost. I'm over it, and although Adrienne is my favorite aunt, I will happily fire her son if I find out he's the one fucking with my bottom line.

Luca closes the app immediately, throwing me an annoyed look. "Mind your business."

"Weren't you just in my business like five seconds ago?"

"I was commenting on your lack of punctuality, not asking questions about your personal life."

Mom gives an exasperated sigh. "Are you two going to bicker all afternoon?"

I punch Luca in the shoulder, laughing when he winces. "Nope. We'll be on our best behavior." I hold up two of my fingers in a gesture that's half salute and half surrender. "Scout's honor."

"You were never a scout," Andreas says as he enters the kitchen through the patio doors that lead to the back yard. Of all three Adler brothers, Andreas is the quietest. He's also the smartest, in that nerdy, bookish way that's revered in the academic world he's chosen to sink his teeth into. People are always impressed when they hear he's the youngest department chair at New Haven University, but when I look at him all I see is the kid who lost his two front teeth on Sunday night and participated in a spelling bee on Monday morning, lisping his way to victory one snaggle toothed smile at a time.

"Tell that to the picture of me in a Cub Scout's uniform that's in the living room."

Andreas rolls his eyes, planting his palms on the edge of the island closest to me. "You attended one meeting and never earned a badge."

"But I did take the Scout Oath."

"You read it off a piece of paper they sent home with you," Luca says. "I don't think that counts."

"Sure it does."

Before either of my brothers can respond, footsteps start to ring out in the hall. The long, heavy strides are ones I know like the back of my hand. I grew up listening for them, training myself to know what they sound like coming from any direction, on any surface. Not because I feared the man whose presence they foretold, but because I knew the moment he entered the room the clock would start ticking, counting down the minutes, or sometimes seconds, before he had to move on to the next thing. The next meeting, the next business trip, the next problem that would demand his attention and take him away from me.

On instinct, my spine straightens and my thoughts start to race. I sift through everything that's happened since last week's lunch when I saw him, trying to find something worthy of the fleeting moment I'll have where his attention is all on me. The only thing that comes to mind is Nadia Hendrix. No matter how many times I push the image of her away, she keeps coming back in vivid detail I didn't process in the moment but my brain is desperate to recall now. The deep hue of her ebony skin. The satin, black perfection of the long tresses hanging down her back and over her shoulder, flirting with the lines of the button-up that was slightly too big for her. A detail that makes me wonder how she'd look in clothes tailored specifically for the lines of her slim, but curvy frame.

When my father walks into the room, I'm trying to think about anything but how tall she is. How when she bumped into me the top of her head had come to my collar bone and when she looked up at me with those eyes, she barely had to tilt her head back at all. I'm failing.

"You boys should be helping your mother with lunch, not sitting around bickering while she does all the work." Everett Adler doesn't speak, he *booms*. His voice is a clap of thunder that inspires action. A strike of lightening that calls stillness in any form complacency and warns you that complacent is the worst thing you can be in this world. So before he's even done talking, Luca, Andreas and I are moving, grabbing bowls, serving platters and whatever else is waiting to make its way to the table while Dad walks over to Mom and gives her a kiss on the lips.

I've always been under the impression that my parents are in love, but the sight of them kissing is rare. In fact, I can count on one hand the number of times I've seen them engage in public displays of affection, and I won't need all of my fingers to do it. My mother's giggles follow me and my brothers to the dining room, and we all share a look laced with the same confusion.

"Are they really making out in the middle of the day like teenagers?" Andreas asks, his clean shaven face crumpling into a frown.

"It's called being in love, you should try it some time, Dre." This smart remark comes from the final Adler sibling and the only daughter. We all turn to see our little sister Zoe sauntering into the dining room with nothing in her hands except a phone. Typical. Dad has always had a soft spot for her, which means she doesn't have to lift a manicured finger if she doesn't want to, and the only time she appears to want to is when she's doing hair down at her salon.

Her entrance prompts a quick setting of the table, so we can all take turns pulling her into bear hugs and kissing the top of her head. When Andreas hugs her, he sneaks in a few tickles that make her squirm and giggle like she used to when she was a baby. Her laughter and desperate shrieks, courtesy of Andreas' need for revenge, is the soundtrack playing when our parents join us in the dining room. Dad pulls out Mom's chair, and we all take that as our cue to sit down as well.

Once we're all settled, Dad splits an approving gaze between the four of us and smiles. "Thank you all for being here."

Luca glances at me, silently asking me what the fuck is going on because like the public kisses, my father's outward expressions of gratitude are rare. I shrug because despite being the most like him, I have no idea what goes on in my father's head most of the time. I've spent my life trying to figure him out, to make sense of the way he's both completely integrated in our family yet apart from us at the same time.

"You're welcome, Daddy." Zoe beams from her seat beside Mom, and we all chime in, offering various versions of the same response.

Mom claps her hands. "Everybody dig in!"

While we fix our plates and pass the dishes filled with food around, she gives us a detailed breakdown of what we're about to eat. By the time I take my first bite of the sandwich she made to go with the salad she was dressing when I arrived, I know that the chicken on it was raised on a free range farm and that the spread on both sides of the toasted ciabatta bread has roma tomatoes, calabrian chiles, garlic, basil and olive oil in it. Everything is delicious, as usual, and we all are sure to let her know that her efforts are appreciated.

"Mom, can you send me the recipe for this sandwich? I think it could fit well on the lunch menu for the rooftop during the summer."

"Sure, sweetheart," she answers, taking a sip of water from her glass. "How are things with the restaurant? You're not working your cousin too hard are you? He said he wanted to come to lunch today, but he couldn't because you had him running interviews."

I wipe my mouth with a napkin and push my plate away. Vince is such a pain in the ass. Of course, he's on the phone whining to my mother about me making him solve a problem he created.

"The restaurant is fine."

Dad raises a brow, immediately noticing that my answer is incomplete. "And Vincent?"

My jaw clenches. Dad is only pushing because he's hoping I'll finally admit he was right when he told me not to hire Vince. Avoiding having to cede that fact to him is part of the reason why my annoying, weasel of a cousin still has a job.

"Vince is good, Dad."

"Liar," Luca says, coughing in his hand in a horribly executed attempt to hide the word while Andreas gives me a look that says I should tell our parents the truth. My brothers and I are close, so they've heard me air my grievances about Vince on more than one occasion. Like Dad, they were both team keep Vince out of your business. I was the fool who let Mom and Aunt Adrienne guilt me with their matching puppy dog eyes over a home cooked meal.

Dad sits back in his seat, eyes trained on my face like he's trying to suss out the lie I haven't even told yet. "Why are you hiring again?"

I shrug, hating the way his question makes me feel like a kid again and completely rethinking the time in the kitchen when I was wishing for his attention. "We're just experiencing some growing pains, getting rid of the people who aren't able to keep up with the demand."

There's no need to admit that I don't know why people are quitting, that I've been too busy working on plans for the Cerros resort along the coast of Santa Monica to get to the bottom of it. Dad wouldn't understand my confusion or approve of my distraction. He'd give me a well-intentioned speech about how there's nothing happening in any of the businesses he owns that he's not aware of. He opens his mouth to respond, but Mom stops him with a hand on his shoulder, changing the subject effortlessly.

"Talia called me yesterday. She said she's coming to town."

At the mention of my ex-wife's name, all of my siblings perk up. They all love Talia, and every time she comes to visit, they each drop everything they're doing to be available when she inevitably calls and ropes them into some random adventure.

"When?" Zoe asks.

"At the end of next month," I say, shaking my head because her brown eyes are already alight with excitement and I don't even want to know what the two of them get into when Talia is in town.

Andreas lifts a brow at me. "What's she coming for this time? Business or pleasure?"

"You know Tally," Luca replies even though no one is talking to him. "Probably a little bit of both."

I glare at the two of them, and they laugh, making me regret the conversation we had last year where I confirmed their suspicions that Talia and I still hook up from time to time. We couldn't make our marriage work, mainly because we're both inflexible assholes who refuse to be wrong about anything, but we've always been good at business…and pleasure.

"Business. She says she wants to run some things by me concerning the resorts in Antigua and Tulum."

Both of my brothers smirk, but it's Andreas who responds. "And she couldn't just send it in an email?"

I asked that same question when Talia sent me her travel itinerary. We'd already had our annual fuck fest, as Luca and Andreas liked to call it, when I flew to Antigua in April, so we aren't due to see each other in person until next year. Whatever she has to say must be too important or personal to be put in an email.

"I guess not."

4

NADIA

Normally, I'd never take a meal from the people who just refused to offer me a job, but there's nothing normal about my life these days. So here I am, sitting at the bar inside the Cerros hotel, scarfing down the very food I was just told I wasn't good enough to serve.

Okay, maybe those weren't their exact words, but that's all I heard when Regina, the interview coordinator, looked between me and my torn resume and said, "We're looking for someone with a bit more serving experience."

I wanted to slap her.

I wanted to slap me.

I wanted to slap the asshole from the lobby who told me I shouldn't waste my time with the interview because I didn't meet the basic job requirements.

"Clearly he didn't know about the free food," I mutter, taking another sip from the glass of Chianti I ordered to go with my Margherita pizza. The smooth red liquid hits my tongue in a rush of black cherry and plum mixed with subtle notes of cedar, sage, sweet tobacco and vanilla, and I close my eyes to hold back the hum of appreciation rising in my chest with nostalgia hot on its heels. The first wine I ever tasted was a Chianti. I was fourteen years old with a wine obsession sparked from a being raised on a vineyard and a father who would give me anything I wanted including a sip of a Chianti Classico while we ate pasta in the Italian town where the formula for it was defined. My mother looked on with loving disapproval as I brought the glass to my lips, and she doubled over in a fit of laughter when I coughed and gagged because it was gross.

In the years since their deaths, I've thought of that day often. Recalling the way the Tuscan sun loved their brown skin and made the natural streaks of brown in Mom's hair pop while revealing the star bursts of gold in Dad's eyes. Those thoughts always lead to other memories that I unpack with an ache in my chest. Sometimes, if I close my eyes tight enough, I can still hear the slight twang of my father's Texas roots in my brain's sad recollection of his voice or remember the weight of my mother's arms wrapped around my body the last time she hugged me. There are so many good memories to choose from, images of a beautiful life frozen inside the warped structure of my mind, it should feel good to remember them, but it doesn't. Because every time I do, I'm left wondering what my parents would think if they could see their daughter now. If they would love this angry, desperate, anxious version of the little girl they raised who hates them for dying and leaving her with nothing.

Another sip of wine washes the bitter taste of grief out of my mouth, and I force myself to follow it up with a bite of pizza to keep it from going straight to my head. Since the accident, I haven't had a single drop of alcohol. Mostly because I've been too afraid to not be in full control of my faculties in case trouble came knocking at my door, but also because I haven't been able to afford anything I would actually want to drink. Being on the run is expensive, which is why I needed this job. Thoughts of my dire financial situation make my head heavy and my shoulders tight. I set my near empty wine glass down and pull in a deep sigh, hoping to expel some of the tension building in my muscles.

"Chin up, doll face, it can't be all bad." The sleazy voice comes from the man taking a seat on the barstool to my left. I turn to him with eyes narrowed into slits and a lip curled with disgust that has nothing to do with his looks because he's handsome in that Jesse Williams / Michael Ealey kind of way that made the girls I used to work with swoon immediately. They'd fall all over themselves to spend the night staring at the perplexing contrast of blue or green eyes against melanated skin only to find that the man underneath was never as beautiful on the inside as he was out.

"It can, and now that you're here, it has."

He grins, baring all of his straight-white teeth. "Feisty, I like that."

"Please stop talking to me."

"I'm Vince." He holds his hand out, completely ignoring my request to be left alone.

"I don't care."

My tone can only be described as nasty and dismissive, but still his smile doesn't falter. Eyes the color of sea glass do a slow sweep of my features, and he tilts his head to the side. "You look familiar."

Now I'm looking at him with renewed interest and panic sliding down my spine. I chose to try to build a life in New Haven because its distance from California— and the people in Los Angeles who prob- ably wish me dead—made me feel like the chances of seeing anyone from my old life were small.

Negligible.

Basically non-existent.

That's what I'd told myself even as I stashed a go bag with a thou- sand dollars in the bathroom ceiling of the motel I've been calling home for a month and some change, and that's what I have been telling myself every day since. And until now, it felt like the truth, not a delu- sion I was force feeding myself to make getting up and facing another day easier.

A slight quiver tries to work its way up my throat, but I push it back down, refusing to let it undermine my confidence. "No, I don't."

"Yeah, you definitely do." Vince rubs at his chin, and every second that passes causes my heartbeat to increase two fold. By the time he snaps his fingers, recognition dawning over his face, I'm close to passing out. "I know! You were in the interviews earlier right? For the server job?"

Relief hits me in a wave strong enough to knock me off the barstool I'm sitting on. My entire body relaxes, and the absence of tension in my muscles is so disconcerting I almost smile at Vince.

"Oh, yeah I was. I don't remember seeing you, though."

"You sure about that?" His brow lifts, and I can see his confidence building with every additional word I give him. Excitement has caused his pupils to dilate, and he's leaning towards me now, just slightly invading my space. "I was sitting at the back. As the manager, it's my job to get a feel for the incoming talent."

The salacious gleam in his eyes makes my stomach turn. Who let a man like this be in charge of anything, let alone a group of workers usually made up of vulnerable women?

"As the manager, wouldn't it be your job to be *running* the interviews, not observing them?" Images of a flustered and overwhelmed Regina flash in my mind, and even though I'm pissed she refused to hire me, I feel bad that she's working with a man who's not just a creep, but a lazy one at that.

"I tend to favor a hands off approach to managing." He inches closer, pitching his voice low. "Unless, of course, you prefer something more hands on."

"I'd *prefer* for this conversation to end."

For the first time since we started talking, he falters. It's a look I haven't had the pleasure of seeing on many men in my life because I've never been able to say no this many times. Actually, I've never been able to say no at all.

"Listen—" He starts, but the rest of his sentence is cut off by the loud tinkling of laughter coming from the group of women who've just walked into the room. They crowd around the bar, taking up all the empty seats and rambling off drink orders the bartender takes down with ease. The ring leader—a short and ridiculously curvy bombshell with skin the color of mahogany and full pouty lips that are painted red—sets her sights on Vince and me almost immediately, abandoning her group of friends to saunter over to us on thick legs that don't so much as quiver despite the mile high heels she's wearing. The hem of her dress rides up her thighs, and Vince, the creep that he is, licks his lips as she settles herself between us. She smells like lemons and sugar, and her hair is a big, blonde cloud of curls that waves her scent around as she looks between the two of us.

In the silence her presence has caused to settle between us, I study her profile and Vince's statuesque features, trying to determine if I'm about to be put in the middle of a lover's quarrel because of a man I didn't want to talk to in the first place.

"Vincent," she says, her voice dripping with sweetness as she places a hand with nails so long they can only be described as claws on his arm. "Are you harassing this poor girl?" She doesn't wait for him to answer, turning to me to get her answer instead. "Is he harassing you?"

I don't hesitate to respond. "Yep."

"Oh, come on!" Vince exclaims, glaring at me like I've done him wrong. "I was just asking you how your interview went."

She ignores him, keeping eyes the color of honey trained on my face."Please don't tell me he used the line about his hands on management style on you."

Judging by the way Vince is shifting in his seat, I can tell my honest answers are digging him into some kind of hole with this woman, but I don't care. "He sure did."

With my confirmation, she swings her head back in his direction, sending more of her citrus and saccharine scent floating up my nose. I watch with undisguised interest as she leans towards him, placing her lips at his ear and whispering something that makes his eyes go wide and his chestnut skin take on a slight blush. When she pulls back, Vince slides off of his barstool and leaves without so much as a glance my way. The woman takes his seat and angles her body in my direction with a triumphant smile on her round face.

"What did you say to him?" I ask, wishing I had those magic words five minutes ago.

She shrugs and gives me a half smile. "Does it matter? I got him to go away, which is what you wanted."

"How did you know I wanted him to go away."

"Because no woman ever talks to Vince willingly."

Her tone is so matter of fact, it surprises a laugh out of me. "I can see why. He's a creep."

"A total creep," she agrees, lifting her hand to get the bartender's attention. "Can I have a Jack and Coke, please? Make it cherry Coke if you have it, and get us another one of whatever—"

She glances at me, and for the second time today, I supply my name. "Nadia."

"Nadia," she repeats. "Another one of whatever Nadia is having."

The bartender nods his confirmation from the other end of the bar where the rest of the women who came in with my own personal Wonder Woman are keeping him busy. Now that I'm no longer stunned by their looks, I'm able to take in their outfits, noticing that they're all dressed like her, tight dresses or skirts, sky high heels and nails long enough to make you question how they function on a daily basis. My heart thumps in my chest as the group of strangers, including the woman next to me, becomes familiar. Known to me in a way that only the women I left behind when I escaped my old life are known to me.

It doesn't take a sex worker to know a sex worker. Anyone can spot them if they know what they're looking for, but it does take a sex worker, former or current, to know a happy one. To know one who chose this life and who was forced into it. Out of all the girls Beau— my abuser, my trafficker, my own private hell right here on Earth—had working under the escort service he built on my back, I was the only one who didn't choose the path we were all on together. I'd watch girls get ready for their dates, jealous of how empowered they felt while I came back from every outing feeling small, dirty, *used*.

Much like the girls I left behind, the ones in front of me are in the life by choice. It's evident in the way they carry themselves, in the easy conversations they have with each other and the absence of shame in the air when they pay for their food and drinks with money they earned doing things that make me cringe when I think of them.

"I'm Desiree," the girl beside me says, sliding me the glass of Chianti she bought for me.

I accept the glass with a brittle smile. "Thank you, Desiree. For the wine and for whatever you said to Vince to make him go away."

"You're welcome." She clinks her tumbler against my wine glass, her red lips curving up into an endearing grin. "Cheers, to alcohol and empty threats!"

"Cheers."

I take another sip of my wine and try not to look like I'm wondering when she's going to leave to go back over to her friends. It's not that I want to be rid of her, I just don't want her to feel obligated to spend any more of her time or money on me.

"So, Nadia, where are you from?"

"Oh, um, all over."

She takes a long swig of her drink, swallowing before pulling a face that tells me how unsatisfactory she finds my answer. "Wow, what a specific answer."

Her sarcasm makes me think of Bianca. The only one of Beau's girls I actually thought of as a friend. She was a smart ass too, and the memory of the first time she called me out on my bullshit is the only reason why I offer Desiree a small bit of truth.

"Texas. I was born in Texas." *But not raised.* I leave that part out because she doesn't need to know I've spent more time in New Haven than the state I was born in. Desiree studies me over the rim of her glass for a long while, like she's deciding if she wants to spend any more time with a liar.

"Anyone ever tell you that you're kind of elusive?"

"Nope. Everyone I know says I'm an open book."

She laughs, drawing the attention of everyone in the room and revealing the gap between her two front teeth as she places her hand on my leg. "You're lucky you're so pretty, Nadia, it makes it easy to forgive the fact that you're full of shit."

Red flags the size of the state I've never actually stepped foot in go up in my mind, and for the second time today, I want to slap myself. I'm not sure how I didn't see it coming. After I clocked her, I should have expected it. All the signs were there. The fake rescue from Vince to start the conversation and garner trust. Buying me a drink to keep me talking. The sudden sense of familiarity followed by an unearned declaration of friendship.

She's trying to recruit me.

God, how could I be so fucking stupid? I fell right into her trap even though I know it's not uncommon for traffickers to send out women to bring them more girls to put to work.

"I don't do that type of work." The words spill out of my mouth and land between me and Desiree in a messy heap of shame and judgment. Her brows pull together into a tight, furrowed line of confusion and offense. She sits back, taking her hand off of my leg and giving me a nasty look that pulls the rest of my thoughts from my head without my permission. "That's what's happening here, right? You're trying to recruit me to come and work for your boss?"

Everything I've said to her in the last few seconds has offended her, that much is clear by the way her features have yet to relax, but she seems especially insulted by the last part of my question.

"My *boss*?" She runs her tongue over her teeth and sets her drink down, pulling in a deep breath that, to my surprise, turns into a huff of laughter. "Girl, I don't have a boss, and I'm not trying to recruit you. Though, now that I'm looking at you, I think you'd pull in a lot of money at Ludus."

"Ludus?"

Desiree nods. Her smile is back, but there's some hurt lingering around the corners of her mouth. "Yeah, it's the club me and the girls work at."

"Oh, like a strip club?" I ask, digging through the terms I learned in the Ancient Greek class I took during college to try to sort out the meaning of the word. From what I can remember, it's the word Greek philosophers came up with the describe love in it's most playful, casual form. It seems fitting for an establishment built on lust and a lack of commitment.

"No, Nadia, not a strip club." She shakes her head like I'm hopeless. "Listen, you're right, me and my girls do sex work, but we don't have a boss or a pimp or whatever the hell else you want to call it, and Ludus makes that possible. It is a sex club, but no one is being forced to work there, and unlike most places, we're the ones in charge. We get to decide who we see, when we work, and how much we charge. The rooms we work in are clean and there's security on every door to make sure we're safe. And, after we pay our yearly operating fee, all the money we make is ours."

It sounds like some fairy tale brothel where everyone is an independent contractor with rights and power. Like a place someone like Beau would never want his girls to know exists because it would mean losing his entire roster.

"I thought you weren't trying to recruit me."

Heat flashes in Desiree's eyes. "I'm not."

"So why are you telling me all of this?"

"Honestly?" She lets out a long sigh. "Because the desperation I read on your face when I saw you talking to Vince didn't go away when he did. He mentioned you were here for an interview, but you don't look like you're celebrating, so I'm assuming you didn't get the job."

"I didn't."

"That doesn't surprise me since you're kind of a bitch." The bartender comes over, placing the bill on the counter. Desiree pulls her card out of the tiny purse slung over her shoulder and slaps it down on top of the sheet of paper without looking at the total.

"So now I'm desperate *and* a bitch."

The bartender returns with her card, two receipts and a pen, and she adds a generous tip to the first copy before signing and leaving it on the lacquered wood surface.

"Yep, you're a desperate bitch, and that resonated with me because once upon a time I was a desperate bitch too and then I found Ludus and everything changed," she says, all of her attention on the back of the second receipt where she's writing something. When she's done, she folds the paper in half and holds it out to me. I hesitate, and she rolls her eyes. "It's just my number, Nadia, I want you to take it."

My hands don't move even though my fingers twitch with the

desire to take the lifeline being extended to me. I don't want to go back to selling my body, but if I want to survive I might have to.

"Why?"

Desiree slides out of her seat and forces the paper into my curled up hand. "Because you're a desperate bitch with no friends, no money and nothing to lose."

5

NADIA

"**S**o *this* is the kind of work you do."

It's been two weeks since Desiree left me with an insult I can't shake off and a phone number I have yet to use, and I'm more than a little shocked to see her standing in front of me with nothing but the cash register I'm working and a belt full of her groceries between us.

Heat floods my cheeks even though there's nothing close to judgment in her voice or in her eyes as she looks at me. In fact, she's smiling like she's happy to see me, to know I feel more comfortable running a check out lane at a bougie grocery store than sleeping with men for money. The truth is, I don't know if I do feel more comfortable here, selling bottles of wine and jars of artisanal jams to New Haven's elite. I'm starting to think I won't ever feel comfortable anywhere.

"Desiree." I grab her bag of avocados. "Nice to see you."

She cocks her head to the side, and her lips—which are tinted with a striking purple stain—pull down into a frown laced with disbelief. "You don't have to lie, Nadia."

"I'm not lying."

With her eyes still on me, she lifts up on her tip-toes and plucks a pack of gum from the impulse buy section, dropping it on the belt with the rest of her stuff. I'm flying through her items, scanning and bagging them with an efficiency that has nothing to do with my growing line and everything to do with the woman burning a hole into the side of my face with her stare.

"Yes, you are. Do you want to know how I know?"

The teasing lilt in her voice as she asks me a question we both know the answer to causes me to miss a number on the product code I'm typing in. With a sigh, I finally meet her gaze, hoping that giving her my full attention will put an end to this interaction.

"Sure, Desiree." I place the dragon fruit on top of the other items in the last of her paper bags without ringing it up. The choice will cost me almost five dollars out of my paycheck. I tell myself getting Desiree out of my line will be worth the deduction, but the clenching in my stomach calls me a liar. "Please regale me with all the things you know about me, a complete stranger."

"Because you looked at me the same way the woman in aisle four did when her husband insisted on helping me get a bag of granola from the top shelf."

"I don't know what look you're talking about."

"Yes, you do." Her eyes skate down the half of my body not blocked by the counter I'm standing behind. "When you were working, you probably got it all the time. You probably still get it. The mix of annoyance and disapproval. The confusion and anger aimed at your audacity to exist. To be sensual and open on top of being beautiful and smart."

My face is hot, and I can't tell if it's because of Desiree's words or the increasingly annoyed gazes of the customers in my line who are probably wondering why she hasn't moved along yet. The man directly behind her shifts his weight from one foot to the other, fingers tapping along the side of the box of diapers in his hand. I know for a fact that if it was another, less attractive, customer in front of him causing a delay, he would have already said something. I guess an extra five minutes in the grocery store is a small price to pay for a prime time view of Desiree's ass.

"Fine." I clear my throat, deciding to go with the truth if it means getting rid of her. "I wasn't happy to see you."

She slaps her hand down on the counter, letting out a breathy, celebratory sigh. "Finally, some truth! I thought I was going to have to stand here all day to pull it out of you."

"Please don't. My boss doesn't like when the lines get too long."

In fact, because of this conversation, my line is already teetering on the edge of infraction. Last week, I watched a girl get fired for not ringing customers up fast enough. Reid, the lanky, power hungry child who manages this place, gave her a whole speech about her 'repeated lack of efficiency' and how it meant she didn't have the competence to do her job. She walked out of here with her head held high, but later that day when I was on break, Beth —one of the deli workers—told me she heard the girl telling Reid she had no idea how she was going to make rent this month if he let her go.

I didn't know the girl, had never had so much as a conversation with her, but that worry resonated deep inside my soul, echoing in the part of my brain that's constantly running, doing the anxious math of survival where the thirty hours of work Reid scheduled me for isn't enough to pay rent at the motel for the next two weeks and save for a new place in a more secure, but no less run down, apartment building. Where chatting it up with Desiree could cost me more than a five dollar dragon fruit. Humor tips the corners of her mouth up as she places her palms on the now empty belt and leans forward.

"You know this would be the perfect moment for me to make a joke about *you* being the one with a boss."

"No, it really wouldn't," I say, watching the woman behind the man eyeing Desiree's ass maneuver her grocery cart from my line to the express lane Reid has just opened up. He throws me an annoyed look over his shoulder, and my heart starts to beat frantically. Before I finalize the transaction, I force a smile onto my face and ask, "Can I get you anything else?"

"Nope."

"Great." My finger slams into the total button harder than necessary. "Your total is $98.14, will you be paying with cash or card?"

"Give me your number."

"What?"

"Give me your number," she repeats.

"No."

One of her brows raises in surprise, and my blood pressure rises right along with it. She glances at the people in line behind her, spreading an easy smile between them, before turning back to me. The smile buys her some good will from her line mates, but it won't do me any good because they'll all still make snide remarks about the wait time as soon as I have their eggs bagged safely. And when I do finally go on break, Reid is going to be in my ass about having to open a register to get the line down.

"Nadia, I'm prepared to stand here all day if you don't give me your number."

"Desiree, *I'm* prepared to call security if you don't pay your bill and get the hell on."

She's still smiling, and this time it's not that fake, sickeningly sweet one she gave to Vince at the bar or even the 'I'm so pretty you can't possibly be mad at me' one she just hit the people behind her with. No, this one is real. Like she's genuinely amused by my rudeness.

"God, you're such a bitch." She tosses her head back and laughs. "I think it might be my favorite thing about you."

This entire interaction is infuriating, but somewhere, in the furthest depths of my mind, I feel myself starting to like Desiree. She's pushy and ridiculous, but she's also honest.

"Cash or card, Desiree?"

"Give. Me. Your. Number. Nadia."

I'm about to say no again, but the word dies on my lips when I lose another person to Reid's line and he shoots me daggers. An exasperated sigh is the first sign of my surrender, but Desiree sees it for what it is. She lets out a cheerful whoop as I snatch a piece of blank receipt paper from the end of the roll and scrawl the number to the flip phone I only bought because every job application I filled out required me to be reachable by something other than email. When I hold the paper out to her, allowing my disdain to show on my face, she doesn't look the least bit remorseful about holding me hostage.

"Thank you," she says, pulling out her wallet and tucking the scrap of paper inside for safe keeping.

"Cash or card?" I ask, hoping the third time is the charm.

The sleek black metal of her card gleams underneath the ambient lighting coming from above, and every patron standing in line, including the diaper creep who has apparently lost interest in Desiree's curves, lets out a sigh of relief.

Desiree blinds us all with a triumphant grin. "Card."

* * *

It takes her two days to call me, and when she does I'm curled up in bed eating a cup of noodles and fuming about handing every dollar of my paycheck over to the greedy ass owner of this shit hole I've been living in. The sound of my phone ringing is so foreign, it causes me to jolt, making the piping hot liquid spill over onto my hand.

"Shit!" I hiss, and it's half pain, half annoyance because I know the only person responsible for bringing chaos into my afternoon of moping is Desiree's annoyingly gorgeous ass. And in true nuisance fashion, she lets the phone ring and ring and ring until I finally pick up.

"Didn't think you'd get rid of me that easily did you?" She asks by way of greeting.

"Of course not, Desiree. I've already accepted that nothing is ever easy with you."

We've only spoken three times, but we've already established a catty rapport that's more comfortable than it should be. Desiree seems to be comfortable in it too, which is good considering how pushy she's been about us being whatever it is we are.

She laughs, introducing yet another alien noise to the quiet of my space. I think it's probably the first joyful sound these four walls have heard since I started existing inside them. How sad.

"I only make things hard when you don't do what I want you to."

"Sounds like a line you've used on one of your clients."

"I haven't yet, but maybe I should."

"Maybe." With the phone tucked between my cheek and shoulder, I lean back against the pieces of cardboard that pass for pillows in this place. "So, what's up? What do you want from me today? My social security number?"

"No, just your eyes."

"My eyes?" Stale air rushes into my mouth as my jaw falls open. "What the hell do you mean?"

"Where are you staying? I'll come pick you up and explain over lunch."

There's no way in hell I'm giving this girl my address. She just told me she wants my eyes, and although nothing about her suggested she was involved in organ trafficking, I don't know her well enough to be sure.

"Girl, I'm going to need a few more details before I give you my address."

"Details?" She asks, a hint of offense in the word. "What kind of details?"

I pull my legs up to my chest, feeding the sudden urge to shield myself from a threat that's not even present. "Oh, I don't know, maybe the kind of details that tell me why you're asking for my eyes."

"Relax, Nadia, I'm an escort not some shady surgeon looking to sell your organs on the black market."

A dry snort escapes me. "You do realize we're practically strangers right? I don't know you from a can of paint."

"You knew me well enough to give me your phone number."

"You coerced me into giving you my number."

I can practically hear her nonchalant shrug over the phone. "Semantics."

"Are you always this exhausting?"

"Only when people insist on fighting me on every little thing."

"Asking for someone's eyes is not a little thing."

"Nadia." She blows out an impatient breath. "Let me be clear—"

"Please," I interject before going quiet, so she can continue.

"When I said I needed your eyes, I meant I needed them on me….while I have sex with a client."

Every conversation I have with this girl gets more and more ridiculous. Honestly, I'm not sure what I expected when I picked up the phone. There hasn't been a single time we've talked or been in each other's presence where she hasn't been making impossible requests. First, it was taking her phone number and thinking about joining some sex club she's a part of. Then, it was my phone number, and now, it's lunch and an exhibitionist show.

"I'm sorry, what?"

"See, this is why I wanted to talk about this over lunch."

"You would have been wasting your money because there's no way in hell I'm doing that."

Just thinking about stepping into the kind of situation Desiree is talking about has me breaking out into a cold sweat. That world, that life. It's not a place where I've ever felt safe. Beau made sure that I never would, and it wasn't always with his hands—though he was fond of using them on me—it was with his words, with the clients he chose that enjoyed debasing me.

"I'll split my fee with you." This is the first time I've heard anything close to desperation in Desiree's voice, and it, plus the monetary incentive she's just dangled in front of my face, gives me pause. "I have this client who's into being watched. Usually, he only comes into town once a month, and he had his normal visit last week. I guess he had to stay longer because he called me this morning asking if I could fit him in tonight. Normally, I'd get my friend Carmen to do it, but she's booked, and I don't trust any of these other girls around him."

"But you trust me?"

She answers immediately. "Yes."

"Why?" It's a valid question. Stealing clients is an act of desperation, of survival, and I'm probably the most desperate person Desiree has come across in a long time. She'd said as much the first time we met, and although I'd resented her saying it, I had to admit that it was true then and it's probably even more true now.

"Because you're done with the life, Nadia."

My brows furrow. "Don't you think that would make me more likely to say no?"

"I considered that, but then I thought about how desperate you looked at the bar that first day, and how worried you were about getting fired by that nerd at the grocery store, and I thought maybe your desperation would encourage you to say yes one more time. It's good money, Nadia, and I know you need it."

She doesn't know. Not really. Because she's not standing in the dark, desolate representation of my need, of my despair. She doesn't know the first night I slept in here, I did so without knowing that the door wasn't fully latched because no one told me the series of secret movements necessary to secure it. She doesn't know there's mold in the bathroom that refuses to come out no matter how many times I bleach it. She doesn't know I walk home every night and expect to find Beau waiting inside my room, allowed in by the greedy owner who would happily sell me out if someone offered him enough cash.

Desiree doesn't know, she can't, but somehow she does, and I find peace in the sadness of our shared understanding. When we met, she told me she'd been desperate before and that the place she worked had changed everything. I thought my change would come in the form of a minimum wage job, but today I've accepted that it won't.

And that knowledge, that acceptance is enough to make me reconsider everything. I swallow, and the question working its way up my throat might as well be a sledgehammer in my hand because I'm about to use it to knock all the boundaries I've drawn around my new life down.

"How much?"

6

SEBASTIAN

"Still can't believe you fired Vince," Luca says, grinning at me over the shoulder of the woman currently grinding on his leg.

"He had it coming." Andreas shrugs and takes a sip of his whiskey.

"Damn right he did." Getting rid of Vince was a simple, but frustrating task that required me to spend weeks after the last round of interviews tracking down every server that quit in the last six months and getting them in the office for a face to face discussion about why they'd left. Only a handful of them agreed to come in, and when they did, they were nervous and defensive. I had to assure them multiple times that they weren't in any kind of trouble, that I was just trying to get to the bottom of our increasing turnover rate. It was only then that they'd relaxed enough to confirm my suspicions that it all came down to Vince.

Vince and his leering stares.

Vince and his questionable comments that bordered on suggestive but were just vague enough to never really cross the line.

Vince and his disgusting behavior that he justified by telling himself, and the women he was supposed to be managing, that harassment was part of the job.

Yesterday afternoon, I called him into my office and fired him on the spot, not caring about how upset it would make Mom or Aunt Adrienne. Not thinking about how long it would take to find a new manager. Not worrying about anything besides getting him far, far away from my business and my employees. After he stormed out, I called my assistant, Regina, into my office and let her know what was what. Thankfully, she'd already seen the writing on the wall. As soon as Vince walked into my office, she'd disabled his employee ID and had his company card deactivated. With that taken care of, I instructed her to contact every server we'd lost during Vince's tenure and notify them that he'd been relieved of his duties and they would be receiving severance checks via wire transfer by the end of the day, contingent on the signing of paperwork stating none of them would threaten or initiate lawsuits aimed at me or Adler Holdings, Inc. Everyone signed within minutes of receiving the contract, and once the transfers were initiated, I breathed a sigh of relief that only lasted for as long as I was able to keep thoughts of hiring a new manager at bay.

A curvy brunette with legs as long as mine runs her fingers over my shoulder as she walks past me and makes her way to Andreas, trying to take a seat beside him.

"Hey, handsome," she purrs.

"Not tonight, beautiful," he replies before she even gets a chance to sit down. The girl, who, if I remember correctly, is named Poppy, isn't put off by his rejection. She just smiles and turns around, setting her sights on me. I wave her away, tilting my head in a silent command for her to pursue someone else.

"Dre, what's up with you, man? You usually love our nights at Ludus. Last time, you were in the back with Poppy before we even ordered drinks."

The concern coating Luca's words loses some of its validity when his hand starts to cut a line across the woman's thigh, hiking up the hem of her already short dress.

"Nothing's up with me," Andreas replies, a slow smile spreading across his face as a busty red head with alabaster skin takes the seat Poppy was just attempting to occupy. He wraps his arm around her waist, closing his eyes when she plants a kiss on his cheek. "I was just looking for something different tonight."

I push to my feet. "Well, I guess this is where I leave you."

"Stay, Seb." The half-hearted plea comes from Luca, slipping out of his lips before he places a kiss to the neck of the woman he's going to be taking into one of the back rooms in the next few seconds. "Finish your drink. Find someone to get your mind off the ass cutting Aunt Adrienne is going to give you when she finds out you fired her precious baby boy."

None of that sounds the least bit enticing, and I leave my brothers to their distractions without explaining for perhaps the thousandth time that for me, Ludus is a business, not a playground. When I started the members only club, it was with the intention of creating a safe space for sex workers to operate without worrying about being abused, cheated out of money they worked hard for, or killed. The idea had been born out of necessity, coming to me in the middle of the night after I'd complied with a police request for video footage from Cerros for the third time in as many months because yet another escort had been assaulted in one of our hotel rooms.

I knew if I didn't do something, and quickly, we'd eventually have a murder on our hands, and so, Ludus was born. Talia had helped me track down the group of escorts who'd been operating in the hotel right under our noses, and we built the club around their specific needs and desires. Of course, their primary concern was security, so we hired the most capable, trust worthy motherfuckers we could find and put them on every door. From there, we branched out, adding on a small operating fee that would give them access to more incentives than they would ever see on the streets—reproductive health training, access to an in-house medical team, workshops and seminars on new toys and tricks, wealth management and rate negotiation—until anyone doing sex work in and around New Haven would be stupid to go anywhere else.

For an illegal operation, Ludus ran smoothly for a long time. We hit our first snag about six months in when a local pimp named Cheese put a price on my head for giving his top earner, Desiree, the strength to leave him and work for herself. Talia was terrified, but I was amused, thrilled by the prospect of unleashing the violent part of me that had no place in the boardrooms I was commanding. Every wanna be assassin that came for me got a choice: walk away or be left bleeding and broken in whatever dark corner they approached me in. They all took one look at the suit and tie and decided to try their luck. I took great pleasure in making each and every one of them regret that choice.

When I finally got to their boss, who showed up with a gun because apparently he was the only one who really meant to get the job done, I beat him within an inch of his life with it. The last thing he heard before he lost consciousness was me telling him to take the stack of hundreds I'd just dropped in the pool of blood next to his limp body and accept it as payment for Desiree *and* the gun.

Since then, things have been good, but I still make a point of staying vigilant, which means when I'm at Ludus, I don't let the beautiful women or their short dresses distract me. Every monthly visit to the club goes the same way. Luca and Andreas insist on coming with me, so I let them. I nurse a drink while my brothers eye fuck every girl that walks by. When they find someone to keep them occupied for the night, I make my rounds, checking on the girls working the floor and the members they're entertaining before going to get a report from the head of security. After that, it's a toss up, and my attention goes to whatever area needs it most. Sometimes it's our cleaning crew requesting additional people or asking if I know of anything stronger than industrial strength bleach. Other times, it's the kitchen and bar staff wanting me to know one of the vendors was short on something.

Tonight, it's the bar that wins out. As I'm leaving the security room, Marcus, a stocky former boxer with a love for mixing cocktails, meets my eyes in a silent plea for assistance that has me heading towards him, ready to deescalate whatever problem he's dealing with. I'm five feet away from the bar when I realize the problem isn't a drunk client or an upset wife—which has been known to happen around here. No, the problem is almost six feet tall wrapped in an intoxicating combination of a black, leather midi dress and ebony skin that shimmers with specks of gold that must have been in whatever lotion or serum she applied to her skin to make it shine under the warm lights of the club. The problem smells like bergamot and amber. The problem is bent over the edge of the bar with bone straight lines of midnight silk trailing down her back, caressing her skin every time she moves her head.

The problem is Nadia Hendrix.

It should be a problem that I've identified her without even seeing her face, but I can't see it that way. I can't see anything but her. Marcus flicks his gaze from Nadia to me, and I kind of feel bad for the guy because he expected me to come over and save him, but I'm not going to do that. Not yet, at least. I take a seat on the barstool next to where Nadia is standing, and she doesn't even look my way. That's how focused she is on the one sided conversation she's roped Marcus into about the ruby red wine in the decanter on the counter between them.

"I specifically requested the '93 Thornehill Pinot Noir, not *this*." She frowns down at the glass in her hand. Her lips curling the way they did when she spoke to me in the lobby the day we met. "What *is* this? Let me see the bottle."

Marcus dries his hands on the bar towel that lives on his shoulder and pulls the bottle from underneath the counter. He reads the label and shrugs before handing it over to her. "Listen, lady, I'm a bartender not a sommelier, and as I told you the other day, you can put in a request, but that doesn't always mean Ruthie will be able to source it. If she can't, she brings the next best thing, which is what you got in front of you."

One look at the label tells me what she has in front of her is a vintage Pinot Noir produced in France and, judging by the tongue twister of a name, costs at least five hundred dollars.

"But I don't want it," Nadia insists, placing the bottle on the tray next to the decanter and wine glasses and pushing it towards him. "I want what I asked for."

Marcus pushes the tray back, glancing at me again to see if I'm going to intervene. "Well, I don't have what you asked for. I have *this*. If it makes you feel any better, the note Ruthie left said it would go well with the duck your client brought in for the chef to prepare tonight."

Something strange happens in my chest when Marcus' words confirm that Nadia is here to work. Based on her outfit and the dramatic sweep of makeup gracing her eyelids, I figured that was the case, but having it confirmed makes me feel...violent.

"You work here?" Those weren't the words I intended to come out of my mouth, but they get her attention. She turns her head slowly, annoyance rolling off of her in waves, and when her gaze meets mine there isn't even a flicker of recognition in her eyes.

"Something like that."

Her tone is clipped and strained with pleasantness she doesn't think I deserve. She turns back to Marcus, whose face is now etched with panic as he looks between the two of us. He opens his mouth, presumably to tell her exactly who she's just dismissed, but I hold up a hand to tell him not to.

"I've never seen you here before."

This time she doesn't even bother to look at me. "There's a first time for everything."

Marcus' brows meet his hairline, and I know he's thinking this is the first time he's ever seen anyone talk to me like this. Again, I give him a silent command to leave it alone.

"Right." I bite my lip to suppress the urge to call her Miss. Hendrix again. If she's working, which I now know that she is, she probably isn't using her real name, and I don't want to blow up her spot. "I guess this is the first time you're going to have to accept that you can't always have it your way." Reaching across the bar, I grab the tray, sliding it towards her until her fingers have no choice but to grip the edge. "Take this, go back to your client and leave the bartender alone."

Now, she's looking at me. Now, there's not only recognition swirling in the puddles of caramel brown, but also anger. It flares her nostrils and makes her take a step back from the bar, clutching the unwanted wine close to her chest. Her mouth opens and closes like she wants to say something but she doesn't know what. When it finally opens again, she's speaking to Marcus, not me.

"Make sure the bottle is comped, have the chef add a cherry coulis to the duck dish and have a complimentary charcuterie board with Gruyère out by the time I pour this first glass."

Her instructions are just as impressive as the effortless stride she uses to walk away after firing them off. Marcus scoffs, muttering something about crazy, demanding women while he wipes down the bar. I watch Nadia, more interested than I should be in who she's going through so much trouble to impress. Since I personally review every member application, I'm not surprised to find that I know the man she's sitting with. His name is Preston Fredericks, and he *used* to be a regular here.

"Marcus," I call his name with my eyes still on Nadia and Preston. When he places his hand on her thigh, I rise from my seat and button my suit jacket. Everything in me wants to go over there and ruin his night, but I reign in that desire, knowing it won't be good for business if paying members see me personally tossing one of their own out on his ass.

"Yeah, boss?"

Finally, I look away from them, pinning Marcus with a hard stare, so he knows I'm serious. "Make sure you do exactly as she says, alright?"

Marcus gawks. "You really want me taking orders from the wine snob?"

"Only if you want to keep your job." I double tap the counter and force myself to walk towards the exit without looking back. Once I'm in my car and headed home, I place a call to Regina. Despite the late hour, she picks up on the first ring.

"Two things," I say without even letting her speak.

"Okay, let's hear them."

"I need a meeting with Nadia Hendrix at Ludus tomorrow. She interviewed for a server position at Cerros, so her contact information should be on file."

"Got it. And the other thing?"

My teeth clench, images of Preston's stupid face cracking into a shit eating grin when Nadia sat down beside him flash through my mind. This isn't a business decision, but it can't be personal because I don't know Nadia personally, so it's something in between. Something primal and necessary. Something dark and possessive that I promise myself I'll only act on this once.

"Sebastian?" Regina calls. "What's the other thing?"

"Preston Fredricks. I want his membership revoked."

"Mr. Fredricks was one of Ludus' first members."

"I'm aware, Regina."

"I know, sir, I'm just not sure I understand—"

"You don't need to understand," I growl, neglecting to mention that I don't understand either. That logic and understanding are a thin layer of glass beneath my feet, creaking and groaning under the weight of the feeling in my chest that doesn't allow me to see reason. "Just get it done."

"Okay, and you would like this to take effect when?"

"Immediately."

"Immediately?" She squeaks, and I can all but see her round eyes going wide with shock. This is unprecedented. I've never revoked a membership to Ludus. Our screening process is so strenuous it's never been necessary, but all I can see in my mind's eye is Nadia hand feeding Preston duck that he washes down with glasses of wine she didn't even want.

"Immediately. Have security carry him out if need be."

7

NADIA

"Nadia, the boss wants to see you in his office."

I've never been called to the principal's office before, but I imagine this is what it would feel like. The low, sinking feeling in your gut that tells you you've done something wrong even though you haven't. The rapid pounding of your heart echoing in your ears, inspired by your name coming over the intercom.

Or, in this case, spoken by Russ—the brutish bouncer who has issued me a guest pass every night for the past month. The first night Desiree brought me to Ludus, Russ chatted her up while I filled out the stack of paperwork necessary to walk through the sleek steel doors behind him. As he took my photo, he cracked jokes about me watching Desiree do her thing, and when my smile didn't reach my eyes, he told me to relax because I was safe here. Generally, I don't make a habit of believing anything men say to me, but I chose to believe Russ because it made it easier to take hold of Desiree's hand and follow her into the room where I made a thousand dollars by doing nothing more than sitting on my ass and watching her do work that, by all accounts, she enjoyed.

When Desiree put the money in my hand—ten crisp hundred dollar bills I gaped at for longer than necessary—she explained that her guy,

Paul something or other, had added a nice tip to thank her for fitting him in on short notice and me for really selling the whole shell shocked look. I was so grateful to her for calling and bullying me into coming, I pulled her into a hug, letting the first rush of truly positive emotion I'd felt in a while spill out of me in a wave of happy tears Desiree wiped away with gentle swipes of her thumb that spoke of understanding.

After that, we drank champagne that triggered unbidden thoughts of eyes belonging to the infuriating stranger I keep running into and ate the best food I've had in months. We danced with the other girls working the floor and I opened up, giving them a thinned out back story that focused mainly on my bad experiences with sex work, which some of them, unfortunately, could relate to. Like Desiree, all of the girls encouraged me to come work at the club, hinging their entire pitch on perks Desiree had already told me about and the money I could make doing things like working the floor and chatting up men who paid for company instead of sex.

None of them, however, mentioned this supposed boss Russ speaks of. I'm not dumb. I know that an operation like Ludus doesn't happen without someone with deep pockets and a lot of connections behind it, but no one has so much as uttered a word about who the man running the show actually is. Given the illegal nature of the operation, it's understandable that the man funding things wouldn't want to be highly visible. I understand hiding to protect yourself. What I don't understand is why he wants to see me, of all people.

"Maybe he heard about you getting into with Marcus at the bar," Desiree speculates, trailing behind me. "Or he might want to talk to you about Preston getting kicked out."

The mention of Preston's unceremonious, and not at all optional, ejection from the club last night makes my heart sink. Desiree and the girls gave me all these assurances about being able to make money at Ludus without having sex, but I'd been hard pressed to find the unicorn they spoke of until Preston came along. I've spent the last two weeks building a relationship with him, gaining tips that got incrementally bigger every night. I had high hopes that last night's tip would be the biggest one yet, the one that would give me just enough money to pay the operation fee at Ludus if I wanted to.

Want.

It's still such a foreign concept for me. Wanting something. Being able to have it. My budding situation with Preston made me feel like I could want things again, like I had options in front of me that were within reach. All of that went away when he got carted off by Russ and another bouncer who's name I think is Bobby. They were stone faced and professional as they escorted an irate Preston out, taking all of my hope with them.

"I don't know anything about why Preston got kicked out."

"Right, which is all you need to tell him."

I stop walking, spinning on my heel to look Desiree in the eye. "Do you really think this could be about the argument I had with Marcus at the bar?"

I don't mention the other person I got into it with. The man I'd met in the lobby of the hotel the day I interviewed for the job at Cerros. The man who appeared out of nowhere with the same smug smile and air of superiority swirling around him as the first time we met. Dark eyes laughing at me, overly familiar hands touching me, a commanding tone sweeping down my spine as he ordered me back to the table with the wrong wine.

"Maybe." Desiree starts moving again, heading toward the staff area where the girls get ready. "Marcus does like to file complaints. For a former boxer, he's kind of a cry baby. I'm sure it'll be fine, though."

I bite my lip, finding myself worrying about losing a job I'm not even sure I want. "Right. It's going to be fine."

"At least try to sound like you believe it." She bumps my shoulder with hers and chucks her chin towards the end of the hall. "Owner's office is down there, come find me when you're done."

"Okay."

She gives me a reassuring smile and turns off, leaving me to make the last of the journey on my own. The hallway isn't long, but it feels like it takes me hours to reach the end of it. My feet are heavy and my mind is racing with possibilities, scenarios that end with me being escorted from the club just like Preston was. Drawing in a deep breath, I lift my hand and knock.

"Come in."

The voice on the other side of the door is dark smoke, billowing through the small crack between the door and its frame in a deep, rasp of a timbre that's too familiar to belong to a stranger. I push the door open, already knowing in some part of my mind, what, or rather who, I'm going to find sitting at the desk in the center of the room.

Pools of champagne greet me first, and tonight they're not laughing. They're serious. Like, deathly serious, as they move from my furrowed brows to my wide eyes to my mouth that wants to drop open to fully convey the shock rolling through my body right now.

"*You're* the owner?"

"Miss Hendrix." He pushes to his feet, and I wonder how he looks bigger today than the last two times I saw him. It takes me a moment to realize it's because he's not wearing a suit jacket. Yesterday, and a few weeks ago at Cerros, the full impact of the broad expanse of his chest and shoulders was dulled by the additional layer of fabric, but today it's on full display. Every slab of well defined muscle emphasized by a white button up and slate gray vest that matches perfectly with his pants, turning his thick torso and even thicker legs into a long, continuous line of power.

Power I can tell he's used to wielding without thought or consideration for the people on the receiving end of it. People who might feel a flare of panic move through them when they realize there's a bull coming towards them and they're wearing red. Power like that on a man like him can only be one thing: dangerous.

I take a step back, giving in to the desire to put some distance between us, and he stops moving. He tilts his head to the side, eyes filled with confusion roll over my features as I push the panic away. Tipping my chin up, I give voice to my own perplexity once again.

"You own this place?"

"Have a seat." The order is punctuated by a wave of his long arm as he gestures towards the chairs in front of the desk. I'm still standing in the doorway, and I can see his impatience building as he lowers himself back into his seat. He's surprisingly graceful for such a large man. "Come in, Nadia, and close the door behind you."

It's only as I hear my name on his lips, that I realize I don't know his. I don't know anything about this man, and now I'm in a room alone with him because despite my instincts telling me not to, I do exactly as he says. The silence in the office wraps around me as soon as the door is closed, and his gaze is a heavy weight on my body. I roll my shoulders back and turn around quickly before I lose my nerve and run out of here screaming.

I take a seat and cross my legs, suddenly aware of the length of my dress that leaves very little to the imagination. To his credit, he doesn't allow his eyes to move away from my face, and I'm quietly appreciative of the fact that he's not a creep. At least he's got that going for him because the rest of his personality leaves a lot to be desired.

"Are you going to answer my question?"

He smirks, and it takes every bit of control I have not to let the growl of frustration building in my chest out. "Yes, Nadia, I'm the owner."

I already knew the answer to the question when I asked it, but something about getting verbal confirmation from him sends my heart free falling into my stomach. It lands in a heavy, broken heap at my feet, crushing the little flower of hope that started to bloom when Desiree first brought me here. Knowing that he owns this place casts our interaction at the bar yesterday in a whole new light. A bright, blood red flood of certainty that spells my demise.

"You're going to fire me."

It's not a question because asking him would be stupid. I was rude to him yesterday. I disrespected him in front of his employees and while he doesn't look particularly upset, I can't imagine he would take that in stride. The chair he's sitting in creaks under his weight as he sits back and links his long thick fingers together, allowing them to come to rest on his stomach.

"That would be hard to do since you don't technically work for me."

He's right. I don't work here. I couldn't work here even if I wanted to. The operational fee is steep, and the money for keeping men company while they work up the nerve to go to one of the back rooms is slow. I've saved every dollar I can—building up a small, cash based, nest egg because I don't trust my new driver's license to hold up under the scrutiny of a bank—but existing is expensive and deciding whether I should pay the operational fee or keep saving to secure somewhere safe to live is hard.

"So what are you going to do?" My voice wants to shake, to convey the fear coursing through my veins at the thought of being at the mercy of a merciless man, but I forbid it. I infuse steel into my vocal chords and through every quivering muscle in my throat. This whole song and dance is a show of power. A reminder that there's a hierarchy here at Ludus, and he's seated comfortably on the top rung while my position at the bottom is secured by nothing more than a harness named Desiree. And although I'm scared, I refuse to cower in the face of it. "Revoke my guest pass and ban me from the club?"

There are other options, of course. Ones that would end with me on my knees or bent over his desk while he reminds me that I'm nothing and he's everything. Beau always chose one of those options, especially for me. If Desiree were here, she'd tell me there's no way the man in front of me would do anything like that. I try to find comfort in that, but all the solace I've taken from the thought is washed away when I remember I don't really know Desiree, so her imaginary guarantees about the stranger in front of me don't hold any weight.

My question makes the dark lines of his brows knit together. "Is that what you would do if you were in my position, Nadia?"

There was a time in my life when I would have been able to imagine being in his position with ease. Not his exact position of course because I don't think I'd ever want to own a sex club but the rest of it. Owning a business, being in charge of a team, paying people well and creating a safe and joyful environment for them to come to work. All of that felt like a forgone conclusion, a path I was destined to walk down because my parents had already paved the way, but that's a distant dream now. One I haven't reached for in years and can't try to grasp right now.

"You still haven't told me your name," I say, switching gears to allow myself some distance from the uncomfortable thoughts his question have caused to surface.

"Sebastian." He leans forward and reaches his hand out to me. I take it and ignore the jolt of energy that passes between our palms, so I can try to figure out why his name sounds familiar.

"Just Sebastian?" I ask, pulling my hand away after a few seconds. "No last name?"

"Adler."

"Sebastian Adler." I test the syllables out on my tongue, frustrated that I still can't place his name. I've heard it before. Not here at Ludus, but somewhere. Sebastian watches me carefully, and I shift in my seat. "Why are you looking at me like that?"

He shrugs nonchalantly. "Just waiting."

"For what?"

"To see if my name rings a bell."

God, he's really a cocky bastard isn't he?

"Should it?"

Amusement creeps into the corner of his eyes. "Yes, Nadia, it should."

"Why? It's not like you have a sign on the door saying 'Welcome to Ludus, owned and operated by Sebastian Adler.'"

"You're right. A sign like that probably wouldn't be wise considering the less than legal nature of the club, but I can guarantee my name appeared more than once on the application."

My brows pull together in confusion. He just made it clear that I don't work for him. I think back to the paperwork I filled out to get a guest pass from Russ. There was a long and detailed liability waiver, a comprehensive non-disclosure agreement, and a surprisingly brief basic information form, but nothing close to an application for employment. "What application?"

"The one you filled out when you applied to work at Cerros."

8

SEBASTIAN

It's more satisfying than it should be to see her caught completely off guard. She doesn't strike me as the kind of person who often finds herself in situations like this, speaking from an uninformed place. I'd seen her trying to put it together when I gave her my first name. Somewhere behind her eyes was a flicker of recognition, a spark of a familiarity she refused to give credence. Now she's kicking herself for not following that thread, for not questioning what it meant to run into me in both of the places she's sought work in New Haven.

My jaw clenches involuntarily at the thought of her working here at Ludus. Anger washes through my gut in a violent wave as visions of Preston touching her and making her smile play out in my mind. I can't stop it or make sense of it. I've never cared about any of the people working here or the acts they've engaged in with our members, and I've certainly never pulled someone's membership just for doing what they've paid a handsome fee to come here to do. Nadia's unsanctioned presence has changed that though. I need to get her the fuck out of here before revoking the membership of every man who looks at her becomes standard practice and there's no Ludus to speak of.

"This is some sort of joke, right?" Nadia asks with outrage etched into her features.

"It's not," I assure her, grabbing the file in front of me and opening it to reveal the copy of her resume Regina sent over last night. "Stay in New Haven long enough, and you'll find my name attached to most everything."

"What makes you think I haven't been in New Haven long?" There's defensiveness coating the words of her question, but there's also something else. Something that suggests she's not comfortable with me being in possession of a fact that's so blatantly obvious.

"Well, for starters, you don't know who I am."

A flash of pink catches my attention, and I find myself tracking the motion of her tongue as it swipes across her full bottom lip. It's interesting how I immediately recognize it as an unconscious act of annoyance instead of something else like anxiety or nervousness. Nadia doesn't seem like the kind of woman who gets nervous a lot, which is probably why it had unsettled me to see her back away when I'd started walking towards her earlier. The concern that had rooted itself in my chest, wrapping around my ribs and forcing me to sit down, was a foreign sensation. I can't remember a single time in my professional life where I've felt so self conscious. Aware of everything from my size and the quickness of my movements to the firmness of my tone and no non-sense expression.

Well, maybe that's not entirely true.

I've been told on more than one occasion that I can be intimidating, that the already harsh lines of my face can become particularly garish in the midst of negotiations and business meetings. I've just never cared enough to adjust.

Until now.

Until her.

I shake my head, refusing to follow that line of thought any further.

"Who are you exactly, Mr. Adler?" Nadia asks, her tone thick with condescension. "Some kind of local celebrity?"

"No, *Miss Hendrix,* I'm not a celebrity. I'm just a well known business man who comes from a well known family. I'm not famous, but most people recognize me, especially when they're standing in one of my many establishments looking for a job."

She uncrosses her legs and pulls down the hem of her dress. It's shorter than the one she was wearing last night, and this time the fabric is a deep red instead of black. The color paired with her curves makes me think of a glass of wine, a full bodied Malbec that explodes on your tongue and demands everything while giving you nothing. Her hair is curled instead of straight, ebony tresses framing her face but doing nothing to soften the sharp edges of her frown.

"And you want me to, what? Congratulate you for being rich and somewhat well known? Apologize for not throwing myself at your feet and begging for a job at *one of your many establishments*?" She pitches her voice low at the end of the sentence in an attempt to mock me. "Or maybe I should—"

"Come work for me," I say, interrupting her.

"What?"

"Come work for me," I repeat. "You have a specific set of skills I feel have been going to waste since you've arrived in New Haven. I'd like to be the first person here to benefit from them."

My eyes are on her sparse resume—which doesn't indicate that she's in possession of the skills I've just attributed to her or is at all capable of performing the duties attached to the position I'm about to offer her—so I miss the moment this already doomed conversation takes a turn for the worst.

Nadia shoots to her feet, and the chair she was just sitting in screeches against the tile floor. It's the sound that catches my attention, but the anger vibrating every inch of her frame is what keeps it. Is what sends the mildest twinge of worry through my gut even as I'm captivated by the sight of her looming over me in all of her furious glory.

"I knew this place was too good to be true." She shakes her head, and I watch self-deprecation roll across her features. "God, I'm so fucking stupid for believing you were running some kind of safe haven for sex workers here. And the constant hiring at Cerros is what? A way to keep your roster of girls full? Do you lure them in with the promise of a normal job that actually pays well and then just pull the rug out from under them, so they're desperate enough to say yes when one of your recruiters comes along. That's what Desiree is right? She's great at her job, so kudos to you for choosing so well. She's that perfect blend of friendly and pushy. Did she tell you it only took one phone call to get me in here? Of course, she did. She probably tells you everything like how last night the only man who thought I was worth something with my clothes on was dragged out of here, leaving me ripe for the picking, ready for the boss to come in and sample the product before making a push for me to sell it."

The surprisingly complex conspiracy theory spills out of her in between agitated breaths that leave no room for me to respond, to refute her allegations with facts and a warning about how watching an excessive amount of true crime documentaries can rot your brain.

"That's not what this is, Nadia."

"Of course it is. I know men like you. I've—" She swallows, choking down the words as she commits to the offensive line of thought that calls my character into question. "So, how do you want me, Mr. Adler?" Her hands go to the hem of her dress and begin lifting it up, agitation making her fingers shake. "Should I get completely naked or just hike my dress up and slip my thong to the side?"

Nadia is a beautiful woman, but there's nothing enticing about the abrupt reveal of her skin or the vulgarity of her words. My stomach begins to churn at the same moment my blood starts to boil. Running Ludus and meeting women like Desiree who, as far as I can tell, has only been a friend to Nadia, taught me that the space I've created here is the exception in the world of sex work, not the rule. Most of the men in my position do exactly what Nadia is accusing me of.

That's the ugly truth of this industry.

I know that. I've known that for years, so it makes no sense for me to be so affected when confronted with the reality of it. For me to want to break the hands of every man that's touched her against her will, to end every person who has treated her like she's something other than precious.

"Nadia." I'm standing now, and I hate the way me rounding the desk to move towards her makes her lips quiver with resignation.

"Let me guess. This is the part where you tell me not to waste my energy screaming because no one is going to help me. You don't have to say it. I won't fight. I won't scream. I already know help isn't coming."

She looks like she's learned that lesson a thousand times over. God, her eyes are so fucking sad now that there's no fire behind them. She's still gripping the hem of her dress, and I note the presence of a long, jagged scar on the inside of her thigh as I step into her space. Tears crowd her eyes, but she blinks them away, maintaining eye contact.

"You think I'm going to hurt you?"

"Please don't lie and say you'll make it feel good," she pleads as one of the tears breaks free, gliding down her cheek. "They always say that, but it never does."

My next breath is a pained shudder because my mind has taken it upon itself to conjure hundreds of images to attach to that statement. Ugly, violent, horrific pictures. It makes me sick to have them in my head. What does it do to her to live with the memories? To believe that every man she encounters is a predator even when there's no evidence to suggest otherwise?

I take a step back, accepting that we can't have this conversation here because she doesn't feel safe being alone with me. The distance between us doesn't make Nadia relax at all, but I'm as far away as I'm willing to be. I sit down on the desk, gripping the edge with my fingers so she knows I'm not going to put my hands on her.

"Pull down your dress, Nadia."

Finally, there's relief. It's tinged with caution, but it's there, calming her features marginally. She hesitates to follow my instruction, glassy eyes searching my face to see if I'm tricking her.

"What? You don't—?"

She lets the question trail off, and I watch her come back to herself a little. Embodying the woman she was in the hotel lobby the day we met, the one she was when she walked in here, the one she was before my coded language made her back slide mentally.

"No, Nadia, I don't." *Not now. Not like this.* The voice in the back of my head adds, surprising the fuck out of me because I don't know where the thought came from. "Please pull down your dress."

My breath comes a little easier when all the soft fabric that was in her hand is back where it should be. Nadia's shoulders are high, tension and embarrassment I don't know how to ease rippling through the muscles. She rubs at her arms, biting her lip but still somehow holding my gaze.

"I'm sorry."

Her voice is small and ratcheted with shame. I know she's playing the last five minutes over in her mind. She revealed so much of herself to me and none of it was intentional, which means it feels wrong to have it.

"Don't be." I run a hand down the back of my neck, only avoiding hanging my head in shame because it would mean not being able to look at her. "This conversation should have happened in a different setting. I wasn't thinking."

"What was in the folder?"

"Your resume."

That wasn't the answer she was expecting. I can tell by the way her brows rise.

"Still as sparse as you remember it?" The question creates a light-ness between us that wasn't there seconds ago. It's not enough to fully dispel the dark cloud lingering over the office, but it's something. "You were right about my lack of experience keeping me from being hired. I thought you were being a jerk when you first said it, but I guess you knew what you were talking about."

"I usually do."

"Are you always this insufferable?"

"Depends on who you ask."

"I'm asking you."

"That's not a word I would use to describe myself, no, but if you think it's fitting I won't argue with you." Nadia almost looks like she wants to smile, but she's not far enough removed from the start of our conversation to access it. Motivated by the need to get her out of here, I push off the desk, placing my hands in my pocket so she doesn't get spooked again.

"Will you have dinner with me?"

9

NADIA

I t's not a date.

I make that clear to him after I say yes and before I follow him into a private elevator that takes us to the mezzanine floor of Ludus.

I've never been up here before because it's only utilized by girls with exclusive client lists that require even more privacy than the ones on the bottom level. Desiree told me there's a separate entrance for the upper levels with it's own door man and elevator attendant who escorts the girls and their clients to the wide open space that's hidden from view by glass that allows the people behind it to see out while keeping everyone else from seeing in. It all sounded pretty impressive, but experiencing it for myself is something else altogether.

"Mr. Adler." The concierge—a stout Black man with a British accent—greets us. "It's an honor to have you and Miss Hendrix in our presence tonight. Shall I seat you at your usual table?"

I don't even bother to ask how this man knows my name. That's just how things work around here.

"That would be great, Albert." Sebastian extends his hand, and Albert takes it with a wide smile curving his lips. "How are Beth and the kids?"

"Doing well, doing well. We'll be moving Claire onto campus in a few weeks."

"She's still going to NHU, right?"

Albert nods, and there's no mistaking the pride on his face as he leads us to our table. I listen to the exchange simultaneously impressed with how much Sebastian knows about his employees and ashamed of how I acted in his office not even twenty minutes ago.

"Forget it, Nadia. I already have." Sebastian's voice is a low rumble in my ear as he pulls out my chair. I lower myself into my seat and start to peruse the menu. Everything sounds so good, but it's hard to focus when my brain keeps replaying the look on Sebastian's face when I pulled up my dress.

He was horrified.

I don't think I've ever seen a man look at me like that. Sad. Worried. Not even Roland—Beau's father and my dad's lifelong best friend who became my guardian after my parents died—showed that much concern after the first time Beau sold me to one of his friends. I'd been gone for a week. Missing for seven whole days, and the man who'd known me for my whole life didn't so much as bat an eye when I stumbled through his front door, bruised in places he couldn't see, blood soaked into the dress I wore to my college graduation.

"Nadia?"

I blink at Sebastian, forcing the thoughts to the back of my mind. "Yes?"

"Albert wants to know if we'd like to order wine."

Heat creeps up my neck as I look up into Albert's patient eyes. "Yeah, sure."

"Any suggestions?" Sebastian asks. His brows raised like he's surprised I haven't already rattled off the name of some vintage bottle that costs more than what I make in a month at the grocery store.

"Oh, uh." I glance at the wine list Albert has just placed in front of me. It's extensive, longer than the one downstairs, which is saying something because that one is pretty long. "What are you planning to eat?"

He doesn't glance at the menu, choosing to hold my gaze instead. "Brown butter lobster with blistered cherry tomatoes."

Just hearing the name of the dish makes my stomach growl, reminding me that I haven't eaten since early this afternoon. "That sounds delicious."

Sebastian seems pleased that I approve of his choice. "We could share if you'd like."

The warmth that spreads through my stomach at his words has no place at this table, no place in my body, no place between me and the man who just recently learned that I've been abused more than I've ever been loved or cherished.

I wave my hand at him, dismissing the offer that's far more generous than I deserve after accusing him of being a predator. "No, that's okay. I can just order my own."

Sebastian leans forward, placing his elbows on the table. "Or, you could get the steak frites, you've been eyeing. The Bearnaise sauce it comes with is incredible."

I don't know how he knows the steak dish has caught my attention. As a meat and potatoes kind of girl, I'm always interested when I see steak frites on the menu, but I rarely order it. Most men expect women to live off of salads and chicken breasts, and when I was with a client it was my job to maintain that illusion. *Eat like a bird and fuck like a porn star.* That's what Bianca used to whisper to the other girls before their dates. I came up with the phrase, using it as a bitter one-liner that encapsulated what clients wanted from us, but she was the one who made it a motto, a motivating reminder to put on a show because the show was the only thing that mattered.

Sebastian is still watching me, so he sees when I pull my bottom lip between my teeth, torturing the soft flesh to keep myself from voicing my refusal. To give my brain enough time to remember that I'm not an escort right now and Sebastian isn't a client, so I can eat whatever the fuck I want.

"You know what? I think I will do the steak frites with a glass of the 2020 Louis Jadot."

Albert nods approvingly. "Excellent choice, Miss. Hendrix. How would you like your steak cooked?"

"Medium, please." I smile and hand him back the menu, aware that Sebastian's eyes are still on me. "And Mr. Adler will have a glass of the 2015 La Comtesse to go with his pasta."

"Very well," Albert says, taking our menus and backing away to make room for the server who is carrying a basket of fresh rolls in one hand and a carafe filled with water in the other. Neither Sebastian nor I speak until she's gone and our water glasses are filled.

"So," I begin, plucking a roll from the basket and sitting it on the small plate in front of me. "This is awkward."

His brows pull together. "Is it?"

"Yes, Sebastian. It is."

"Why?" He crosses his arms and leans back in his chair. His posture is rigid but also relaxed. A fitting contradiction for a man who confuses the hell out of me.

"Because of what just happened in your office."

I refuse to mince words. We both know that sitting down for dinner after I just bared my skin and soul to him is weird. He pulls in a deep breath, and the movement causes the fabric across his chest to strain.

"Nadia, I'm not holding any of the things you said or did against you, so you shouldn't hold them against yourself. I wasn't aware of how triggering the setting and the language I used during the conversation would be for you. I should have been more considerate."

His features have crumpled into a grimace that tells me I'm not the only one giving myself a silent lashing about how things happened downstairs.

I shake my head. "It wasn't you. It was me. I overreacted. I let my fear and anxiety run rampant and didn't stop to check the facts of the situation."

That's perhaps the most embarrassing thing of all. My reaction to the things he said made no sense. He asked me to come work for him, made mention of skills he felt I wasn't utilizing, and I immediately jumped to the darkest conclusion. Accusing not only him, but also Desiree, of being underhanded liars who prey on vulnerable people because life under Beau's reign of terror had taught me not to expect anything else. Every act of kindness came with strings and handcuffs attached, and for every real smile or laugh there were a thousand tears. That was my life for a really long time, and even though that's not the case anymore, my brain doesn't always remember.

Sebastian stares at me, and it's a long and thorough look, like he's seeing past what I've just said and right into my brain, into that dark space where the person Beau made me cowers in the corner, waiting for the next shoe to drop or, with the way my life has gone, the next punch to be delivered.

"Let's just agree that we both made mistakes in how we approached the conversation and agree to do better in the future."

Humor and the desperate need to lean into the positive energy he's infusing into the conversation has a smile pulling at the corners of my mouth. "I guess that could work."

"I think it can," he says, eyes sparkling as the server places our individual glasses of wine in front of us. His long fingers curl around the stem of his glass before he raises it in the air and tips it towards me. "To the future."

I pick my glass up and clink it against his. "To the future and what-ever it entails."

Stirring the conversation back to his botched job offer wasn't my intention, but that's exactly what my addition to his toast does. In an instant, Sebastian turns serious, not that dangerous kind of serious that made me want to run earlier, but something else. Something softer than before but still commanding and weighted.

"Are you ready to hear my offer?"

Anticipation rushes over me in a wave that I attempt to squash by pulling in a deep breath. I don't know what Sebastian wants from me, and I'm not confident I'll be able to deliver, but I can listen.

I guess.

My wine glass is at my lips before I make the decision to take a drink, and Sebastian waits patiently while I savor the buttery white wine. After a long silence and a less than lady like gulp, I set the glass down. "I'm ready."

"I want you to come work for me."

"So you said."

"True, but you didn't let me get past that part last time."

"You're right." The laugh that passes my lips surprises me. It surprises Sebastian too. I can tell by the way his eyes widen just a bit. He's trying not to make a big deal of it, but his expression suggests that he didn't think I was capable of a sound like that. "So, let's hear it. You want me to come work for you at one of your many establishments."

"At Cerros," he specifies.

"Doing what?" I sit back and cross my legs. "You already told me I'm not qualified to be a waitress at your restaurant."

He rubs at his chin, fingers moving through the thick, dark hair of his beard as he tries to figure out if this conversation is about to go left like the last one did. "To be fair, your resume didn't indicate you were qualified to do much of anything."

I could argue with him but that would probably mean having to tell him why my resume doesn't reflect any of my actual skills, and *that* would mean getting into things I don't feel comfortable discussing with Sebastian or anyone else for that matter.

"And yet, you still want to hire me."

"I do."

"To do what?"

"To manage the restaurant you wanted to be a server at."

I don't know what I expected him to say, but it wasn't *that*. My mouth drops, and a shocked laugh spills out from between my lips. Sebastian doesn't look the least bit amused. "You're kidding right?"

He shakes his head. "No, Nadia, I'm not kidding."

My chance to respond is stolen by the appearance of two servers with our food. As expected, Sebastian's pasta looks amazing. The nutty aroma of the browned butter and the slight sweetness of the tomatoes makes me wish I felt comfortable enough to take him up on his offer to share.

"Is everything to your liking, Mr. Adler?" Albert asks, appearing out of nowhere once the servers are gone.

"Everything looks perfect, Albert."

Albert turns to me. "Miss Hendrix, can I get you anything else?"

I glance down at my plate, appreciating the fullness of the heap of fries underneath the sliced steak. They're clearly hand cut and fried perfectly. I couldn't be happier. "No, Albert, I think I'm fine."

"Very well." He taps the edge of the table twice and smiles. "You two enjoy."

The moment he's gone, I pop a fry into my mouth and let out a happy sigh around the crispy goodness partially scorching my tongue. Sebastian is still staring, but I don't care. Nothing is going to stop me from appreciating a good french fry, not even this confusing man who apparently wants to hire me.

"Why me?" I ask after I swallow the fry and wash it down with another swig of wine.

Sebastian is quick with his response, pausing mid bite to say,"Why not you?"

My brows pull together, and I'm tempted to ask him if he's having a stroke or something. We've already established that I've never worked in a restaurant before—though technically that's not true— so I'm not sure what makes him think I can run one.

"Besides the obvious reasons?"

He wipes his mouth with the cloth napkin that was resting on his lap. "Last night at the bar when Marcus didn't have the wine you requested, you could have panicked but you didn't. You found a way to make what you had work and flipped it into an amazing experience for your client." The muscles in his throat constrict when he says 'client' and I wonder if it's the word in general or the person it refers to. I don't have time to ask because he starts talking again. "You demonstrated the ability to think on your feet in a high stress situation. That's something that can't be taught, and I need someone with that skill running things on the rooftop."

"Don't you already have someone up there running things?" I arch a brow and take a bite of my steak, hoping none of the juice from the tender cut of meat has dripped onto my dress. Sebastian grimaces like thoughts of Vince send chills born of displeasure and annoyance rushing down his spine as well.

"We parted ways."

"Amicably?" I spent all of five minutes in Vince's presence, but I can pretty much guess that it wasn't. Still, I feel the need to ask, to make sure that he's being as honest with me as possible.

"No, it wasn't amicable."

He takes a sip of his wine, and I watch appreciation skate across his features as the crisp, acidity of the dry white cuts through the rich, buttery notes of the sauce coating his pasta. What I don't see on his face is surprise, which kind of catches me off guard. It's almost as if he had no doubt in my ability to choose the perfect wine pairing for his meal. Sebastian doesn't strike me as the kind of man who gives away his confidence easily, so for him to extend it to me, not just in relation to his dinner, but to his business means a lot.

"Did I make a good choice?" I ask, just to be sure I'm reading him correctly.

He nods, licking his full bottom lip to capture the minuscule droplets lingering there. "You did, but then again, I knew you would."

"You have a lot of confidence in someone who's a virtual stranger to you."

Storm clouds gather inside the pools of champagne he calls eyes as they bore into me, and I get the sense that he's trying to figure out if I'm always this hard to give a compliment to. I want to tell him that it's been years since I've received one that had nothing to do with how soft my breasts are or how tight my pussy is. I want to tell him that I used to be a different person, a girl with confidence in her looks, but more importantly, in her mind. That's the woman my parents raised, not the one sitting in front of him wondering why his vote of confidence makes her feel, for the first time in a long time, that she can find her way back to herself. Sebastian taps his fingertips on the white linen table cloth, regarding me with a stare that makes me squirm in my seat. When his lips finally part, I let out a silent breath of relief.

"I know talent when I see it, Nadia."

"Do you also know a hot mess when you see one, Sebastian? Because that's what I am." A self-loathing laugh punctuates the proclamation, and I'm so ashamed of the sound, I turn my attention to my plate, using my fork to push my food around so I don't have to meet his eyes. "I know wine, and I know that free shit always stops people from whining about what they didn't get. You say it's talent, but I know it's just a result of eating at a lot of nice restaurants with a lot of impatient men."

Suddenly, there are fingers under my chin, tipping my head up so I have no choice but to look him in the eyes. He's barely shifted in his seat, but I guess that's not really necessary when you have the kind of wingspan he does. Everything about him is just so damn big and long. Even his fingers are thick, so thick I think it'd probably take two of mine just to make one of his. I meet his eyes, and there's impatience there. The emotion is so familiar on his face it makes me want to laugh, but there's no place for humor here. Just the disconcerting echo of his touch spreading through my body. Just the lethal slash of his thick brows as they pull together to form one, dark, disapproving line.

"I don't care about what you've done in the past. The choices you had to make in order to survive aren't anything to be ashamed of, and they damn sure don't disqualify you from the future you were trying to create for yourself when you applied to work at Cerros."

I wrap my hand around his wrist and push his hand away. "It was just a waitressing job, Sebastian."

"It was a conscious decision to seek out something different from the work you were doing before."

"Sex work. Don't try to tell me it's not something to be ashamed of if you can't even call it what it is."

"Sex work," he repeats, nostrils flaring. "Applying for the job at Cerros was a conscious decision to seek out something different from sex work."

He's grimacing again, and I don't know why. Obviously, he doesn't have an issue with sex workers or else he wouldn't own a place like Ludus. I study him, trying to figure out if there's another reason why he looks like I just forced him to swallow glass and coming up empty.

"Maybe I just wanted a change of scenery."

"Or maybe you wanted to prove to yourself that you could earn money on your feet instead of on your back."

The urge to slap him is so strong my palm vibrates with the desire to collide with his face. "Do you really think being an asshole is going to increase the likelihood of me taking you up on your offer?"

"No, I think being honest with you is going to increase the likelihood of you taking me up on my offer."

He's not wrong. I prefer his cut and dry assessment of my thought process when I applied for the job at Cerros to the pretty euphemisms meant to motivate me into believing I can do a job I know I can't.

Not because I'm not qualified.

Honestly, I'm more than qualified. The degrees I hold in Viticulture & Enology and Hospitality and Restaurant Management plus a lifetime of watching my parents run one of California's most successful Black owned vineyards have more than prepared me for this job. The problem is those degrees and that experience belong to someone else. Not just in name, though that's definitely an issue because Nadia Hendrix has no degrees or relevant job experience to speak of, but also in spirit.

I'm just not that person anymore. That girl who was so sure she could lead, teach and inspire, who learned the ins and outs of running a business from her father and the intricacies of hospitality from her mother is gone. Maybe Sebastian caught a glimpse of her last night. Maybe that's who he's looking for, but she's not here. I am.

And I am broken and scary and anxious. I am a hollowed out shell who can't be trusted with her own future let alone that of a restaurant.

We've both given up on the illusion of eating, so I push my plate to the middle of the table. "Can I also be honest?"

He nods. "Please."

"I don't trust you."

"You don't know me, Nadia. It would be dumb to trust a stranger. You don't strike me as dumb"

One corner of my mouth tries to lift up into a half smile, but I bite it back. "My life is complicated right now. I don't know how long I'm going to be in New Haven. Your team needs stability, especially after Vince's departure, I don't think I'll be able to give them that, and I know I won't be able to sign a contract for an extended amount of time."

This piques his interest, and I think I see something akin to panic flicker in his eyes. He leans forward, elbows back on the table, fingers steepled and resting under his chin as his gaze turns thoughtful. I don't know when this became a negotiation, but that's exactly how he's treating it.

"So we go with a shorter contract term. It can be month to month if that's what you want. Just tell me what you need, Nadia, and I'll make sure you have it."

"Sebastian, you're not listening."

"Yes, I am." Earnest and triumph are battling it out to be the primary emotion taking over his handsome features. "You're laying out your terms, and I'm demonstrating my willingness to meet them. Please, continue."

I shake my head. "No, I'm telling you that I'm not the right person for this job."

"And I'm telling you that I disagree. Every obstacle you can think of is nothing more than a condition to your employment, a term for us to agree upon. You need flexibility in your contract? You've got it. You want more money than Vince was making? Consider it done. I was going to pay you double his salary anyway. So what else is there?"

Everything sounds simple when it comes out of his mouth. So simple I almost forget the point I was trying to make.

"You have a whole team to consider, Sebastian. They don't need another person coming in and changing everything up just to disappear on them in a few months."

"They work at a restaurant where everything, from the weather to the menu, changes depending on the day. I'm sure they can adjust to a new manager."

His brows lift in a silent demand for my rebuttal, but I don't have anything else to say besides the truth he refuses to hear. "I can't do it."

"Nadia," he breathes my name, a soft utterance filled with desperation. "Can you at least try? It can be a trial run. Sixty days of you giving it your all, and if, for some reason, you still believe you're not right for the position, I'll help you get set up doing something else. I know a lot of people in a lot of places, Nadia, I can get your foot in any door you want to walk through."

Kindness isn't something I've come to expect from this world, and it's not something I trust coming from men as powerful as Sebastian. I stare at him, trying to see the strings attached to the offer he's just extended to me because it feels too close to good to actually be true.

"And if I agree to this, that would make me what? Some kind of charity case? Your good deed for the year?" My voice shakes. The steel I'd forced down my throat earlier all but gone. "I don't need a sponsor, Sebastian."

Pity.

That's his answer to my words. Pure, undiluted pity that shows me how bewildered he is by my brokenness. That tells me he's confused by the layers of it, by the way it goes on and on and on, radiating from the crack in my sternum Beau gave me the first time I tried to run away. He didn't know before, but now he does, now he sees that it's endless. That his words and his kindness will never be enough to seal it up, to make me whole.

I expect this to be the moment when he finally gives up. When he pats himself on the back for trying to be kind to the pathetic ex-sex worker with no prospects and goes on about his day, but instead his jaw clenches, setting with an unerring determination that scares me.

"You're right, Nadia, you don't need a sponsor, but you do need a job and options and maybe even a friend to show you that everyone in this world isn't out to get you."

"And that's what you want to be? My friend?"

His expression is unreadable. "If you'll let me."

Silence descends on our corner of the room, creating a bubble of consideration around Sebastian and me. He's staring again, almost like he's willing me to give in, not because he wants to best me, but because he wants what's best for me. I don't know how that's possible when we're virtually strangers, but there's a part of me, deep down and tucked away, too afraid to actually be seen, that believes it to be true.

My shoulders slump with resignation at the same time my heart lifts with excitement. "A sixty day trial run."

Sebastian's face splits into a wide grin. "With the option to renew."

* * *

LESS THAN TWENTY four hours after agreeing to be Sebastian's new restaurant manager, I return to my motel room with a bag of freshly thrifted business casual clothes I hope will make me look the part in my hand and a pep in my step. But when I see the bouquet of white lilies in front of my door, the pep dissolves into paralysis and the bag of clothes falls out of my hand, landing at my unmoving feet.

I'm distantly aware of the fact that I'm standing in the middle of the parking lot and at any given moment one of the many tenants who make a habit of driving under the influence could come flying through here and turn me into roadkill, but it still isn't enough to make me move. To take a single step closer to the familiar arrangement of fragile petals I've only received from one person in my entire life.

Beau.

Just thinking his name sends a sharp, urgent rush of fear sweeping down my spine. Suddenly, it feels like there are eyes on me, and the hairs on the back of my neck rise as I try to will myself to move, to seek shelter, to find somewhere safe to go even though if he's found me nowhere is safe. None of that matters though, because I can't move. So I just stand. I just wait. I just look at the flowers blowing in the gentle, humid heat of a July wind and surrender to the memory their appearance has pulled to the surface.

The tears have gone, so there's nothing to accompany the sobs wracking my body. My despair is the only sound in the room until the door creaks open, followed by his heavy footfalls as he walks over to the nightstand. He shoves my diploma to the side to make room for the glass vase full of freshly bloomed white lilies. His hands are pale and smooth, indicative of the soft life he's led courtesy of the money my parents left for me that, only days ago, I learned he and his father blew through the last of a few months ago.

Up until yesterday, those hands had never posed a threat to me. They'd only ever been kind, maybe sometimes a little too familiar, but they'd never been violent. _He'd_ never been violent. Not until I threatened to go to the police and report him and his father for drugging me at the dinner they insisted on having to celebrate my college graduation and selling me to a stranger who raped and abused me for days on end. When I made that threat, I'd unleashed a monster, and now that he's been set free, Beau refuses to pull back his fangs.

The mattress sags under his weight as he settles on the bed beside me. His hand is on my thigh. The metal on the gold signet ring he always wears is cold against my skin, but I don't flinch. I'm too weak to move or fight, too scared to push him away, so I just stare at the flowers and cry without shedding a tear.

"You like the flowers?" he asks, fingertips tracing over the bruise he left when he kicked me in the back. "They were my mom's favorite."

"I know that, Beau."

They're the ones he lays on her grave every year on the anniversary of her death. I always take tulips for my mom and carnations for my dad. Beau and I would take turns driving down to the cemetery on the anniversary of their deaths, reminiscing about the last holiday we spent together as a unit before they boarded the flight that claimed all of their lives.

I don't know how to reconcile that person with the man sitting in front of me, with the man who would do the things he's done to me, so I don't try. I just stare at the lilies and wait for it to be over.

"Did you know she wasn't supposed to be on that plane with your parents? They insisted she come with them."

"That's not true."

His hand goes still over a particularly sore spot, and as a reward for my disagreement, he pushes down on it, causing it to throb. "Yes, it is. My dad told me that your mom insisted..."

"_Your mom_ insisted," I spit the words out, forcing them past the scream lodged in my throat. "She wanted to ask my dad for a loan because your father's gambling habit had eaten through their savings and was about to cost them the house."

I've always known that Belinda's last minute addition to the trip was because of the financial stress Roland's gambling was causing, but Beau and I never talked about it. When he flips me over onto my back and climbs on top of me, wrapping his fingers around my throat, I wonder if now was the best time to bring it up.

"Take it back!" He screams, his face turning red, veins popping out of his forehead as he begins to squeeze. "Take it back you worthless, fucking whore!"

Black spots begin to cloud my vision, and I panic, calling up the only bit of strength left in my body to try to fight. I claw at his fingers, his wrists and his arms, using my body to try to buck him off of me, but he doesn't budge. He doesn't stop. He just keeps squeezing and screaming.

"Don't fight. You can't win."

He's right. I can't win on my own. In a desperate, hail Mary attempt, I try to wheeze out his father's name. Roland didn't stop him from beating me yesterday, but maybe today he's in a different place. Maybe today, he'll draw the line at murder.

"He's not here," Beau laughs, squeezing so hard his finger nails dig into my skin. "No one is coming to help you. Do you hear me, you stupid bitch? Help isn't coming."

A blaring horn behind me is the only thing loud and strong enough to pull me back into the present, back to a reality where the threat Beau poses to my life and safety hasn't been made real yet. It's enough to get me moving.

"Sorry," I call out to the impatient driver behind me. They flip me off and speed out of the parking lot mere seconds after me and my bag of clothes are out of the way. I don't even have the energy to be offended by their rudeness because all of my attention is on the bouquet. Pressing my lips together, I move forward, using the kind of slow, cautious steps most people reserve for approaching rabid animals or bombs. When I get right up on it, I notice there's a card nestled in the center of the arrangement. I stop, unsure of whether the card will make me feel worse or better. Just as I decide to reach for it, my phone rings, causing me to jump out of my skin.

"Jesus, Nadia, get it together," I mutter to myself, pulling the phone out of my back pocket and flipping it open. When I see that the call is coming from a number I don't have saved, my mind starts to race with all kinds of possibilities, trying to determine the likelihood that Beau has not only found me here in New Haven, but also somehow come across a phone number I've only given to a handful of people.

Beau is a lot of things—violent, hateful, sleazy—but he's not smart. He's never been smart. If he had found me, *he* would be waiting on my doorstep, not a bouquet of flowers. He'd be laying hands on me right now, not calling to torment me. Satisfied with my reasoning, I answer the phone and hope I was right.

"Hello?"

"Did you get the flowers?" Sebastian asks, a smile folded into the layers of his otherwise serious sounding baritone. All of my muscles relax, and I sag against the door, my body heavy with relief.

"I did. Thank you."

"Are you okay? You sound…winded."

I place a hand over my pounding heart, trying to calm it. "I'm fine. You just caught me in the middle of…something."

Great, Nadia, that doesn't sound suspicious at all.

"Okayyy," Sebastian says slowly, and I know if I could see his face right now, his eyes would be laughing at me. "Well, I won't hold you. I just wanted to make sure the flowers got to you okay."

I glance down at the bouquet at my feet. Now that I know they're from him, they don't feel like a threat. "They did, and they're beautiful."

"I'm glad you like them. They're supposed to symbolize rebirth, so I thought it was fitting for your new beginning."

"Oh." I bite my lip to hold back the sudden onslaught of emotion coursing through me. "That's very thoughtful of you."

"Don't sound so surprised. I can be thoughtful."

Any verbal response I might have wanted to give him is crowded out by the lump building in my throat. I don't know where the happy sob was conceived, but I do know that it wants out, to be birthed, to come into the world loud and fast, announcing the arrival of goodness in my life.

"I have to go." I'm amazed when the words come out relatively normal and decide to push my luck by adding something else. "Thank you, again, Sebastian."

The expression of gratitude is meant to encompass more than this one act of kindness. I hope Sebastian gets that because I can't elaborate.

"You're welcome, Nadia," he says, and the softness in his voice tells me that he does.

10

SEBASTIAN

"**Y**ou're welcome, Nadia," Luca repeats in an annoying rendition of what's supposed to be my voice. I'd stepped away to make the phone call to Nadia to avoid being overheard, but of course my little brother doesn't understand or respect boundaries. I slip my phone into my pocket and grab the bottle of olive oil Mom asked me to get from the pantry off the shelf to my left.

"Shut up, Luc."

I brush past him, but of course he follows. There's a bounce to his stride as he catches up to me, clapping one of his large hands on my shoulder as we cross the threshold of the patio where Mom decided we should have our impromptu Sunday dinner.

"Who's Nadia?" He asks loud enough for everyone at the table to hear. As expected, Mom, Dad, Zoe and Andreas all turn their attention to us as we take our seats at the end of the table.

"Nadia?" Mom asks, her brows lifting to meet the soft curls at her hairline. "Who's Nadia?"

"Don't ask me," Luca says, smiling wide because Mom has just played right into his hand. "Ask Seb. He's the one who was on the phone in the pantry, whispering to someone named Nadia."

In true younger brother fashion, he uses his thumb and his pinky to make a fake phone and pretends to murmur into it with his face warped into some kind of love sick expression.

"Oh, Nadia," he whispers. "You're so welcome, baby."

I roll my eyes when Zoe and Andreas both laugh at his antics. "I didn't call her baby."

"But everything else about that—" Dad asks, gesturing to Luca who is still going. "Is accurate?"

I give him a look that urges him to be serious. "No, Dad. Nothing about that is accurate."

Mom laughs and passes Zoe a wooden bowl filled with pasta salad. "Then please, Sebastian, give us an accurate recount of your conversation, so Luca can stop doing whatever that is."

"It's called acting, Ma," Luca exclaims, placing one hand on his chest to feign hurt.

"Don't quit your day job," Andreas says, taking the bowl from Zoe and handing her the platter filled with chicken kabobs.

"That would require him to actually have a job, Dre."

Zoe's comment is what gets Luca to finally end his imaginary phone call. His mouth drops open. "Zo, I thought I was your favorite brother. How you gone play me like that?"

Our little sister shrugs, her lips pulled up into her signature, joyous smile. Before I met Nadia, I never thought about how easily Zoe's smiles come to her. How their regular appearance on her face speak of the shelter she's thrived under for her whole life. Not just the money she's grown up with but the family she's grown in. Two, loving and attentive parents. Three older brothers who would lay down life and limb for her. Zoe's smile is the smile that belongs to a person who knows what it means to be safe, to be protected, to be loved. Nadia's smiles are few and far between, and they never look quite right.

Joy is a stranger to her features.

The thought occurred to me when we shook hands last night over the cold remnants of our meal. She was excited about the job, but she was too afraid to let it show. I kept catching glimpses of it though, the anticipation and excitement lingering under the layers of self doubt she's always so comfortable with revealing to the world. I sent the flowers because I wanted to bring the other, more positive emotions to the surface even if I wasn't there to bear witness. It was enough just to know she experienced them.

That was the lie I told myself before the images my brain conjured of her rare smile stole what was left of my self control and forced me to call her. She'd sounded strange on the phone, but the thanks she'd given was genuine. It made the risk I'd taken sending the flowers to the address she put down on her application worth it.

"I don't have a favorite brother," Zoe says finally, which only makes Luca look more hurt.

"How can you say that when I'm the one who laid the floors in your salon?" he asks.

Zoe rolls her eyes at him. "You paid someone to do it."

"And *I* had to pay someone else to remove them and get new ones put down." My addition to the conversation brings all eyes at the table back to me, and I immediately regret reminding everyone how I had find a quick solution when Luca's hired help left Zoe with warped floors and crooked baseboards the day before her opening.

"That's right, Seb, you're a regular ole hero." Luca grins at me, taking a sip of his lemonade. "Did you save the day for Nadia too? Is that why she was calling to thank you?"

Andreas snorts when I roll my eyes and let out a heavy sigh. "Should have seen that one coming."

"You're right. I should have." I sit back in my seat and resign myself to divulging the details of my conversation with Nadia so Luca can finally let it go. "Everybody listen up because I'm only going to explain this once. Nadia is the new manager for the Cerros rooftop, and she didn't call me, I called her to make sure she received the flowers I sent to celebrate her joining the team."

Mom makes a semi-disapproving noise in the back of her throat. "I still can't believe you fired Vince. Every time Adrienne calls me it's the first thing she brings up. You know he's moved back to LA, right? She's worried sick about him."

I love Aunt Adrienne, and I love my mom more, but neither of them are going to make me feel bad about getting rid of Vince, and no amount of subtle pouting is going to make me take any kind of responsibility for the bender he's probably on out in LA. Aunt Adrienne is only ever worried sick about Vince when he's in a hole somewhere, gorging on drugs, women and alcohol.

"He wasn't right for the job, Mom."

She nods like she understands even though I think there's a part of her that wishes I would have kept Vince on in some capacity if only to save her from the constant stress of discussing it with her sister.

"And you think this Nadia person is?" Dad asks between bites of his food.

"I do. She's smart, passionate and quick on her feet. Her knowledge of wine is extensive, and she knows how to craft an experience that makes people want to come back for more."

That makes *me* want to come back for more.

Ever since our first encounter, I've been holding my breath until the next. I can't remember the last time I've just wanted to be around someone like I want to be around Nadia. Talking to her, learning from her, challenging the lies someone told her about who she is and what she deserves.

Every member of my family is looking at me, but it's Mom's face that tells me I've revealed more about my interest in Nadia than I intended. Her eyes are bright with excitement.

"She sounds lovely, Sebastian. Maybe we should have her over for lunch one day."

The image hits me immediately. Nadia sitting beside me while we share a meal with my family. Zoe would obsess over her hair and talk her into coming to the salon for an appointment. Mom would have her in the kitchen tasting every component of the latest dish she came up with on a whim. Dad would steal her away and dazzle her with the contents of the wine cellar we used to play hide and seek in as kids. And Luca and Andreas would do what they're doing right now: stare at me to try and find a crack in an expression designed to give away nothing.

My jaw clenches with sudden discomfort and the need to deflect. "She's exactly what the restaurant needs."

"Exactly what the restaurant needs or exactly what *you* need?" Luca asks through the smug grin pulling at his lips. It makes me want to pluck every hair of his beard out one by one.

I glare at him. "My relationship with Nadia is strictly professional."

Zoe twists her lips and casts a doubtful look in my direction. "I don't know about that, Seb. You sent her flowers."

"And?"

"*And* you don't send people flowers," Andreas says, his tone flat.

"He's right," a voice, husky but feminine and definitely not currently present at the table chimes in, causing every head, including mine, to turn toward the source of the sound.

Talia West.

She's never been an Adler because she refused to take my last name when I made her my wife. Her almond eyes glow with pleasure when everyone lets out their own unique sound of surprise, and her back length microlocs sway around her shoulders as she sashays towards us, spreading hugs and kisses around the table before she comes to sit beside me.

"You never brought me flowers, Sebastian, and I was your wife."

"Still not sure how he managed to talk you into marrying him," Luca snickers, grabbing Talia's hand and pressing a kiss to her knuckles. "You know you should have chosen the best Adler brother."

"I would have, Luca," Talia purrs, slipping her hand out of his grip. "But Andreas was taken."

Her dig at me and Luca sends laughter skittering through the group, and I hope the infusion of humor plus Talia's sudden appearance will be enough to get and keep us off the subject of Nadia.

"So," Talia says as she turns assessing eyes on me. "Who's the lady lucky enough to get flowers from Sebastian Adler?"

Luca is the first to pipe up. "Nadia. Sebastian's new restaurant manager."

Talia cocks a brow at me. "Sending flowers to your employees, Seb. That's definitely not your style."

I push out a harsh breath. "She's new in town. I was trying to be nice."

Most people wouldn't be at all interested to hear someone they know talk about trying their hand at kindness, but Talia isn't most people. She has intimate knowledge of who I am, of how I do business and interact with my employees. Luca, Andreas and Zoe might think they know, but Talia is the only one who has a real idea. On more than one occasion she's encouraged me to get to know the people who work for me past their job titles and skills, but I've always resisted. Getting to know an employee on a personal level is how I ended up with a wife I only talked about business with.

"Nice," Talia repeats, her lips curling around the word.

"Leave it alone, Tal."

The note of warning in my tone is enough to send a hush over the entire table, and after a moment of awkward silence, the conversation turns to something that doesn't make the vein in the center of my fore-head throb with irritation.

* * *

THE REPRIEVE IS BRIEF, only lasting as long as Talia and I are around my parents and siblings. The moment we walk into the house we shared when we were married, Talia's hands go to my belt, and the questions begin.

"Are you dating her?" She asks, her brows knit in concentration as she tries to navigate the button on my jeans with the talons she calls nails.

"Talia."

My harsh tone doesn't deter her the way it did when we were in front of my family. Her deep brown eyes mock me for even trying to deploy it.

"I don't care, Sebastian. I just want to make sure I'm not stepping on anyone's toes by sitting on your dick." Her lips are on my neck now, and we're walking backwards, stumbling towards the couch in the center of the open-concept living area. No one has been in this house since the last time she visited New Haven, but everything is in pristine condition courtesy of the cleaners I pay to come out every month.

We land in a heap on the couch with me and my back and Talia on top of me. She straddles my hips, pulling her shirt off to reveal the perfect tear drops that are her breasts. We've been doing this so long it takes no time for my body to respond to hers. In seconds, my dick is hard, straining against the seam of my half-opened jeans. Talia smiles and grinds down on me.

"If you're in a relationship, *he* certainly hasn't gotten the memo."

"I'm not in a relationship."

Nadia and I aren't even friends. We're barely colleagues. We're nothing to each other. Less than nothing, but I'd be lying if I said I didn't want to be something.

Talia slides down my body, dropping down on her knees in front of me. Her hands are back at my waist, working to free my erection from my jeans. She doesn't speak until my dick springs free. "But you want to be, right? You sent her flowers, so you must like her."

If it were any other woman, I'd be confused, maybe even a little outraged, that they were asking about my relationship goals with someone else while literally staring at my dick, but this is Talia we're talking about, and nothing, least of all her blasé attitude about sex, surprises me anymore.

I thought it was cool at first, to have a wife who didn't care if another woman caught my eye, who encouraged me to explore my desires even if it took me outside of her bed. I never did because I was determined to have a marriage that looked like what my parents had. I wanted a good partner. Someone who wouldn't bat an eye when I put everything I had into my business and gave them whatever was left after that. Talia was all of that and more. She was as passionate about my business as I was, pouring everything into building Cerros as a brand and taking the resort chain international. We were a good team, equally matched in all the ways I thought mattered. Putting her on projects I didn't have the bandwidth to handle was a no-brainer because she was essentially me in female form. Where we differed, though, was in the way we approached our marriage.

Meaning, I was being faithful, and she wasn't.

The revelation of her affairs didn't happen like they do in the movies. There was no big production, no emotional underscore that spelled heartbreak and despair. Just a deadpan confession and a question about why I wasn't using her extended stays in Antigua or Mexico as opportunities to sleep around. Apparently, she'd thought my lack of rebuttal to her persistent encouragement to fuck other women meant I was down to open our marriage. I was stunned when I found out because we'd never had such a glaring misunderstanding before, but I wasn't hurt. The idea of her in bed with other people didn't bother me in the slightest. That was when I realized we were better off as friends, business partners and occasional sexual partners.

Talia lowers her mouth to my tip, and the warmth of her breath forces my brain back into the moment.

"I'm not talking about Nadia with you."

"Refusing to talk about her with me, just means there is something to talk about." She swipes her tongue along my shaft, and I know the instant her flesh connects with mine that I can't do this with her today. My hands go to her shoulders, and she freezes. There's no hurt in her eyes when they meet mine, only intrigue, which kind of makes me wish I did want to fuck her, if only to take both of our minds off of Nadia.

Talia stands, and I do too. She slips on her shirt while I button my jeans and hope that us both being clothed will make this whole situation less awkward. It doesn't.

"Damn." Talia laughs, putting her hands on her hips "You really like this woman."

I shake my head. "She works for me. It's not like that."

"You won't even fuck me, Sebastian. It's like something."

"Maybe I'm just not in the mood. You weren't supposed to get in until tomorrow."

We both know the timing of her appearance doesn't have anything to do with it. Under different circumstances—which would be any circumstance where I'm not discussing my new employee with my ex-wife—I would have already pulled two orgasms out of Talia and had her on her way to the third, all without wondering why she's in New Haven sixteen hours earlier than she should be.

Talia rolls her eyes, crossing over to the kitchen and pulling a bottle of water out of the refrigerator. "You were hard, Seb. Your body was willing, but your heart wasn't. The only thing that's changed is that Nadia is in your life."

"She isn't in my life."

But she is because I insisted that she should be. I talked her into taking a job she didn't want and told her we could be friends. I pushed, and she gave in, so now she's in my life. The thought sends a twinge through my chest, and it's made of equal parts fear and excitement.

"You *really* like her." Talia looks amazed, like she didn't know I was capable of liking someone. She gestures at the barstool across from her. "Sit down. I want to hear all about her."

"I have to go, Tal." I fish my keys out of my pocket, choosing an abrupt departure over subjecting myself to whatever line of questioning she's preparing to throw my way. Her knowing laugh follows me out the door, proceeding a statement that sounds like a threat and a promise all wrapped up in one.

"I'll be at Cerros at noon. I can't wait to meet Nadia for myself."

11

NADIA

I'm all nerves and thrifted clothes that don't fit quite right when I walk into Cerros for the second time in my life, and having the official, if temporary, title of the manager of the rooftop restaurant doesn't help at all. I'd thought it would make me feel like less of an outsider in this place that screams glamour and luxury, but it doesn't.

My clothes still feel cheap.

My shoes still fit wrong.

The only thing that makes me feel like I'm in the right place is Regina at my side. When I arrived this morning, stepping into the lobby hoping I would be spared the embarrassment of having to ask where I should report to on my first day of work, Regina was there waiting with a cup of coffee and a warm smile.

If she has thoughts about me going from an unqualified waitress hopeful to a managerial position, she hasn't let it show, and for that I'm grateful. So far, she's taken me to the security room on the first floor, so I can take my employee photo and get the ID card that will grant me access to all the spaces that fall under my domain.

"You can also use your ID to bypass the hotel floors and go straight to the part of the building we use for Adler Holdings," Regina explains as we step onto the elevator. She gives me a tight smile and gestures for me to press my ID to the scanner on the panel next to the buttons. When I do, the panel beeps and the buttons for the higher floors light up, signaling that they're available to be pressed. I look at Regina for further guidance, and she laughs. "Your office is on the twenty-ninth floor."

"Right." I press the button and swallow the shocked gasp creeping up my throat. I didn't realize I would have an office. "This building is pretty impressive. I didn't know Adler Holdings was also housed here."

"Mr. Adler didn't see the point in maintaining another office space when we could easily fit our offices in the top seven floors of the building."

"Also doesn't hurt to be able to offer exclusive lodging and food options to potential business associates."

"Exactly."

"There are thirty floors total, right? Plus the rooftop."

Regina nods. "Yes, twenty-two floors dedicated to the hotel, seven for Adler Holdings, and the top floor houses the kitchen for the rooftop as well as the indoor dining room for customers who want to take advantage of the view without being exposed to the elements."

"He really thought of everything."

"Mr. Adler is very good at anticipating people's needs and meeting them before they're ever expressed."

The elevator glides to a stop, and the doors slide open with a low ding that announces our arrival onto the floor. Regina exits first, turning to the right and looking back to make sure that I'm following her. I am, but I have to jog a bit to keep up with her quick strides. For such a short woman, she moves fast as hell. The hallway she's leading me down is nothing but a blur of glass windows and natural light. I glance back towards the elevators to see what's on the other end of the hall and spot a massive conference room as well as a pair of stately French doors with opaque glass and a name plate I can't read from this far away.

"That's Mr. Adler's office, and this is yours," Regina says, stopping

in front of a set of doors that are a mirror image of the ones I just spotted. There's a name plate here too, and the letters etched into the gold
plated metal spell my name. I gape at it, refusing to believe that the
space behind these doors belongs to me. I haven't even seen it yet, but
I already know it's too much.

More than I could ever need, possibly more than I deserve.

"This is too much." The words are a quiet murmur only meant for
my ears, but Regina is standing right here, so she hears them. She
shakes her head as she opens the door.

"Mr. Adler said you would say that."

"Do you always call him Mr. Adler?" I ask, following her on
cautious feet into a space I still can't believe is mine. It's even bigger
than I thought. I could probably fit five of my motel rooms inside of
here and still have room to move around comfortably. For such a big
space, it's cozy with several sitting areas strategically placed
throughout for more casual conversations and a large conference table
off to the side, perfectly positioned to give every person sitting at it
their own unique view of downtown New Haven. In the center of the
room is an L-shaped desk made of light oak with shelves just begging
to be filled with books built into the sides.

I move over to it, placing my purse, cup of coffee and ID badge on
top, so both my hands are free to roam over the smooth surface. To
touch what feels like a tangible representation of my future.

"Not always," Regina says, reminding me of the question I asked
her before my office decor rendered me speechless. "Sometimes when
he gets on my nerves, I call him Sebastian."

Her response makes me laugh. "Does he get on your nerves a lot?"

"Endlessly." She tilts her head to the side, assessing me. "But he's a
good boss, if that's what you're trying to figure out. He can be
demanding and a little curt sometimes, but he's always respectful. If
you decide to stay on past your sixty day trial, I don't think you'll
regret it."

Hearing Regina mention the contingencies around my employment
adds an unwelcome dash of reality to what has been an otherwise
lovely morning. My heart does a free fall into my stomach, landing

with a splash that has nothing to do with the time constraint, because I could walk into Sebastian's office right now and take the sixty day trial off the table, and everything to do with why it's there in the first place.

Me and my mess of a life.

Me and my self doubt.

Me and my fear of putting down roots just to have Beau appear and force me to yank them back up again.

As I sink into the chair behind my desk, I school my features into an expression I hope hides the fact that I don't know where I'll be living, let alone working, in sixty days. "I guess we'll just have to see how it goes."

Regina looks like she shares my lack of confidence in my ability to make it through this trial period. I don't know if that makes me feel worse or better.

"Right." She claps her hands and rounds the desk. "Let me show you how to log in to your computer, so you can get started with your tasks for the day."

"Oh, okay." I slide to the right, making room for her to type in what I assume are my credentials to bring the desktop to life. "I thought I would at least get to meet with Sebas—I mean, Mr. Adler, before I got started."

"He'll be in meetings most of the day, so you probably won't see him."

"Oh." The disappointment held in the one word is loud, and I cringe as it settles into the space between me and Regina. I don't know where it came from. The disappointment, that is. It's not like I spent every minute since our phone call yesterday entertaining the foreign sensation of butterflies in my stomach when I thought about seeing his face again.

"Don't worry. He's given me a list of items for you to review that will probably keep you busy for the rest of the day."

"What kind of things?" I ask, watching her fingers fly over my keyboard as she starts to log me into my work email. "I can do that myself, you know. All you have to do is give me the login information."

For the first time since we've met, Regina looks apologetic. Red tints the top of her cheeks as she straightens and backs away from the computer. "Right, my apologies, Miss. Hendrix."

"It's fine." I give her a smile to let her know I'm not offended or upset. "And please, just call me Nadia."

My new name used to feel odd on my tongue. Every time I would say it, it would feel like I was testing it out, trying it on for size, but lately, specifically since I've heard it on Sebastian's lips, attached to all his beliefs about who I am and what I can do, it's started to feel like mine. I don't even stumble over the syllables when I tell Regina to use it in place of the formal Miss Hendrix.

"Nadia," she says, sliding the piece of paper she has my username and password written on over to me. "This is your login for every system we use, including email. I would suggest changing it today, so no one has access to your computer and files except for you."

"Got it. I guess I'll add that to the list of things Mr. Adler left for me to do."

"Oh, yes!" She exclaims, pulling an actual to-do list from the clipboard under her arm and handing it to me. "Everything you need to get done is written down here. You'll find that I've already included changing your password right at the top."

She taps the empty check box with the nail of an index finger, and I almost laugh at the excitement on her face. "Thank you, Regina."

"You're welcome, Nadia. Can I get you anything else?"

"No, I think I'm fine. If I need anything, I'll come find you."

"Oh, that won't be necessary." My focus is already on the detailed list of action items Sebastian has left for me, but my eyes fly to her face when I hear the mild flare of panic in her voice. "If you need me, just dial one of your phone and I'll come to you."

My brows pull together in confusion. "You're not my assistant, Regina, I don't expect you to be at my beck and call."

"Mr. Adler has left me with strict instructions to see to your every need until you can hire your own assistant."

On the surface, it seems like a thoughtful gesture, but something about Regina's expression makes me feel like her hovering is more about oversight than assistance. I press my lips together to stop myself from voicing the assumptions swirling around in my mind.

"That's sweet, Regina, but absolutely unnecessary."

Her lips pull into a tight line. "Mr. Adler deems it necessary, therefore it is necessary."

I feel like I'm missing something, but I'm not sure what exactly it is. My mind, of course, is ready to fill in the blanks, ready to tell me that Sebastian has assigned Regina to shadow me and report back, to let him know whether or not I'm capable of doing this job. It's the only plausible explanation, but something about it feels wrong because out of the two of us, Sebastian seemed to be the only one certain of my abilities.

Blowing out a slow breath, I decide to let it go. "Okay. Well, I'll let you know if I need anything."

Relief washes over her features. "Perfect. I'd like to show you one last thing before I go if that's alright with you?"

It doesn't really feel like I have a choice. "Sure."

I rise from my seat and follow her to the far right corner of the room. At first glance, the wall we're facing doesn't look any different from the others, but then Regina presses her palm to part of it and a panel pops open, revealing a small hallway.

"Through here, you have a private bathroom, complete with a shower and a small wardrobe for you to keep a change of clothes in case of emergencies." Everything she's just described is housed in the room to my right, and my jaw drops as I look inside, taking in the marble walls and gold finishes. I'm past the point of surprise. Now, I'm just plain flabbergasted. "And over here, you have your own private elevator that provides direct access to the kitchen on the floor above."

"This is it right? Because I don't think my heart can handle another hidden feature."

"That's it. I promise." Regina laughs, leading me back into the main part of the office. I go back to my desk while she heads to the door. Her fingers rest on the handle. "Well, I guess I'll leave you to it."

"Thanks for helping me get settled," I say, genuinely meaning it.

"You're welcome."

She departs with a soft click of my office doors, leaving me to lose myself in the work Sebastian has left for me to do. After I change my password, I check it off the of the list and move on to the next thing which is checking my email. Since my account is fairly new, there aren't many messages, but I do see one from HR that's titled **Offer Letter + Benefit Details.** I'm just about to click on it when a notification from the leave management system comes through, pulling my attention away from my email and over to the app where an employee named Sarah has just submitted a request for time off. Deciding what to do with the request sends me down a rabbit hole of employee records, previous leave requests, and current work schedules that, in most cases, don't align with the preferred hours listed on the employees application.

It takes me hours to sort through it all and come up with my own to-do list that includes scheduling a staff meeting, creating a new preferred hours form for everyone to fill out and figuring out the best way to disperse it. By the time I'm done, it's well past noon, and my stomach is staging a riot. I push back from my desk with a sigh and glance around the expansive office that has a private bathroom and elevator but not a single snack in sight. Regina told me to call her if I needed anything, but it feels kind of icky to call her about food when I can go get something for myself.

My logic is sound, but I still hesitate when my fingers wrap around the handle that will take me outside of my office. I can't shake the feeling that Regina, and maybe by some extension, Sebastian, wants me to stay tucked away in here. The mere idea of me walking around made Regina look like she wanted to tether me to my desk, though I can't for the life of me understand why.

"Maybe you're just being paranoid," I say, offering up the possibility like it's not *my* brain I'm trying to reason with.

Paranoia is always a possibility. At this point, we're reluctant bedfellows. I mull it over, and find the explanation wanting because it doesn't account for Regina's reactions. She was worried about me leaving the office without her by my side, which suggests that I'm being hidden away. But why? And from whom? All my desire to answer those questions dies when my stomach lets out another reproachful groan that reminds me I have access to a private elevator that will take me right to a kitchen with plenty of food and no people.

Grinning because I've solved the issue of my hunger without upsetting whatever precarious balance Sebastian has assigned Regina to protect, I rush over to the door that leads to the hidden hallway. Within moments, I'm deposited into a room full of gleaming stainless steel appliances. I glance around, nodding my appreciation for the state of the art commercial kitchen. It meets all of my expectations, except for one: it's not empty.

"Uh, can I help you?" The woman standing at one of the prep stations asks, tossing a harried look at me as she presses a sesame mixture into the flesh of an ahi tuna steak. When I don't respond, because I'm honestly too captivated by the contrast of the white of her chef's jacket against the vibrant depth of her blue-black skin, she rolls her eyes. "How'd you get up here?"

"I used my badge." I hold it up, and she gives it a long, hard look then nods.

"Great, so at least I know you're not crazy." When the sesame is perfectly affixed to the tuna, she leaves them to rest on a plate and moves over to the sink to wash her hands. "Now, tell me what you're doing in my kitchen."

"Your kitchen?"

Her eyes narrow into slits, and she looks prepared to take back her earlier declaration about me not being crazy. "Yes, *my* kitchen. I'm Chef Elle O'Dea, who the hell are you?"

"Sorry, Chef. I'm new here, so I don't know everyone on staff yet." I step forward and extend my hand, wondering if this is why Regina wanted me to stay in my office. "I'm Nadia Hendrix, the new manager for the rooftop restaurant."

Elle doesn't take my hand. Instead, she brushes past me and sets about preparing the pan to sear her tuna. "Is there something I can help you with, Nadia Hendrix?"

"Oh, um." I bite my lip, searching my brain for a plausible lie. "No, I was just—"

Whatever lie I was going to tell is interrupted by the loud and long growling of my stomach. Chef Elle turns around, her dark lips curled into a knowing smile. The gentle expression makes her already stunning features even more breathtaking, allowing me the chance to appreciate her round, dark eyes and high cheekbones.

"Let me guess, you came up here hoping to get something from the walk-in that could hold you over until you got home?"

"How'd you know?"

"Girl." She laughs as she adds a thin layer of avocado oil to her pan. "You'd be surprised how often I get staff members up here taking a piece of fruit here or a vegetable tray there."

"So you wouldn't mind if I grab something real quick? I promise I'll be in and out."

"Sure, you're more than welcome to do that, or you can wait about five minutes and have this extra tuna steak I'm about to have on hand."

Her offer comes as a shock to my brain and a delight to my stomach. "Are you sure you won't need both?"

"No. I always make an extra when Mr. Adler has meetings, but he only eats one."

I hate the way my spine straightens when I hear his name, but I'm thankful that Elle is too busy tending to the fish to notice. "And what about his guest? Won't they notice if their plate comes out with everything but the protein?"

I'm asking the question like my stomach hasn't already staked its claim on that second tuna steak, but I have to be sure I'm not eating someone else's food. It would be so embarrassing to explain to Desiree that I got fired over a piece of fish.

"No," Elle says, shifting the pan off of the eye that's still glowing red. "His wife doesn't eat meat."

12

SEBASTIAN

"Ludus: Antigua," I muse in response to Talia's pitch, throwing a napkin over what's left of my lunch. "You want to take an illegal enterprise international?"

"Sex work is legal in Antigua, Sebastian."

"But brothels are not, Talia."

"Might I remind you that neither of those things are legal in the United States? We won't be breaking any laws in Antigua that we aren't already breaking here."

Technically, that's true, but in Antigua we'd be breaking laws without the protection of the connections I have stateside. I rub at the back of my neck, considering the wisdom of diving into this further. Talia watches me, and everything about her gaze tells me that she's not about to let this go. I let out a sigh.

"Where's this coming from?"

Victory dances in her eyes. She knows as soon as I start asking questions, she's got me on the hook. "The same place it came from last time. The resort is attracting escorts, and we don't have the manpower necessary to provide constant supervision for the villas. So far we haven't had any issues with things getting violent, but we both know it's only a matter of time before cops are knocking on my door."

Just the thought has me frowning. I don't like the idea of anyone, least of all some assholes with impulse control issues fucking up what Talia and I have worked so hard to build. The Cerros resort in Antigua was our largest undertaking, and the most risky. Not just because of the size, but also because of the kind of people we serve. Talia wanted to take advantage of the exotic backdrop to really lean into the more primal urges of our clientele. Under her instruction, Cerros Antigua has become one of the top hedonistic resorts in the world, hosting events that cater to kinks and fetishes of all varieties. What she's built is important to her, which means it's important to me.

"We can't have that."

"No, we can't." She gives me a broad smile and then sits back in her seat, her shoulders sagging with relief. "If it makes you feel better, I already have a spot scoped out."

"That depends on the number attached to the spot you scoped out."

"Oh, please, we both know money is not an issue."

It's not. I could buy the entire island twice and still have more money than I'd ever be able to spend in this lifetime or the next. The problem is the only person I'd pay to handle the Ludus build in Antigua is giving me the run around about a job in California. I guess I've got to learn how to trust someone with a contractor's license besides Dominic Alexander.

"Start with the land, and we'll go from there."

"Perfect." Talia finishes off her glass of water. "Now we can get to the second order of business."

"Second order of business or the real reason you're here?"

"What makes you think the conversation we just had isn't the real reason I'm here?"

"Because we could have discussed a land purchase over the phone or via email."

She purses her lips. "True, I guess I kind of wanted to look you in the eyes when I told you that I'm getting married."

"You're engaged?" There's no way to keep the shock out of my voice. "You just had my dick in your mouth yesterday, and you're engaged?"

"Sebastian, you more than anyone, know that a ring isn't going to stop me from fucking who I want when I want." She's right. The flawless diamond I put on her finger didn't keep her from falling into bed with any and every one who caught her eye. "And for the record, I was engaged the last time your dick was inside me."

"Great, that's great, now I've gone from the man you cheat on to the man you cheat with."

Talia rolls her eyes. "It's not cheating when you and your partner have an understanding."

"*Do* you and your partner have an understanding?"

"Yes, Blue and I are both clear on the parameters of our relationship." She gets out of her seat and moves around to my end of the table. "I'm not making the same mistakes I made with you."

Her hands go to my shoulders and glide down to my chest until she has her arms wrapped around my neck. It's an innocent embrace, and I lean into it, laying one of my hands over hers.

"Well, that's comforting. I'm so glad I could be your learning curve."

"I'm glad you could be too." She presses a kiss to my temple. "You were a terrible husband, Sebastian, and I was a terrible wife. But I think I might get it right this time around."

"What changed?" I ask, glancing up at her. "After the divorce, you swore you wouldn't get married again."

"I didn't think I would. Then Blue came to work at the resort, and it was like…"

"You finally found the thing you didn't even know you were looking for," I finish her sentence, surprising Talia and myself. I don't know where the words came from, but they feel right. They perfectly encompass the way Nadia's presence in New Haven has interrupted my existence. She walked into my life and cracked open my reality, upsetting the delicate balance of control and predictability I've thrived in for so long. Now, I'm just like Talia's sentence: fractured.

Waiting.

Wanting.

Wondering about how we could fit together. Not physically—

because I have no doubts about the way her long legs would wrap around my waist or the perfection of her curves in my hands—but spiritually.

I have questions about her soul. About the pain it holds and the joy it might find intertwined with mine. I have thoughts in my mind I only want to share with her. Secrets I don't even know yet that can only be heard by her ears and seen by her eyes.

I used to think what Talia and I had was all I was capable of giving someone. Now I know I can give more, and I want to. None of it makes sense to me, but Talia nods like she understands.

"Exactly. Is it that way with you and Nadia?"

I shrug her off, blowing out a breath of frustration. "When are you going to stop asking about her?"

"When you finally let me meet her."

"That's not going to happen."

"Oh, come on, Seb, please. I mean how can I not want to lay eyes on the woman when you talk about her like *that* and send her flowers just to be nice?"

"Oh my, God. Can we please let the flower thing go?" If I had known they were going to cause this much commotion, I wouldn't have sent the flowers at all.

Okay, that's a lie.

The truth is nothing would have stopped me from sending those flowers to Nadia, from showing her how happy I am to have her on my team, and in my life. I wanted her to have the best first day possible. The flowers were my first attempt at ensuring that, and keeping Talia out of her way is the second.

Talia hasn't made it easy.

She brings Nadia up almost as often as she crosses my mind, which makes it hard for me to *stop* thinking of her. Wondering what she's doing, if she likes her office, whether she's already made her way through the to-do list I left her and how annoyed she is that Regina's only assignment for the day is keeping her from running into Talia. I know she's noticed. She's too smart not to, and Regina isn't exactly subtle.

Talia pushes her lips out into a pout that's supposed to make me give in. "Why don't you want me to meet her?"

"Because it's her first day, and she needs to get her bearings without you asking her invasive questions or, worse, flirting with her and making her uncomfortable."

Everyone who knows Talia knows she's a relentless flirt and a fiercely protective friend. While I appreciate those qualities about her most of the time, I don't want to subject Nadia to them just yet. I know I won't be able to keep them apart forever, especially if Nadia stays on past her trial period, but I can prevent their worlds from colliding today.

"Does she look uncomfortable when you flirt with her?"

Talia's question brings images of Nadia's panicked eyes that night in my office to the front of my mind. My stomach flips, awash with anger and disgust for my earlier thoughts about her legs wrapped around my waist. I shouldn't be thinking of her like that. I shouldn't be thinking of her at all.

I push to my feet, trading my spot at the table for the chair behind my desk. Talia watches quietly as I shift through the stack of folders on top of it, moving things around just to have a reason not to look in her in the eyes. "I don't flirt with my employees."

"You flirted with me," she tosses back, bringing up the other reason why I'm determined to keep her and Nadia apart. Our relationship started when Talia was working for me. I don't want Nadia to know that just yet. Not before she gets the chance to know me, to learn that I'm not the kind of man who makes a habit of using his employee roster as a dating pool.

"And look how that ended up."

"It wasn't all bad. We had lots of fun before things imploded."

"You really believe that don't you?"

"I do." She plops down in one of the arm chairs across from me and kicks her feet up on my desk. "You don't feel the same way?"

"We had lots of fun," I concede. "But I think we got married for all the wrong reasons."

For me, proposing was a no-brainer. A decision born out of rationale and void of emotion. One day I woke up and realized we'd been doing everything together—living, sleeping, working—and thought the only thing we had left to do was get married. I still don't know why Talia said yes to my proposal. I've made job offers that have been more romantic than when I asked her to be my wife.

Talia nods. "For sure. It was all business and no emotion. You didn't even get down on one knee."

"And you didn't even want a ring."

"I was surprised you thought to get one."

We stare at each other. Both of us staying quiet, taking a moment of silence in observation of our failed union before we burst into collective laughter. I come up for air first.

"We were doomed from the start."

"We really were," Talia agrees. "But just because we couldn't make things work, doesn't mean we can't get it right the second time around."

I give her a sincere smile. "I hope that's true for you and Blue."

"It is," she replies with certainty etched into her features. "Maybe it will be for you and Nadia as well."

Refuting her genuine articulation of goodwill feels wrong, so I smile and accept it even though I know there will never be anything real between me and Nadia Hendrix because the shadows lurking in her past, the ones keeping her from seeing the good that could be her future, won't allow it.

13

NADIA

B y the end of my official first day of work, I'm tired of looking at Regina and my office. After she found me in the kitchen with Elle, enjoying a rather delicious, and conveniently free, lunch, Regina escorted me back to my cell and refused to respond when I asked her if Sebastian's wife was the reason she'd been on my neck all day.

Ex-wife.

The voice in my head says, reminding me of Elle's last minute correction which was promptly followed by an explanation about how everyone on staff still refers to Talia West as Sebastian's wife because it's common knowledge that they still fuck whenever she's in town and he hasn't dated anyone since the dissolution of their marriage three years ago. Despite the weird energy that laced our initial interaction, Elle actually turned out to be quite nice and extremely gossipy. She told me everything I wanted to know about Sebastian and Talia, and some things I didn't, while I ate, and she didn't look the least bit remorseful when Regina scolded both of us for talking about the boss behind his back.

I wasn't remorseful either, but Regina definitely made me regret my trip to the kitchen when she rewarded my little field trip by attaching herself to my hip for the rest of the day. From twelve thirty to five, my office became her office too. A shared space for my anxiety about the email I sent to the entire staff requiring their attendance at a meeting tomorrow, and her disapproval, which was so strong it's still scenting the air even though she left thirty minutes ago.

I would already be gone too, but I made a last minute decision to print out employee files, so I could take them home and review them. Since I don't have a laptop and therefore no way to access any Cerros systems at home, printing everything out had felt like a smart decision. But right now, when I'm trying to stuff a stack of papers the size of my head into my cheap faux leather bag, I'm second guessing myself.

"How was your first day?"

The only good thing about spending my nights replaying every conversation I've had with Sebastian over in my head is that I know his voice by heart now. If that wasn't the case, I would probably be jumping out of my skin right now because there were no footsteps or anything else to announce his impending arrival.

"Great," I respond without even looking at him. I tell myself it's because all of my attention needs to be on the stack of papers and the bag that refuses to hold them, but deep down I know it's because I'm not ready to look at him yet. "I especially loved the part where my office became a maximum security facility where Regina was the warden."

The papers are finally inside the bag, so I pull the zipper shut and breathe a sigh of relief that becomes a huff of frustration when the seam pops and the metal mechanisms holding everything together clatter onto the floor.

I glance heavenward, shooting a glare to the ceiling and directly at God because apparently He still has it out for me. "Perfect, that's just perfect."

"Do you need help?"

Sebastian has gone from lingering inside the door to standing just on the other side of my desk, so when I turn my withering gaze on him, I get to see him flinch. "No, I don't need help, and I also don't need a baby sitter, so I hope you and Talia have concluded whatever business you needed to attend to today because tomorrow I'll need to actually leave this office to do my job."

Dark eyes rush over my features, documenting my anger with vivid interest. "Regina told you about Talia?"

"No." Now, I'm the one studying his features, watching for any micro expression that might confirm Elle's suspicion about Sebastian's lingering feelings for his ex-wife. "Regina didn't say anything to me about Talia, which means she neglected to explain to me why you felt the need to hide me from her."

I don't voice any of the assumptions I've made about why he felt the need to go to such great lengths to keep me and his ex apart, but they bounce around in my head, taking turns launching themselves off of the inside of my skull. All of them centering around my lack of qualifications and Sebastian's embarrassment over hiring me. Each one telling me that the moment he realized Talia and I were going to be in the same place at the same time, Sebastian decided it was best to spare her from having to interact with me. The worthless whore, the incompetent slut who can't hold a candle to the woman he still trusts to oversee some of the most integral parts of his business on her best day.

Shame is a sharp current, cutting down my spine as I realize that the voice speaking the harsh words swirling around in my head is mine. Not Sebastian's. Not Beau's. Not even the regal, and maybe even a little snooty, lilt I assigned to Talia in my mind. Just mine. I don't know when that happened. When *I* became the person feeding me lies about who I am and what I deserve.

Sebastian dips down to pick up what's left of my bag's closure and places it on the edge of my desk. His movements are precise and unhurried, like he has all the time in the world to respond. I guess he does, because I'm not leaving this office until I hear what he has to say.

"I wasn't hiding you from Talia," he says finally, still watching my face to measure my reactions. "I was hiding Talia from you."

"What? Why?"

In the seconds between my question and his response, I see Sebastian fight a battle between his desire to tell me the truth and the need to keep the inner workings of his mind to himself. His jaw clenches, and a vein in the center of his forehead pops out and begins to pulse before he speaks.

"Because Talia and I met when she was working for me, and I didn't want you to hear that and think I'm the kind of guy who sleeps with every woman whose check he signs."

I open my mouth to tell him that I wouldn't think that of him, and then stop because we both know my mind is capable of jumping to some outlandish conclusions. Heat floods my cheeks, and my eyes drop to the floor, shame preventing me from holding his gaze.

"Oh."

"Hey," he says softly, urging me to look at him without touching me like he did last time. "That's not an indictment of your reaction to our conversation at Ludus. It was just me trying to be cautious. I didn't mean for my concerns to interfere with your day, though, and for that I apologize."

Him apologizing for being thoughtful feels wrong even if his decision was a bit misguided. For some stupid reason, probably because I'm still not used to people thinking of me or considering my feelings at all, unshed tears sear the back of my eyes.

"That's not what I was expecting you to say."

Amusement turns his mouth into a jagged line, his lips caught somewhere between a smile and a frown. "What did you think I was going to say?"

"I just thought you would reach for one of those lines men love so much when they want a woman to forgive them without actually admitting they're wrong."

"Ah." He crosses his arms, and it's the first time I take notice of his outfit.

Today, he's in an outfit that's as casual as I'll probably ever see him. A cream polo that gives me a dissatisfying peek at his impressive biceps. His shirt fits like the cloth was cut to his exact dimensions, tapering at his waist and disappearing into the band of a pair of white pants.

White.

The man is wearing white pants, and there isn't a single spot on them. Why does that impress me? Upon further inspection, I mark the presence of a thin gold chain around his neck that matches the small hoop dangling from his earlobe. It occurs to me then that I've never seen his ears before, and that I'm only seeing them today because his locs aren't in their usual ponytail. Instead, someone—I'm trying really hard not to think about who—has created several rows of rolled twists at the front and pulled the rest up into a bun that's secured at the top of his head.

"You expected me to reach for the old 'you're overreacting' or 'it wasn't even like that' excuse?" He asks, forcing me to return my attention to the conversation.

I clear my throat, which is suddenly dry. "Something like that."

Sebastian laughs, and the sound is a rich cloud of humor that washes over me. "I don't do excuses. If I fuck up, I own it and do what's necessary to make it right. So tell me, Miss Hendrix, what can I do to make this right?"

There's no reason for a shiver to run down my spine when he calls me Miss Hendrix, but it does. It most definitely does, and it causes my brain to short circuit for a second.

"You can start by having Regina stay in her office tomorrow."

He laughs again, stroking his beard with long fingers. "That one will be easy since she told me if she had to spend another day trying to keep tabs on you, she'd quit."

"Damn, was I really that bad?"

"Apparently, so. She said something about spending her lunch break looking for you and finding you upstairs with Elle?"

"Yeah, I went up there hoping to sneak a small snack back to my prison cell and ended up hanging with her instead."

His eyes narrow. "So you're the one who ate my second piece of tuna?"

I nod enthusiastically, not the least bit sorry. "I am, and it was good too."

"Wow, you just gone brag about it right in my face?"

I arch a brow. "Would you prefer I do it behind your back, Mr. Adler?"

Something strange happens to his face. Emotions I can't name clamor for my attention behind his eyes before he shuts them all down and turns serious again. Feeling self conscious about making things weird with my potentially flirty comment, I turn my attention back to the broken bag in my desk chair. I feel Sebastian's eyes on me as I haul it onto the desk to try to get a closer look at the damage.

"So," he says, "HR let me know they haven't received your counter yet."

"My counter?"

"To the initial salary offer we made."

"Shit." I toss my head back and let out a groan. "I knew I was forgetting something! I never even looked at it."

"Nadia, it's fine, you can send it in tomorrow."

I shake my head and sit back down at my desk, shaking the mouse to call the screen back up. "No, I can do it now. I just need to log back into my computer."

I glance up to give him a reassuring smile only to find him giving me another strange look. "Why don't you just look at it on your phone?"

"Because they don't have email on these." I pull my phone out of the pocket of my bag and hold it up. Sebastian's jaw drops, and horror dawns his features, making his disdain for the obsolete technology in my hand clear. He reaches out and plucks it from my hand, holding the relic gingerly. When my desktop finally presents the login screen, I split my attention between the keyboard and his face, watching as he glances from the phone in his hand to the bag on the desk filled with papers.

"Do you have some kind of aversion to technology that I need to know about?"

"Not exactly."

"You have a flip phone, Nadia, and you printed off employee records when you could have just logged in to the system remotely. Surely, that's indicative of some kind of issue with technology."

"Or, it's indicative of a lack of means," I say, scanning my now full inbox for the email from HR I neglected to open earlier. I find it close to the bottom, buried underneath a bunch of responses from my staff letting me know they'll be at the meeting tomorrow. "The flip phone was all I could afford when I got here, and a laptop, tablet or whatever other gadget I'd need to access the system remotely, has never been in my monthly budget."

Sebastian sits my phone on the desk, his expression sober now that I've reminded him about the glaring wealth disparity between the two of us. "Take a look at your offer letter," he says, pulling out his phone and tapping at the screen with his brow furrowed in concentration. "Now that you're working here, you'll find there isn't much that's out of your budget."

I double click on the offer letter attached to the email and gasp when I see the numbers underneath the extensive, and extremely generous, list of benefits. Sebastian didn't over state things when he said there wouldn't be much I couldn't afford with my new salary. He did, however, fail to mention all the things that would come along with it. The words that detail my compensation swim around on the screen in front of me, and I have to blink several times to get them straight. My voice comes out in a stunned whisper as I read the paragraph out loud.

"We will be offering you an annual gross salary of $242,000 as well as a $10,000 stipend to cover any relocation fees and an $8,000 clothing allowance that will be deposited into your account on the 1st of every month."

He's lost his mind.

That's the first thought that pops into my head after I add all those numbers together to get a staggering total that is more money than I could ever need. I turn my wide eyed stare on Sebastian to find that he's still preoccupied with his phone.

"You expect me to *counter* this?"

"Yes."

"But why? It's already too much?"

He tucks his phone into his pocket, finally done with whatever it was he was doing, and levels me with a stare I know shakes even more the most formidable business men to their core. "Because even when someone is offering you something good, you should always remind them that you deserve better."

I shake my head in disbelief as he turns and strides towards the door. I can't believe this. I don't know what to say, but I have to say something, right? Maybe he doesn't know that six figures is far more than any other restaurant manager in New Haven is making. Maybe he doesn't know that relocation fees and clothing allowances aren't really a thing. Maybe….he's just being nice.

There's that word again. That reminder of the existence of good in a world that's only treated me to evil lately. I used to believe in good. I used to have good all the time. I could look around and find it anywhere. In my mother's smile. In my father's eyes. In the halls of the sprawling estate they built together. In the hills of our vineyard and the sweet squish of ripe grapes under my toes. Good used to be everywhere, and then they died and it was gone. I don't know what it means that it's decided to reappear in my life in the form of this man.

"Sebastian," I call out, but he doesn't turn around.

"Submit your counter before you leave for the night, Nadia."

* * *

IT TOOK me forty-five minutes to work up the nerve to send the email to HR asking for an additional fifteen hundred dollars, but it only took two for Sebastian to respond, countering my counter and telling me to think bigger.

By the time I accepted the offer, my salary was fifteen thousand dollars more than the initial offer and both my stipend and clothing allowance were sitting at a cool ten thousand. And just when I thought I was free to go home and relax after a long day of work, I got a follow up email from HR asking for my direct deposit information.

The request sent me into an hours long tail spin that I'm still caught up in when I walk through the doors of the bank Desiree recommended when I told her about my concerns over dinner last night. They've only been open for a few minutes, so there's no one in line when I make my way to the first teller I see. She glances up, her countenance caught somewhere between pleasant and annoyed.

I flash my brightest and friendliest smile, so she doesn't read my nerves as nefarious intent and press a silent alarm of something. "Hi, I know you're just getting settled in, but I was wondering if I could talk to someone about opening an account?"

Acknowledging that she's just getting her day started buys me some good will. The annoyance fades away, making room for a genuine smile. "Of course, you'd need to speak with one of our associates in the offices over there." She nods towards the wall of offices behind us. "Typically, they don't get in until eight thirty, but Cara is always early. If you take a seat by the office on the end, I'll text her to make sure she knows you're waiting for her."

"Perfect. Thank you."

"You're welcome. Have a great day."

My anxiety reaches an all time high as I sit beside Cara Armstrong's closed office door. Ten quiet minutes pass by with me tapping my foot on the gleaming tile floors before one of the tellers turns on a TV, putting the channel on the morning news. The volume is down low, but there's still no one in the bank, so I hear the exact moment the broadcast turns to a national news segment where the woman at the desk is talking about how authorities in Florida are still looking for information about a wreck that left an unidentified man brain dead and on life support.

Beside her head, a picture of the totaled car appears. It's wrapped around the thick trunk of a stately tree. The reporter doesn't say it, but I know that the car used to be a canary yellow Lamborghini. I also know that the reason why they're having such a hard time identifying the man is because he stole the car from some rich asshole in Miami, and less than twelve hours later, I took his wallet, with all of his identification, off of what I thought was his corpse. I kept the cash and tossed the rest out somewhere between the dark road in the Everglades where we'd crashed and the women's shelter in Jennings, Florida where I paid one of the regulars there to put me in contact with someone who could make me into someone new.

Nadia Hendrix was born in the sketchy basement on the Florida/Georgia state line. She was made with the assistance of a man named Ray who took my new driver's license photo against a white backdrop I'm certain was made from a sheet and advised me to pick a name with the same initials as my old one so my signature would still be authentic.

That is who I am.

Not the girl who climbed out of the wreckage still being displayed on the TV screen. Not the destitute girl Beau sold to men he didn't know well enough to trust, the one who hasn't seen the inside of a bank in years and never thought she'd have an account of her own, let alone anything to put in it.

The reminder of how drastically my life has changed since I climbed out of that car and left everything behind is enough to soothe away the last of the anxiety lingering in my bones. Enough to make me confident in my yes when a woman, who I assume is Cara Armstrong, pauses at the door beside me and asks if I'm here to discuss opening an account.

It takes all of twenty minutes for Cara to set me up with a checking and savings account, print me off a bank verification form and provide me with a temporary debit card, so I don't have to hold off on making any immediate purchases that can't be covered by what's left of my last check from the grocery store. I thank her for her efficiency and rush to work, hoping I won't be late on my second day.

Thankfully, the bank is only a few blocks over from Cerros, so I get there at right on time, managing to snag a spot on an elevator that's packed with hotel guests and Adler Holdings employees. Since Regina isn't on my heels, herding me around like cattle, I feel comfortable making a stop on the twenty-sixth floor to give Heather in HR my direct deposit form before heading up to my office. I pass through the glass doors that lead to my space and look around cautiously, half expecting to find Regina lying in wait, ready to scold me for daring to wander outside my domain.

When it's clear that she's not, I laugh at myself for being silly enough to entertain the thought and approach my desk, stopping short when I see a stack of boxes that weren't there when I left last night sitting next to my desktop. Next to the boxes, which vary in length and size, is a bouquet of flowers. My heart starts to beat rapidly, and I realize that for the first time in a long time the increase in my heart rate isn't tied to some negative emotion like fear. This time it's linked with something else, something positive, something sweet like the scent of nectar coming from the honeysuckle buds that are nestled among the daisies in the bouquet.

I run tentative, but appreciative, fingertips over each petal before I set the vase to the side and take a closer look at the boxes waiting for me. Now that I'm closer, I can see that the larger one, which is on the bottom of the stack, contains a laptop—the latest edition to Apple's Mac collection. On top of the laptop, is an iPad, and on top of that is what's sure to be the newest iPhone. I'm already dancing on the edge of overwhelm when I see the note stuck to the phone. I pick it up and revel in the newness of the experience that is Sebastian's handwriting, in the way seeing it makes me picture him sneaking into my office early this morning, or late last night, with his arms full of gifts for me and stopping to write something he knew would make me smile.

__Welcome to the 21st century, Nadia.__

14

SEBASTIAN

Nadia is a born leader.

I was certain of it when I hired her, but there's something so different about seeing it in action, about seeing *her* in action. As soon as I heard about the staff meeting she'd set up, I shifted my schedule around so I could be here to witness her in her true form. Not in the cloak of shame and self doubt, but in the power she hides underneath it. It's there in every stride of her long legs as she walks back and forth across the front of the indoor dining room attached to the rooftop. In the firm but motivating tone she uses to convey her expectations for her team and the changes she plans to make.

And I'm not the only one who sees it.

I'm standing off to the side, in the room but removed from the conversation, which gives me the opportunity to scan the faces of the servers, hostesses, chefs, and busboys. There isn't a single person here who isn't engaged, who isn't nodding or smiling at the things she's saying, or, in some cases, specifically with the college age kids who like to be teacher's pet, taking notes. No meeting I've ever seen Vince run has gone this way. In fact, the days after his staff meetings were usually when people were most likely to quit. He always said it was because people didn't want structure or respect authority, but I know it was just because he was wrong for the job.

Nadia, on the other hand, was made for it. When she talks, people listen, and when she smiles, it makes them want to do whatever the fuck she says. She's smiling right now, and the sun is pleased by it, sending streams of light and adoration to wash over her form through the glass windows in the room, making her look radiant in the cream and yellow sundress she's wearing today. She's paired it with a blazer and a pair of heels to make it look more professional, but I know it'd be the perfect ensemble for a more casual setting. A picnic on a beach at sunset or dinner with my parents on their patio…

"Okay, guys, last thing." Nadia's voice snaps me out of my thoughts. "I've sent out a calendar link with a few time slots throughout the day for anyone who wants to have a one on one meeting with me. One on ones are not mandatory, but you should feel free to use them if you want to talk privately about something. This would be the perfect time to let me know what jobs you'd like to be cross trained on or bring me any questions you have about the new scheduling system."

When the meeting finally breaks, I feel the strongest surge of pride run through me. I knew she could do this, but it feels so fucking good to see the evidence of her growing belief in her abilities on her face. It feels even better to watch some of our more reluctant staff members from the kitchen approach her with compliments and praise about the changes she plans to make. I know I shouldn't linger any longer, but I can't bring myself to move just yet. It's not until our eyes meet over the head of one of our newest servers, that I realize it's because I'm waiting for her.

I want to talk to her. To congratulate her on a successful meeting and ask if there's anything I can do to support her initiatives. I'm not usually this hands on with my managerial staff, and I damn sure don't make a point of personally offering my support, but I've accepted that Nadia is different. Not just because she's new at this job and doesn't have any documented experience doing it, but because she's her.

Whatever that means.

"Mr. Adler." Her lips pull up into a smile that curves around my name and makes my heart skip a beat. She comes to a stop in front of me, and I notice the tablet I bought to make sure she never has to lug home another stack of paper in her hand. She glances at its screen and then back at me. "I don't remember getting your RSVP to this meeting."

"You didn't send me an invite," I return, eyes skating down her frame to take in her relaxed demeanor. She's different today. More confident, less worried about whether she belongs here. The air of certainty looks good on her.

"Well, I figured you'd have better things to do than attend a lowly staff meeting."

As the CEO of a multi-million dollar company, there are a number of things I should be doing right now besides standing here with her. On my desk alone are five urgent, and potentially expensive, issues that need my immediate attention, but she's my priority.

"I just wanted to make sure no one gave you a hard time. I know the kitchen staff can be pretty temperamental."

"Oh, no, everyone's great."

"They all seem excited about you being here."

Her eyes light up, delight dancing in pools of caramel and gold. "They do, don't they?"

I nod, happy she can see it too. "Yeah. It sounds like you have some great ideas about how to make things run smoother. Make sure you let me know if there's anything I can do to help you execute them."

For a moment, she looks like she wants to tell me that won't be necessary, but then she remembers that I'm a relentless bastard and acquiesces. "I will. Thanks."

"You're welcome." We stare at each other, silence neither one of us knows how to fill stretching between us. Not wanting to make it awkward, I clear my throat and take a step back, breaking the hold she has on me. "Well, have a good rest of your day."

I turn and walk away, heading for the door that leads to the stairwell and feeling good about what might be our only interaction today. Moments later, I hear her heels slapping against the floor as she hits a jog to close the distance between us.

"I almost forgot!" She says, not the least bit winded from exerting herself. "There is something I wanted to talk to you about. Do you have a minute?"

Her legs are about as long as mine, so I only have to slow down a bit to give her time to fall into step beside me. "For you? Always."

I don't look at her because I don't want to see her reaction to what I've just said. If she looks horrified, then I'll feel terrible. If she looks intrigued, then I'll probably ask for permission to taste her lips right here in the middle of this stairwell.

It's a no win scenario, so I keep my eyes trained on the ground, silently counting every step we're taking on our descent to the twenty-ninth floor.

"I wanted to ask if you'd noticed that the number of reservations coming from people that aren't staying in the hotel are down. Like way down?" Her attention is on the screen of the iPad, so I chance a glance at her face. She's biting her lip, and there's a regretful dip in the middle of her forehead, right between her two perfectly arched brows. "It's almost like we aren't doing any outside marketing, but that can't be right, can it?"

"I wish I could say it wasn't, but unfortunately, I don't know. When my cousin was managing the restaurant, I didn't keep a close enough eye on things."

We're back on our floor now, closer to my office than hers when Nadia stops walking and gawks at me like I've just told her I'm best friends with a serial killer.

"Your cousin?" She asks. "Vince is your cousin?"

"Unfortunately."

"That really is unfortunate. He's such a fucking creep." A shiver runs through her, and she pulls a face that makes me think she's speaking from experience. "Is that why you guys had to part ways?"

"I'd rather not talk about this in the middle of the hallway. Would you like to come into my office?"

"We're the only two people with offices on this floor, Sebastian, I don't think there's anyone around to overhear."

"Normally, that'd be true, but HR is having a team building seminar in the conference room that'll be starting shortly. Heather will have my head if she hears me discussing termination agreements in public."

I give her a reassuring smile and hope that it's enough to make her feel okay about being alone with me in a space that's solely mine. The last time has me scarred, and I'm determined to be cautious, to make sure we don't lose all the ground we've covered because of a misstep on my end.

Nadia blows out a steadying breath, and I watch her psych herself up, doing the mental work necessary for her to extend this bit of trust to me. "Okay, yeah, I guess that makes sense."

"We can leave the door open, if that'd make you feel more comfortable."

As soon as she processes my offer, the tension melts out of her muscles. She takes one step forward, and then another, and another until she's passing through the doors of my office first, leaving me to follow. Once she's inside, I open both doors and secure the latch at the top that will keep them propped open. When that's done, I turn to find Nadia making herself at home in my space.

It's a mirror image of her office. The same layout with different furnishings. Mine are darker, more traditionally masculine, built large to accommodate my height and weight. Nadia's tall, with a frame that's both slender and curvy but not dainty by any stretch of the imagination, but even she seems smaller among the furnishings. She watches me with eyes that try to appear relaxed as I move to take a seat behind my desk, allowing it to act as a barrier between us and hating the way she seems to be put at ease by it.

"Thank you for being so...accommodating."

I shrug like it doesn't bother me that the woman I can't stop thinking about doesn't feel comfortable being alone in a room with me. "It's not a problem. Now, where were we?"

"Umm, I believe we were talking about you firing your creepy cousin."

"Right." I heave a sigh and then launch into an amended version of the sordid tale of Vince's employment. Nadia listens intently, and when I'm done she pushes her lips together and lets out a short whistle.

"Wow. That sounds like a disaster."

"It was."

She shakes her head. "And here I was thinking I got the short end of the stick because he hit on me at the bar."

"He did *what?*" I try to sound calm, but I can tell by the look on Nadia's face that I've failed. Her eyes are wide, and her lips are parted but there are no words coming out because she doesn't know what to say.

"It was nothing, Sebastian."

I can't make her tell me. Honestly, I don't even need her to because knowing the details aren't going to change the outcome. She could say he did something as simple as glanced at her breasts or something as fucked up as slapping her ass when she got up from her seat, and it won't matter because knowing he made her uncomfortable is enough. The second the words left her mouth, I made the decision to whoop Vince's ass the next time I see him.

Luckily, I won't have to wait too long because I'll be in California this weekend.

My original plan was to take Nic straight to the job site in Santa Monica and get him excited about all the amazing things we could do with the beach front property, but now I'm mentally amending my plans, adding a stop in Los Angeles to the agenda just so I can find Vince and knock a few of his teeth loose.

When my vision is no longer clouded with red and my desire for violence has gone dormant again, I swallow the words I wanted to say and tell Nadia what she needs to hear. "Allow me to extend my sincerest apologies to you on behalf of my cousin. I don't know what he did or said to you, but I can promise you it's not a reflection of how the men in my family treat women."

"I know that, Sebastian."

Her response soothes a part of me that is constantly worried about fucking things up, about never being able to gain her trust and make her believe that she's safe with me. We still have a long way to go, but that sentence, those four words, make me believe that one day, we'll actually get there.

"Good, I'm glad." I clear my throat, expelling the emotion wrapped around my vocal chords. "Now, tell me what your plan is for solving our marketing problem."

The way she switches back into business mode is impressive because it happens quickly. One second she's showing a bit of vulnerability, and the next she's all command and confidence.

"Well, since our primary concern is getting people through the door who aren't staying at the hotel, I think we should turn our focus to events aimed at the public."

"Makes sense, that way the restaurant's revenue isn't tied to the hotel's revenue."

She nods enthusiastically. "Exactly! I didn't expect to meet with you about this today, so I'm just spit balling here. If you hate any of these ideas, don't hold it against me."

I can't imagine hating anything that comes out of her mouth, but instead of telling her that I just gesture for her to continue.

"Okay." She sits back in her chair, tapping her nails on the leather arm. "Right off the top of my head, I think monthly wine tastings with an exclusive menu crafted by Chef Elle could be amazing. We'd run ads in the paper and online to sell tickets, push all the tables together to create a communal dining experience."

"Are you thinking a different bottle for each course or multiple courses planned around one bottle?"

She tilts her head to the side to consider my question. "Different bottle for each course."

"Great. I love it. What else do you got?"

Shock colors her features, rendering her speechless for a few seconds. "Sip and Shop on the Rooftop?"

"Are you asking me or telling me?"

"Telling."

"Oh, okay, 'cause for a second there it sounded like a question."

She rolls her eyes, but when she says the name of her second concept again, it's not a question. "Sip and Shop on the Rooftop. A weekly event where local artists and businesses set up tables and people come and shop, have drinks, enjoy brunch style finger foods while a DJ plays music."

I'm quiet for a second, working out the logistics of what that might look like. While I think on it, Nadia grows tense. "This is you spit balling?" I ask, finally.

"Yeah, I mean obviously, I'd take some time to really plan these events out, but I think they could be exactly what we need to draw in more people." She pulls her lower lip between her teeth. An act that makes her appear adorably self conscious. "We don't have to do any of them, though."

"I want to do all of them."

Her eyes go wide. "Really?"

"Really." I grin at her, letting the pride swelling in my chest show in my eyes. "Take the ball and run with it, Nadia. I trust you."

"You know, I'm actually starting to believe you when you say that."

"Good, because I mean it."

The smile she gives me happens slowly. I watch it rise, the happiness it's inspired by lapping in the corner of her eyes like gentle waves, and when she finally stops fighting it, letting it take over the soft lines of her features and transform the full line of her mouth, she's even more beautiful than usual.

"You're nothing like I thought you'd be as a boss."

I lean back in my seat and rub at my chin, contemplating whether or I should ask her what exactly she thought I'd be like as a boss or just take the compliment at face value. There's a part of me that doesn't want to know, that doesn't need to hear her describe me the way everyone else does—impatient, distant, exacting—but then there's another part of me that's greedy for a glimpse into her mind.

"What did you think I was going to be like?"

Nadia presses her lips together for a second like she's considering not answering my question, but then she shrugs and throws all caution to the wind. "Well, I kept thinking about the first time we met in the lobby when I bumped into you and you said '*don't be sorry, be attentive.*'" She snorts when I pull a face to demonstrate how little I appreciate her recreation of my voice.

"I don't sound like that."

She dismisses my complaint with a wave of her hand. "Anyway, it made me think you were going to be this rigid stick in the mud with no personality or desire to think outside the box, but you're not."

"So what am I?"

Her lips part, and my heart starts to race. I didn't know when I started this conversation, that I'd be waiting with bated breath for her to tell me who she thinks I am, to reveal how she sees me. I should have expected it, but I didn't, which probably makes me as stupid as Nadia is beautiful.

"You're supportive and encouraging." She laughs softly, and the sound is half disbelief and half joy. "You make me feel like I can do this job."

"You can do anything you want to do, Nadia."

She swallows hard. Her throat working to contain the emotions swelling in her chest. "And you say things like that and do things like buy out a whole Apple store to bring me into the 21st century. That was completely unnecessary by the way."

"It was three things and completely necessary because I won't have any employee of mine walking around with a flip phone."

"I was going to replace it when I got my first paycheck."

"Well, now you don't have to. I hope it's okay that it came with a new number. I would have ported over your current one, but that would have rendered the relic you're using inoperable, and I didn't think you'd appreciate that."

"You're right, I wouldn't have, but I do appreciate the phone, and the iPad, and the laptop, *and* the flowers."

When she lists them off that way, it makes me realize that I might have gone a bit overboard. The first bouquet was already out of the ordinary, but the second one in addition to the full Apple collection will have more than Luca, Talia and the rest of my family asking questions about me and Nadia. I should pull back, but I know I won't. I know I can't. If Nadia needs or wants something, and it's within my power to give it to her, she'll have it. Consequences and questions from everyone outside the bubble I've built around me and her be damned.

"Am I interrupting?" The question comes from behind Nadia, but I don't have to look up to know that it's Nic. He saunters into my office without waiting for an invitation, and both Nadia and I rise from our seats. I come around the desk, inserting myself between the two of them even though I know Nic doesn't pose a threat. He looks at me like I've just insulted his intelligence and questioned his integrity.

"No, we were just wrapping up." I reach out and offer him my hand, which he takes, greeting me with a handshake that seems to get more complicated every time we do it. When we release each other, he turns his attention to Nadia in a silent request for an introduction. "Nadia, this is Dominic Alexander, owner of Archway Construction. He's the man who handled the rooftop conversion and designed our office suites. Nic, this is Nadia Hendrix, the new manager for the Cerros rooftop."

Nic extends his hand, and she takes it. The contact sends a flare of possession running through my chest. "Nice to meet you, Nadia."

"It's nice to meet you too, Dominic."

"Nic," he corrects her. "Everyone calls me Nic."

"Nic." Nadia repeats, giving him an easy smile. I find myself grinding my teeth as I count the seconds until they're no longer touching. Five. It takes five whole seconds for Nic to let go of her hand, and another two for her to look back at me. I know as soon as our eyes connect that I'm not doing a good job of hiding what's going on inside my head. Nadia gives me a quizzical look that I don't address because I don't know how to. It haunts me all the way back to my desk, weighing me down as I lower myself into my seat.

"Well, I guess I should get going," Nadia says, clearly feeling awkward. "I'll keep you updated on the progress of the projects we discussed, Mr. Adler."

"That sounds great, thank you, Nadia."

She gives me one last discerning look before tucking her tablet under her arm and making her way to the door, leaving me to stare after her, wondering exactly when I lost my mind and if she's ever going to give it back.

15

NADIA

Desiree's nails click against the screen of my laptop when she pushes it closed. I barely have time to move my fingers off the keyboard before it slams shut.

"Des! I was in the middle of sending an email."

"It's Friday evening, Nadia. You've officially made it through your first week of work, which means you should be getting dressed so we can go out to celebrate instead of sending a stupid email."

"It's not a stupid email." I grumble, opening the laptop back up to make sure she didn't crack my screen when she slammed it down.

"Close the computer, Hendrix!" She orders, marching over to her bookshelf to turn on the speaker. In seconds, ass shaking music fills the room, and Desiree's hands are in the air. She's topless with a mixed drink that's mostly tequila in hand. "We're getting fucked up tonight!"

"I'm happy to get fucked up with you AFTER I send this email."

Technically, this could probably wait until Monday morning, but I don't like leaving loose ends lingering over the weekend, especially when I've had such a productive week. After my meeting with Sebastian about new marketing efforts, I hit the ground running, meeting with Elle to hash out the finer details of the wine tasting. She had a notebook full of dishes she'd been dying to try, so we went through her culinary wish list and built a menu we were both excited about.

Based on the ingredients Elle decided to highlight and the flavor profile she wanted to create, I recommended several wines I thought would make them shine. Elle loved my recommendations and suggested that I reach out to Ruthie, Sebastian's go to wine contact, to source them. Ruthie, however, is a hard woman to get into contact with. Regina told me she prefers emails, and since I want to get the ball rolling sooner rather than later, I'm using what's left of my Friday to reach out in hopes that we'll have a meeting on the books by Monday morning.

"Well hurry up and send it," Desiree demands, shaking her breasts in my face. Her nipples graze my cheek, and I swat her away, not the least bit bothered by her nakedness. At this point, there's no such thing as a private part between me and Desiree. I've seen her face down, ass up, and tits out more times than I can count, and somehow, the transparency has made us closer. She's the first person I've called a friend since Bianca. I find myself thinking of her a lot lately, mostly when I'm with Desiree like this, laughing and talking and having fun. I think about how Bianca and I never really got to have what me and Desiree do. We were never free together because Beau was always there, lingering, waiting for the chance to steal any bit of joy from me. He hated how close we were, and I still think our friendship is the only reason he started sleeping with her.

He used their relationship to create a void between us, and it wasn't long before he had poisoned Bianca against me, convincing her that I was the reason she wasn't getting the clients she wanted when really it was him sending me out to work even though I didn't want to. The day I left for the Florida job that granted me my freedom, we got into it. Bianca got in my face, calling me selfish for stealing the job from her when I knew she needed the money to help take care of her sick mom. I just sat there and took it, unable to defend myself, to explain that the money the client paid would never touch my hands.

Despite the way we left things, I still miss Bianca. I still regret that we will never get to know each other outside of the cloud of toxicity that lives around Beau.

I hit send on the email to Ruthie and close my laptop, signaling the true end of my work week. It feels good to have my first five days behind me and even better to have my own money to contribute to the celebration Desiree insisted we have tonight.

"Finally!" She says, bouncing on her tip toes and making the alcohol in her cup slosh over the side and onto her hand. "Put the computer and all your work shit in the guest room and grab a glass, you're already two drinks behind."

"How have you already had two drinks?"

"Because you took forever to send that email."

I flip her off on my way to the guest room where she insisted I sleep tonight. This isn't my first time staying the night at her apartment, but I feel like it is my first time really *looking* at it. Seeing it through the eyes of someone with money and options as opposed to someone pinching pennies and barely getting by. Now that I have a salary and a healthy bank account, I'm eager to get the hell out of the motel, but I don't know where to start my search for new digs.

"Do you know if there are any units available for rent in your building?" I ask Desiree, completely un-surprised that she's followed me from the living room.

She plops down on the bed next to the bags I brought over. Among them is a shopping bag containing a dress from a high end boutique I stopped by after work. I bought several pieces, including a slinky, backless number to wear out tonight that made me grateful for the outlandish clothing allowance that hit my bank account this morning.

"Why? You trying to be my neighbor?"

"Maybe. Will you check with the leasing office to see?"

"I could do that," she says, shifting my brand new leather duffel bag to the other side of the bed. "Or, you could just move in with me."

"As much as I appreciate that offer, I'm going to have to pass."

She shrugs. "Suit yourself. I don't want a roommate anyway. Then I'd have to stop walking around naked."

"You're literally sitting on the bed with your tits out, Des."

"Yeah, but I have on shorts."

I shove my laptop into the work bag that matches my new duffel and laugh. "Right. My mistake. I forgot all about the booty shorts that barely cover your ass."

Desiree taps her temple. "Key details, gotta remember the key details."

I sit down on the foot of the bed and hold my hand out for her drink. She gives it up without argument, and I take a sip, cringing when I realize that it's just tequila tinted with juice. "What time are Carmen and the rest of the girls getting here?"

"They should be here in a few."

Handing her drink back, I arch a brow. "Are you going to put a bra on before then?"

"Probably not, since my dress doesn't allow for it."

"You never showed me what you were wearing."

She pops up suddenly, downing the rest of her drink before she dashes to her room and returns with a red satin jumpsuit and a pair of silver heels. "This!"

"Ohhh, that's cute!" I take it from her and stretch it out on the bed then pull out my dress and lay it out next to it.

"Damn." Desiree gives me a mischievous smile, running her fingers over the short hem of my black dress. "You're about to look so good in this. How are you going to wear your hair?"

"I was thinking sleek pony?"

Her expression turns considerate, then she nods. "Yes, I love that."

"Perfect, because you know I'm going to need you to do it for me."

She lets out an exasperated sigh, but when the time comes, she wrangles my hair into submission, giving me a ponytail that's somehow secure and comfortable. It doesn't so much as budge as we indulge in a night of debauchery that takes us to several different clubs in New Haven and ends with us having dessert at a cafe that opens at midnight and serves boozy milkshakes along with their fresh baked goods.

I'm sipping on something called a Drunken Cookie—a blend of vanilla ice cream, chocolate vodka, Irish cream and chocolate chip cookies they make in house—when a familiar face fills my admittedly distorted vision.

"Is that Preston?" The music inside the cafe is loud, but Desiree, who's sitting next to me, hears my question. Her head turns as she follows my gaze to the bar where Preston Fredricks was just sitting. I say just, because now he's standing and walking over to us.

"Yep, and he's coming over here!" Desiree says, tapping my leg and using subtle movements to push me out of the booth.

"*Desiree!*" I hiss, glaring at her as I gain my footing.

"Harper." Preston comes in for a hug as soon as I turn around. He's all confidence and familiarity as he calls me by the name I used when I was working in the club. It's not the first time we've embraced, so my body doesn't do that thing where it panics at the sensation of a foreign touch.

I ease back, looking up into brown eyes that are happy to see me. "Actually, it's Nadia."

Preston takes the correction in stride. In fact, he smiles at me, which makes the cleft in the middle of his chin pop. He's a handsome man with umber skin and jet black hair he keeps cut close to his scalp. He always looks like he just left the barbershop and smells like he recently starred in a commercial for Tom Ford cologne.

"Nadia." He tilts his head to the side and nods. "I think it fits you better than Harper."

"Thanks. I think so too." We both take a small step back from each other, but Preston's hand stays on my waist. "It's nice to see you again."

Images from the last time we were in the same room play in the back of my mind, and I can tell by the look on his face that Preston is thinking of it too. His usually happy facade cracks a little, a bit of bitterness shining through before he pushes it away.

"You too. I've missed being in the presence of a woman who's as beautiful as she is intelligent."

A blush sends heat sweeping over my cheeks. "Preston."

"I'm serious, Nadia." And his eyes convey just how serious he is. They bore into mine, making it hard for me to look away. "I have thought about you every day since my membership at Ludus was revoked."

"I still can't believe that happened."

Preston shakes his head and lets out a dry laugh. "Me either. I mean, kicking out a founding member with no explanation? That's just bad for business."

For some reason his words make something like defensiveness come alive in my chest. It's stupid since what he just said has nothing to do with me personally. Preston doesn't notice my silence, he just keeps talking.

"They make it impossible for ex-members to get in touch with the girls, and trust me I tried."

"You shouldn't have. They have those rules in place for a reason. They keep everyone safe." Especially the sex workers who don't have money and influence to protect them if people from the club decide to follow them home at night.

"Right." Preston says, maintaining his smile even though it has faltered a bit. "You're absolutely right. I didn't mean to imply that the rules weren't necessary. I just wanted to let you know that I *wanted* to get in touch with you."

"For what?"

The question isn't completely necessary. I can tell by the way he's still gripping my hip, his fingertips resting on the skin left exposed by the cut of my dress, that he wants more than a friendly run-in that happened by chance. My heart starts to slap against my ribs. The force of it makes my chest hurt.

"Well, I was hoping we could get to know each other outside of Ludus, maybe over dinner?"

The last person who *asked* me out on a real date was a guy named Wade who was in my economics class in college. We went out on one date and realized we had nothing in common except that class. I don't think I actually liked the guy. I just said yes because I had squandered my college years pursuing a double major and putting off everything that would interfere with my plan to use my trust fund to buy my parent's vineyard back from the people Roland sold it to. When things didn't work out with Wade, I wrote it off as a fluke and told myself I'd have plenty of time to date after I got the business back on its feet.

That never happened.

So this is my first time being asked on a date as a grown woman with full control of her life and the ability to say no if she wants. The trouble is, once Preston's question settles in the air between us, I'm not able to say anything at all. And that's where Desiree comes in. She pops out of her seat and dazzles Preston with her smile.

"Dinner?" She asks, ignoring my scowl that tells her to sit the fuck down. "Nadia *loves* dinner."

16

SEBASTIAN

"**W**hy do I feel like I'm pitching you this project instead of the other way around?"

Nic huffs out a dry laugh at my question and stretches his legs out in front of him, looking far too comfortable for a man refusing to commit to a multi-million dollar contract that will keep his company in the black for several years.

"Because I don't pitch myself to anyone. My work speaks for itself."

I'd be annoyed by his cockiness if I didn't respect it so damn much. Nic is the best at what he does, which is why I'm working so hard to get him to take on this resort build in Santa Monica. Out of all the commercial contractors on the list Regina compiled for me, he's the only one I've pulled out all the stops for. Flying him out to view the site in person, promising to pay for housing for the two years it would take to complete the build, guaranteeing a space in the Adler Holdings satellite office in Los Angeles for him to operate out of when necessary. None of it has been enough to get him to give me a hard yes.

Taking a sip of bourbon from the tumbler in my hand, I study him, trying to get an idea of where his head is at. As usual, his expression gives away nothing, and I laugh at myself for even bothering to try.

"Level with me, Nic, tell me what you need in order for you to take this job."

He takes a bite of his burger and chews thoughtfully. "You to accept that I'm not moving to California for two years to do it. I need to be in New Haven."

My patience is waning, but I consider him a friend, so I don't let it fully expire. I've known Nic for close to four years now. We met just a few months after his best friend and business partner, Eric Kent, died, so I understand his limitations. He's gone from running a company with a trusted partner to handling everything on his own. That in and of itself poses challenges to my request for him to personally oversee this project.

"You don't trust Andre to handle things while you're here?" I ask, and we're both surprised that I remembered the name of his number two.

Nic wipes his mouth with a napkin before tossing it onto his plate. "I'd trust Andre with pretty much anything, including the lead on this project."

"No, I don't want your flunky. I want you."

"You just asked me to leave the man in charge of my entire operation, but when we're talking about putting him in control of building your resort he's just a flunky?"

"Anyone who isn't you is a flunky to me."

"Damn, Seb," he teases, leaning back in his seat. "Just say you love me and get it over with."

I flip him off. "You're such a pain in the ass."

"Don't try to flip the script now, tell me more about how desperate you are to have me bid on this job."

"I'm not going to beg you."

"Good, because it'd be a waste of your time. I'm not available for any projects outside of New Haven at the moment, but Andre is."

My brows furrow. All this time I thought he was just being a stubborn asshole and giving me the run around, but this is the first time he's mentioned that he *can't* take the job. I search my brain, trying to remember if I've heard about any large scale projects happening in

New Haven that might rival the size of the contract I'm offering Nic. I come up empty.

"What are you working on?"

Nic gives me a thin smile. "Nothing yet, but I'm hearing whispers that the contractor on the La Grande Nuit renovation is about to jump ship."

"And you want to pick up where he left off?"

"Something like that."

"That doesn't make any sense." I know the project he's talking about. The small hotel is just a few blocks away from Cerros and owned by some guy named James Robinson. He's been working on it for a while now, with hopes of opening in October, but he keeps running into delays because his contractors keep quitting on him. "Why would you be interested in taking that on?"

"I have my reasons."

I can't imagine what they might be, and judging by the way Nic's looking at me, I'm not going to find out any time soon.

"Well, I guess there's nothing left for us to discuss."

"I guess not."

We both stand, and I toss a few hundreds on the table to cover our food. Nic extends his hand, and I take it, allowing him to turn the simple handshake into a brotherly hug. "Thanks for the trip, though. That was my first time on a private jet," he says, laughing.

I shove him away, but I'm also laughing as I leave him to find his own way back to his hotel. "Let me know if your availability changes."

"I'll start prepping Andre on the specifics of the project," he calls out, tossing one last bomb of rejection at my back. I'm still shaking my head when I get behind the wheel of my car, frustrated with his stubbornness. Something told me the day would end with me feeling like this, which is why I planned to visit Vince right after dinner. When I pull up to his place—which is really just our grandparent's home that his mom moved out of a few months ago to follow him to New Haven —adrenaline and the sweet anticipation of violence pulse through my veins.

I walk up to the front door with a smile on my face, and it stays firmly in place even when Vince opens the door. His eyes are blood-shot, his pupils are the size of saucers, and there's a bottle of beer in his hand. All of these things would make a better man pause to reconsider what he's come here to do, but all it does is piss me off because here he is pumping his body full of poison, that he probably paid for with the money from the severance check I gave him, without a care in the world while everyone else cleans up the messes he's made.

"Seb, what are you—"

His sentence is cut short by my fist colliding with his jaw. The bottle in his hand falls to the floor and shatters. I crush shards of glass to follow him over the threshold, my hand wrapped around the neck of his shirt, so I can guarantee that the next blow lands where I want it. Vince groans and doubles over, forcing me to let go of him. I step back, allowing him time to catch his breath, to get mad enough to fight back, so I can have a reason to come at him harder.

"What the fuck, man?" He straightens, wiping the blood from his lip. "Are you insane?"

"No, but you are. You had to be if you thought I wouldn't find out what you did."

"What are you talking about? I haven't done anything besides the shit you made up, so you'd have a reason to fire me."

I don't even bother dignifying that part of his statement with a response. We both know my reasons for firing him were more than valid. Besides, I'm here to talk about the only person he's harassed that actually matters to me. "Nadia Hendrix."

His face turns red, but he tries to act like he doesn't know who she is. "Who?"

"Nadia Hendrix." I step to him, enjoying the flare of panic in his eyes when he realizes he's pinned between me and the wall. "You met her at the hotel bar after the last round of interviews you oversaw."

"I don't remember her."

"Well she remembers you," I sneer, my lips curling in disgust as I imagine what he must have said to her.

"You flew to LA to tune me up based off the word of some random chick I don't even remember?"

The jab to his stomach comes in so quick he doesn't have time to try to block it. He folds over again, and I grab his shoulder to push him up. "I'm here on business, dropping by to beat your ass is just an added bonus."

His face crumples, and at first I think he's about to cry, but then he barks out a rough laugh. "You fucking her? You gotta be fucking her because otherwise you wouldn't give a damn about a conversation I had with her weeks ago. Tell me, did she cry about all the nasty things Big Bad Vince said to her before or after she climbed in your bed?"

"Actually, she told me all about it when I gave her the job you were too incompetent to do correctly. She's amazing at it, by the way."

He rubs at his jaw, and I note the presence of a fresh bruise already forming there. "Shit. Talia did a number on you didn't she? You've gone from being married to a hoe to hiring a whore in hopes that she'll give you some pussy. A desperate girl like that, you could have bought her for the rest of the year and paid less than the salary you're giving her."

Something about the way his words touch on every insecurity Nadia exposed to me at Ludus during our second interaction sends rage flooding through my system. My vision is red again, and when I hit Vince, my fist connecting with his nose with so much force it breaks on impact, the white walls in our mothers' childhood home turns a garish shade of crimson to match it.

* * *

I'M RUNNING my tongue over the cut in my lip I got when Vince finally got the nerve to hit me back when Nadia walks into my office on Monday morning. We both pause and look at each other, shocked for two completely different reasons. Me, because she walked in without knocking which indicates a growing level of comfort between us. Her, because there's a bruise underneath my cheek in addition to the cut splitting my lip.

"What the hell happened?" She shocks me again when she moves over to me, her face screwed up and brows knit with worry as she rounds my desk. I turn in my seat, so when she stops in front of me and grabs hold of my face, she's standing between my legs. "Who did this to you?"

Her grip is firm and it doesn't hurt a bit to have her touching me, but I still wince because the moment her skin touches mine, my nervous system lights up. Nadia reads it as pain though, and she tries to pull away.

"Don't." I stop her retreat with gentle fingers that wrap around her wrist and hold her hand in place. "You're not hurting me. You just surprised me is all."

"Oh. Sorry. I should have asked for permission to touch you." She bites her lip, a bit of self consciousness passing over her features. "I just really hate seeing people bruised like this. Just thinking about the violence that leads to it…"

I don't know a lot about Nadia's past. Actually, I don't know anything at all besides she used to do sex work and has probably, on more than one occasion, been a victim of sexual assault. Now, I know that she's also sensitive to violence, which is probably a result of being on the receiving end of it. The knowledge breaks my heart.

"I'm okay. I just got into it with Vince when I was in Los Angeles this weekend."

Some emotion passes behind her eyes too quick for me to catch or attach a name to.

"Vince is in LA?"

"Yeah, he went to school out there and lived there for a while before I hired him. He moved back after I let him go."

We're still touching, locked in a moment I didn't expect to have. Her scent, those same notes of bergamot and amber, wraps around me like a cloud of citrine sweetness, teasing my senses and making me want to close my eyes. I don't though. I keep them trained on Nadia, on the frown on her lips and the soft slope of her nose.

"It doesn't seem like you like him very much, why'd you go and see him?"

It doesn't occur to me to lie to her. "To beat his ass for disrespecting you."

"Sebastian! Why would you do that? I told you it was nothing."

"He made you feel uncomfortable, that's not nothing."

Frankly, it pisses me off to hear her minimize it. Vince doesn't get a free pass just because he didn't subject her to the same level of depravity the people who hurt her in the past did. And when I learn who those people are, I'm going to find them and give them something worse than a broken nose.

Nadia looks like she wants to scold me, to say something dumb and untrue like she isn't worth all this trouble, but my eyes stretch in a silent plea for her not to. Not because I don't want to hear that I was wrong—especially since I know I was right—but because I don't think I can downplay the way I feel about her when she's this close to me.

She sighs, and her breath is warm as it passes over my face. "I still can't believe the two of you are related. Vince is so creepy and predatory, and you're...."

My brows lift. "And I'm what?"

Her teeth sink into her lower lip again. "You're you."

"That almost sounded like a compliment, Miss Hendrix."

The sultry smile she gives me is almost enough to take away the sting of her letting me go. *Almost.* "It might've been, Mr. Adler."

Even though we're no longer touching, we're still in a moment. Currents of something unspoken and unnamed pass between us, building up momentum until it feels like I have to do something, to say something, so it doesn't pass us by. I push to my feet, and Nadia gulps and takes a small step back. She's not running, just making space for me and this thing growing between us that seems too big for the room. She feels it. I know she does, but I still hesitate because I have to be careful with her.

That hesitation costs me everything when Regina comes barreling through the door with the tablet she uses to manage my schedule in her hand. She's so preoccupied with it, she doesn't see Nadia and I step back from each other, our moment dissolving into nothingness.

"I was able to move everything but your first meeting of the day. It's with the director of the New Haven Victim Assistance Network. She's in the conference room waiting for you. While you're dealing with that, I'll watch some YouTube tutorials on how to cover bruises," she says, finally looking up. "Oh! Hi, Nadia. I didn't realize you were in here."

"Hey, Regina." Nadia turns to face her, angling her body away from me. "I just stopped by to speak with Sebastian about something really quickly, but I'm on my way out."

She only manages to take one step towards the door before I catch her hand in mine. "Wait. What did you come to talk to me about?"

Nadia glances at Regina, who couldn't care less about our exchange, and pulls away. "Nothing important enough to delay your meeting."

"You sure it can wait?" She nods, already moving away. My body rejects her departure, forcing me to blurt out more words. "I'll stop by your office later, so we can discuss it."

"Sounds good. Maybe I can help you out with your face."

"What's wrong with my face?" I ask, just for the pleasure of hearing her giggle echo in the hallway.

17

NADIA

Sebastian Adler was going to kiss me.

And I think I was going to let him.

Who am I kidding? I was definitely going to let him. Thank God Regina came in when she did because I don't think there's anything smart about making out with your boss in your second week of work. Not that there's ever a good time to get involved with the man signing your paychecks, who has the power to snatch back the financial security he has so graciously given you.

Sebastian wouldn't do that.

The voice in the back of my head tells me, choosing to believe in the continued goodness of the man I've come to think of as a friend. I don't know when that happened, when I started to like him and not just be grateful he plucked me out of the obscurity that was my existence at Ludus. When I started to trust him and stopped searching for an ulterior motive behind every kindness he extends to me without me having to ask.

I take him at face value.

And when I was in his office this morning, that face wanted to kiss me.

I guess it's kind of my fault that things escalated. After all, I was the one who initiated physical contact. The act spoke of familiarity we don't have and tap danced all over the boundaries I insisted on. In less than five minutes, I undermined them all. Walking into his office without knocking. Touching him without his permission. Leaning in when I should have backed away.

The walking into his office without knocking part wasn't that bad. At least that's what I've spent the last hour telling myself. I had a valid reason for being there, something important I needed to tell him about yet another thing his cousin failed to do when this office was his.

"Knock, knock." I glance up from the event request form I'm responding to and find Sebastian standing just inside my door. "Can I come in?"

My heart wrestles with my brain for control of my mouth, and since I can't trust either one of them to say something appropriate, I just nod. Sebastian moves into the room, leaving one of the doors open in a silent acknowledgment of my discomfort around being in a room alone with him. A discomfort that doesn't seem to exist anymore.

"You can close it."

My words give him pause, catching both of us off guard. "You sure?"

"Yeah, I'm sure."

"Okay." He turns and pulls the door shut, then resumes his walk back to my desk. I watch him drop down into the arm chair across from me in hopes of getting a read on him, to figure out if he's obsessing over what could have happened in his office earlier. His face gives nothing away.

"How's your day going so far?" he asks, stretching his legs out in front of him.

"Good, how about yours?"

"Can't complain." He smiles, and my eyes drop to the cut on his lip just as he runs his tongue across it. "It doesn't hurt, Nadia."

"Yeah, but that doesn't mean it isn't an eye sore."

His eyes glitter with humor. "You requested my presence in your office just to call me ugly?"

I gape at him. "I didn't call you ugly!" It's actually the last word I would use to describe him, but he doesn't need to know that. "I also didn't request your presence in my office. You insisted on coming by."

"Yeah, because you stopped by mine first."

"I had something I needed to discuss with you!"

"Which was?"

My skin flushes under the weight of his gaze. I clear my throat, willing my ability to speak coherently to rise to the surface as I grab my tablet and stand. Sebastian is quiet as I move around the desk and sit in the chair next to him.

"When Regina set up my email, it was also linked to the event request email for the rooftop," I explain, pulling up the account so I can show up what I'm talking about.

Sebastian slide to the edge of his seat and leans over, so he can see the screen. "Let me guess, Vince was ignoring event requests?"

I turn my head and immediately wish that I didn't because our faces are so close I can feel his breath on my lips. His scent surrounds me, taking me back to the first day we met when I thought the layered notes of spiced rum and sugar cane was as pretentious as he was.

"I don't think he was even checking the account. I've found requests that date back six months." To demonstrate my point, I swipe several times, scrolling down what seems like a never ending page of requests. "There's no telling how much revenue we've lost out on because he failed to approve these."

His nostrils flare. "I should have hit him harder."

An involuntary shudder runs through me at the thought. Sebastian's knuckles are bruised, which means he didn't just hit Vince once. He hit him multiple times, and he did it hard enough to draw blood, maybe even hard enough to break bone. I'm not uncomfortable with him fighting with his piece of shit cousin, not really, I just hate the way that the aftermath of the brawl makes me think about the marks Beau used to leave on me.

"I don't think that would have solved anything."

"You're probably right. My aunt is already going to have my head for what I did to him this weekend."

"Did you really do it because of what he said to me?" I've had a hard time wrapping my head around that. Sebastian has known Vince for his whole life. They're blood, and I'm...I'm just the woman he almost kissed in his office.

"Which part of what happened this weekend bothers you more? The violence or the fact that it was done in your name? Because I can promise you that I'll never be violent towards you, but I can't say that I'll never be violent *for* you."

"Sebastian, please be serious."

"Do I look like I'm joking, Nadia?"

He doesn't. In fact, he's wearing that deathly serious expression that makes his champagne colored eyes darken and leaves nothing up for discussion. I want to answer his question, but doing so would just lead us right back to that moment we were in earlier, and that's a place I cannot go.

Like a coward, I turn my attention back to the tablet in my hand. "I've already started responding to some of the newer requests. The event calendar is filling out quite nicely. I wanted to get your thoughts on what to do with the older ones, though. Do we just leave well enough alone or reach out with an apology and maybe an offer for a free bottle of wine upon their next visit to the rooftop?"

I can tell he doesn't appreciate the change in topic—the vein throbbing in the center of his forehead says as much—but he allows it to happen. "Make it a meal and also put a time limit on it. They'll need to redeem the offer within sixty days or it expires."

"Sixty days, got it." Pushing to my feet, I move back to the other side of my desk, so I can make note of his suggestions. With our conversation done, I expect him to find a reason to excuse himself, but he stays seated. "Umm, did you need something else?"

The heat from his gaze sears my skin, and I struggle against the urge to fan my face with my hand. "Yes."

"Okay. Am I supposed to guess or are you going to tell me?"

"You made the offer, Nadia, I'd expect you to remember it." His cocked brow jogs my memory, and I snap my fingers.

"Right! Your face." I pull my purse from the bottom drawer in my desk and begin to rummage through it, dumping brochures for apartments out so I can find my makeup bag. As fate would have it, it's at the bottom of the Coach tote I bought over the weekend when I went shopping with Des.

While I'm digging through my junky bag, Sebastian picks up the stack of glossy tri-fold papers touting the amenities of the few buildings in town with apartments coming available in the next month.

"These places are nice."

"Yeah, they are." I grab the brochures out of his hand and tuck them back inside my bag. "Let's go cover your bruises."

Sebastian follows me to the private bathroom attached to my office, settling himself against the edge of the sink while I rummage through our options. I'm so grateful that I was able to invest in better products because the stuff I was using before wouldn't have done a damn thing for the angry bruise under his eye.

"I need a closer look," I tell him.

He opens his legs and spreads his arms wide, welcoming me into his space. I step forward with my focus on the tubes of concealer and color corrector in the bag instead of on where my feet are going and end up stumbling over one of his legs. My body pitches forward, and I brace myself for a collision that never happens because Sebastian's hands fly to my waist. His long fingers span my sides and settle somewhere along the small of my back, refusing to budge even when I'm no longer in danger of falling.

Our eyes meet, and I consider, for the briefest of seconds, asking him to let me go, but ultimately decide against it because inside the bracket of his arms is the safest place I think I've ever been.

I lift a tentative hand to his face, tracing my fingertips around the uneven lines of the bruise, identifying the color hiding underneath the stained bronze of his skin.

"Purple," I breathe, setting the bag on the edge of the counter next to him.

"Purple?"

"Your bruise. It's purple."

"That matters?"

"Yeah." I feel the weight of his gaze on my face, as I dig out a face wipe from the bag and use it to cleanse the area. "The color of the bruise determines what concealer we'll use to hide it."

"Oh."

I know there's more he wants to say, more he wants to know, but he remains quiet while I work, using primer to prep his skin then applying a green color corrector to the bruise and blending it out with a small brush. I'm in the middle of blending the foundation with a sponge when he finally finds the courage to speak the words he's been holding in.

"Did you get your knowledge of covering up bruises the way I think you did?"

I toss the sponge into the sink and pull out some translucent powder to set the makeup. "That depends on how you think I got it."

"Someone hurt you." I feel his fingers flex through the fabric of my dress. "Someone hit you regularly, and you had to find a way to cover up the evidence."

There's no point in lying when he knows, so I just nod. "But no one hurts me anymore."

"Because you got away."

It's an oversimplification, but it's still accurate, so I don't correct him, don't offer any more of myself than I have to. "I did. And now, I only use my makeup to cover up the bags under my eyes from lack of sleep."

He tilts his head to the side, searching my face for signs of sleep deprivation, and I have to use the hand not holding the makeup brush to force his head back into the position I had it in before.

"You're not sleeping?"

"I manage to get a little rest between midnight and three, but after that the baby is up every thirty minutes crying."

"The baby?"

When I step back to admire my handiwork, it forces him to let me go. Annoyance at our distance is the only change to his other wise calm expression, which surprises the hell out me. I'd been deliberately vague, leaving room for him to assume that the baby keeping me up at night belongs to me just so I can see how he'd react to that. Only, he doesn't seem to be reacting at all. Where most men become flustered at the mention of a child attached to the woman they're attracted to, Sebastian is nonplussed. His breathing hasn't picked up, and his face is still enough to rival stone.

And it doesn't matter, because I have no children to speak of, but his calmness tells me that I could have a whole brood running behind me and it wouldn't make any difference to him. I don't think I've ever met anyone so accepting.

"In the room next to mine," I say finally, grabbing my makeup bag and putting everything back inside. "She's real cute. I met her when she and her parents arrived this weekend. Apparently, she has colic."

"That's rough," he says, turning to look at himself in the mirror. I guess he's satisfied with my work because he doesn't offer any critiques.

"*You* know what colic is?"

"Yeah, Zoe, my little sister, had it when she was a baby. It was really hard on my mom."

I cross my arms and lean back against the wall behind me, surprised by how easily he's shared this small part of him. It makes me realize that I don't know that much about him. "How many siblings do you have?"

Sebastian mimics my stance, resuming his position against the edge of the vanity. "Three. Two brothers, one sister."

"You're the oldest?"

"Yep."

"That makes so much sense."

"Does it?"

"Yeah, you have older brother vibes."

"Older brother vibes," he repeats with snark all up and through his tone. "What exactly does that mean?"

I don't have an older brother, or any siblings at all, so I'm really just going off of what I think an older brother should be like. "It means you're used to being in charge of everything, and you always think you know what's best for everybody."

He smirks, and I hate that I wasn't able to do anything about that cut on his lip. "Not everybody."

"Just your siblings?"

"And you."

One day I'll learn to stop walking through doors just because he opened them, but today is not that day. "You think you know what's best for me?"

My mind immediately goes to how he most definitely knew what was best for me as far as this job is concerned, and I bite the inside of my cheek, hoping he won't bring it up.

"I knew this job was best for you."

Why did I even bother with hope? I should have known better, should have been prepared for him to reach for the example that's literally right in front of his face.

I shrug, trying to appear nonchalant. "I was broke and in desperate need of a better job. Anyone with eyes could see that."

He huffs out a dry laugh. "Right. And anyone with eyes could also see that the apartment buildings you're looking at won't provide the kind of security you need to feel safe."

"You looked at those brochures for all of three seconds, how would you know what those buildings have to offer?"

"Because I own them."

I throw my hands up in exasperation. "Is there anything in this town that you don't own?"

Sebastian glances heavenward, giving me the distinct impression that he's doing a mental run through of his real estate catalog. "The motel you're staying in now."

"Makes sense. It definitely feels a little too low budget for you."

"It's a little too low budget for you as well."

His eyes skate down my frame, taking in the sleeveless blazer dress I'm wearing. It's sky blue with gold buttons holding together the tweed fabric that's just long enough to cover the scar on my leg. I paired it with pearl earrings and a pair of slingback pumps from Dior with a four figure price tag. It's safe to say that I've been putting my clothing allowance to good use, but that's not the point Sebastian is trying to make.

"Yeah, well, it was all I could afford at the time, and the buildings I'm currently looking at are the only ones with openings in the next month."

"They also don't have doormen or building security."

The fact that he knows how much the additional layers of security mean to me makes my chest feel all warm and fuzzy. I kind of hate it.

"I know, but I can't wait six months for a unit that meets my exact needs."

"You don't have to. I can get you in to see some places you'd actually feel safe in as soon as tomorrow."

"Sebastian, no." I shake my head, grappling for the words I need to explain that I can't be on the receiving end of another act of kindness so soon. "You don't have to do that."

"I know I don't have to." He pulls out his phone and starts tapping on the screen, wearing that same mask of concentration he had on when he solved my tech problem. "I want to."

"You've already done enough." *You've already done too much.* That's what I really want to say, but I can't because I'm too busy crossing the room to cover his phone screen with my hand. He looks up at me, surprise and maybe some confusion etched into his features. "I appreciate the offer, really, I do, but I want to do this on my own, okay?"

Reluctance casts a dark cloud over his features, but he nods his acceptance. "Okay, but I'll be here to help when you need it."

18

NADIA

W hen.

At the end of our conversation about my apartment hunt, Sebastian said he'd be there when I needed him, not *if* I needed him. It takes me multiple failed apartment visits and damn near the whole month of August to realize his word choice was deliberate. That he knew I was going to need him because the real estate scene in New Haven is a hellscape, and he, apparently, is its dark master.

Within twelve hours of me caving and asking him for his assistance, I'm standing in the middle of an immaculately decorated penthouse in one of the safest buildings in town with Sebastian and his personal realtor in tow. We've seen several places over the course of the morning, but this by far is my favorite. The high rise building is just two blocks from Cerros, so I can walk to work every morning. There's a doorman, security, a gym, and a grocery store that takes up the entire second floor, in addition to two units on the penthouse floor.

"It's perfect," I gush, unable to contain my excitement or hide my smile even though Sebastian has the smuggest grin I've ever seen on his face.

"I told you I was saving the best for last."

"Shut up." I shove his shoulder with my hand, and he laughs, looking at me the way he always does when I touch him. Physical touch became something of a necessity for our relationship when I had to regularly take time out of my work day to cover up his bruise. Every morning for over a week, Sebastian would report to my office as soon as he got in, and I'd stand between his long legs, using my hard won makeup skills to hide the evidence of the violence he committed in my name. The bruise is long gone and the cut on his lip has healed, but the familiarity between his body and mine is still there.

We both feel it, and in moments like now when I'm not as guarded and he's not as cautious, it comes out, pushing its way to the surface and daring us to stomp it back down.

I avert my gaze, turning my focus to the realtor, Nikki Washington. She's been giving us weird looks all day, like she's trying to figure out what we are to each other. We're too friendly to just be the colleagues Sebastian told her we are and too distant to be the couple the hand he places on the small of my back when we're navigating hallways suggests we might be.

"Is the furniture included?" I hope it is because putting together furniture with no one but Desiree for help sounds like a nightmare.

Nikki's brown eyes flit from me to Sebastian. It's a quick glance, but I clock it just like I clocked the others. Every time I've asked her a question about this place specifically, she's looked to him before answering. I guess it makes sense because The Ivy—a stately twenty-four story skyscraper in the middle of New Haven—is yet another one of Sebastian's properties, but it's still a little annoying.

"Yes," she says, her focus back on me. "The owner actually just purchased everything, so it's all brand new. They've also just had a security system installed for an added layer of protection along with a doorbell camera that you'll be given access to once you sign your leasing agreement."

I was already thinking that the owner and I might be the same person because every piece in this place, from the canopy bed in the master to the large, plush sectional in the middle of the open concept living area is something I would have picked out myself. But now that

Nikki has told me about the security, I'm certain this mystery person and I are one in the same.

"Perfect. That's perfect."

"So you'll take it, right?" Sebastian asks. His voice is all gravel and temptation in my ear.

"I don't even know how much the rent is yet."

Nikki opens her mouth to answer that question, but Sebastian cuts her off. "Whatever it is, you can afford it."

"You don't know that."

"Yes, I do."

Arguing with this man is impossible, especially when he's right. I roll my eyes. "Okay, fine, but I'd still like to know the exact number, so I can budget accordingly."

Nikki flips through the clipboard in her hand, presumably searching for the listing where all the finer details about the space are written down. "You'd be looking at four thousand a month with utilities included."

"Four thousand? With utilities?" I split a disbelieving look between her, Sebastian and the three thousand square foot space with floor to ceiling windows and panoramic views of the city. "That can't be right. They could get three times that amount for the space alone, and that's before you throw in the utilities and furniture."

Again, Nikki looks at Sebastian before addressing me. "Well, the owner is very motivated to fill the space, so they're doing what's necessary to make the unit more attractive."

"I guess I get that, but there's a difference between motivation and bad decision making. They might as well be paying me to live here."

She tucks a strand of hair behind her ear and nods. "It's a great offer."

"Which is why you should take it," Sebastian adds. "You won't find a better deal."

As usual, he's right. We looked at three different places before we came here, and all of them were asking twice the rent for half the space. I would be a fool to pass this up.

I chew on the inside of my cheek, and both Sebastian and Nikki watch me, waiting for an answer I can't give yet. I turn to Sebastian.

"Do you know the owners?"

"I'm familiar with them."

"Familiar enough to tell me that this deal is legit? Because it's all sounding a little too good to be true, and I don't want any weirdos knocking on my door saying I need to pay the rest of my rent on my back."

Sebastian's eyes darken with murderous intent that should scare me but just makes me feel safe. "That won't ever happen. You'll be safe here. No one will bother you."

He says those words, and it feels like more than standard reassurance. It feels like a vow, like a sworn oath to make my safety his priority. I drop his gaze, forcing my brain to let go of the images of Sebastian standing guard outside my door, acting as a shield against dangers he doesn't even know about.

"Okay, I'll take it."

Relief washes over Nikki's features as she strides over to the island. "Great, let's get the lease signed, so you can get your keys."

My brows pull together in confusion, but when Sebastian nudges me forward, I follow her to the kitchen. By the time I reach her, she's already got a pen and a small stack of papers on the counter waiting for me.

"Lease? Isn't there an application process or something? Don't you need to run a credit check? Verify my employment?"

I'm not sure why I'm pressing for additional eyes on my fake identity, especially when it could jeopardize my employment and, thus, everything I've built here in New Haven, but it just feels strange to get a place without going through those steps.

Suddenly, Sebastian is at my side, placing a reassuring hand over mine. I meet his eyes, borrowing the calm he's trying to lend me. "All of that has already been taken care of, Nadia. When I called Nikki yesterday afternoon, I gathered all of the information she needed from your employee file and sent it over, so she'd only take us to places you were pre-approved for."

All of the apprehension leaves my body, melting into a puddle of anxiety at my feet that calls me silly for thinking that Sebastian wouldn't have thought of everything. In the weeks that I've known him, he's proven himself to be thoughtful, considerate, and attentive over and over again. I don't know why I thought that wouldn't be the case today. With Sebastian in my life, I don't have to face anything alone. He treats every concern, issue or minor inconvenience like a hurdle for us to jump together, an obstacle for us to face head on and hand in hand.

I don't know why he's decided to make this part of himself available to me, but I'm grateful that he has.

"Oh." My fingers curl around his. "Thank you."

His eyes go all soft, and my heart turns to mush. "You're welcome. Now sign your lease, so I can take you out for an early dinner to celebrate."

* * *

OUR DINNER IS part celebration and part business, which just means that we talk about how things are going at work while we sip on glasses of champagne and eat from the assortment of small plates the tapas bar Sebastian insisted we try is known for.

"Are you sure Nic doesn't want us to go all out tonight? I mean if it's a first date then, he should do something special."

Sebastian laughs, washing down the firecracker shrimp he just ate with some water. "He's reserved the entire rooftop, so they can have a private meal. I think that's special enough, don't you?"

I shrug. "I guess, but I'd love to do something more. We could get a string quartet, clear off all the tables and cover the terrace with flower petals."

"It's a first date, Nadia, not a wedding."

"Fine," I concede while making a mental note to at least put some fresh cut flowers on the table to up the romance factor. Nic's request for a private meal came at the last minute via his personal connection to Sebastian, and despite the fact that it's left my team with the ugly work of having to cancel reservations, I'm excited about playing a role in the budding relationship between him and his mystery woman. "Do you know who the woman is he's bringing?"

"No idea. He refused to give me any details."

"Why'd he call you instead of contacting me?"

"Because you don't owe him any favors."

His answers sparks my interest. Both my brows rise, and I wiggle them at him. "What kind of favors do you owe Dominic Alexander?"

"*Owed*," he stresses, pushing one of his plates to the center of the table. "I owed him a few favors, and he cashed all of them in today."

"Damn." I pick up my glass and polish off the last of my champagne. "She must be someone special for him to give up having you in his debt just for a meal with her."

Sebastian settles his gaze on me. "I'm sure he didn't even think twice about it. There are some people you meet that make you just want to do everything for them, no matter what it cost you."

My heart jumps up into my throat because he's sucked me into yet another moment. Another bubble of possibility where he and I are the only people that exist. How does this keep happening?

I sit my glass back down with shaky fingers. "You sound like you're speaking from experience."

He licks his lips. "Maybe I am."

"Nadia?"

The moment stretches and snaps at the sound of my name, and Sebastian and I both turn to see who's responsible for the frayed edges at our feet. I'm stunned to see Preston standing over us, two rows of straight white teeth gleaming between lips pulled up into a smile that turns strained when he aims it in Sebastian's direction. The abrupt change feels weird to me, but then I look over and see that Sebastian is glowering at him. Everything from the curl of his lip to the narrowing of his eyes demanding Preston to justify the interruption that is his presence. Since it was my name he called, I assume he's here for me.

"Preston, hi."

"Hey, gorgeous."

He swoops down, pressing a kiss to my cheek. Heat immediately rushes to the spot his lips touched, and the reaction is based on two things: the gentle press that spells the beginning of intimacy and the knowledge that Sebastian is watching. Unlike Desiree's client with the exhibitionism fetish, I don't have a thing for being watched, so the second part of my two fold reaction stems from something else. Preston doesn't give me time to dig out the roots, though, because the moment the kiss is done, he turns to Sebastian.

"Adler."

Sebastian doesn't miss a beat. "Fredricks."

I've never seen these two men interact, but it doesn't surprise me that they know each other. They have to since Preston's membership at Ludus was only granted after a personal interview with Sebastian. What does catch me off guard is the reproach coating both of their tones. I didn't realize there was bad blood here, but I probably should have since Preston seemed especially bitter about being kicked out of Ludus. It didn't occur to me until just now that he might blame Sebastian for that.

Preston straightens and places a possessive hand on my shoulder. "I didn't realize you two knew each other…socially."

One of Sebastian's eye brows lifts like he wants to say something, but he looks to me, creating space for my voice in a conversation that's quickly becoming awkward as hell.

"Sebastian and I work together," I say, turning in my seat slightly to bring Preston's attention back to me. I'm not desperate for it, but I am desperate to get him and Sebastian away from each other before whatever is happening between them explodes all over this restaurant.

Surprise lights the corners of Preston's honey brown eyes. "Really? And what is it you do when you're not dazzling the men lucky enough to haunt the halls of Ludus?"

Something about the way he phrases the question doesn't sit right with me, but I shrug it off, contributing it to the tension in the air between the three of us.

"Oh, I don't work at Ludus anymore."

"She manages the restaurant on the Cerros rooftop." There's no mistaking the pride in Sebastian's voice when he chimes in. I know it's probably shining in his eyes as well, but I don't allow myself to look at him to find out. I don't think I could take it.

"That's amazing," Preston says, looking like he genuinely means it. "Maybe you can tell me all about it when you finally let me take you out to dinner."

Sebastian stands, causing Preston and me to look his way. Tension laces the hard line of his jaw as he excuses himself, leaving us with some excuse about going to take care of the bill. I watch him go with a weighted ball of anxiety in the pit of my stomach. I haven't done anything wrong, but I feel like I have. I stand too, and Preston backs up.

"Preston, it was so nice to see you." My attention is split between being polite to the man in front of me and being concerned about the man who just walked away. I can see the wide span of Sebastian's shoulders cutting an urgent line through the tables and chairs in the restaurant to the front where our server is talking to the hostess. Preston clears his throat, and my eyes snap back to his face. I give him a thin smile. "I'll have to give you a call about dinner."

"Or, if you give me your number, I could give you one," he says, reminding me that the last time we ran into each other—when Desiree accepted his dinner invitation on my behalf—I took his number but didn't give him mine.

The idea was that having his number would give me some semblance of control over this whole date situation. That I'd have the time and space I needed to be brave enough to step out on this limb with Preston. The courage never came. Probably because I've been over thinking it, doubting whether I can have a normal introduction into the dating world. Apparently, if it's left up to me, I'll never find out, so I make a split second decision to leave it up to someone who already knows what they want, to put the ball in the court of a man I chose and see how it all plays out because it can't be any worse than what I've already lived through.

Preston watches my internal battle with patient eyes that light up when I hold my hand out to him.

"Give me your phone, and I'll put it in."

I've never seen a man move so quickly. Within seconds, his phone is unlocked and waiting in my open palm. I type my number in and save my contact, then give it back to him.

"My schedule is pretty busy, but I'm usually able to make evenings work," I tell him, grabbing my purse so I can finally follow Sebastian. Before I walk away, I give him a smile that's completely genuine, followed by words I'm surprised to find I mean. "I can't wait to hear from you."

"I hope you mean that, beautiful, because I'm going to be reaching out real soon," Preston calls out as I walk away.

Tossing my purse over my shoulder, I head toward the front of the restaurant in search of my disappearing companion. By the time I make it to the hostess stand, he's nowhere to be found, so I go outside, hoping to find him there. Sure enough, he's standing on the sidewalk next to his car with the door on the passenger side already open for me.

"Done?" he asks, his tone all censure and quiet disapproval.

"Yep."

I don't know what to do with him in this mood, so I just slide into the buttery leather of the seat and latch my seat belt. Once I'm secure, Sebastian closes the door and rounds the car, slipping into the driver's seat with what can only be described as a grimace on his face. I allow him the chance to merge into oncoming traffic before I ask the question burning a hole in the back of my throat.

"Are you mad at me?"

He's in the middle of switching lanes, but he glances at me. "Why would I be mad at you?"

Every answer to that question sounds valid in my mind, but I know it will sound ridiculous coming out of my mouth. In the end, I go with the facts and leave all of my assumptions about jealousy to fester and die in the same place they were born: my head.

"I don't know. The way you got up and left made me think something was wrong."

"I went to pay the bill."

"You could have waited for our server to come back and given her your card like any normal person."

He takes the hand not currently on the steering wheel and scrubs it down his face. A sign of annoyance if I've ever seen one before. "I was trying to give you privacy, Nadia. I didn't think you'd want to set up a dinner date in front of your boss."

Your boss.

The words, while an apt description of his only clearly defined place in my life, slice me open. Cutting through skin and muscle to hit bone. Making me feel foolish for thinking of him as a friend, a source of support and safety that has nothing to do with the financial security I've gained from my job.

"Is that all you are? My boss?"

What I mean to ask is if that's still how he sees us after working so hard to make me think of him as something more. Employer and employee. Supervisor and subordinate. Two people who, outside the confines of professional boundaries, don't mean anything to each other. That he would even suggest that's all we are to each other feels like a slap in the face.

"I've always been your boss, Nadia."

"Okay, but that's not all you are. You're also my friend, right?"

Sebastian's jaw clenches, and he doesn't take his eyes off the road. "Yes, Nadia, I'm also your friend."

Relief slips down my spine. I feel silly for needing verbal confirmation of his friendship, but I'm grateful to have it because it makes me feel comfortable broaching the next subject with him.

"What's with the weird energy between you and Preston?"

"There's weird energy between me and Preston?"

"Sebastian!" I go to slap his shoulder with my hand, but he catches it, holding my fingers hostage between his. Our linked hands hover over the gear shift, and my heart makes a home at the base of my throat.

"The only thing between me and Preston is a revoked Ludus membership."

"I was there that night he got removed from the club," I tell him. "Security came out of nowhere and had him carried out."

He uses his free hand to turn into the parking garage underneath

Cerros. Once the car is in park, he turns to look at me. "I'm sorry you had to see that."

"It's okay. It wasn't traumatic or anything. I just always wondered what happened that led to his removal."

Sebastian smirks, seeing straight through my subtle segue way. At first I think he's going to give me an answer, but then I see him mentally shift gears. "Does it matter? I mean you don't really want some guy you're dating spending his nights chatting up other women do you?"

At the moment, when Sebastian's fingers are warm and snugly wrapped around mine, I don't care what Preston does or who he does it with.

"We're not dating."

Champagne eyes rove over my features. "But he wants to be, and you're considering saying yes."

"Isn't discussing this some kind of breach of professional and personal boundaries?" I ask, like we're not holding hands. Like those lines have ever existed for us. Our professional relationship was made with an offer of friendship and understanding attached to it, and while I never thought I'd actually call any man a friend, that is exactly how I think of Sebastian.

As a friend, and something more…

"You're the one who brought him up."

"To ask about his Ludus membership, not to discuss our relationship."

His brow lifts. "Oh, so it's a relationship now?"

"No, I just meant—"

My fumbling explanation is brought to a halt by the ringing of Sebastian's phone. He drops my hand to answer the incoming call from his mom using the flashing green button displayed on his dashboard.

"Hey, Mom."

"Hey, Sebby." The smooth silk of her regal tone washes over me. Love is woven into every note, and I close my eyes, soaking it in even though it wasn't meant for me. "We missed you today at brunch."

When I open my eyes again, Sebastian is looking at me, concern etched into his features. I give him a reassuring smile that doesn't feel like it reaches my eyes. He extends his hand, turning his palm up in a silent request for us to resume the comforting act of pressed palms.

"I know, Mom, I'm sorry I missed it too."

And he does look genuinely sorry, which tells me everything I need to know about his family life. Children who come from dysfunctional homes can't wait to get out of them, to escape their parents and their nonsense. Children who come from good, stable, loving homes, can't get back to their safe space soon enough. Sebastian is lucky enough to fall into the latter group. I would have too, if my parents were still alive. The thought sends a sharp ache through my chest.

"That's okay, baby," Mrs. Adler is saying now. "Will you be able to make it to dinner tomorrow or will you still be helping your friend look for a place?"

Hearing his mom refer to me even in the vaguest terms sends shock trickling down my spine. I hadn't realized Sebastian was talking to his family about me. He reads my surprise clear as day and squeezes my hand to get my attention and make sure I see his reassuring smile.

"No, we're all done with the apartment hunt. She found the perfect place today."

"Oh, that's great news," his mom gushes. "Tell her I said congratulations."

"Tell her yourself, Mom, she's right here and she can hear you."

"Sebastian!" She admonishes. "What did I tell you about putting me on speaker phone without warning me first? You don't know what could have come out of my mouth. I don't want Nadia getting the wrong impression."

"Don't worry about that, Mrs. Adler. I've heard much worse from your son."

"I'm sure you have." She laughs, and even the sound of her amusement is laced with adoration for her child. "And call me Madeline, please, darling."

"Madeline." I can't help but smile as the warmth that must surround her in person radiates through the phone. "It's nice to meet you."

"And you as well. I keep telling Sebastian to bring you out to the house. Everyone wants to meet you."

"Mom!" Sebastian frowns his disapproval at his mom's unwitting admission. "We have to go. I'll talk to you later."

"Oh, okay. Goodbye, Nadia! I do hope I'll be able to meet you in person soon."

"I hope so too, Madeline. Bye."

When the call disconnects, I look at Sebastian and find him shaking his head.

"Remind me never to trust her with any pertinent information."

"She's your mom, she already knows all your pertinent information, and mine too, apparently."

He rolls his eyes. "I had to give her a reason for missing brunch today."

"I get it. Moms want to know everything."

My mom used to be the same way. She made it a mission to know every single friend I made and class I took. She knew what I was struggling with and where I was excelling. She knew when to push me to go harder and when to pull back. She was the best, and while I miss her every day, hearing Sebastian talk to his mom made me miss her a little bit more.

"We can talk about it if you want," he offers, his piercing gaze seeing straight through to the jagged line running down my broken heart.

I pull away from him, letting palms still warm from his touch comes to a rest in my lap. "Talk about what?"

Sebastian pushes out a dry, disbelieving laugh. "Nadia."

"Yes, Sebastian?"

"Look at me." I do as he says and immediately regret it because I'm now face to face with his most serious, compassionate face. "You know you're not as good at hiding as you think you are, right?"

I smooth a hand down the long line of my pants leg. "What's that supposed to mean?"

"It means there's no point in playing coy because I already see you, I already know you."

Truthfully, Sebastian knows more about me than anyone else in New Haven, but having more information than anyone else doesn't make him some kind of expert on me even if he thinks it does.

"You don't know me. Not really."

My mind runs amok with all the things he doesn't know about me. With all the things that would render him speechless and leave me without a friend or a job.

"Yes, I do," he insists.

Irritation claws at my chest, and I blow out a harsh breath, turning in my seat to face him completely.

"Okay. If you think you know me so well, then tell me something about me that I haven't told you yet."

19

SEBASTIAN

I've built several successful businesses and made a name for myself in the world by never, and I mean never, backing down from a challenge. And despite the fact that my brain is telling me not to go through with it, today isn't going to be any different.

For weeks now, Nadia has kept me at arms length, breaking apart moments that could be something more with an averted gaze or swift change in subject. I've allowed it because I understood she was skittish and untrusting, afraid of being perceived, scared of being hurt. Any other day, I'd be feeding those fears right along with her, letting their existence keep a wedge between us, but today, I can't do it.

Maybe it's because I had to watch Preston fucking Fredricks hone in on territory he hadn't earned access to, and it pissed me off. Maybe it's because when he kissed her cheek and touched her like he had the right to, it made me want to remind her what it felt like to have a man's eyes on her when he cared enough to look closely. To see past the stunning features, long legs and rich ebony skin down to the core of her existence. To be held in the gaze of a man who would spend centuries unearthing every precious facet of her soul, and longer still polishing them until they shone like new.

"Well?" Nadia asks, tipping her chin up.

One last alarm bell sounds off inside me, but I silence it. "Okay. I know that you're running from someone, and that that same someone is probably the one who hurt you and made it necessary for you to know what you know about covering bruises."

Her lips part, presumably to tell me that I've yet to say anything we haven't already established as fact, but I hold my hand up and continue.

"I also know that before you came to New Haven you were alone in this world."

"How could you know something like that?"

"Because no one with a good family escapes from a bad situation and runs somewhere that isn't home." I've suspected for a while now but seeing her reaction to my phone call with Mom really solidified the assumption for me. Her parents are either gone or not a part of her life, and since she's one of the most amazing people I know, I can't imagine them choosing to be away from her. "Am I right?"

She nods, pressing her lips together before speaking. "My parents died when I was 16. I was an only child."

I consider stopping there, letting this moment of revelation die a quiet death in the silence of Nadia's tacked on fact, but then I decide against it because I want to know if I'm right about one more thing.

"I also know that Nadia Hendrix isn't your real name."

Her eyes go wide. I see fear cut a harsh line across her features, so I rush to reassure her. First with my hand settled over the fingers fidgeting in her lap and then with my words. "I don't care about that, Nadia. Honestly, I'd be surprised if you didn't given what I've learned about your past. The only reason I brought it up is because I wanted to tell you that one day I want to know your real name. The name your parents chose for you when they first gazed upon your face. The one they called you by when they needed your attention or wanted to reassure you of their love. The one that was probably the last thing on their lips when they knew they weren't coming back home to you."

I leave it there because the tears shimmering in Nadia's eyes tell me she can't hear anymore, but there's no end to the list of things I want to know about her. Facts I know I'm not entitled to but feel like belong to me anyway. The way something does when you're the first one to care enough to unearth it, to lay eyes on it, to hold it in your hands and declare it precious. Sacred.

That's what Nadia is to me, sacred. Her name is a divine proclamation. Her past consecrated ground it's my birthright to walk on. And that's why watching her with Preston made me feel like I was being eaten alive with jealousy and rage, my heart pierced with a dagger laced with something that felt so close to betrayal I couldn't breathe. When I got up from the table, I couldn't see straight, couldn't think of anything but the lovely shade of red that tinted her cheeks when his lips touched her skin or the way the moment he appeared, she only had eyes for him.

Watching the exchange between them didn't make me angry, it made me sad. It made me question myself, doubt whether the things I felt when we were in these moments were real, wonder if I was reading her right when the changes in her breathing and severity of her stare told me she was feeling it too. This whole time I've been going slow, holding back because I thought she wasn't ready for anything romantic, but now I have to consider that maybe she doesn't want anything romantic with me and maybe she never will.

Except right now, when her hand is still in mine and her eyes are asking how I see her so clearly, that doesn't feel within the realm of possibility. And that should be comforting, but it's just confusing.

She's confusing. Our entire friendship with underlying currents of romantic interest is confusing, and I don't know if I can trust myself to be gentle as I unravel the tangled web of us. I want to rip the threads apart, split fibers and strands until we're both laid bare and have no choice but to face this. But Nadia doesn't want to. I see the hesitance in her eyes every time we get too close. It always shows up first, and then it's only a matter of time before the walls rise and her open expression closes, shutting me out.

I'm watching it happen in real time. She rebuilds the wall between us brick by brick all while holding my hand. Even though it pains me, I release her from my hold, wanting to have some say in the matter of our untangling.

The apology written all over Nadia's face breaks something inside me. I don't want her to be sorry. I want her to be comfortable. I want her to know that I'll never make her regret trusting me with her heart.

She grips the door handle. "I should go. Sarah says Elle is already here, and I want to talk to her about the wine tasting before she gets swept up cooking."

We both know that things will be mind numbingly slow for Elle with Nic and his date as the only guests on the rooftop tonight, but I accept her excuse, knowing she needs time to recover from our conversation.

"Okay. I'm going to head over to my parents' to see how they're doing."

Her foot is halfway out the door, but she pauses, turning back to me. "Are they okay?"

The question is an echo of the one in my mind. The one sparked by Mom's insistence on having multiple family gatherings during the week. We used to have one standing lunch on Mondays, but now she's added on brunch on Saturdays and dinners on Sunday. At this point, I feel like I'm living with them again, and I'm not sure why.

"Yeah, I think so."

Her brows furrow, and there's that concern again that makes me think she's the best thing I'll never get the chance to actually have. "Are you sure?"

I'm not, but I don't have the energy to infuse any more uncertainty into our dynamic. "Yes, Nadia, I'm sure."

"Will you let me know if they're not?" she asks, seeing right through my act.

"Yes, I'll let you know."

She climbs out the car, holding the door open like she doesn't actually want to go. "Sebastian?"

"Yeah?"

"Thank you for today, for your help with finding a place. You went out of your way for me. You *always* go out of your way for me."

More tears gather in her eyes. Their appearance sends a quake through my soul, but it's the waver in her voice that sends my self control sliding off the edge of a cliff. Within seconds, I'm out of my seat and around the car, pulling her into my arms and letting the tears skating down her cheeks soak into my shirt. She surprises me by wrapping her arms around my back, allowing me to hold her.

"You're so good to me. I don't know what I'd do without you," she gasps into my chest.

I press a kiss to the top of her head. "You won't ever have to find out."

When she pulls back to look at me, her eyes wet with tears and her full lips quivering, I wish I could say more, give her more, promise her more and feel confident that she was ready for it.

"You really mean that don't you?"

I don't even have to think about my answer to that question. "Yes."

Her response isn't verbal but physical. It starts with a determined blink and then a slow ascent on her tip toes that brings her face level with mine. I suck in a shocked breath and force my body to go still, my heartbeat to go quiet. Doubt flirts with the corners of her mouth, and for the briefest of seconds, I think she's not going to go through with it.

It being whatever she's planning on doing to me. It could be anything from a kiss on the lips to a literal kick in the teeth and it wouldn't matter because as long as it's coming from her, I'll be glad to have it.

She puts me out of my misery a minute later with a kiss that lands at the corner of my mouth. Her scent invades all of my senses, momentarily stealing my ability to truly appreciate the feel of her lips on my skin. By the time it comes back around, Nadia is walking away from me. The wide legs of her black pantsuit swinging back and forth with every stride, teasing me with fleeting views of her ankles as she moves away, draining perhaps our most important moment of all its potential.

* * *

My mind is still on Nadia when I walk into my parent's house, but I'm not so preoccupied that I don't notice the quiet. The silence that indicates my siblings'—and more specifically Luca's—absence.

I find Mom and Dad on the couch, sharing a bottle of wine and what's left of a grazing board. Mom's face lights up when she sees me, and she starts to rise from her seat next to Dad, but I wave her off.

"Don't get up, Mom. I'm sure you're tired from all the cooking you did today."

Apparently, brunch was quite the experience, surpassing the level of expansive culinary complexity we've all come to expect from Mom.

Dad puts his arm around her waist, pulling her close. "She is tired, but I don't think it has anything to do with brunch."

My stomach turns at the insinuation. "Dad, please. I don't need those kind of images in my head."

"Oh grow up, Sebastian. How do you think you got here?"

"Dropped off by a stork?"

Mom cackles. "You weighed thirteen pounds when you were born, I don't think a stork could have carried you."

"You're probably right."

"So what brings you by, son?" Dad asks. "Your mother and I were enjoying a quiet evening *alone.*"

"Everett! Don't say it like that, you'll make him think we don't want him here."

"I don't want him here right now. I want an evening alone with my wife."

I scrunch my nose up, more offended by the sexual innuendo in his words than anything else. "And I'll make sure you have that right after you two answer a question for me."

"What question is that?" Mom asks, crossing her legs and leaning back into Dad's hold. He curves his arm around her waist and lays a kiss on her temple.

The two of them look so relaxed together. More relaxed than I've seen them in years. There's always been an ease between them, but this is something different. Something peaceful and accepting that comes with decades of marriage and four children. I wonder if I'll ever have anything like that. It was never going to happen with Talia. We're too much alike. Neither of us knows how to bend, how to give, how to compromise, and we never made each other want to learn. Our marriage rested comfortably in the challenge of being opponents while never accessing the intimacy of true partnership.

I can look at my parents and tell that's what they have. It's not something I've ever noticed before, and I can't tell if I'm aware of it now because Nadia's presence in my life has made me think about how I would do things differently the second time around or because they've just started openly displaying it.

"What's going on?"

Dad frowns. "I'm afraid you're going to have to be more specific, son."

"Well, we've gone from having a standing lunch on Monday to multiple gatherings throughout the week that are starting to feel less optional and more mandatory, so, again I ask, what's going on?"

My parents raised us to be fiercely independent, while also making sure we felt loved and safe with them. Which means that by the time we were all grown, we felt ready to take on the world on our own. We all moved out at eighteen, securing our own jobs and finding our place in the world. By some miracle, we'd all found those places in New Haven, able to stay close to each other and our parents. That proximity never came with more than one obligatory family engagement a week, now we're working our way up to three.

Mom's round eyes cut to Dad who looks more uncomfortable now than he did when he sat me down to give me a talk about sex, condoms and consent when I was 14.

"Tell him, Everett," she says and her words cause my throat to constrict because they seem to confirm my fear that something is wrong.

My eyes fly to my father's face. "Are you sick?"

He hasn't even answered my question, and I'm already reeling. Trying to imagine what him saying yes would mean for our family. Him stepping back from the business I never wanted to run. Hospital stays and doctor's visits. Prescriptions for medicines impossible to name. His large frame yielding to physical exhaustion, every cell in his body turning against him, conspiring to take him away from us.

My thoughts must show all over my face because Dad moves from his place on the couch by Mom to the ottoman in front of me. He puts a hand on my shoulder, squeezing tight to demand my attention.

"Look at me, son." I do as he says, and I feel like a little boy again. Searching his face for reassurance, depending on his calm to ground me. "I'm not sick. A few months ago my doctor found a blockage in my heart, so I had to get a stent placed. It was a minor procedure, and I'm doing fine."

"*A few months?*" A strange mixture of disbelief and relief coats the words. I look over at Mom, and her features are still the way they always are when she's trying to hide the fact that she doesn't agree with her husband's decision but went along with it anyway. "You knew about this?"

She brings the glass of wine in her hands to her lips, taking a swig before answering me. "Yes, I was the one who made him go to the doctor when he was having chest pains."

"And you hid that from me?"

I don't make mention of my siblings because as the oldest the information pipeline always sends knowledge flowing my way first. And I'm the dam, holding everything back to protect them, only opening up to release something when it all gets to be too much. When that happens, I loop in Andreas, and if we can't hold it together, we call in Luca. Nothing ever touches Zoe if we can help it.

"It was my decision," Dad says, narrowing his eyes in a silent reprimand for questioning my mother, and by extension, him. "There was no need to worry you when everything went fine."

"What if it hadn't gone fine though, Dad? Then what? Do you have any idea what it would have done to us to just wake up one day and find that you're gone?"

My question sends images of a younger version of Nadia's face flitting through my mind. She was sixteen when she lived the exact reality I'm asking my father to imagine for me and my siblings. It's been over a decade and that pain is still so fresh for her. The grief of it was heavy on her tongue when she said the words in the car.

"Sebastian, please." Mom's hand goes to her chest, and I see the beginning of a sob working its way up her throat. I don't know what it is about today that has me making every woman I care about cry. She tries to fight it back, but the sob refuses to be delayed especially when Dad turns from me to her. The second their eyes lock, it hits the air, a jagged note of devastating possibility.

"*Maddy*." Dad calls, reaching for her. She brushes him off as she rises from her seat.

"I'm fine," she lies. "I just need a moment. You two keep talking."

We watch her go, both of us fighting the urge to go after her. Me, to apologize for upsetting her. Dad, to console her. Neither of us move, though, because we have things we need to say to each other.

"She gets upset every time we talk about the procedure."

"And what could have happened if you hadn't gotten it in time."

He rubs at his jaw with hands that look like mine, grimacing at my addition to his statement. "Yes, she thought I was having a heart attack."

"You weren't far off."

"No." He shakes his head. "I wasn't. I got lucky, and I won't ever forget that."

"What brought it on?"

"Stress. Your mother and my cardiologist seem to believe I've been working too hard and not taking good enough care of myself."

That sounds about right to me. Dad doesn't know how to take a break. For decades, he's worked himself to the bone day in and day out, never taking a day off or indulging in a vacation. He's carried the entirety of the family business on his back, taking on all the stress and responsibilities. When I graduated with my MBA, I was supposed to step into the CFO position at Adleron Enterprises. Doing so meant helping take some of the stress off of Dad and also getting the hands on training necessary to eventually fill the CEO role when he retired. Instead, I decided to take a leap of faith and start my own company. Everyone was shocked at the choice, but Dad was the only person whose opinion meant anything to me. He was sad about not being able to pass the company on to me like his father had passed it on to him, but he was also supportive. That support made it easy for me to feel good about my choice, and I've never regretted it.

Until now.

Dad sees it all over my face, and he shakes his head, refusing to give my guilt room to blossom. "No, don't you dare do that. You made a choice for yourself, and I've never resented you for it."

His words don't help. They don't move the needle or quiet the racing thoughts in my mind that are riddled with guilt and responsibility.

"Yeah, you're right, and look at what it almost cost us."

"Sebastian." He sighs heavily and pushes to his feet. I watch as he starts pacing the length of the floor in front of me. "Your choices have nothing to do with my health. The truth is I've been pushing myself too hard for too long. Your mother has been asking me to slow down and take better care of myself for years, but I haven't listened. This—" he gestures at his heart "—is a result of me not listening to my wife or my doctor's warnings about lifestyle changes."

I gaze up at him, forcing myself to take him in as he is, not how my fear is trying to make me see him. He's the same man he was on Monday when we sat out on the patio discussing the land Talia and Blue think we should purchase for Ludus: Antigua. The same man who raised me, who took me to buy my first car and forced me to negotiate the terms even though we could afford any price the salesman came up with, who sat me on his lap while he commanded meetings in board rooms with our name on the door.

He's still him. Healthy, strong, larger than life. The way he's always been for my entire life. The lack of change in his appearance offers me some comfort, allows me to focus on something else, like the positive changes his health scare have brought about instead of the negative outcomes we've narrowly avoided.

"Do those lifestyle changes include more family gatherings?"

Dad laughs, turning to me when I stand as well. "That's all your mother. She thinks we need to spend more time together, and she's using my health scare as a way to make me cooperate."

"She's a smart woman."

He slips his hands into the pocket of the khakis he's wearing. "That she is."

"And you're okay? Like really okay?"

He nods. "Yes, son. I'm really okay. All of my check-ups have gone well, and my blood work is clear."

"No more chest pain?"

I find myself staring at his chest, trying to envision the small scar that's probably there under the light fabric of his cotton shirt. Dad must be self conscious because he covers the spot with his hand. The other goes back to my shoulder. We share a long look, and I'm comforted by the strength of his unwavering gaze.

"That's right. No more chest pain. I'm okay."

"You're okay."

The relief flooding through my body causes me to sway on my feet. Dad holds me steady, refusing to let me fall even when my taller, larger frame starts to crumble around him.

The tears come, and he holds me like he did when I was a thirteen and my whole world fell apart when my girlfriend of a week broke up with me. He holds me like I'm a baby and not a thirty-two year old man who has stood taller than him since his sixteenth birthday. He holds me until Mom comes back and joins in too, and then I'm wrapped in both of my parents' arms, enveloped in love that for some reason, makes me think about Nadia and the length of time she's gone without it.

20

NADIA

Turns out moving is quick and painless when your apartment comes fully furnished with brand new everything and you have nothing to your name but a growing wardrobe made up of designer clothes and a go-bag with five times more money in it than you originally started with.

I spin around in the middle of the floor, barefoot and happier than I've been in a while because every time I close my door and lock it, it stays shut. Because everything is clean and nothing smells like mold and despair. Because I have a home for the first time since my parents died, and I feel safe.

After Beau I didn't think that word would ever belong to me, and when I climbed out of that car, finding freedom but not security, I was certain it would never be mine again. I thought I would never sleep peacefully, never walk into a building without first looking over my shoulder, never answer the door without my anxious brain telling me that Beau is on the other side of it not the person I'm actually expecting.

Today that person is Desiree, and she all but pushed her way in, carrying a bag of takeout from the Indian spot around the corner and fussing at me about not letting her help me move in. She's still ranting right now, standing at my island in a purple sundress with cutouts that expose the lush curve of her hip and some of her belly. Her hair is in its signature cloud of wild curls, and the lemon and sugar scent that I now know comes from the body scrub she uses every time she showers, fills my nostrils as I trace her steps to the kitchen. She glares at me when I sit down on the opposite side of the island and reach across to grab my mango lassi and a straw.

I take a long sip and close my eyes to fully appreciate the goodness before I address the daggers she's shooting my way. "Why are you looking at me like that?"

"Because!" She slides me a take out tray that, judging by the smell, has lamb biryani in it. "You really moved in without letting me help you."

"The place came fully furnished, and it took me all of five minutes to pack up all my shit from the hotel and bring it over here this morning. I didn't need any help, Des."

"So what? I still wanted to be here with you."

In my old life, I'd go months without crying, and it would drive Beau crazy because my tears were his most prized possession. He'd beat me to get them, and I'd deny him the pleasure of having them every time. When I was in Los Angeles, there was a wall between me and my emotions, I used it to protect me, but here in New Haven? That wall is slowly crumbling, dissolving under what seems to be a constant stream of happiness flowing from my eyes because I now have people in my life who care enough to help and get upset when I don't let them.

Happy tears leak from the corners of my eyes, dropping onto that invisible wall, onto the bricks I added when Bianca chose Beau over me, and Desiree throws me a questioning look as she bites down on a lamb skewer.

"Damn, bitch, why you crying?"

The laugh her cheeky question pulls out of me is wrapped around a half sob that's been sitting in my chest for ten days, ever since Sebastian helped me find this place and then followed up the act of kindness with a declaration about always being by my side.

I ball up the paper from my straw and throw it at her, hitting her square in the forehead. "I hate you."

"No, you don't. I'm your best friend."

For some reason that statement—which is about as true as anything has ever been—sets me off again. *"You really are."*

Des looks at me like I've lost my mind and rushes around the island to wrap a supportive, but reluctant, arm around my shoulders. She looks down at me, confusion written all over her features. "You on your period or something?"

I burst out laughing, but the tears are still coming, so I feel crazy. I must look it too because Desiree's eyes go wide, and I can all but see her wondering if she's going to have to get me admitted to a hospital for a seventy-two hour psych hold.

"No, it just went off" I gasp, leaning against her shoulder. "I'm just happy."

"People don't usually sob when they're happy, babe."

"They do when their life suddenly starts going really good after years of everything always being bad."

A commiserating silence falls between us, and I know I don't have to say anymore. Desiree doesn't know much about my past, but I've given her some hints. Some glimpses into the hell that rained down on me when my parents died.

"You're right." She says, pulling me in closer and breathing the words against my skin. "You cry all the happy tears you want because you are finally free."

"Were you this emotional when you got away from Cheese?"

We both cringe at the dumb nickname of the man she had to escape on her way to freedom. I don't know much about how she came to work for him or even really how she got away. I just know that she did, and if that's all I ever get to know about it, then I'm okay with that.

"Sometimes. I was mostly just angry though. When I got out from under him and realized the shit I was accepting because I didn't think there was better out there for me, I got so pissed off. Sebastian had to talk me out of going back to kill him several times."

I twist in my seat, brows furrowed as I look up at her. "Sebastian?"

"Yeah, he's the only reason I left Cheese and started working at Ludus."

She starts to pull away, and I let her go, allowing her to return to her plate on the other side of the island. I don't bother looking at my food because I know I can't eat right now. There's something sour churning in my gut, washing out the joy and appreciation that was just there and replacing it with something else.

"Oh." My fingers go to the abandoned cup in front of me, but I don't pick it up to take a drink. I just spin it around on the counter absently, waiting for Desiree to elaborate. When she doesn't, I resign myself to continuing the conversation. "I didn't realize Sebastian played such a huge part in you starting at Ludus."

"That makes sense, considering that I never told you."

She laughs, but I can't even crack a smile. My brain is too busy drawing lines between what I think he's done for her and what I know he's done for me with ink from a pen that runs green. It makes no sense. Desiree is my best friend, and Sebastian is...well, he's not anything to me that would justify me feeling like he owes me the exclusivity of his kindness. But knowing that doesn't make me want to own it any less.

"Tell me now."

We're both caught off guard by the demand. Desiree's eyes go wide as she takes a bite of garlic naan, and I take another sip of my drink to try to seem casual even though my mind is running rampant with images of an imagined relationship between two of the most important people in my life.

"Umm, well, when Ludus first opened, it wasn't even on my radar. I didn't know anything outside of Cheese and the box he allowed me to exist in." She gives me a sad smile that makes my heart ache. Even though she didn't go into detail, I know. I know the horrors she must have lived through inside that box. "I bet it still eats him up that he's the reason I found out about Ludus in the first place."

"What do you mean?"

"He would have these poker games with his friends and make me and some of the other girls work the room. We'd serve drinks, food, give a random blowjob here and there. You know, usual stuff. One night during a game, one of his friends, Kirk, started going on and on about how he was losing girls to some club owned by a guy with enough money to buy girls their freedom with no strings attached."

"No one knew it was Sebastian?"

"Not at first. The club was only a few months old then."

"How did they figure it out?"

Her cheeks turn red. "I told them."

"How did *you* know?"

"Cheese sent me in to find out. I clocked Sebastian almost immediately because everyone moved different when he was around. Plus, he was the only guy there who didn't try to fuck me."

I hate the way my shoulders start to relax after she says that.

"What happened after you realized he was the owner?"

She dips a kebab into a small container of the yogurt mint sauce it comes with. "I sat on the information for a while."

"Why?"

"Because I didn't want to leave. I've always liked sex, but Ludus was the first place I enjoyed doing sex work, you know?"

I nod even though I don't know. Not really. There hasn't ever been a time or place where I've felt good about having sex for money, and because of Beau, I doubt there ever will. But the lack of first hand knowledge doesn't mean I don't understand. Desiree isn't the first girl from Ludus to say something similar to me. Her friend Carmen and some of the other girls have as well, and while their stories are all different, the thing that's always the same is their appreciation for the autonomy and control they found within the walls of the establishment Sebastian built.

"Is that why you decided to stay?"

Desiree shakes her head. "No, Sebastian made that decision for me when I came clean with him about why I was there."

"And when was that?"

"About a month after I started at Ludus. Cheese beat Sebastian's name out of me because he was tired of me using the search as an excuse to be at the club all the time."

"He wanted you back out there making money for him."

It's not a question, but a statement because I'm intimately familiar with the greed that comes along with exploiting others. Beau had it too. He'd berate me for refusing to work when my period was on, cursing me out for complaining about cramps and bloating, assigning me clients with a thing for blood who didn't care about my comfort.

"Exactly. I was his top earner, so he didn't take it well when I said I wasn't coming back. I had to go tell Sebastian the truth with two broken ribs." Her eyes take on this far away look, and I know she's remembering that day. The day her life changed forever. I wonder what it means for us to have both found freedom and goodness on the other side of broken bones and brutality. "He wasn't even mad. He just sent me to the doctor with the promise to pay my hospital bills and told me to come back when I was ready. When we found out about the hit, I thought for sure he was going to show his true colors, but he didn't even blame me. He just kept rolling with the punches. Literally."

"THE HIT?!" I shriek, and Desiree's eyes snap back to my face.

"Relax, girl. This was years ago. Cheese tried to get him killed for stealing me away, but Sebastian took care of it. I haven't seen or heard from that man in years."

I sit back in my seat, slumping against the back of the barstool. "Wow. I'm really glad you got out of that situation, Des."

I genuinely mean it. There's no world in which I would ever wish continued violence and pain on Desiree or any other woman for that matter. There is, however, a world where I'll feel hurt, and maybe even a little angry, to find that nothing Sebastian has done for me is out of the ordinary. That saving women like me and Desiree is just a pastime for him, a benevolent indulgence that makes him feel good about himself. That among all the things I am—an orphan, an ex-sex worker, a capable restaurant manager—I am not and will never be, special.

Not to him.

Deep down, I think I've always known that, which is probably why I've never allowed myself to fully be in those moments we share even though they feel so natural and come so easily. My heart twists in on itself, and I suck in a deep breath.

"You okay?" Desiree asks, concern pulling down the corners of her mouth.

"Yeah, I'm good. I was just thinking—"

"About your date with Preston tomorrow?"

I'm grateful for her interruption because it keeps me from having to come up with something to say besides the truth, but I'm also slightly irritated by it because just like this conversation my thoughts when I agreed to go to dinner with Preston were all about Sebastian.

What he would think if I said yes.

What he would think if I said no.

Now, I'm wondering if he'll even care at all.

"Yeah, I'm not sure what I'm going to wear," I say finally.

Des is back to eating her food now, absolutely devouring the remaining kebabs with no idea as to what is going on inside my head.

"Did he tell you where you guys were going?"

"Some placed called Cream?"

She nods like she knows the place I'm talking about. Given that she's lived in New Haven for most of her life, she probably does. "That's a good choice for a first date. It's upscale but not snooty. You'd be comfortable in something dressier like that leather midi skirt you just bought or a pair of nice jeans and a blouse."

Grabbing my uneaten plate, I move over to the fridge and put it away. "Do you have my whole wardrobe memorized?"

"Just about," she quips. "You're not eating?"

"I'm saving it for later. I have to get ready for work."

Truthfully, I should have been at work fifteen minutes ago double checking everything for the wine tasting event Elle, Ruthie and I have worked our ass off to make happen, but I didn't want to kick Des out as soon as she got through the door.

"Oh yeah!" She exclaims, following me down the hall to my bedroom. "I forgot all about your event! Are you excited?"

"Excited is what I will be when it's over."

Planning this event hasn't been hard per say, especially not with people like Ruthie and Elle on my team. But it has been daunting. Mostly because I've been doubting myself at every turn, letting little things like wait staff calling in sick or a glitch in the ticketing system make me feel like I couldn't really pull it off.

Des plops down on the chaise in the corner of my bedroom near the closet, watching as I carry a few clothing options to the bed.

"That one," she says, pointing to the last outfit sprawled out on my comforter. It's the cream leather midi skirt she was just talking about paired with a camel colored cross neck halter top made from the same material. "It's sexy and professional, and it will look good with the little up-do you have going on."

The hairstyle in question is a low bun that's settled at the nape of my neck with curtain bangs that frame my face and random, wavy tendrils set loose in random places to make the style appear effortless and sexy. I pick the top up and hold it to my body, turning towards the mirror to find that, as usual, Desiree's clothing suggestion is spot on.

She watches me get dressed, giving her opinion on accessories and shoes, and then drops me off at Cerros, blowing me a kiss before pulling off into evening traffic. When I get to the kitchen, everything is in full swing and running smoothly, so I leave before Elle has the chance to kick me out, taking the hallway the servers use to the rooftop.

Mid-September air that's warm with a little chill to it greets me, but that's not the cause of the goosebumps popping up along my arm. No, that honor belongs to the man in front of me, standing by the door like he's been waiting for me to walk through it. That honor belongs to the man in the suit as dark as his eyes are right now with his locs in a neat bun at the top of his head. That honor belongs to the hand he places on the small of my back and the kiss he plants on my cheek, to the gravel in his tone when he puts his lips at my ear and says, "You're late."

A full blown shiver runs down my spine, and I forget for a moment the conclusion I came to at my apartment less than an hour ago. The one where I decided I wasn't special because as far as I can tell he treats every woman in his life like this. Despite that thought echoing in my mind, I find myself leaning into him, extending my neck to place a kiss that lands at the corner of his mouth and allows me to breathe in the perfection of his scent. Together, we're a cloud of spices and flowers, a bubble of decadence begging to be indulged.

"Dinner doesn't start until eight."

I step back, trying to pop the bubble Sebastian seems determined to keep in tact. His hand follows my body's retreat, maintaining firm pressure at the spot just above the curve of my ass.

"True, but all staff was supposed to be here at five."

"I'm not staff, Sebastian, I'm the boss who came in at five with everyone else, troubleshot several staffing issues and did a full inventory check with Elle and Ruthie before going home to shower and get dressed."

His eyes take on an odd glow that makes my insides turn to liquid. "Say that again."

"Say what again?"

"You're the boss."

Heat washes over me, adding what I'm sure is a red tint to every inch of my skin. Sebastian tracks the change with his eyes, and I want to order him to look away and also ask him never to take his eyes off me again.

"No."

"Nadia."

A helplessly nervous laugh slips past my lips because there's a part of me that wants to do exactly as he asks. "Sebastian, no. I have things to do."

Using the hand on my back, he pulls me closer, until the amount of space between our bodies is so small it's negligible. My breath leaves my lungs in a quiet whoosh as he gazes down at me, a playful smile on his lips.

"Those things can wait. I want to hear you say it again."

"Why?"

"Because it's the truth. It's always been the truth, but it's the first time you've said it out loud, and I want to hear it again. *Please*."

My teeth sink into my bottom lip, and I hate him for noticing things like what he's just pointed out. I hate myself even more for conceding, repeating a statement that both appeases him and affirms me.

"I'm the boss."

"And I figure you saying that means we're no longer doing the trial run thing, right? You're all in?"

Something about the warmth of his gaze on my face makes me feel like there's a hidden meaning behind his words, like he's asking me for my verbal commitment to this job and something more. Something that makes my heart flutter. Something that makes my brain swirl with possibilities yet to be realized. Something that makes me feel brave.

"I'm all in," I whisper, making the expression of commitment a private thing. Something just for his ears and my lips.

The hum of approval that rumbles through his chest startles me because I never thought such a deep, guttural sound could come from a human man, and because it causes a delicious clenching of muscles in my lower extremities that is unfamiliar but not unwelcome. I bury my reaction behind a frown and a slap to his chest that causes him to finally release me. The self-satisfied smirk curving his lips makes me roll my eyes.

"You're so annoying."

"Does that mean you don't want to meet my family?" he asks, turning to the side to reveal a group of five seated at the end of the table closest to us. Something about his tone when he poses the question makes me feel like the world has fallen out from under me. I grapple to find my footing, to remember that this isn't special, that I'm not special, that he probably introduces colleagues and friends to his family all the time and it means nothing.

"Of course, I want to meet them."

"Fine, but I should warn you, they're just as annoying as me," he jokes, returning his hand to the small of my back and leading me over to the group. Everyone tries to act like they aren't paying any attention to the two of us. Well, everyone except the older woman with long curly hair and smooth, umber skin. She's looking right at us with eyes that remind me of Sebastian's and shine with interest, especially when they sweep over me and her son.

"Everyone, this is Nadia Hendrix," Sebastian announces, his voice loud and sure as it demands their attention. They give it easily, all their eyes leaving whatever thing they were pretending to be focusing on to come to rest on my face. "Nadia, this is my mom, Madeline, my father, Everett, my brother Andreas, my other brother Luca, and our younger sister, Zoe."

I follow Sebastian's hand as he gestures to everyone, matching names I've heard before with faces. "Hi, everyone. It's so nice to meet you all."

"The pleasure is all ours, Nadia," Madeline says, rising from her seat to pull me into a hug I'm not expecting but sink into anyway. No one's hugs feel like my mother's, but Madeline's feel close. She applies the perfect amount of pressure and holds me for the exact right amount of time. Then she pulls back and grips me by my shoulders, looking between me and Sebastian. "You're even more gorgeous than Sebastian said."

"Mom!" This comes from Zoe, the youngest Adler sibling and the only girl. I don't envy her positioning in this family, under the reign of three older brothers who are all formidable in their own right and a father who could cut down a giant with one look. "You could at least try to be subtle."

Madeline moves back, leaving space for Zoe to join us in our little circle of femininity. She gives me a hug too, and even though it's quick, it's no less welcoming than her mother's.

"Sebastian hasn't talked about you *that* much." I don't know whether I should take comfort in her statement or not, so I just smile. "In all of the times he's talked about you, he's failed to mention how beautiful your hair is. Who does it?"

"Umm, I do?"

"Really?" Her brown eyes stretch wide as she circles me to do a full appraisal of my tresses. "All of this hair? It must take you hours. Are you natural or relaxed?"

"I'm what I like to call a straight natural."

Meaning I don't relax my hair, but I always wear it straight because my natural curls are too damn thick. Zoe seems to know exactly what I mean because she's smiling when she comes to a stop in front of me.

"Are you looking for a stylist? I'd love to have you in my chair."

"Not actively, no, but I am in desperate need of a wash and trim." I can't remember the last time I've had hands that aren't mine massaging my scalp and just the thought of it has me a little weak in the knees. "When's your next opening?"

Zoe pulls out her phone and checks her schedule. "Tomorrow afternoon, around four."

My brows go up as surprise etches itself into my features. Sebastian told me that Zoe is a very popular, extremely busy stylist, so it seems unlikely that she would have an opening so soon. When she sees the look on my face, Zoe pauses.

"What? That doesn't work for you?"

"No, that's actually perfect. I was just surprised that you have availability on a Saturday."

"Oh, I'm usually closed on Saturdays, so I didn't have anyone on the books." Zoe laughs when my brows go even higher. "I make my own hours. Sebastian did tell you I own a salon, right?"

"Of course he did. He's very proud of you and the work you've done to make it a success."

Sebastian said as much to me the other day when we were eating lunch and Zoe called just to say hi. After they hung up, the conversation we were having about the restaurant turned personal. He told me about Zoe's salon, Andreas' hallowed academic career and Luca's struggle to find his footing inside Adleron Enterprises, their family business. I wasn't able to share anything, but I soaked every bit of information he offered up because I wanted to be prepared for this moment.

Zoe beams at her oldest brother. "Aww. Thanks, Sebby."

I glance at Sebastian who has gone from smiling at his little sister to glowering at her in a matter of seconds. "Sebby?"

He shakes his head. "Don't even think about it."

"Call him whatever you want," Andreas says, adding his quiet energy to the group. He doesn't come in for a hug, but Luca does. He bursts into my personal space with a wide, welcoming smile that sets me at ease despite the abrupt show of physical affection.

"Damn," he mutters, stepping back and allowing his eyes to skate down my frame. "I would buy you so much more than one bouquet of flowers."

Sebastian opens his mouth to correct him, but it's Everett's voice that calls Luca's name, snapping over his head like a crack of lightening that makes the youngest Adler son hold up his hands in surrender.

"Sorry. I'm sorry." He gives me a roguish grin as he bows dramatically. "Please forgive me, Nadia."

I can't help but smile back at him, shaking my head. "Consider it forgotten."

"Don't indulge him, Nadia," Everett says, pulling Luca back and extending his free hand to me. I take it, noting that he and Andreas are the only members of the Adler family who haven't tried to hug me. Sebastian warned me that they could be standoffish. He also said he shared their detached temperament, but I can't tell because he's never been that way with me. "He's like a stray dog, if you feed him once, he'll keep coming back for more."

"Damn, Dad. Tell me how you really feel." Luca places a hand over his chest, a frown on his face that's as deep as it is disingenuous. It's clear to me that he's used to being the butt of his family's jokes, his sense of humor and relaxed demeanor keeping things light in an otherwise serious dynamic.

"Thanks for the advice, Mr. Adler."

"Everett," he corrects me the same way his wife did over the phone. "It's very nice to meet you, Nadia."

"It's nice to meet you too, Everett." I split a warm gaze between all the people looking at me. "Thank you all for being here tonight."

Madeline waves a dismissive hand at me. "Oh, you don't have to thank us, sweetie. Sebastian told us how hard you've been working to make this night happen. We wanted to make sure you knew you had the support of the entire Adler family."

"Mrs. Adler...I mean, Madeline, I don't know what to say."

"Say you'll come over for lunch on Monday," she says. "I've been trying to get you over to the house for weeks now."

"Mom. Nadia is very busy."

I glance back at Sebastian, noting the tension making his jaw tight and hating the way it scrapes right across the insecurities my conversation with Desiree brought up. The way it tells me that his mother's invitation has revealed a line in the sand neither of us realized had been drawn until this very moment. The way it says that I'm good enough to be his friend, to meet his family in a setting like this, to go to his sister's salon and sit in her chair, but I'm not good enough for this.

For his parent's home and the sacred nature of their weekly family lunch.

"He's right, Madeline." My smile is bone dry, brittle enough to fall right off of my face. "I am."

Once again, Madeline waves her hand through the air, dismissing all excuses. "Nonsense, if Sebastian can make it to lunch every week, then so can you. You're coming, and I won't take no for an answer."

I glance around, looking for help from someone else in the Adler family and coming up empty. Seems that no one, not even Everett, wants to intervene on my behalf. I don't look at Sebastian because I don't want to see whatever emotions will take over his face when I accept the invitation his mom won't let me refuse.

"Then I guess I'll see you Monday."

21

NADIA

My appointment with Zoe at 5th Street Salon starts off rough, and it's all my fault. I was so excited about the prospect of having her capable hands in my head, I didn't stop to think about why she's usually booked out eight months in advance or how she can afford to be closed on Saturdays when most stylists are wide open.

The first indicator of my mistake were the ring lights and cameras at every station in the salon. The second was the live stream she was on when I walked through the door. I paused just inside the threshold, holding the door open partially in case I had to take my garment bag and make a run for it, and watched as she restocked products and chatted with what is apparently a very active and dedicated fan base. When she caught me watching her, she waved me forward with eager eyes that made me feel bad for shutting her down with a curt shake of my head. I was grateful when she didn't ask again, choosing instead to end the live and tend to me, but that feeling only lasted for a few minutes before she sat a ring light and a camera in front of me and asked if I minded being recorded.

In this age of social media, I know most people only ask for permission to record as a formality. The assumption is always that the answer will be yes, that you'll be eager to be featured on social media platforms with hundreds of thousands of followers that could possibly lead to an increase in your own numbers. But, here's the thing, that stuff only matters when you have socials to follow, and I don't. That stuff only matters when you're not hiding from a man who spends all day trolling Instagram looking at hair and makeup pages in hopes of finding another hot girl to recruit to his escorting operation. That stuff only matters when you're a normal girl with no fears or anxieties about thousands of strangers seeing your face and learning your name.

Unfortunately for me and Zoe, none of that stuff matters to me.

As soon as I said no, trying to make my choice to avoid social media sound like a cool lifestyle decision and not a security measure, the energy in the room changed, and we've been sitting in the cloud of discomfort for close to an hour. It has lingered around the edges of stilted conversation while Zoe took my hair history, floated above the wash bowl and whined over the hum of the dryer right up until five seconds ago when the power went out and the entire shop went quiet.

Our eyes meet in the mirror, and then all the weird energy falls away and we both burst out laughing. Zoe is laughing so hard she drops the blow dryer on the tray beside her and folds at the waist.

"Oh, my God." she wheezes, her body still shaking from the giggles filling the air. "This is like the worst appointment ever."

I shake my head, trying to reassure her even though I'm cracking up too. "No, it's not."

Zoe looks at me, and I can see how hard she's working to try to pull it together. "No, it really is. Half of your head is wet, and the power just went out for no reason. You've been uncomfortable since you walked through the door because I tried to force you onto a live."

I spin my seat around to face her. "You didn't try to force me. You asked and I declined because social media—"

"Isn't your thing," Zoe finishes for me as she drops into the styling chair next to mine. She's not laughing anymore, and neither am I, but the lightness that's filled the air remains in place despite our fading humor. "What's with that anyway?" she asks, pulling out her phone. "I don't think I know anyone who isn't on at least one app."

"Well, now you do."

Her arched brow tells me my elusiveness didn't escape her attention, and I'm thankful when she chooses to make a phone call instead of pressing the issue any further.

"Hey, Dad," she says, smiling into the phone even though he can't see her. Grief and pain claw at my chest as I listen to Zoe describe the electrical issue to her father because it reminds me that I don't have a father to call when something goes wrong in my life. That I don't have anyone besides Sebastian, and after his obvious hesitance around bringing me, the charity case in designer clothes, to his childhood home, I'm pretty sure I don't have him either.

"No, I didn't check that," Zoe is saying now, rising from her seat to go to the glass door at the entrance of the shop. She opens it and peeks her head out then pulls it back in. "Yeah, you're right. No one on the block has power."

I fight the urge to throw my head back and laugh because of course there's a power outage in the middle of my first salon appointment in years and of course I scheduled that appointment right before my first real date in forever.

"Real subtle," I mutter under my breath, aiming the acrimonious words to the indifferent deity hellbent on keeping me humble. Zoe glances at me, and I shake my head to let her know I wasn't talking to her.

She turns her back to me, peeking out the front door again. "Dad, I've got Nadia here, and she's half blow-dried. Could you come start the generator?" Everett's response is lost on me, but judging by Zoe's tone, it's less than satisfactory. "No, I can't leave her like that," she says. "Because it's bad for business, and she's got a date in an hour!"

A panicked gasp tries to work its way up my throat, but I suppress it, telling myself it doesn't matter if Everett Adler knows I'm going on a date because that doesn't mean Sebastian will find out. Then I put my head in my hand and ask myself who I'm kidding because of course Sebastian is going to find out. I told his sister—because it was the only way to explain why I brought a garment bag with the black corset, cropped blazer and matching high waisted slacks inside to my appointment—and now his dad knows, which means it's only a matter of time before information I purposefully kept from to myself, finds its way to him.

Zoe, who is completely unaware of the anxiety her words have just sent racing through my veins, bounces on her toes and lets out a high pitch squeal that tells me her father has finally said something she wants to hear.

"Yes, that's perfect, Daddy! Thank you." She turns and gives me a thumbs up to confirm my suspicion. "Okay, bye!"

When she hangs up, she does a happy little dance and comes to sit back down across from me.

"Got it all worked out?" I ask, hoping she did and that, by some miracle, that solution has nothing to do with her oldest brother.

"Yep," she says, all smiles and happiness that comes from having so many people in her life that she can count on. "Dad said Sebastian is on his way."

It takes him twenty minutes to the salon and another five to get the generator going, and I use every second of those twenty five minutes preparing myself for the moment he chooses to question me about information I know was passed along to him by his father. He waits until my hair is done and I'm fully dressed to broach the subject, which I would probably appreciate if it didn't feel so calculated.

"So, you're going on a date." He's got his arms folded across his chest as he leans against the door frame of Zoe's office in a black ensemble that matches mine perfectly.

I lift my hair off of my neck, freeing it from the inside of my blazer and fully appreciating how soft and bouncy Zoe got my curls. Sebastian waits for my answer to his non-question, and I take my time because we both know I don't really owe him one. When my curls are settled back around my shoulders and face, I turn away from the mirror and face him.

"Yes, Preston and I finally made plans."

He rubs at his jaw, and a grimace casts a dark shadow over his eyes. "You're really going out with that guy?"

I let out a long sigh that contains every bit of doubt about my worth and importance in his life that I've felt over the last twenty four hours and leaves nothing in its wake but annoyance.

"Yes, I'm really going out with him because at least he wants to share a meal with me."

One of his dark brows lifts. "Are you suggesting that I don't want to share a meal with you, Nadia? Because we eat together all the time."

"You're right, which is why it's all the more confusing that you don't want me to come to lunch at your parent's house on Monday."

"What are you talking about?"

"Yesterday your mom invited me to lunch, and before I could even say a word, you jumped in with some excuse about me being busy to keep me from accepting."

"You're managing a restaurant and planning events with little to no help from the people I literally pay to assist you, you *are* busy."

Frustrated, mainly because he's making a good point, I plop down in Zoe's desk chair and set about digging out my shoes. I find them at the very bottom of my garment bag and drop them on the floor, eyeing the buckles at the end of the straps and cursing myself for choosing a pair that is so hard to get on by myself.

"That's not the point, Sebastian."

He steps into his sister's office, stopping at the edge of her desk where he's close enough for me to smell him, for me to look into his eyes and see my reflection staring back at me.

"Then what is the point, Nadia?"

"The point is you don't want me there!"

And that truth hurts me, but I don't know why.

"I never said I didn't want you there"

"You never said that you did."

"I didn't say that I did because I didn't want you to feel pressured to come, because I know how overwhelming it can be for you to be around people you don't know or trust, because—"

His jaw clenches, and the vein in his forehead starts to pulse. His eyes are trained on my face, pupils filled with some emotion I can't name, and that's all it takes for us to be swept up in another moment. In the push and pull of warring waves of emotion spilling out from pools we're too afraid to dive in.

"Because what?" I ask, searching his face for answers before he has the chance to give them. When he speaks, his voice is hoarse, like he's fighting to maintain control of something that refuses to be tamed.

"Because I know you're not ready for the things I want from you, and I don't want to be sitting in front of my parents and siblings when you shut me out again."

My heart slams against my rib cage repeatedly, stealing my ability to breathe for a moment. I turn his words over in my head, hoping the repetition will help them make sense. It doesn't. I can't fathom Sebastian Adler wanting anything from me that would evoke the emotions sweeping across his features, softening the lines of his thick brows and filling his champagne eyes with earnest.

"You want—" I stop, clear my throat and try again. "You want things from me?"

This isn't the conversation I should be having with my boss, with my friend, with the first man I've trusted in forever. It's too risky. Because if things get fucked up—and based off of how things in my life usually go, they will—then I'll lose all those things. I'll lose him.

That's why I've been shutting him down, why I've been cutting our moments short. Not because I'm not ready to have the things Sebastian wants to have with me, but because I'm not ready to lose them.

"Nadia," he breathes, dropping to his haunches in front of me and placing a hand under my chin. His fingers are warm on my skin, and his grip is tight but firm. "You seem to be under the impression that you're not the most precious thing in my life. There is no end to the list of things I want to have with you and give to you, chief among them is time. Time to heal. Time to trust. Time to prepare your heart for what mine wants to ask of it." The pad of his thumb swipes over my bottom lip, and he drops my gaze to trace the motion with his eyes. "How could you ever think I don't want you around after all the things I've done to keep you in my orbit?"

Every other moment we've shared before this, pales in comparison to this one. To the sincere emotion Sebastian has layered into every word and pressed into my flesh. To the heat in his eyes that matches the molten lava scorching my veins and giving me startling clarity. Suddenly, I can see everything. Not just Sebastian's handsome face looming in front of me in a haze of tears, but also everything he's done to demonstrate the truth he's just laid bare.

I reach for him with tentative fingers that sift through the surprisingly soft hair covering the hard line of his jaw and force a laugh past the lump in my throat. "I thought you were just being nice."

The smile he gives me is dazzling with razor sharp edges that cause desire to unfurl low in my belly. "I'm not nice, Nadia."

"Yes, you are. Desiree told me what you did for her. You saved her from that guy, gave her a job at Ludus and helped her take control of her life again."

His eyes search my face, seeing the hidden meaning between my words. "You know that's different right? Even if what you're saying is true and I did save Desiree's life, I didn't save yours, Nadia. You saved yourself. You didn't need me then, and you don't need me now, but I want you to want me."

His hand moves from my chin down my throat, and I swallow against his palm when he grips my neck. I can't breathe, but it's not because of the way he's holding me, it's because of the way his touch makes me feel like there's never been anything else in the world that's mattered to me more than it.

Sebastian leans forward, planting a kiss on my jaw with warm breath and gentle lips. "Do you want me, Nadia?"

I nod, unable to lend my voice to this confession. Sebastian's not having it though, he pulls back, leveling me with a demanding gaze. "*Say it.*"

"I want you."

22

SEBASTIAN

Those words leave Nadia's lips, and it's all I can do to be gentle when I put my free hand on her waist and pull her to the edge of the seat. Her legs already had a small gap in them, but she opens them wider, surprising the fuck out of me when she locks her ankles at the base of my spine and urges me forward. I go willingly, shifting my weight from the balls of my feet to my knees so that I'm kneeling in front of her. It feels right, assuming this position of reverence, demonstrating my desire to worship her. It's the only place I've wanted to be since the day I met her, since the moment the words 'I'm all in' left her lips on the rooftop the other night.

She gazes down at me with wide brown eyes that drip gasoline over the open flame licking at my ribs. The need to go slow, to be gentle, is a song on repeat in the back of my mind, but I've waited for this for so long that it's hard to hear the lyrics. And when Nadia brings her hands up and grabs my jaw, running her fingers over the hairs in my beard, it becomes nearly impossible. She's touching me so freely, but I'm going slow. The fingers of the hand not wrapped around her throat exploring the soft curve of her waist a quarter of an inch at a time while hers move through my locs in swift strokes that send tingles through my scalp.

"I want you to kiss me," she says, and I love the strength hidden in the quiet whisper vibrating against my palm. She looks good with my hand around her neck, but I slide it down her chest, over the mesh panels of her corset that are covering her stomach and let it come to rest on her side. "Sebastian?"

"I heard you, precious."

She sucks in a breath at the nickname. I don't know where it came from, but it feels right. I search her face for any indication that she dislikes it and find nothing but appreciation glittering in her eyes. That, paired with the mischievous tilt of her lips when she winds my locs around her hand, makes my dick throb.

"Then what are you waiting for?"

"I'm just giving you time to change your mind." I lean in, placing my lips on her neck, relishing the way her pulse spikes when I continue. "To run. To push me away and walk us back from this line I'm so *fucking* desperate to cross."

Nadia squirms as I open my mouth and pull delicate skin between my teeth, kissing and biting my way down to the hollow point at the base of her throat that I don't hesitate to dip my tongue into. Her hand is a vice at the back of my head, pulling thick strands of hair taut and making me wonder how her instincts are in such perfect alignment with what I like.

"I want you, Sebastian." She tugs on my hair, forcing me to abandon the home I've created in the curve of her neck. "I'm not going to change my mind."

Her reassurance is the only invitation I need to dive into the lushness of her mouth. Kissing Nadia is like nothing I've ever experienced before. She's sweet and soft and receptive. She's commanding and impatient, using her grip on my hair to hold me still and control the kiss. I let her. Because her comfort trumps my need to lead. Because she gives me more when I give her less and what she's giving me is all I've ever wanted from her. Desire laced breaths. A seeking tongue plundering my mouth with want on its tip. A quiet moan that comes from deep in her chest and comes to live in mine. A kiss that goes on for forever, erasing everything from my mind that isn't me and her.

"*Whoa!*" Zoe's voice, colored with shock and maybe a little bit of disgust, comes from behind us, announcing her sudden and unwelcome intrusion. Nadia breaks the kiss, her panicked eyes flying to my little sister's face. I look at her too, but I have to turn around to do so, and when our eyes meet, mine aren't panicked or apologetic, they're narrowed and filled with the kind of annoyance a big brother can only have for his little sister.

"Get out."

"Sebastian, this is my office," she reminds me with her hands on her hips.

"You're not using it, Zo. Go home, I'll lock up for you." I start to turn back to Nadia, determined to finish what we've started even if it means defiling Zoe's office, but when I see that my sister isn't moving, I pause. "Did you need something else?"

"The only I need is the image of this—" she waves a hand at Nadia and me "—wiped from my brain, but I don't think the man waiting for Nadia outside will be so easily appeased."

"Oh my God! Preston!" Nadia shouts, untangling herself from me with a quickness that leaves my mind and body reeling from the sudden loss of contact. I push to my feet, watching as she tries to wipe smudged lipstick from around her mouth.

"Don't." I reach out and grip her chin, turning her head to make her face me. Her eyes are pools of caramel that simmer with heat when I rub my thumb across her lip. "You look perfect like that."

Zoe gags, which makes me laugh and Nadia blush. "I'm going home now. Nadia, text me later so we can get you another appointment on the books. I don't think that silk press is going to make it past tonight."

"Bye, Zo."

She flips me off and blows Nadia a kiss before departing, leaving us to figure out what to do with Nadia's date. In my head, there's only one option—send him home with his tail between his legs and his heart broken because there's no way Nadia's leaving here with anyone but me—but keeping Nadia's autonomy in tact is paramount.

"How do you want to play this?" I ask, opening up the door for all manner of possibility.

Nadia stands up and straightens her blazer even though it's not messed up. She doesn't have her shoes on yet, and the difference in our height makes me realize that I've never seen her barefoot. That I've never seen her without makeup or in anything less than a perfectly coordinated outfit. The observation creates a need to know her outside of those parameters, to witness her in the comfort of her home, with sex mussed hair and one of my shirts swallowing her frame or with a scarf on her head and a glass of wine in her hand.

"Umm." She bites her lip as her voice pulls me out of my head and brings my focus back to the task at hand. "I guess I should go talk to him?"

"What are you going to say?"

"That tonight isn't going to work for me."

"Just tonight?" I ask, lifting a brow. "Are you planning on being available to him some other night?"

She hasn't even answered the question, but my chest is already aching at the thought of sharing her. Not just with Preston, though that fucker isn't worthy of a second of her time or an ounce of her energy, but with anyone.

One kiss.

A singular encounter with the unique flavor of desire on her lips.

That's all I've had, and it's all I need to know that sharing her isn't an option.

"No," she says finally, lifting her hand to my face so she can stroke her fingers through my beard. "I just think it's best to let him down easy."

"And slowly."

She frowns, making it clear that she's caught the note of apprehension in my tone. "Sebastian, I'm just trying to be nice. I don't want to hurt his feelings."

I nod like I understand what she's saying even though I don't give a damn about Preston's feelings. "You don't have to."

"What does that mean?"

I step back and give her a grin that can only be described as devilish. " It means, I'll hurt his feelings for you."

"Sebastian!" She calls out, her tone filled with admonishment that rings in my ears as I stride through Zoe's salon and out the front door to find Preston leaning against the passenger door of his car with his hands in his pocket and a smile on his face that disintegrates the second he sees me.

"What are you doing here?" he asks, pushing off the car to meet me on the sidewalk. I'm several inches taller than him, so he has to look up at me, which seems to only piss him off more.

I glance down at his empty hands and cock my head to the side. "You didn't even bring her flowers?"

"The fuck are you doing here, Adler?" He attempts to look around me, but I move with him, blocking his view because I don't know where Nadia is and I don't want to risk him seeing her. "Where's Nadia?"

"She's unavailable. I came out here to tell you that she won't be able to make it tonight or any other night because she's no longer interested."

"Bullshit! When I called her on Thursday to ask her out, she was excited."

Doubt flickers in his eyes, making me think those weren't Nadia's exact words. She was probably just being polite again, trying to avoid hurting his feelings while using this date with him to hide from her feelings for me.

"She changed her mind."

And I made sure of it, which had been my intention all along. When Zoe called Dad about needing the generator turned on, I was sitting next to him on the couch listening to every word. I wasn't trying to eavesdrop, but the moment I heard Nadia's name in the same sentence as the word 'date' I tuned out the game we were watching and tuned in to the conversation. Nadia hadn't even told me she'd solidified her dinner plans with Preston, probably because she knew that would be the final straw for me, the thing that would make me throw caution to the wind and act on the feelings I've been keeping at bay for her comfort.

I know now that it wasn't her comfort I should have been worried about. In fact, it was the space I was giving her in the name of comfort that was causing the true issue between us. Making her believe that the man I am to her and the things I do for her are the result of some inherent kindness I give to everyone in my life instead of a quiet demonstration of the love I have for her.

I won't be quiet about it anymore, though. Once I'm done with Preston, I'm going to make it my mission to spend every day loving Nadia out loud, to spend every day showing her that no one owns the parts of me that she does.

Preston scoffs. "She doesn't get to change her mind."

"Excuse me?"

"You heard me, Adler."

"No." I shake my head, a dangerously deceptive calm coating my words. "I don't think I did."

There's a part of me that hopes he won't repeat himself because I don't want to turn my sister's salon into a crime scene, but there's another part of me—the one with a short fuse that becomes nonexistent where Nadia is concerned—that wants to know what his skull will sound like when it hits the sidewalk.

Preston, being the idiot that he is, decides to provoke my less rational side, looking me square in my eyes as he repeats himself. "I said, she doesn't get to change her mind. I've invested too much time and money playing this little game of cat and mouse with her, and tonight, I plan on getting a return on that investment, so go in there and get her."

"I'm right here, Preston."

We both turn toward the sound of Nadia's voice. Her heels click on the sidewalk as she moves over to us. My heart swells with pride and satisfaction when she stops beside me, making us a united, and extremely pissed off, front.

She crosses her arms and pins him with a hard stare. "Now what were you saying about a return on your investment?"

"No…I…it wasn't—" Preston stammers, and Nadia and I share a look that's confusion, humor and anger all wrapped in one.

I crack my knuckles, preparing for the inevitable moment when I have to punch him in the face, and sigh. "Don't lie to her, Fredricks. If you're going to be a disrespectful piece of shit, at least have the decency to be an honest one."

He ignores me, angling his body towards Nadia, which is a mistake because she looks like she wants to hit him too. Maybe I'll let her.

"Nadia, please. I didn't mean it that way."

She purses her lips. "I don't really think there's another way you could have meant it, Preston. Did you honestly think this date was going to be an extension of the time we spent together at Ludus?"

"I mean…yeah? Why wouldn't I?" he asks, which makes Nadia's nostrils flare.

"Maybe because I told you I was no longer working at the club? Because I gave you my real name and my real phone number and told you about my real job? What about the interactions we've had over the last few weeks made you think the rules at Ludus—which still wouldn't have guaranteed you a second in bed with me—still applied out here in the real world?"

"Because you were playing the same game out here that you were in there." He's glaring at her now, but it's the slight rise in his tone that has me stepping forward, placing myself between them.

Nadia's head rears back and her brows knit themselves together. "What games? I was very clear about my boundaries at the club. Sex was never a part of the deal. You paid me for my time and conversation."

"Oh come on! We both know that was just an act. Girls do it all the time to stand out from the competition. And even after I got kicked out of Ludus—" he pauses, glancing at me, "—thanks for that, by the way"

"You're welcome," I return, unashamed of following my instincts when they told me to get him far away from Nadia.

"And even after you got kicked out of Ludus, what?" Nadia says, prompting Preston to return to his original line of thought.

His eyes return to her face, bitterness curling his top lip. "Even after I got kicked out of Ludus, you were still playing hard to get. Taking my number but refusing to give me yours. Not calling for weeks. Then finally giving me your number and taking days to return a text. All of it is just mind games—"

"Or disinterest," I say, cutting him off. "You're too damn old not to know what that looks like on a woman."

Nothing I know about Preston suggests that he's a fighter, so it makes sense that I see the punch he throws coming from a mile away. That I'm able to stop the sloppy attempt at a jab with one hand and upper cut him with the other, sending him flying into the door of his car. His body hits the steel frame so hard the alarm starts to blare, drowning out the sound of Nadia's exasperated sigh.

"Sebastian!" She shouts, outraged but not upset enough to help Preston who looks dazed and confused. "You can't hit every man who talks to me crazy."

"Oh, precious." I turn to her, snaking a hand around her waist and pulling her in close. "I absolutely can."

23

NADIA

I don't know what's crazier, the fact that I watched Sebastian punch Preston in the face and then help him to his car or the fact that not even an hour after it happened, we're perusing the aisles of the grocery store inside my apartment building, looking for something to make for dinner. I told Sebastian we could just go out to eat, but he insisted on cooking for me, saying he didn't want to risk us having any more interruptions tonight.

Sebastian is pushing the cart while I trail behind him, admiring how completely domestic he is in this moment. He looks right at home in the produce section, examining heads of butter lettuce and palming avocados to check for their ripeness. When he finds a few that meets his standards, he bags them and puts them in the cart.

"What if I don't like avocados?" I ask, sitting the red onion he told me to grab beside the item in question.

"You love avocados. Whenever you get the Cobb salad from Twisted Sistas, you always ask for extra."

I snap my fingers, pretending to be put out by how closely he pays attention to me even though I'm sure he's aware how much I love it. "Damn, can't get anything by you."

"That's right, precious, you can't."

The first time he called me precious I thought it was a mistake. A slip of the tongue that caused him to confuse an adjective with a verb, but he's done it several times now, which let's me know it's intentional. When he uses it, it's not just a descriptor—a thing I happen to be some of the time— it's an endearment, a title I'll always hold when I'm with him.

With him.

Am I with him? I don't know. We haven't exactly had time to put a label on anything, and I guess now is as good a time as any to ask. I put a hand on Sebastian's arm, stopping him from grabbing the radishes on the shelf in front of him. His eyes find mine, and the smile that softens his features makes me melt.

"I have a question."

Amusement makes the corners of his mouth quirk. "I figured."

I bite my lip, suddenly feeling nervous with his eyes on me. "Are we..uh, are we together? Like together, together?"

"Together, together?" Sebastian laughs, which breaks up some of my nervous energy, allowing it to transform into something else when he steps into my space, placing one hand on my hip and using the other to tuck an errant strand of hair behind my ear. "Nadia, are you asking me if I'll be your boyfriend?"

He's teasing me and normally I'd hate that because I'm asking for reassurance, but right now I don't mind because there's fire in my veins and his scent has invaded my lungs and all I really care about is the answer to my question and whether or not it's going to lead to us kissing again.

"No, I'm telling you that after you punched my date in the face and made me waste a perfectly good outfit on the grocery store in my apartment building, you better want to be something more than friends with benefits."

"Well, don't get me wrong, I *want* the benefits." The hand on my waist slides up my body, caressing my side, grazing my breast, stealing my breath. Sebastian catalogs my reaction to his touch with heated eyes that skate across my features with vivid interest. He licks his lips before continuing. "But I want to be more than your friend, Nadia."

I swallow and find that my throat is suddenly dry. "So you do want to be my boyfriend?"

As quickly as he advanced on me, he retreats, leaving me flustered and needy next to the eggplant while he smirks. "That's where we'll start."

My mind swirls with a million responses to his statement, but none of them leave my lips. I watch in stunned silence as Sebastian continues down the aisle, proceeding to grab items from the grocery list that exists in his head, wondering how the hell I went from running from this man to running after him, desperate for him to elaborate on a topic that just yesterday I was afraid to broach. When I catch up with him, he's adding a piece of ahi tuna to the cart.

"What are you making?"

It's not the question I want to ask, but I don't have the mental fortitude to process the answer to the one bouncing off the walls of my skull. *If boyfriend is where we'll start, where does he think we're going to end up?*

"Cobb salad with seared ahi," he says. "Is that okay with you?"

Truthfully, I don't have an appetite, but he seems determined to feed me, so I nod. "That sounds good."

It also sounds quick, which means we can eat sooner and move on to other more interesting things like kissing each other senseless. Being this obsessed with his kiss feels a bit juvenile, but I don't care. When I was working as an escort, I never allowed my clients to kiss me. It was the one bit of control I had over my body, the one place they couldn't touch, the one thing they couldn't have when they were already taking everything else. Somewhere along the way, I forgot kissing was a thing people enjoyed, that it was a thing *I* could enjoy. But the second Sebastian's lips collided with mine, that desire, that craving for the gateway to true intimacy came alive again. And it isn't just a want anymore, it's a need that pulses inside my body, incessant and loud as Sebastian pays for the groceries, demanding and impossible as we enter my apartment.

Sebastian must feel it too because the second we're inside, he catches me by the waist and pins me to the wall. The bags in his hands fall to the floor, and a perfectly good avocado rolls underneath my couch.

"You keep staring at my lips," he says, and the heat in his voice tells me the groceries won't be making it to the kitchen and the only meal in my future is the man in front of me, which is fine because I absolutely want to devour him. "Do you want me to kiss you again?"

"Yes." I'm breathless, aware of every inch of his body that's pressed into mine, of the way his pupils dilate when my heavy breaths cause my breasts to rub against his chest. "And this time, I don't want you to stop."

"Careful what you wish for, precious," he whispers just before he swoops down and takes my mouth for the second time today. This kiss is different from the one we shared in Zoe's office. More passionate, more thorough, more…everything. Sebastian urges me to open for him with a nip to my bottom lip that makes my knees weak. Literally. I feel them buckle and my ankles wobble, but I don't care about falling physically when I'm already in the midst of an emotional free fall.

This man just brings it all out of me. Everything I've trained myself not to feel, not to want, not to hope for, it doesn't just exist with him, it blooms. It grows. It *thrives*, turning sweet and fragrant like ripe grapes on a vine that only fall when they're overflowing with goodness, ready to be picked up and made into something new.

When Sebastian picks me up, prompting me to wrap my legs around his waist, I wonder if I'll be transformed at the end of this, if his reverent hands and adoring tongue will make me into something new too. If this moment of gentle desire will erase years of abuse and exploitation and what feels like a lifetime of being coveted but not cherished, kept but not loved. If anyone's touch can do it, Sebastian's can.

He moves us away from the wall, maintaining the kiss while he takes determined strides down the hallway to my bedroom. I shed my blazer and all my inhibitions during the short trek, leaving them to linger on the floor with my questions and doubts.

I want this.

I want *him*.

Those are the only things that matter.

Just as I make my peace with that decision, Sebastian pauses and pulls back. We're right outside my bedroom door, and I know what this is—a check in, a moment to pause and reflect. He searches my face, the question written in the wrinkles between his eyebrows.

"I'm sure, Seb." And to prove just how sure I am, I roll my hips into the tip of the thick erection he's been strategically holding me above. The contact sends a rush of liquid heat to my core and makes Sebastian curse.

"Don't do that, Nadia."

He sounds like he means it, but he moves me down his body, aligning the parted lips of my throbbing sex with his dick. Sparks of pleasure trail down my spine, and I chase them with slow rocks of my hips that drag my pussy up and down the bulge behind the seam of his jeans . Sebastian groans and leans forward, resting his forehead against mine. His locs brush my collarbone, and I'm hit with an image of him above me, his bare chest to my bare chest, my legs wrapped around his waist, the tips of his locs grazing my collarbone every time he works his length in and out of me.

"Take me to bed, Sebastian," I beg, completely unconcerned about the note of desperation in my voice. "Please. I promise you I'm not going to regret this."

His jaw is clenched and his eyes are on fire, but he doesn't refuse me. I don't think he can because he wants this as much as I do. He surges forward, using his foot to push the door open and stepping into my most sacred space. It feels right to be doing this with him here, in the home he found for me, in the space he made it possible for me to have. A wave of gratitude rushes through me, making my chest tight.

Sebastian lowers me to the bed, and as he stands over me, his black jeans tented because of his helpless reaction to me, muscles tight with anticipation, I feel like a star at the center of his universe. And when he kneels at the edge of the bed, removing my shoes and then my pants and corset until I'm naked, wet and wanting, I'm certain that's exactly how he sees me.

Even with the scar.

"You're exquisite," he breathes, his lips running a trail up my right leg, going from my ankle to the top of my thigh where the raised skin and jagged edges reside. "It's not fair for you to be this fucking gorgeous."

Him saying that when he's literally looking at the part of me I'm most self conscious about is both confusing and gratifying. I lift my head from the mattress, gazing down the line of my body to find him already looking at me.

"Let me see you."

Within moments of the words leaving my mouth, he's on his feet, pulling his black t-shirt over his head to reveal a wide chest and biceps that are even more impressive outside the expensive fabric I'm sure he has tailored to enhance their appearance. Next, are his shoes, then his pants, and finally the black briefs containing his erection. When those hit the ground, all of my breath leaves my body and my eyes go wide.

"You've got to be fucking kidding me."

I've seen a lot of dicks in my day. Far more than I'd have liked to, but I've never seen anything like this. Given his stature, I knew Sebastian would be working with considerable length or substantial girth, but I wasn't expecting him to have *both*. His dick is almost as thick as my forearm and nearly as long, and there's no way on God's green Earth that all of *that* is fitting inside me.

Sebastian grins, gripping and stroking the battering ram between his legs that's pointed right at me. "Don't worry, precious, I'll go slow."

His promise is delivered in a deliciously dark tone that has my knees falling away from each other and my core clenching with anticipation. Suddenly, I don't care about how big he is or how long its been or the fact that I've never done this consensually, all that matters is I'm empty and he's the only person that can fill me up.

I pull in a deep, calming breath, banishing all thoughts of pain to the back of my mind and nod to let Sebastian know I heard what he said. "Come here."

His eyes go soft, ripples of appreciation and wonder interrupting the still surface of pools of champagne as he climbs onto the bed and settles himself between my legs. He leans in for a kiss, and the flared tip of his dick nudges my entrance. Our breaths come together in a tangled hiss that demands us to do anything but stop. Anything but abandon lust for logic and desire for reason. And even though I know we both know better, we obey the primal order without a second thought.

Sebastian surges forward, and I meet his thrust with a roll of my hips that seats him at the end of me. He moans in my ear, and his locs brush my cheek repeatedly as he sets a rhythm that contradicts his promise. There's nothing slow about this, but it feels right because slow wouldn't have my bed frame knocking into the wall. Slow wouldn't have beads of sweat blooming on Sebastian's back and ass as he pounds into me. Slow wouldn't have the euphoria that's always eluded me spreading through my limbs like the first spark of a wildfire hunting for something to turn it into a real flame.

"Sebastian!" I cry out, holding on to him for dear life, something close to panic rolling through me as my body starts to come apart underneath his.

"Don't fight it, precious," he murmurs in my ear, tracing the shell of it with his tongue. "You deserve this, don't you, baby? You deserve to be fucked like this. To come so hard you can't see straight on a dick big enough to touch the end of you and still go deeper."

To prove his point, he pushes further, stretching me to my absolute limit with one deep stroke after another while I dig my nails into his ass and grind my clit into his pelvic bone. It's all so fucking perfect. The man. The dick. The filthy, filthy words he's chanting in my ear that make my muscles seize and my core melt.

Sebastian recognizes the tremors that indicate my orgasm before I do. When they start, he lifts up just enough to treat me to a triumphant smile that I hold in my mind's eye as my body cedes to an onslaught of pleasure the likes of which it's never seen before. It obliterates me, rendering me motionless as Sebastian increases his pace, finding satisfaction at the tail end of a set of rhythmic strokes that have his dick pulsing as he empties himself inside of me.

We're both panting and sated as he collapses on the bed next to me, close enough that the ragged breaths leaving his mouth shift my hair which, as Zoe predicted, has been ruined by our efforts. Sebastian turns on his side and loops an arm around my waist, pulling me back into him. I turn over so I can face him, tossing my leg over his hip.

"That really happened," I muse, fighting back tears for some odd reason.

Sebastian clocks the glossiness in my eyes immediately and frowns when it turns to actual tears. "You okay? I didn't hurt you, did I?"

"No, you didn't hurt me." I'm doing that odd smiling/crying combination I did with Desiree yesterday, and he looks far more concerned than she did. I guess it's a bit more alarming when you're lying in bed with the person caught between two very different emotions. I wipe my tears away with an impatient swipe of my fingers. "I'm fine. I promise. I just, I didn't know it could be like that."

His fingers walk a line up my back, tracing the notches in my spine. "What? Sex?"

"Yeah, I've never…" I pause, trying to choose my words carefully so my trauma doesn't ruin this moment. "Never mind."

But it's too late, Sebastian has already gone still, the wheels in his brain working to try to put the pieces together. "You've never what?"

"Just leave it alone, Sebastian." It feels kind of counter intuitive to tell a man to mind his business when you've literally got his cum leaking out of you, but I'm willing to do whatever is necessary to salvage our night.

"Don't do that. Don't shut me out, not after what we just shared."

The smile from my weird emotional combo is now gone, leaving me with nothing but tears and memories I'm scared to lend my voice to even though there's a part of me that wants to share, that's tired of carrying shame that doesn't belong to me all on my own.

I let out a long sigh and call up every ounce of strength I can muster, knowing I'll need it for the conversation we're about to have. Sebastian is quiet, and his breathing is shallow, and I hope that silence and stillness means he's preparing himself for some ugly truths.

"I was a sophomore in high school when my parents died." Just saying those words has my heart rate kicking up a notch. I try to calm myself by touching the tips of each of my fingers to the center of the hand resting against Sebastian's back. "I don't know what that grade was like for you, but for me it was the most confusing year ever."

Sebastian's fingers are gentle as they push some of my hair out of my face. "Your parents died, baby, of course it was confusing for you."

"Right, but it wasn't just that. It was my parents dying and the world continuing to spin. It was my supposed best friend telling me about how she lost her virginity in the back of her boyfriend's Range Rover at the repast. It was coming back to school and finding that everyone was suddenly having sex."

"Everyone except you."

"Exactly. Because no one wants to hook up with the depressed girl with the dead parents."

"Did you want to hook up with them?"

I shake my head, remembering what I was like that year. Crying all day and all night, sleeping in class, skipping school and stealing Roland's car to drive out to the vineyard just to feel close to my parents. Sex was the furthest thing from my mind.

"No," I say finally. "All I wanted was for my parents to come back and for my life to return to normal, but of course, that didn't happen. If you can believe it, life actually got worse. My guardian sold the house I grew up in without even asking me and moved us away."

"Us?" Sebastian asks. His unwavering gaze a grounding weight on my face that makes me want to elaborate even though I know I shouldn't. I want to give him names, dates, locations, every detail that would allow him to truly know me, but I can't.

"Me, my guardian and his son."

My voice doesn't change when I refer to Beau even in the vaguest of terms, but somehow Sebastian still knows. When I say 'his son', his eyes turn dark and stormy and I shiver as an image of the two of them meeting flits through my mind. The thought makes me sad. Sebastian is the only man I know who would put himself between me and Beau, but I would never ask him to. I would have to leave him before it ever came to that.

"By the time I got started at a new school, I was coming up with a plan to get away from them," I continue, smiling a little when Sebastian pulls me closer, like the mere mention of me planning to leave makes him want to hold me tighter.

"What was your plan?"

"To keep my head down and focus on school, so I could get everything my guardian sold out from under me back. I worked my ass off, graduating high school early, earning two Bachelor's at once."

Surprise etches itself into his features, quickly followed by pride. "I knew that resume was bullshit."

I laugh, grateful for the levity he's just infused into the moment because things are about to take a turn for the worse. Sebastian catches on as soon as my mood turns somber again, and he reaches back to grab my hand, threading our fingers together and bringing them to rest between our bodies.

"I kept telling myself I would have time for a relationship and everything that came along with it after I graduated college and got away from them, but that never happened."

"What did happen?"

"I went to dinner with my guardian and his son to celebrate my graduation and woke up in a stranger's house." Sebastian curses, and I close my eyes, unable to look him in the eyes as I say the rest. "They sold me. They sold me to him to pay off gambling or drug debt, I'm not sure. I don't remember. I guess it doesn't really matter. What does matter is that when I went into that man's house, drugged, gagged and bound, I was a virgin, and when he carried me out, I wasn't anymore. What matters is that every sexual encounter I've had before today has happened with everyone's consent but mine, which is why I didn't know it could be that way." My eyes are still closed, but that doesn't stop the tears from rushing down my cheeks. Their appearance sets Sebastian in motion, and he goes from laying beside me to hovering over me with his hips notched between my open legs.

"Look at me, Nadia."

I follow his order even though I know the moment I gaze into those turbulent champagne pools, I'm going to break wide open.

"I didn't get the chance to find out," I gasp. "I ran out of time, and no one told me it could be this way."

"No, you didn't run out of time, baby," he says. His hand goes to my cheek, and his thumb smooths the tears into my skin. "You didn't run out of time. It was stolen from you, but you have time now. *We* have time, and I'll show you how good it can be, okay? Do you hear me, precious? I'll show you that it can be so much better."

Hiccups mixed with shuddered breaths tear through me, ripping me apart at the seams until Sebastian's lips cover mine. He murmurs reassurances into my mouth, literally speaking them into me, and I feel my soul go quiet in observance of his promises. The pain subsides, retreating to make space for the quiet bloom of desire.

I wrap my arms around Sebastian's neck and my legs around his hips, pulling him down. He's already hard, but his face is conflicted as he gazes down at me.

"Nadia, we don't have to."

"I know, but I want to." I pull him down further and kiss him, slow and sweet. "Show me how much better it can be."

24

SEBASTIAN

I spend the whole night showing Nadia.

Teaching her, pleasing her, making my body a slave to hers.

We don't fall asleep until the wee hours of the morning, which is why it pisses me off exponentially to hear my phone ringing from the pocket of my jeans that are somewhere on Nadia's bedroom floor. With aching muscles and an empty stomach, I sort through the mess of clothes we left at the foot of the bed and dig it out, grimacing when I see who's calling.

"What the fuck do you want, Luc?" I whisper, throwing myself back on to the pillows next to Nadia's sleeping form.

She's naked and her bonnet is halfway off her head, and my fucking chest swells with pride because the scarf I insisted she put on is still in place. She wanted to throw the bonnet on and call it a night because it was the closest thing to her, but I wasn't having it. I went to the bathroom and grabbed her scarf off of the sink and a brush before coming back to bed. She was half asleep when I made her sit up, but she moaned her appreciation when I ran the brush through her tangled strands and placed the black, satin fabric around her edges, securing it with a bow I had to retie several times because she said it was too tight. Once I was done, she slapped the bonnet on her head and curled up under the covers, ordering me to turn off the lights and come back to bed to hold her.

Cuddling has never been a part of my post-sex routine. Talia and I never bothered with it because we were both always so eager to get to the next thing. There was no desire to pause, to connect physically without the goal of an orgasm. And with every other woman I've slept with, I've never stuck around long enough after sex for them to ask me for anything let alone more of my time.

But when Nadia asked, well, technically, ordered, me back to her bed to hold her, I didn't hesitate because there was no where else I wanted to be. As soon as I put away the abandoned groceries, armed the security system and turned off all the lights, I climbed into bed and hauled her onto my chest, planting a kiss to the top of her head while she breathed a sigh of content and passed out. We stayed that way all night, neither of us moving, and as soon as I'm laying down again, Nadia curls herself back around me, resting her head over my heart.

"Why are you whispering?" Luca asks, loud as all hell. "Is Nadia still sleeping?"

My hand tightens around the phone that I wish was his neck. "Don't say another word."

I love Luca, but there are few things in the world he takes seriously and I won't have what happened with me and Nadia be diminished by his humor, whittled down to nothing more than a punchline for one of his jokes. The censure in my tone gives him pause.

"Chill, Seb. I wasn't even about to talk shit. I'm actually happy for you."

The sincerity coating his words is the only reason I don't hang up on him. "Thanks, but how did you even know?"

"I mean technically, I didn't know. Zoe told me about the two of you kissing in her office when me and her went to the movies last night, and I just filled in the blanks for myself."

"Don't you two have anything better to do than sit around talking about my love life?"

"Love life? Oh, you in love now?"

"Fuck off, Luca."

His knowing laughter is the last thing I hear before I hang up the phone and toss it onto the nightstand. It lands with a loud thump that causes Nadia to groan. She cracks one sleepy eye open and squints at me. I run my hand down her back and place a kiss on her forehead.

"Sorry. I didn't mean to wake you."

"Then you should have left the room."

I can't stop the smile that curves my lips or the familiar spark of joy that rushes through me every time I learn something new about Nadia. It doesn't matter if it's a big something, like how old she was when she lost her parents, or a small something, like the fact that she's a grump in the morning, it's all valuable information to me.

"But that would have meant leaving you," I reply, letting my fingers skate over the light smattering of hair at the small of her back I never would known existed if last night didn't happen.

She rolls her eyes. "Don't make me want to kiss you when I have morning breath."

"You can kiss me anytime you want, precious. Even when you have morning breath."

"Oh, Goddd. Please don't tell me you're a morning person."

With a dramatic sigh, she flings herself onto her back, and I follow her, settling my weight between her legs as I bury my face in her neck. She smells like me. Like my sweat and my cum and the last remnants of my cologne. It's not the first time I've noticed how perfectly our chosen scents blend together, but it is the first time I've gotten to revel in it. Nadia cards her fingers through my hair and starts to massage my scalp.

"I'm a *you* person."

I lay a kiss on her jaw and flex my hips, letting the tip of my dick sink into the moisture gathered between her thighs. It's a mixture of me and her, a silken representation of a repeated lack of control on her part and mine.

"We didn't use condoms," Nadia says, her mind clearly in the same place as mine.

"No, we didn't." I push forward, loving the feel of her muscles clenching around me. "Is that a problem for you?"

"No," she whimpers, trying to focus despite the fact that I'm teasing her with shallow strokes designed specifically to make her lose her train of thought. "I'm on birth control, and you know I'm clean."

She's right. She had to submit a clean bill of health to get a guest pass to Ludus. If she wasn't clean, she wouldn't have been allowed to interact with members.

"I'd die before I put you at risk, so trust me when I say, I'm clean."

I pull back and drive back in with a thrust so hard it causes her breasts to bounce. Nadia brings her knees up until they're pushing against my elbows, giving me the space I need to go deeper.

Her nails dig into my back as she moans her response. "I trust you, Sebastian."

It's all I've ever wanted. Her trust. Her openness. Soft eyes on my face and lush curves in my hands. The chance to cherish her in a way she hasn't been in years. It'll last beyond this moment, my endeavor to lavish her with affection. I'll be at it for years if she'll allow me, decades, a lifetime.

Forever.

That's what I want with her, that's where we'll end up. She wanted me to say that last night when we were buying groceries for a meal we never got to eat, but she wasn't ready to hear it. She's not ready now, either, and that's okay because we have time.

Time to heal.

Time to trust.

Time to bask in the moments of connection we've been running from for so long.

We're in one now. A moment. And unlike all the other times we found ourselves wrapped up in each other, Nadia is right here with me and she shows no signs of wanting to leave.

I slip my hands under her back and flip us over, so she's on top. The sudden shift surprises Nadia, but she doesn't miss a beat. As soon as my back hits the headboard, she's on me. Her arms around my neck, her long legs on either side of my body, a life ruining arch to her back as she pushes her ass into my hands and slides onto my dick.

"*Fuck,* Nadia."

She smirks, tangling her hands in my hair and crushing her lips to mine so the moans rolling off of her tongue can meet the ones breaking free from my chest. My hands go from her ass to her head, removing her scarf and bonnet in one fell swoop, so when she throws her head back and tosses a moan into the air, her wild tresses are free. They flow around her shoulders and cover her breasts, the blunt ends tickling my stomach every time she grinds down on me.

"Sebastian," she cries, sinking her teeth into her lower lip. It's meant to be a warning, but I already know what's coming. I can tell by the way her walls begin to pulse around my shaft, by the way her movements become faster and less fluid.

She's going to come.

"I got you." My hands go to her waist, gripping tight to hold her in place while I take control of the rhythm. "I'll always have you, precious. You don't have to be afraid to let go."

I thrust up into her over and over again, and every stroke makes my balls slap her ass. Nadia's eyes roll back into her head, and her neck arches, the muscles in her throat straining as she screams my name. Falling apart with so much force and beauty that it leaves me no choice but to surrender to the pleasure building at the base of my spine. I come with a groan that Nadia steals from the air with greedy lips that cover mine, pulling me into a kiss that lasts for all of five seconds before it's interrupted by a rumbling in her stomach.

She breaks the kiss and gives me a sheepish smile. "I think I might be hungry."

"Might be?" I drop a quick peck on her lips, unable to resist the urge to taste her again. "It's sounding more like a definitely."

"Shut up!" She shoves my shoulder, trying to look upset even though there's happiness radiating off of her in waves. "You're the one who didn't feed me."

"That was your fault. You were the one staring at my lips."

"You could have waited until after I ate to notice."

"Oh, so now I'm in trouble for paying attention?"

"No," she says quietly, shaking her head. "I like that you pay such close attention to me."

Nadia is one of the most guarded people I know, so these random moments of vulnerability are rare. I try not to make such a big deal out of them, but it's hard to appear unaffected by it when I'm still inside of her.

My thumbs rub tiny half circles on her sides. "What else do you like that I do?"

She twists her lips to the side, trying to appear thoughtful. "How about I tell you *after* you feed me?"

Her need for food is emphasized by another long growl from her stomach, so I have no choice but to concede.

"Fine." I reach over and grab my phone off the nightstand, checking the time. "If we leave now, we can make it to my parents' house in time for brunch."

"I thought you guys did dinner on Sundays."

The observation comes just as she's lifting off my dick, and the slow drag of her warmth over my stubborn erection temporarily steals my ability to put together a coherent thought. It doesn't return until Nadia is standing next to the bed looking at me with furrowed brows.

"We try to," I say, sliding to the edge of the bed and pulling her close because I can't seem to let her go. "But it changes from week to week, and today Mom wanted to do brunch instead of dinner."

Her breath hitches when my mouth closes over one of her nipples. "And you want me to come?"

It physically pains me to pull away from her, but I do so because I know she needs verbal confirmation more than anything else. When she revealed to me yesterday that she felt like I didn't want her at my parents' house, it broke something inside of me. Finding out that something I had said or done made her feel unwanted even for a second didn't sit right with my soul.

"I want you with me whereever I go, Nadia."

For a second I think she's going to cry again because her lip starts to wobble but then it changes, shifting into an expression of pure joy. "Only you could make a brunch invite sound like a request for a lifetime commitment."

"We already have one of those, precious." I smack her ass,

hoping the sting will distract her from the severity coating my words. From the way they try to tell her that our bond is set in stone, etched into the very fabric of time. It was created the day we met in the lobby of Cerros, substantiated by the friendship we've built over time, and consummated last night with hours of love making that was about nurturing our emotional connection as much as our physical one.

"Sebastian!" She yelps, her face scrunched up in an expression that's a cross between arousal and pain. "That hurt, you ass!"

"I'm sorry, baby." I push to my feet and hug her. "I would let you get your lick back, but unfortunately, you have to go take a shower now."

Spinning her around, I gently urge her to the bathroom door, pushing her through it while remaining on the other side. Nadia turns to look back at me, her face still scrunched up, one of her hands rubbing at her ass. "You're not joining me?"

My eyes rove down her body, making note of every curve and inch of satin skin. Nadia is walking temptation, and me getting in the shower with her wouldn't do anything but ensure that we starve to death.

"No, precious, I have to run over to my place to shower and change."

She pushes her lips out into a nearly irresistible pout. "Can't you just stop by your place and change after we get done here?"

"No, I really can't."

Nadia frowns, suspicion rolling over her features like a storm cloud. "Why?"

"Because if I stay here while you shower, you'll distract me with all of that—" I gesture at the magnificence of her naked form "—and it'll be quicker to leave from here."

I find myself holding my breath, sending up a silent prayer that she doesn't push me for further explanation because I can't get into it with her right now. Thankfully, she doesn't.

"Oh, okay." She opens the glass door to her shower and reaches inside to turn on the water. Almost instantly, steam starts to fill the room. "Well go ahead and wash your stinky balls and hurry back to me."

"Yes, ma'am." I laugh, backing away from the door and leaving her to handle her business. As soon as I'm out of her sight, I deflate a little, hating the fact that I lied to her about why we couldn't go to my place. Hating even more that she believed me so easily.

After I get dressed, I grab my phone and my keys and leave Nadia's. Her heavy door slams shut behind me, and even though I know she's in the shower, I still glance back to make sure she's not around to see me turn to the left instead of the right, heading for the door of the only other unit on this floor instead of the elevator.

My heart pounds in my chest, and I feel stupid for being nervous about walking into my own place, but that's what I am. Nervous and guilty because Nadia and I have been together for less than twenty-four hours and I'm already keeping things from her. The trouble is I don't think she'd appreciate or understand why I decided to move into this unit the day after she signed her lease for hers. She wouldn't get that even then I had this pressing need to be close to her, to take care of her, to keep her safe. All things that couldn't be accomplished from my place across town.

It was always my intention to settle down here at The Ivy. Out of all the buildings I own, it's my favorite. The old world charmed mixed with modern luxury makes me feel right at home, and the proximity to Cerros and Adler Holdings, is an added bonus, making it the perfect place for me. And Nadia too.

When she walked into the lobby and immediately fell in love, pointing out all of the same design aspects I appreciated, I knew this would be the place she chose to put down roots, so I did what I had to do to put down roots beside her, to grow next to her until she trusted me enough for us to grow together.

Knowing that I'm actively undermining that trust weighs heavy on my heart, and I spend the duration of my shower and the time it takes me to get dressed, convincing myself that it's not a big deal, that the perfect moment will present itself for me to tell her that I'm her neighbor and explain exactly how that came about. For the most part, it works, and by the time I'm standing in front of her apartment, announcing my arrival with a quiet rapping of my knuckles on the door, I almost believe it.

Nadia opens the door with the same smile on her face she had when I left her, and one of the two shoes she needs to walk out the door on. "You got back quick!"

I linger in the doorway while she moves toward the couch in search of her other shoe. "I told you I wouldn't be long."

"And you meant it too."

"I did. You look beautiful."

Her outfit is simple, a pair of light washed jeans with a crisp white button down and gold accessories that highlight the warm undertones of her skin. She's got her hair pulled back into a slick bun, which means I can easily see the small gold hoops in her ears that look a lot like the one currently threaded through my lobe.

Nadia slips her left foot into the mate of the white sandal she already has on and glances down at herself. "You don't think it's too simple?"

I hold out my hand, beckoning her forward. She grabs her purse and crosses the room, linking our fingers together. I pull her in, pressing a kiss to her forehead. "I think it's perfect, just like you. Now, let's go eat."

25

SEBASTIAN

We arrive at my parent's house just as Mom is plating french toast made from challah bread and stuffed with strawberries and whipped marscarpone. Everyone is surprised but delighted to see Nadia on my arm, and we field questions about what we are to each other from each of my siblings and both of my parents over the course of our meal. Despite the inquisition, the meal goes well. We sit around the table talking about everything from our childhood antics to the stock market, and I watch Nadia soak it all in with some hints of sadness, but mostly joy on her face.

It makes me happy that she's here, enmeshed in the family I want her to be a real part of more than anything.

"She's good for you," Mom says, sitting the serving platter with nothing more than cold bacon crumbles on it in the sink. I'm standing at the counter, watching Nadia and Zoe say their goodbyes to Luca and Andreas instead of scraping food from our plates into the trash like I'm supposed to. The last thing I want to do is look away from her, but I do, letting my eyes land on my mother.

"You think so?"

"Oh, absolutely. I knew there was something between the two of you when I saw you together at the wine tasting event, but I didn't think it was so serious."

"Serious?" I raise a brow. "What makes you think it's serious?"

"Sebastian Everett Adler." She wags her finger at me, reminding me of when Luca was a baby and she used the same motion to tell him something was a no-no. "Don't play coy with me. I'm your mother, I know what it looks like when you're serious about someone."

"Maddy, I thought we agreed we weren't going to meddle," Dad says, walking into the kitchen with more serving trays in his hand. I take them from him, the instinct to accommodate him stronger than it's ever been before, causing me to act without thinking. Dad sighs and shakes his head, exasperation written in the lines of his face. "And I thought *we* agreed that you weren't going to baby me, Sebastian."

"Guess we're all going back on our word because I could have sworn you told me you were going to take it easy."

"I *am* taking it easy," he says, clapping a strong hand over my shoulder when he joins me at the sink. "Tell him, Maddy."

"Yeah, yeah, you're taking it easy," Mom says, moving over to us. "Can we get back to the conversation at hand?"

I pour dish soap onto a sponge and wet it. "What conversation is that, Mom?"

"The one where you tell me how you got that gorgeous girl out there to fall in love with you."

"Mom!"

"Maddy!"

The disbelief in my tone blends with the surprise in Dad's and Mom rolls her eyes at the both of us. "Relax, you two, it's not like she can hear me."

"Like who can hear you?" This, from Zoe who appears out of nowhere with Nadia in tow. All at once, Mom, Dad and me all turn around to find Nadia and Zoe coming up behind us. The two of them look between the three of us, and there's a moment of awkward silence that Dad breaks.

"Nadia, has Sebastian told you about the wine cellar?"

"No, Everett. I don't believe he has."

She throws me a wide eyed look that's all fake accusation, and I stick my tongue out at her. "My apologies for not giving you the full specs of the house, precious."

The nickname slips off my tongue easily, and I regret allowing it to when Mom and Zoe both press their lips together to suppress what I'm sure is a squeal.

Nadia smiles, a slight hint of red creeping into her cheeks as she holds my gaze. "I'm sure I'll be able to find it in my heart to forgive you."

"Thank you."

"*After* your dad shows me the wine cellar."

In a move that shocks the hell out of me, she loops her arm through Dad's and smiles up at him, allowing him to lead her out of the kitchen. My heart does something odd as I watch them walk away, leaving us all to linger in the wake of a conversation about storage temperatures and humidity percentages. It aches and swells at the same time, hurting for the part of Nadia that's suffered at the hands of so many men, rejoicing for the part of her that feels safe with not only me but my family. My father, my brothers, my sister and Mom. She's opened up to each one of them today in different ways, showing glimpses of who she is when she feels safe, and it's only made me love her more.

Clearly, I'm not the only Adler that feels that way.

"You know Dad is going to have her down there for hours, right?" Zoe asks, hopping up on the counter beside me.

"Nadia won't mind," I assure her, ringing out the sponge to get rid of the excess water and suds. "Wine is her favorite thing to talk about."

I still haven't quite figured out why that is, but if I had to guess I'd say it has something to do with her parents. There are some interests that only become passion through the loving guidance of a parent. It can be a bright, positive thing born at the intersection of a parent's knowledge and a child's desire to connect on a level beyond familial obligation. If the parents are lucky—the way my dad was with me and business, the way I suspect Nadia's parent's might have been with her and wine—the child's interest will grow as they get older, creating a long-standing dedication to a love they both share.

"Oh, Everett will love that," Mom sighs wistfully from my other side. "He'll finally have someone to obsess over his collection with."

"Thank God! That means I don't have to go down into the cellar with him any more." Zoe shivers dramatically, which makes me and Mom laugh. "It's way too dark down there."

I dry my hands off on a kitchen towel, ignoring my sister's antics. "Mom, when did Dad start building his wine collection?"

"Around '94, I think. Why?" As soon as the question leaves her lips, her eyes light up. "Are you thinking about starting one for Nadia? That would be so lovely, Sebby!"

"Mom, calm down." Zoe places a hand on her shoulder, giving her a concerned look. "What's going on with you today?"

"Nothing! I'm just excited. It's nice to finally see one of my children in love."

"And this is where I leave you," Zoe says, hopping down off the counter and giving me a sympathetic look. "You know as soon as she starts talking about us falling in love that means grand-baby talk isn't far behind."

"Well, I'm not getting any younger!" Mom says, the words landing somewhere along Zoe's retreating back.

"Later, Mom. I love you! Seb, don't let Dad keep you and Nadia here all night."

We don't stay all night, but it is late when we get back to Nadia's place. And even though she's tired, she's still smiling as she tells me about all the amazing bottles Dad has in the cellar I haven't seen in years.

"I seriously can't believe he had the 1945 Romanée- Conti." She shakes her head, kicking off her shoes by the door I just closed and locked. "Do you know how much that bottle costs?"

"No, precious. I have no idea." I put my hands in my pocket and lean against the door, content to be standing in her space again, watching her shed her clothes and free her hair from the bun.

She's halfway down the hall with her fingers in her hair, presumably massaging her scalp, when she notices that I'm not following her to her bedroom. When she turns back to face me, her brows are pulled together in a line of confusion.

"What are you doing? Why are you still standing there?"

I shrug. "I thought maybe I'd spend the night at my place, give you some space."

Her hands go to her hips. "Who said I wanted space?"

"No one. I just figured—" I let the sentence trail off because I don't really know how to finish it. All I know is that I don't want to overwhelm her, that I don't want her to panic and shut down because it all got to be too much.

Nadia frowns, tilting her head to the side as she studies my features. "Do *you* need space?"

My answer is immediate. "No."

"Well, neither do I."

"Oh." That's all I can say because this woman continuously shocks the hell out of me. She's gone from shutting me down at any hint of connection, to being all in, and I don't know how it happened, but I'm damn glad it did.

She strides over to me with her shirt half unbuttoned and her hair doing everything but laying down, but she's still the most beautiful thing I've seen in my life, the most precious thing I've ever held in my hands.

Her arms go around my waist, and she turns her face up to mine, pursing her lips in a silent request for a kiss that I grant immediately.

"I don't want space, Sebastian. I want you *in* my space. I sleep better when I sleep next to you, so please stay."

26

NADIA

My favorite thing about Sebastian is that I only have to tell him I want something once. One statement about wanting him in my bed leads to another sleepover that's more sex than sleep. One request to be held on our first night together means being unable to escape the powerful circle of his arms while I sleep. One off hand comment about liking to start my Monday mornings with an Americano and apple danish from the cafe on the corner weeks ago means him returning from a quick trip to his apartment to get dressed for work with both of those things in his hand.

I'm standing in front of the floor length mirror in my living room checking out my outfit for the day—pleated, tan trousers paired with a white blouse for a simple but professional combination that suggests I haven't spent the entire weekend being folded like a pretzel by my boss—when he walks through the door. He lets out a long, low whistle of appreciation as he strides over to me, looking like walking temptation in a black, three piece suit with his jacket undone.

"What you got there, handsome?" I ask as I run a hand over my unruly hair.

"Breakfast." He sets the cup and the pastry bag down on the

counter and crosses his arms, meeting my gaze through the mirror. "I thought you were ready."

"I thought so too, but my hair just refuses to cooperate." All of Zoe's hard work has been undone by her brother. She joked with me about it at the house yesterday and told me to call her so she could come by and fix it. I had put her off, telling her I could make do until our appointment in two weeks, but after last night, I might have to take her up on her offer. And find a Sebastian proof hairstyle.

"I think you look beautiful," the destroyer of silk presses says, sliding his arms around my waist and placing a kiss to my neck.

"Well, thank you, but I don't think your opinion counts since you're my boyfriend."

"Why does my position in your life invalidate my opinion on your looks?"

"Because you've got the rose colored glasses on now. All the newness of our relationship and the good sex keeps you from being able to see me clearly."

The intensity of his stare threatens to shatter the mirror. "Do I strike you as the type of man whose vision gets distorted easily, Nadia?"

I swallow as an unfortunate wave of desire rushes through me, soaking my panties. "No."

"Then why would you think our relationship would make me see you as anything other than exactly what you are?" His fingers flex against my hips as he straightens to his full height, which brings him several inches above me. "I see you more clearly now than I ever have, precious."

The heat from his body bleeds into my back, and I find myself leaning into him, admiring our reflections in the mirror. We look like we belong together, and it's not just the designer clothes or our complimentary heights. It's the possessive grip he's got on my waist, and the happiness swirling around us. It's those champagne eyes on my face and the synchronicity of our breathing.

"You're quite the romantic, Mr. Adler."

Warm lips press a kiss to my temple. "Only with you, Miss Hendrix."

Our transition into formality is playful at first, but then it turns into something else when I remember that we're about to take our changed dynamic into Cerros, and we haven't discussed how that's going to work.

I spin around to face him. "You know, we never discussed how we were going to navigate *this* at work."

His hands skate over my ass. "How do *you* want to navigate it?"

The smart thing to do would be to keep us under wraps and avoid all the speculation about whether I got my job because I'm sleeping with the boss, but that just doesn't feel right. For a long time, my life was nothing but one horrific thing after another, and now that I have some goodness, I don't want to hide it, I want to shout about it from the rooftops.

I wrap my arms around his neck. "I don't want to keep us a secret."

A heart-stopping smile curves his lips, and I taste joy on his tongue when he leans in to kiss me. It's a short, sweet peck that makes me squirm with anticipation for more.

"Good," Sebastian says, his eyes dancing with humor because he can see on my face that I'm now hungry for things we don't have time for. "Because I have every intention of walking into work together, holding hands."

It's such a sweet, juvenile desire. You would think it's too simple a show of possession for a man who is the master of his universe, but when we walked into Cerros hand in hand, Sebastian's expression was all satisfaction and open affection. No one seemed surprised to see us together. Regina was especially unaffected when she found us kissing outside of my office door. She didn't so much as gasp, just waited patiently for Sebastian to turn his attention to her so she could sweep him off to meetings that keep him from me for most of the day.

By the time lunch rolls around, I'm hungry for food and Sebastian's attention. Since food can be acquired anywhere at any time, I prioritize my desire for attention, abandoning a half written email just to seek him out. I find him in his office behind his desk but realize too late that he's in the middle of a video call. I pause, mid-stride and try to back out as quietly as possible, but he spots me.

"Hold on, Talia," he says, glancing up from his phone to set questioning but pleased eyes on me. "Where are you going, precious?"

I hook a thumb over my shoulder. "Back to my office."

"Why? You just got here."

"Because you're in a meeting, and I don't want to interrupt."

He frowns and beckons me forward with two fingers. "You're not interrupting anything."

Except a call with his ex-wife who he went to great lengths to keep me from meeting the last time she was in town. I hesitate to go to him, wondering if this is an attempt to right that wrong, to prove that he has no qualms about showing me off to her.

"Sebastian, really, I can come back later."

His gaze darkens. "Come *here*, Nadia."

With a huff that's half annoyance, half arousal, I go to him. He pushes back from his desk and turns, opening his legs so I can stand between them. I'm aware of the phone in his hand and the silence on the other end that tells me Talia is listening to this whole exchange. I wonder what she thinks of it.

"This is completely unnecessary," I tell Sebastian. "I just came to say hi."

"Then come say hi."

He grabs my hand and tugs, pulling me down onto his lap. I land on one of his hard thighs and glare at him, which only makes the smile on his face spread wider.

"So *this* is Nadia," a husky voice says from inside the phone. For the few seconds I've been in front of the screen, I've made a point not to look at it, not to look at her, but now I don't have a choice.

Talia West is stunning.

Her skin is ebony perfection, and her jet black microlocs look like they've been growing for as long as Sebastinan's have. There's something sharp about her smile that makes her look predatory, like a pantheress with dinner in its direct line of sight. Except on her it's more sensual than sinister, which is surprising but a little less unsettling.

Sebastian's placing his hand on my thigh. "Yes, this is Nadia. Nadia, this is Talia."

I force a nervous smile. "It's a pleasure to meet you, Talia."

"Oh, the pleasure is all mine, Nadia," she purrs. "Sebastian has told me so much about you. It's a shame he's just allowing us to meet. We could have had so much fun when I was in New Haven."

There's no mistaking the note of flirtation in her tone, but I still look to Sebastian for confirmation. He gives me a subtle nod to let me know I've read it right, which sends a small shock wave down my spine. I don't know how I expected this meeting to go, but this isn't it.

"Talia," Sebastian says, and there's caution tape wrapped around the one word. "Stop flirting with my girlfriend."

"Girlfriend?" Her eyes light up, and I can see she's genuinely happy for him, which makes me relax a little. "Congratulations, Seb!"

He looks at me, pride swimming in his eyes. "Thank you."

"Nadia, trust me when I say I know what a handful that man can be. If you ever need a break, just have him send you to Antigua. You would *love* the Cerros resort here."

During our gossip session on my first day here, Elle told me about the Cerros resorts and how Talia oversees both international locations but spends the majority of her time in Antigua. In my head, I imagined that the resorts were just like the hotel but on a larger, more exotic scale, but when Talia's invitation pulls a displeased grunt from Sebastian, I realize I must have missed something.

"Goodbye, Talia."

He ends the call with an abrupt stab of his finger, and Talia disappears. The screen goes dark, reflecting my stunned expression back at me.

"That was rude."

Sebastian sits back in his chair and pulls me with him, tucking me into the curve of his body. "She knew it was coming."

"Because she invited me to the resort?"

"Because she flirted with you, then invited you to a resort that caters specifically to hedonism and is known for group sex sessions she regularly leads."

"*Oh.*"

His rumble of a laugh vibrates against my cheek. "Yeah, it'll be a cold day in hell before I leave you to fend off Talia and Blue on your own."

"Who's Blue?"

"Talia's fiance."

I sit up, so I can see his face and make sure he's serious. "She's engaged?"

"Yep. She told me about it the last time she was here."

"Are they in an open relationship or something?"

"Every relationship Talia is in is open in one way or another."

"Even your marriage?" I ask, finding myself wanting to hear him say it even though Elle already told me as much.

He nods, but there's no bitterness or anger in his eyes. "Yeah, but that happened without my consent."

"That must have been hard for you."

I can't imagine that it was easy. In the short time that we've known each other, he's demonstrated himself to be extremely protective over what he considers his. He must have torn the world apart piece by piece when he found out Talia was cheating on him. I shudder at the thought, hating the idea of him being jealous and possessive over someone else even though I know it doesn't make sense because she was his wife and, at the time, he didn't even know I existed.

"No," he says, pulling me out of my thoughts. "It wasn't."

His answer shocks me, but it also makes a lot of sense. Most men wouldn't be able to be business partners and friends with a woman they resented for cheating on them.

"Why? Didn't you love her?" I regret the question as soon as I ask it because I don't want his answer. I shake my head, trying to walk it back. "Never mind. You don't have to tell me."

Sebastian pulls me back down to him, and I tuck my head into the crook of his neck, forcing myself to focus on my breathing so I don't pass out when the man I'm pretty sure I'm in love with tells me how much he loved his ex-wife.

"I adored, Talia," he says, and my heart twists itself into a knot. "I still do, but I don't think I ever loved her. We got along great, we worked well together, we had great sex." My jaw clenches, and he laughs, running a soothing hand over my leg. "Nothing like the sex you and I have, precious," he adds before continuing, "but none of that was enough for love or marriage. To have those things, you just need... *more*."

For some reason, my heart is racing and my mind is rushing with thoughts of what more means to him and if he thinks it exists between us.

"Do you think you'll ever find it? The more you're looking for?"

"I think I already have."

We both go quiet in observation of what he's just confessed, and I curse myself for not being able to say something meaningful back, for not being able to be open the way he always is.

"It's okay, precious, you don't have to say anything back," he says, obviously aware of what's going on inside my head.

"I don't pray, Sebastian," I blurt out, needing to say something, to lay some part of myself bare to him as a means of reciprocation for his vulnerability. "I don't pray, but on the rare occasion I find myself in conversation with God, I talk to him about you. Even before we were us, I spoke your name to Him, submitted it to the heavens at the top of a list of the few things in this world I'm thankful for. I don't believe or trust in anything, but I trust you. I believe in you. And I know that maybe that's not enough—" my voice shakes and all my words disappear.

"It's enough," Sebastian says, dropping a kiss on my head that tells me I don't need to say anything else. "It's more than enough."

* * *

AFTER OUR EMOTIONAL conversation and a delicious lunch straight from Elle's kitchen, I head back to my office to finish out my work day. I send emails and make staff schedules and field phone calls from an anxious bride who is having her wedding reception on the rooftop on a day when it's supposed to pour down raining. She cries to me for fifteen minutes about how the weather will ruin her bridal hair, and after I reassure her that we have a contingency plan in place if the forecast is correct, I hang up the phone and call Zoe to make an appointment to fix my hair. She laughs as she goes through her appointment book and finds me a slot for later on in the week.

I'm in the process of adding the appointment to my calendar when I see a reminder in there about the birth control implant in my arm expiring in three months. I've had it in for close to three years now, and I've been hoping to establish care with a gynecologist in town to talk about other options, but I haven't had time to do any research about where I can or should go. And I still don't. Pulling out my phone, I shoot off a text to the only person whose recommendation I trust: Desiree.

> Nadia: Hey, who's your gynecologist?

She gets back to me immediately.

> Desiree: Why you need to know that?

> Nadia: Because I have a vagina, and I need someone to look at it every now and again and tell me everything is alright.

> Desiree: Isn't that Sebastian's job now?

I roll my eyes, cursing myself for bringing her up to speed on the new developments in my relationship with Sebastian while he was at his place getting dressed for work.

> Nadia: Someone with a medical license, Des.

She sends three eye roll emojis and then an actual response.

> Desiree: I see Dr. Suffrant at the New Haven Women's Center. She's the best.

Nadia: Thank you.

I close out the thread before she can respond and find the number to Dr. Suffrant's practice. The receptionist answers immediately and she's very friendly, which I take as a good sign, but the good vibes end when she tells me Dr. Suffrant is booked until the end of November and asks if I'm okay with waiting that long. Since I have plenty of time before it expires, I agree and add yet another appointment to my already busy calendar.

Just as I'm closing out the calendar app, a notification from my bank comes across the top of my phone screen. I click on it, opening my banking app to reveal a payment reversal from the realty company in the amount of my first and last month's rent plus my security deposit.

"What the hell?" I mutter to myself, slamming my phone down on my desk so I can use both hands to dig through my purse and find Nikki Washington's card. I find it at the bottom, wrinkled but still legible, and dial her number. She picks up on the first ring.

"Nikki Washington of Washington Realty, how may I help you?"

"Nikki." I smile even though she can't see me, hoping it will infuse some kindness into my agitation laced tone. "This is Nadia Hendrix, Sebastian Adler's—"

"I know who you are, Miss Hendrix," she says, cutting me off. "What can I help you with today?"

"Oh, well, I just got a notification about a payment reversal from your company back to my account. It looks like it's everything I paid the day I signed my lease."

Silence greets me, and I assume she's just as shocked as I am, but when it lingers, going on for longer than I expect, I pull the phone away from my face to make sure she's still on the line.

"Nikki?"

"Yes! I'm so sorry. I was just trying to pull up your file." Since I don't hear her fingers clicking on the keyboard, it sounds like a lie, but I don't call her out for it. "Okay, I'm not seeing the payment return here on my end, but let me look into this for you and call you back. Best case scenario is it was a glitch in our system."

"A glitch in your system," I repeat, slowly. "That resulted in

27

NADIA

The automated message instructing me to leave a message plays in my ear, and I think about chucking my phone at the nearest wall. Instead, I push out a steadying breath and say the same thing I've said to Nikki Washington's voicemail everyday for the last month and half.

"Nikki, this is Nadia Hendrix giving you a call again. Please get back to me as soon as you can." I don't bother elaborating because I know she knows what I'm calling about. Just like I know she knows that her explanation about a glitch in her payment system is bullshit. Frustrated, I set my phone on the counter and turn my attention back to the pot of mashed potatoes I made to go with the braised short ribs I've had in the oven for close to two hours.

October swooped in and brought a chill with it that apparently is going to carry over into the month of November, so I decided to make a warm and cozy dish that has the added benefit of reminding me of home. I've been thinking about my parents a lot lately, the way I always do when the anniversary of their death is closing in on me. Every year for the last fourteen years, between the last few days of October and the beginning of November, my brain is flooded with thoughts of them. Memories of the last few weeks I got to spend with them mixed with regrets about the moments I didn't. The conversations I was too busy with my friends to have, the dinners I missed and the hugs I cut short because I was determined to get to the next thing. I'd give anything to have them back, to be standing in the sunlit kitchen I grew up in chopping onions, carrots, and celery while Mom sears the short ribs in the dutch oven and Dad pours wine into the decanter before getting started on the mashed potatoes.

I tried to recreate those vibes tonight, but it doesn't feel the same. The house is too quiet because I'm alone and the only wine I want to drink with this dish can't be found on any shelf in New Haven. I know because I've checked. I considered having Ruthie check too since she has more resources at her disposal than I do, but I just couldn't bear the thought of her search coming up empty too, proving that Beau and Roland were successful in their obliteration of my parent's legacy and my family's name.

The front door opens, and I don't even bother to look up because I know it's Sebastian. The app on my phone that's connected to the doorbell camera announced his arrival, and I watched him use the key I gave him two weeks ago to let himself in. Deciding to give him a key was an easy decision because he was spending every night at my place anyway. I didn't even panic when he moved what seemed like half of his wardrobe into my closet the same day. I didn't mind. I meant what I said when I told him I like having him in *my* space. I'm most comfortable here, and his constant presence only adds to that feeling.

"I've got a surprise for you," he says, by way of greeting.

I look up to see him walking into the kitchen with his hands behind his back and a smile on his face. "You know I hate surprises, Sebastian."

"You'll like this one, I promise."

I grab a kitchen towel and wipe my hands, tossing it over my shoulder as I round the island to meet him. "What is it?"

His gaze drops to my lips. "Give me a kiss first."

I roll my eyes, but do as he asks, rising up on my tip-toes to press my lips to his. It's a short kiss, really more of a peck, but when I pull back he looks extremely satisfied, so I hold my hand out.

"Surprise, please."

He shakes his head and laughs. "Thought you didn't like surprises."

"I don't, but I could use the pick me up today."

"You okay?"

We haven't seen much of each other since this morning because he's been in meetings all over town, which means he hasn't been around to witness the beginnings of my annual bout of depression.

"Yeah, just missing my parents a little bit more than usual."

His smile melts into a sympathetic frown. "I'm sorry, precious. Do you want to talk about it?"

Every day I spend with Sebastian it feels less realistic to keep hiding from him behind the wall I built to safeguard my present from my past. He wants to know me, every part of me, and I want him to, but I'm also scared. Scared that a conversation about my parents will lead to one about Beau and that speaking his name will conjure him like a dark spirit, bringing him straight to New Haven, straight to my doorstep.

"Not today."

"Okay." Sebastian lets me go, and I read the disappointment on his face before he's able to tuck it away. He's been more patient than any other man would be, but I know my reluctance to share is weighing on him. "Ready for your surprise then?"

"Yes, please."

The enthusiasm in my answer wins me a smile. "Close your eyes and hold out your hands."

"*Sebastian!*" I whine, hating him for drawing this out even more.

He doesn't even respond, just blinks at me until I do what he asked. As soon as I'm in compliance, I feel something smooth and cool to the touch in my hands. I run my fingers along the object, feeling the width taper as I get closer to the end of it.

"A bottle of wine?" I ask, hoping it's a nice full bodied red to go with the dinner I made.

"Yes," he says, excitement layered in his tone, "but not just any bottle, open your eyes."

Once again, I follow his instruction and find myself holding a bottle I never thought I'd see again. My eyes rove over the black bottle and black label with distinctive gold foil that denotes the name of the brand in a flowing script font made from my mother's handwriting. My lips part because I have so many questions, so many things to say, but not a single sound comes out.

"It's the '93 Thornehill Pinot Noir, the bottle you were looking for that night at Ludus," Sebastian says, reminding me of the day when I almost wasted this perfection on Preston Fredricks. "Ruthie helped me track it down. She says it's one of the last bottles left in existence from a vineyard in Sonoma."

Tears blur my vision and sadness becomes a tremor in my voice. "Did you know it takes two years for Pinot Noir to age?"

"No, I didn't know that." There's a world of caution in Sebastian's voice when he answers me, which lets me know that he's caught on to the change in my mood. "So that wine was actually processed and barreled in..."

"1991," I interject. "The year I was born." I look up and give him a watery smile, wanting to sob because I miss my parents so badly and holding this bottle makes that pain more acute, wanting to laugh because suddenly I don't have a desire to talk about anything except them. "I guess we *are* talking about my parents today."

"We are?"

I nod. "Yeah, we are, but first I need to decant this."

As soon as the words leave my mouth, the timer I set for the short ribs goes off.

"I'll get it," Sebastian says, moving around me to the oven. While he gets the short ribs situated, I pull out the decanter, cork screw and two wine glasses, sitting everything on the counter but freezing when it comes time to open it. My fingers shake as I run them over the label, tracing the letters that spell out the name I haven't dared to speak in months. Thornehill. It's a combination of Hawthorne—my father's last name—and Hill—my mother's maiden name—but to me it has only ever sounded like home.

Sebastian's questioning gaze is a heavy weight on the side of my face. "Do you want me to do it?"

"No, I got it." I sound so confident, but my hands still aren't moving. *I'm* not moving. I'm just standing here, barely breathing, staring at the bottle like if I look hard enough my parents might appear in the black glass.

"Nadia."

Pulling in a shaky breath, I start talking, saying the first thing that comes to mind with no regard for if it makes sense or whether it's the best place to start.

"When I was a kid, my dad would repeatedly tell me about how harrowing it was to have a newborn with colic and a quarter of an acre of grapes with thin skin and a sensitivity to everything."

Sebastian's brows dip inward. His expression a silent question that compels me to elaborate.

"Pinot Noir grapes are notoriously difficult to grow. They're completely unforgiving, reacting to every little change in their growing environment. And if you do manage to get them through growing season, you still have to worry about their tendency to rot during wine making."

His head bobs up and down, signaling his understanding. "Your dad made wine."

"My dad made *this* wine." I spin the bottle around, so he can look at the label, so he can fully appreciate the fact that he unknowingly brought home the key to the safe that holds all of my secrets. "And it was his favorite because despite the challenging circumstances, he managed to get everything exactly right that year, and two years later, he put out a small batch of his first Pinot that went on to win several distinctive awards." Sebastian stares at me in awe, and I take his silence as license to continue. "Instead of framing his success as a result of overcoming the difficulties of having a new baby who refused to sleep anywhere but in his or his wife's arms, he attributed that success to me. Saying that taking care of me taught him how to be patient and more nurturing, which is exactly what the grapes needed most."

I turn the bottle back towards me and shake my head. The motion sets the tears lingering at the corners of my eyes free. "I can't open it."

"You don't have to." His hands cover mine, and I look up, wondering how I missed him moving over to me. "We don't have to drink it. *Ever.* Tell me something else about them. About your parents."

The gentle request sets memories I haven't accessed in years free, and I see everything, I *feel* everything, and it's just too much. I crumble under the weight of it all, sinking down to the floor as heavy sobs wrack my body and waves of tears pull me under, drowning me in a current of grief. Sebastian doesn't crumble, but when I hit the floor, he hits it with me. Actually, he hits it mere seconds before me, allowing me to use his body as a cushion to soften the blow. I curl in on myself, and he wraps his arms around me and lifts his legs up, drawing me in closer, cradling me like a baby.

By the time I finish crying dinner is cold and my throat is raw. I've barely got a voice, but I still want to speak. I still want to tell Sebastian everything there is to know about me.

"My mother's name was Corrine Hill, and my dad was Maxwell Hawthorne." Just speaking their names makes my throat burn, my vocal chords feel like they're being seared by grief. "He had this great, big laugh that only my mom and me could get out of him. With everyone else he was super serious, borderline grumpy."

I close my eyes, trying to recreate the boisterous sound of his laughter in my mind and failing.

"Sounds like my kind of guy," Sebastian muses, and I smile.

"You two would have gotten along really well….eventually."

His laughter shakes my body. "Right. He probably would have hated me in the beginning, threatened to take me out if I hurt his baby girl."

"Exactly, and he was from Texas so there probably would have been a gun involved."

"Texas?"

I nod. "Houston to be specific. He was born and raised there. I think most of his family still lives there."

"You have family in Houston?"

"Yes, on my dad's side. Grandparents who didn't want me to exist and aunts and uncles who were happy when their youngest brother left the fold because it meant one less person to split the Hawthorne empire with."

Sebastian has been rubbing small circles on my arm, but the last words in my sentence make him pause. "Hawthorne. As in Hawthorne Energy?"

"One in the same."

I knew he would put it together, but I'm impressed that he did so quickly. My paternal grandparents own and operate the largest Black owned oil and energy company in the United States. Like Sebastian, my father came from money, and just like me when I came to New Haven, my mother came from nothing. By the time she got to Texas Southern, where she met my dad, she was all alone in the world. Her parents were dead, both of them surrendering to drug habits they'd fought her whole life. She had no siblings or extended family to speak of because everyone had either died or wrote her parents off after years of broken promises to get clean.

"So they didn't approve of your dad and your mom."

"Nope. They were against them from the jump, but they didn't say anything because they thought their relationship would fall apart when they graduated from college."

"But they didn't."

"Nope. Mom got pregnant with me then Dad proposed and all hell broke loose. My grandma tried to pay off my mom to get an abortion and leave town. When Dad found out he confronted his mom, and everyone took her side, so he cut them all off. They lived together in this small apartment near the school until they graduated. I was born a few weeks later, and then they moved to California."

When my dad used to tell me the story of him and Mom, I used to get so annoyed, but now I'm glad that I listened, that I stored the information away for a moment like this because sharing these details with Sebastian feels like reaching a new level of intimacy.

"How'd your dad go from drilling for oil to running a vineyard?"

The question makes me laugh because it's one that everybody would ask when they found out where he came from. No one could fathom why an heir to an oil fortune would want to spend his days pruning vines and tending to grapes.

"He said he always had this desire to use land for something beautiful, to create something from it instead of leeching it dry like his family had for generations."

"That's admirable," Sebastian says, and I hear the respect in his voice. "Did your mom share his dream?"

"Oh, yeah, she left all the farming and science to Dad, but she loved the business and the people. She had all the good ideas like vineyard tours and wine tastings, and all the staff loved her because once a week she'd cook these big family meals to feed everyone. It was her way of checking in. Your mom reminds me of her a lot."

"She loves you, you know, and I know it won't make you miss your mom any less, but I'm happy to share her with you."

I know he means it because he already is sharing her with me. Honestly, he's sharing his entire family with me. Over the last month and half, I've built my own relationship with each member of the Adler family, and I don't have any plans on letting any of them go.

Sitting up, I place my hand on his cheek and look deep into his eyes, losing myself for just a second in the calm of the champagne orbs. "I think I'll take you up on that offer."

"Smart woman." He drops a kiss on my lips. "Do you want to tell me more or are you done sharing?"

I consider stopping but find that I don't want to. The more I say about my parents and myself, the more I *want* to say. And so I tell Sebastian everything there is to know about me while we sit on the floor of my kitchen. It takes forever, and every time I mention Beau and Roland, his hand turns to a fist at my waist. He gets especially upset when I tell him about them blowing through all the money in my trust while I was in college.

Eventually, we get off the floor and reheat the dinner we let get cold. Then Sebastian sits me on the island counter and feeds me straight from the pots with a spoon he takes bites from when he's not busy kissing me, which he's doing right now.

"I have one more thing I want to tell you," I murmur against his lips.

Sebastian pulls back, his eyes serious as they move over my face. "What is it?"

"My name."

28

SEBASTIAN

Nyla Hawthorne.

That's Nadia's real name. The one Maxwell and Corrine chose for her. The one she trusted me enough to say out loud. The one I asked her for permission to share with the person I trust most with sensitive information—Russ Cooper, the head of security at Ludus. Nadia was hesitant at first, but when I explained that Russ was who I would be giving that information to, and provided a few details about his military intelligence background, she agreed.

Once I had her permission, I gave Russ a call. We had a short conversation about what I wanted him to dig up, and twelve hours later, he's in my office with multiple files in hand, ready to lay everything out for me. I asked Nadia if she wanted to sit in on the meeting, but she refused, saying she preferred to stay focused on the life she has now, not the one she escaped from. Apparently, that includes keeping the name she chose for herself when she carved out her new beginning.

"Where do you want to start?" Russ asks, laying the thick files out in front of him on the conference table.

"Beau Montgomery."

The name of the man who abused, exploited and victimized the love of my life tastes like acid on my tongue. I want to know everything about him including the exact location of the rock he's currently hiding under.

"Okay." Russ opens the folder directly in front of him, like he knew that was where we would begin. "Beau Montgomery, the only son of Roland and Belinda Montgomery. A born and bred sociopath with a history of drug and alcohol issues. His mother, Belinda, passed away in the same plane crash that killed Corrine and Maxwell. Email communications between Belinda and Corrine indicate that she intended to ask Maxwell for a job at Thornehill."

"Why the secrecy? Their families were extremely close, right?" Nadia explained that her father and Roland grew up together, and their friendship was the only remaining link to his life in Texas.

Russ pulls a page from the folder and slides it across the table to me. "Bank statements indicate financial problems, probably due to Roland's gambling habit. My guess is Roland was trying to keep it under wraps, hiding it from everyone, including his wife."

I pick up the paper, a bank statement that's over fifteen years old. I don't even bother asking Russ how he got it. The people he knows and the access they have to things they shouldn't even be aware of are why I keep him around and pay him so well. Why I prefer to have him at Ludus, the most vulnerable arm of my business because of its lack of legality, instead of anywhere else.

"Financial problems," I repeat, scanning the bank statement that shows regular four and five figure withdrawals from the Montgomery's joint banking account. The code next to each has them designated as ATM transactions at a casino. "They were broke."

Russ nods. "And in danger of losing their house. Once Belinda found out, she started trying to contain the damage, emptying out Beau's college fund to catch up house payments, and then, when that wasn't enough, going to the Hawthornes for a job."

For every fact Russ spews, he slides a paper or two across the table to back it up. His word is more than enough, but I appreciate the picture being painted by the documentation.

"Do we know how much Beau knew?"

"My guess is not a lot. He was too busy partying, drinking, taking every drug he could get his hand on and beating up his girlfriends whenever he got a chance."

"Was he ever charged?"

"No. Apparently he had quite the talent for making the girls think they deserved it. Most of them never went to the police, and the few that did recanted their statements immediately."

"So Nadia wasn't his first..." My teeth clench around the word, and I have to force it out. "So Nadia wasn't his first victim."

Russ shifts in his seat as he pulls a thin file from the back of Beau's folder. He hesitates to open it, which lets me know what's in it is probably something I don't want to see.

"She wasn't," he says, meeting my eyes. "But he was particularly brutal with her."

My stomach turns. "When did it start?"

Nadia told me about the abuse, but she never gave me specifics. And I want the specifics because those details are what I'll have in mind when I find him and take his fucking life.

"Best guess would be after she graduated from college. That's when the hospital visits started."

"Hospital visits?"

Russ nods. "They started out slow. She'd be seen at the ER every now and again for little things like repeated broken fingers that were easily explained away. Then Roland Montgomery died, and she was seen four times in one month for a broken arm, bruised ribs, multiple black eyes and a fracture to her sternum she attributed to a fall."

I can't sit any longer. Listening to Russ catalog Nadia's injuries, knowing that the proof—hospital records, pictures, or maybe even both —are inside the folder in his hand. All of it makes me want to set fire to something, to leave this office and seek Nadia out so I can hold her in my arms and reassure myself that she's here and she's safe.

"There are photos," he says, confirming my thoughts as he slides the folder across the table. "A nurse in the ER took them, she gave them to the police, but they never followed up."

I snatch the folder up, but I don't open it. "What the fuck do you mean they never followed up?"

"By that time, Beau's escort operation was pretty large...."

"And large operations require police protection," I finish for him, knowing that Beau must have used his connections with the local police to avoid charges. It's not an uncommon practice. In fact, it's one I've seen utilized by men in New Haven who are no better than Beau Montgomery, men I put out of business by creating Ludus.

"He had connections in LAPD that helped him keep it all under wraps. In exchange for their protection, he'd make girls available to them free of charge."

"*Fuck.*" The folder turns in on itself when my hand tries to become a fist. "Everybody failed her. At every fucking turn, they failed her."

But I won't. I won't fail her. I won't let another person in this world hurt her, especially not Beau Montgomery.

I return to my seat and push the folder back to Russ. I don't need to look at those photos, to see Nadia battered and bruised, that would be too much like looking backward, and I need all of my attention on a path forward, on finding the man that hurt her and ensuring he never gets the chance to do so again.

"Where is he?"

Russ grimaces, and I already know I'm going to hate what he says next. "His current address shows him living in a bungalow in the Cypress Park area. We know that he likes to frequent a few clubs in—"

"Russ, I don't give a fuck about any of that. I want to know where he is right now."

He sighs and clasps his hands together. "I don't know."

"You don't know?" I slam my fist down on the table. "You can pull bank statements and emails from fifteen fucking years ago, but you can't find him? You can't tell me where the fuck he is *today*?! He could be in New Haven right now."

"I don't think he's in New Haven."

"But you don't know!" My blood is boiling, and I'm seething as I push up from the table again. I'm done with this meeting. "*Find him.*"

I leave my office and head straight for Nadia's, nearly putting my fist through the wall when I walk in and find it empty. I need to see her. That's the only thought in my head as I storm through Elle's kitchen, the indoor dining area, and the roof where I finally find her. She's up here all alone, her elbows resting against the glass and metal panels that line the roof's edge, brown eyes studying New Haven's skyline. Slowing my steps is a hard task when the need to touch her is an urgent thrumming in my veins, but I force myself to do so because I don't want to alarm her. The last thing she needs is the stress of helping me process traumas she endured. When I'm sure that I won't raise any red flags, I move towards her.

"Penny for your thoughts."

Nadia doesn't jump or scream or do any of the things people usually do when they've been caught off guard, which means she knew I was here and probably gave me the time I needed to gather myself before I came to her. She glances at me over her shoulder, her eyes cautious as they skate across my face.

"I was actually thinking of you," she says, turning back to the view in front of her. "How was your meeting with Russ?"

I step up behind her, wrapping my arms around her middle and folding my front over her back. She sighs like she needed this moment as much as I did, and I bury my nose in her hair, pulling in deep lungfuls of that combination of bergamot and amber I've come to love.

"Difficult," I admit on an exhale. "But nothing I can't handle."

"You don't know him Sebastian. Beau is…" she pauses, shakes her head. "Beau is a snake, and you never see him coming until he's close enough to strike. Close enough to hurt you."

The fear wrapped around her words breaks something inside of me. I hear it shatter, feel the shards piercing my heart and my lungs making each breath I pull in ragged and uncertain. I hate this. I hate that she's afraid. I hate that she thinks I can't protect her when I'd die doing so.

"He won't ever get close enough to hurt you, precious."

She turns around and the tears in her eyes when she wraps her arms around my neck threaten to unravel me completely. "I'm not worried about me, Sebastian. I'm worried about *you*. If I stay here, Beau will find me, and you'll try to put yourself between me and him, and I don't...if something ever happened to you because of me, I'd never forgive myself."

When the tears start to fall, she buries her face in my chest, and I cradle the back of her head with tender hands that tremble with the need to destroy something.

If I stay.

The words play in my head on an endless loop that sends flares of panic reverberating down my spine. I've never been as afraid of losing anything—wealth, property, connections, resources—as I am of losing Nadia.

"Don't cry. Nothing is going to happen to me or you. I promise." It's not enough to convince her or soothe the ache caused by the fear clawing at my chest.

"You can't promise that, Sebastian."

"Yes, I can." Leaning back, I slip my fingers under her chin and urge her to look at me. "Have I ever broken a promise to you? Have I ever told you I was going to do something and didn't follow through?"

She shakes her head, teeth digging into the flesh of her bottom lip. "No, but—"

"No buts," I say, cutting her attempt at expressing doubt short. "*I* will take care of you. *I* will keep you safe. Tell me you believe me."

Nadia pulls in a shaky breath. "I believe you."

I kiss her as soon as the words are past her lips, losing myself in the salt laced perfection of her sweetness. She reacts instantly, her fingers tangling in my hair and holding tight while my hands explore her curves, skating over the butter soft cashmere skirt she's wearing that matches her sweater. I don't know when I make the decision to pull it up, but one second I'm just touching her, gripping her ass, and caressing her hips and the next I'm guiding it up her thighs, exposing her skin to the coolness of the wind and enjoying the way it juxtaposes the heat between her thighs.

"*Seb*," Nadia hisses, breaking the kiss and looking up at me with wide eyes that ask if we're really about to do this. My answer to her silent inquest is a hand cupping her sex then gripping the lace of her panties and yanking hard so they relinquish their hold on her. It's two hands on her waist, lifting her up and sitting her on the wide ledge, and two bent knees that put my face level with her pussy.

I look up at her, taking in her silhouette against the backdrop of the city where she found safety and security, where she found *me*. Her eyes are wide, her expression half fearful and half trusting. "Legs on my shoulders, precious." Like the good girl she is, she obeys, and I kiss the inside of her thigh, running my tongue over the jagged lines of the scar I still don't know how she got. "Good. Now cross your ankles behind my head." Once again, she does exactly as I say, and I reward her with a swipe of my tongue over her clit. My intention was to take it slow, but the moment her sweetness hits my taste buds, I lose it, devouring her with hungry, open mouth kisses and unrelenting swipes of my tongue over her heated flesh.

Nadia squirms, and I squeeze her hips. "Stay still."

"I can't," she says, both sets of her fingers tangling through my hair until she's holding them like reigns. "It feels too good."

Her breathless confession turns into a helpless moan when I drive my tongue into her pussy and moan when I feel her muscles ripple around me.

"*Sebastian!*" She screams, trading her grip on my hair for the ledge and dragging her nails down the metal. It groans in protest, but the sound is no match for the broken cries pouring from Nadia's lips as she surrenders to the wave of pleasure rolling through her. She's still in the throes of her orgasm when I pull her down off the ledge and spin her around, placing my hand between her shoulder blades and urging her to bend over. I use my knee to push hers apart and slip two of my fingers into her heat, testing how wet and ready she is for me.

"You're soaked, Nadia."

She rolls her hips, grinding her pussy down on my hand and whimpering when I take it away so I can free my dick. The whimper turns into an anticipatory moan when I run my tip through her folds, grazing her clit before pulling back to line myself up with her entrance.

"I want it hard, Sebastian. Fuck me until I forget."

It's not a request so much as it is a demand, an order I'm bound by heart and blood to obey, and by the time I'm done with her she's forgotten everything that's not my name and the slow glide of my dick moving inside of her.

* * *

"I'M STILL SORE," Nadia grumbles from across the table, glancing around to make sure no one overheard her.

We're at Roku waiting for Nic and his new fiancé, Sloane, to arrive. When I heard the news that he'd gotten engaged to his late best friend's widow, I was shocked. And when he told me about how he'd been secretly pining after her for over a decade, I congratulated him on finally growing some balls and offered to take them out to dinner to celebrate. They chose Roku—a Japanese place not too far from Cerros —because apparently it's one of Sloane's favorite spots.

"You're the one who said you wanted it hard."

A lovely red tint seeps into her cheeks, and she smiles, which makes me smile because it feels like she's finally returning to herself after a few days of being in her head about everything related to her past and Beau.

"Yeah, but I didn't think I'd still be feeling it a week later."

I shrug. "What can I say, baby? I like to leave an impression."

Nadia rolls her eyes, but her lips are still curved into a smile, so I know she's not really annoyed. She goes back to perusing the menu while I split my attention between her face and the door, watching for Nic and Sloane. They arrive a few minutes later, both of them looking a bit disheveled despite trying to hide it. One side of Sloane's cloud of curls is flatter than the other, and Nic has some of her lipstick on his neck. Despite the small imperfections in their appearance, which were clearly caused by a moment of carnal indulgence, they look good together. I tell them as much when they finally get settled at the table after a brief round of hugs and introductions. Sloane is seated beside Nadia and the two of them spend the first half of dinner exchanging compliments on everything from their hair, nail color, clothing and purses.

"Did we even need to be here?" Nic asks. The question is directed at me, but it's Sloane who answers, cutting hazel eyes at him that are dancing with amusement.

"Don't tell me you're jealous, Dom."

"Not at all, angel. I was just wondering when you two were going to include us in the conversation."

"Sounds like a bit of jealousy to me," Nadia quips. "I would apologize for stealing all of your fiancé's attention, Nic, but I'm not really sorry because she's kind of amazing."

"I know, that's why I asked her to marry me."

"Should I be jealous?" I ask, pinning Nadia with a questioning stare. "I don't think you've ever called me amazing."

"I have," she says, taking a sip of wine. "Just never to your face."

"Oh, I have to do that too," Sloane adds, smiling. "You can't give them too many compliments because then their heads get all big and their egos get super inflated." She shudders for dramatic effect. "Who wants to deal with that?"

"No one," Nadia replies, clinking her glass to Sloane's.

I look at Nic. "You regretting this yet?"

He sighs, chewing a piece of sushi he just stole from Sloane's plate. "You're the one who insisted on getting together."

"Next time we can just stay at home."

"That'd be perfect actually," Sloane says to Nadia who giggles. "Then we can invite my best friend Mal and make it a girl's night."

"Yesss! I'll bring my best friend, Desiree, and we'll have a ball."

Even though I'm listening to Nadia actively plan to leave me in the dust for Sloane, Desiree and Mal, I can't find myself to feel anything but happiness because making plans for the future, even in the most general of terms, means that Nadia is creating a life here in New Haven. Developing bonds and friendships outside of me that I hope will make it harder for her to give in to her instinct to run if things get to be too much.

Since our conversation on the rooftop about Beau, I've made it a priority to put her in situations where she could do just that. Taking her over to Mom and Dad's house for dinner, going to the movies with Zoe and Luca, attending a boring ass lecture Andreas gave at the college, and now, this dinner with Nic and Sloane. All things to remind her that she is not alone in this world anymore, so she doesn't have to run. She can stay and fight, and we'll stand beside her.

I'll stand beside her.

By the time we leave Roku, Nadia and Sloane have exchanged numbers, and I have been roped into making the rooftop available for an engagement party Nic didn't seem aware they were having at the end of the month. As I drive us home, Nadia is alternating between writing down ideas in her notes app and bouncing in her seat with excitement.

"Sloane sent me pictures of the engagement set up! Did you know Nic built her a house out of candles?" She's gushing and her voice is pitched high. "I think we should line the perimeter of the rooftop with the same kind of candles for the party. It'll be such a nice tie in."

"That sounds amazing, precious." My attention should be on the road, but I can't stop looking at her, can't stop soaking in the joy pouring off of her in waves. "You're really excited aren't you?"

"I love a good party, Seb. Especially one that's all about love and has no budget to speak of."

"You're going to make Nic regret saying that aren't you?"

"No." She laughs, and the lights from the city stream in through the moon roof, highlighting the smile lines around her eyes. "My mom always said just because you have the money doesn't mean you should spend it, so I'll make sure to get the best deals on everything and only splurge on the important stuff like wine."

"Nic doesn't drink, precious," I say as I turn into the parking garage underneath our building. The look on Nadia's face tells me the reminder was a waste of my breath.

"Yeah, but everyone else does."

"I guess you're right."

"I am." She's on her phone now, probably emailing Ruthie and Elle to ask them for their assistance.

"What date did you and Sloane settle on again?"

"The 27th. It'll be tight, but I think I can pull everything together in time."

As I pull into the parking spot designated for Nadia's unit, I run the date through my mental calendar, making sure I don't have anything on the books. "That's the Saturday after Thanksgiving, right?"

Nadia's brow furrows. "Is it?"

"I think so."

I watch her close out her email and open her calendar to confirm. "Yeah, it is. God, this month is flying by, I guess I need to figure out my plans for Thanksgiving."

"You mean other than having dinner with me and my family?"

"I didn't...I didn't realize I was included in your Thanksgiving plans."

"You're included in all of my plans, precious."

"Oh." Her eyes go all soft, pools of brown melting into liquid caramel. "Do you guys usually have dinner at your parents' place or are y'all one of those weird families that go out?"

"We usually eat at Mom and Dad's, but I was thinking we could do things a little different this year."

"How so?" Nadia asks.

I reach over and grab her hand. "I was thinking we could host. Give Mom a break from cooking, keep Dad from trying to burn the house down deep frying another turkey."

The idea is freshly formed, but as I say it, it feels right. As the oldest son, I always assumed that holidays would eventually become one of my responsibilities. I thought it'd come when I got married and had a house, but as much as everyone in my family adores Talia, it never felt right. She didn't have the desire to host or entertain, two things Nadia seems to enjoy.

"Sebastian." She shakes her head, looking at me like I've just asked her to join a cult. "Thanksgiving is a family thing—"

"You are family. You're *my* family."

Her fingers squeeze mine, and I send up a silent prayer that she's not about to refute that statement because if she does I'll have to prove it to her, and the only way to do that is by asking her a question she isn't ready for.

"One day I'd love to host Thanksgiving with you, but not this year okay? I'm still finding my footing in New Haven, in this relationship, in your family, and we both know Luca will never let me live it down if I fuck up the macaroni and cheese on the most important eating day of the year."

29

NADIA

I hate turning Sebastian down, but I love that he takes my refusal in stride. That he hears my reservations and doesn't minimize them, doesn't try to talk me out of feeling the way I feel. It makes me feel safe, it makes me feel seen, it makes me feel loved.

We haven't said those words yet, but they're here, floating around us, layered in every touch we share and breath we exchange. But most of all, I see it in Sebastian's eyes, and it thrills me as much as it scares me.

Which is a lot.

Every time I think he's going to say the words, I lose the ability to breathe. And not in a good way, in a way that would probably lead to me passing out and ending up concussed instead of saying it back.

I'm not sure if I *can* say it back, and that in and of itself is frustrating because if I don't love Sebastian Adler, I have never loved a single thing in my entire life. He's the kindest, most patient man I've ever known, more considerate than I deserve, showering me with more compassion and care than any one person has the right to receive in a single lifetime, going out of his way to demonstrate how he feels about me even when it means doing ridiculous things like trying to put me in charge of the single most important meal of the year.

After I refused to host the entire dinner, we landed on a compromise of me assisting his mom with the cooking. Sebastian called her as soon as we got inside the penthouse, letting her know that she would finally have some willing help in the kitchen this year. I didn't stick around to hear her response, heading to the bedroom just in case she wasn't as excited as Sebastian said she would be. I'm in the bathroom removing my makeup when Sebastian comes in with a wide grin on his face.

"Mom is over the moon," he says, padding over to the shower and turning it on because he's got my evening routine memorized. "She's already plotting what dishes she can have you make."

The warmth of acceptance spreads through my chest, and I find myself mirroring Sebastian's grin. "As long as it's not the macaroni and cheese, I'm down for whatever."

"I'll make sure it's not on your list of duties."

"Thank you, sir." I turn around to face him, knowing I should be wrapping my hair up because steam is already filling the bathroom but holding off because a random question just popped up in my head, and now that I'm thinking of it, I have to know the answer. "Hey, where would we have done Thanksgiving at anyway? If I would have said yes to hosting, I mean."

He closes the shower door and looks at me. There's something odd about his expression. "Umm, I hadn't thought that far, but probably here."

"Here?" The bathroom is growing more humid by the minute, so I turn and grab my scarf, rushing through the process of wrapping my hair while Sebastian watches. "Why wouldn't we do it at your place?"

Even with the steam billowing around us, I can still read the discomfort on Sebastian's face. It's in the shifting of his eyes and the press of his lips, in the tensing of his jaw and the seconds he lets pass by in complete silence while I wait for a response.

"Because I'm in between places right now," he says finally, and if he was anyone else—like a man whose wealth I have not only benefited from but seen with my own two eyes—I'd be worried that he was on some con-man, drifter shit.

"In between places," I repeat. "Is that rich people speak for I own so much shit I can sleep at a different place every night of the week?"

His lips curve into a brilliantly cocky grin. "Something like that."

My response, which is more of a request for him to elaborate on how many places we're talking about specifically, is interrupted by the unmistakably loud whirring of a power tool. Sebastian and I share an incredulous look, and he glances at his watch.

"Who the fuck is doing construction right now?"

"Maybe the neighbors?" I can't get any more specific than that because I've been living here for almost a month now, and I've yet to see anyone but the construction guys I spotted the other day coming or going from the other unit on this floor. "When I came home from work last week, I saw some men taking in some glass panels and metal frames." Sebastian frowns and pulls out his phone, which makes me wonder if maybe there is another problem. "Is that not allowed?"

"What?" He glances at me. "Oh, yeah, construction is fine as long as there are permits. The issue is with the timing. No one should be using power tools at this time of night."

"Oh, well maybe it was just a one off."

"Maybe."

Now that my hair is wrapped, I set about shedding the heather gray sweater dress I wore today. Sebastian runs appreciative eyes over my frame, and when I take off my bra, revealing hardened nipples that are pointing right at him, he sucks in a deep breath.

"Are you going to join me in the shower?" I ask, shimmying out of my lace panties.

"Do you really have to ask?" He murmurs with dark eyes set on me. His hands go to his waist, his fingers are on his belt. My mouth is watering with anticipation when the charged silence between us is broken once again by whatever is happening on the other side of the wall.

I see the exact moment Sebastian decides he's going over there and immediately protest. "Just leave it alone, babe, come take a shower with me."

He shakes his head, dropping his hands to his side. "Take your shower, precious. I'll be right back."

"Sebastian!" I call for him, but he's already gone. And since I'm naked, going after him isn't exactly an option, so I take my shower and hope he won't be in handcuffs by the time I get done.

When I emerge from the bathroom, wrapped in a towel and still a little damp, he's just returning to the bedroom. I pause in the middle of the floor, while he lingers in the doorway.

"Did you take care of it?"

"I did," he says, closing the space between us with long, confident strides. One of his hands go to the overlapping edges of the towel and tugs, sending the soft cotton flowing to the ground. "Now you can be the noisiest thing on the floor."

* * *

MY HEAD IS STILL on all the pleasure-laced noises Sebastian wrung from my body the night before when Zoe appears in the doorway of my office. It's a little after one in the afternoon, and I'm neck deep in several emails, but I'm happy to see her.

"Hey, Zo! What are you doing here?"

I start to get up, but she waves a hand at me. "Don't bother, I'm only staying for a minute."

Despite her proclamation, she takes a seat on the opposite side of my desk and kicks her pink Converses up on my desk, making herself comfortable. I raise a brow at her.

"You sure about that?"

"Yeah, I just came to see Seb, and he told me about volunteering you to help Mom with Thanksgiving dinner."

I sit back in my seat, studying her face for any signs that she's upset. "Is that okay with you? I mean, I don't know what kind of traditions you guys have, but Seb made it seem like—"

"Oh, no, Nadia, I'm not upset!" The words come out in a rush, accompanied by a laugh. "I have no interest in getting in the kitchen with Mom on any day, but especially not Thanksgiving. She can be kind of...intense."

"Oh, okay." I find myself smiling. "Thanks for the warning, I don't think she could be any worse than Elle is during the dinner rush though."

"You're not in the kitchen cooking alongside Elle during the dinner rush, Nadia," Zoe deadpans.

"Sooo, should I be scared?"

"Not scared, just vigilant."

"Got it. Anything else I should know about navigating my first Adler Thanksgiving?"

She twists her lips to the side, gazing heavenward. "Umm, it's usually just us, but I think Aunt Adrienne will come this year since she just moved to New Haven."

"Aunt Adrienne, that's Vince's mom, right?" I fight to hide the tremor of disgust that runs through me when I say Vince's name.

"Yep, she's very sweet, though, you'll like her.

"Will Vince be there?"

Zoe's brows pull together. "I'm not sure, but he usually goes wherever Aunt Adrienne does during the holidays. He's a huge mama's boy."

I laugh when she rolls her eyes. I'm sure she's spent her whole life exasperated by her brothers' and cousin's obsession with their mothers.

"I hear you. Thank you for the info, Zo."

"Of course," she says, hopping up out of her seat. "I knew I had to come give you the 4-1-1 because Sebastian wouldn't. He thinks threatening everyone to be on their best behavior around the woman he loves is enough to make everything go well."

The woman he loves.

My heart flutters and then starts to pound. Zoe must sense that something is wrong because she pauses and gives me a strange look.

"Did he..did he say that to you?" I wheeze my way through the question. "That he loves me?"

"I don't want to be the one to tell you how Sebastian feels about you, Nadia," she says with a frown. "But if he hasn't said it to you, he's definitely shown you."

There's that panic again. Those ice cold fingers of anxiety wrapping around my throat and squeezing until my breathing becomes labored.

Zoe comes around the desk and grips my shoulder. "Nadia, are you okay?"

My chest hurts, and my head is spinning with thoughts and questions that are all over the place, ranging from wondering when it got so hot in my office to why Zoe insinuating that her brother is in love with me has triggered the first full blown panic attack I've had in months.

I can't answer her. I can't say anything, all I can do is grab at my chest while my breathing grows increasingly labored. Zoe's eyes go wide and she starts to back away from me. I don't know when she leaves the office or how long she's gone, but when she comes back Sebastian is with her. He's in front of me in seconds, his hands on my face and then moving to my arms. He takes my hands in his, linking our fingers together.

"Look at me, precious," he orders, his voice gentle and harsh all at the same time. My eyes snap to his. "Good girl, now focus on my face, focus on me, and *breathe*. Nice and slow through your nose. I'll count, okay? Listen to me count."

I squeeze his fingers and nod, letting him know that I hear him, that I'm listening. It's not much, but it's enough to get him to the start the box breathing technique I taught him a few weeks ago when he asked me how I dealt with my anxiety.

He counts from one to four, his voice low and even, a melody in my ears that tells me when to start each breath and when to end it. I don't know how long we stay like that, Sebastian counting and me breathing, but when it's over, and I'm calm enough, Zoe is gone and the office is quiet.

Sebastian disentangles his fingers from mine, bringing one of his hands up my jaw, cradling my face with a gentleness that brings tears to my eyes, that makes me wonder why the thought of this man loving me scares me so badly.

"What happened?" he asks.

"Nothing, I just—"

"*Nadia.*" He shakes his head, disapproval pulling his lips down into a flat line. "Don't lie to me. Tell me what's wrong, so I can fix it."

My heart shatters into a million pieces because I know that no matter how much he might want to, Sebastian can't fix me.

I clear my throat, hoping the momentary delay will give me courage. "Zoe and I were talking, and she…she said something about you being in love with me."

Sebastian's hand drops into my lap, and there's no denying the hurt turning his eyes into storm clouds. He pushes to his feet, and I reach for him, but I'm not fast enough to catch him. Thankfully, he doesn't go far, taking a seat on the edge of my desk.

"And the thought of me loving you scared you so badly that you had a panic attack?"

He's not trying to be hurtful, but the question still sends pain shooting through my chest. It seems to match the wound I've given him, the one I've allowed to fester because of my fear.

"No, Sebastian, it's not like that."

"Then what is it like, Nadia?"

I can't stay seated any longer, so I stand and push my chair under the desk to give me room to pace. The movement is necessary, it helps me think, helps me explain things to him that even I don't fully understand.

"It's like when you look at me, you see me. You see me so clearly, more clearly than I've seen myself in years."

"And that's a bad thing?"

"No! Yes." I scrub a hand down my face. "I don't know. I don't think it's a bad thing, it's just you look at me and see this woman who's strong and capable—"

He crosses his arms. "Because that's who you are."

"Except it's not, Sebastian!" My voice cracks. "You fell in love with a version of me that doesn't exist. I'm not strong, I'm not capable, I'm not whole." I gesture at my chest, at the invisible hole in the center of my body that refuses to close.

"Nadia, you are—"

"Broken, Sebastian. I'm broken. I'm always going to be broken. That's why the thought of you loving me scares me because you don't know, you don't *see...*"

The ugliness. The scars. The bruises, cuts and broken bones.

Sebastian stands, and when I think he's going to go, that he's finally realized that I'm a lost cause, he comes closer, he pulls me in and puts his fingers under my chin, forcing me to look at him.

"I see you, Nadia. I see the woman in front of me, and I love her." Tears gather in my eyes and skate down my cheeks. He wipes them away and continues. "I see the hurt and traumatized woman lurking in the shadows of your eyes, and I love her. I see the woman I'll build a future with, and I love her. I see my wife, the mother of my kids, the partner I'll trust with everything and deprive of nothing, and I love her. *I love you.* I know everything there is to know about you, and what I don't know I'll learn. You don't have to run from me, Nadia, and you don't have to be scared. I don't just want the polished, perfect version of you. I want the broken one too. I want every version of you because every version of you belongs with me."

Gentle fingers move the hair in my face behind my ear, gentler eyes hold me hostage, and I surrender to their hold. Allowing myself to disappear in pools of champagne that promise me a life beyond my fear, an existence not dictated by my doubts. Knowing that this is what Sebastian meant on our first day together when he said our commitment was just the beginning.

A stepping stone we'd use to launch a future where running is a thing you do because you're in a rush, not because you're scared for your life.

Where pain is a possibility but not an expectation.

Where love is loud and grief is quiet but not lonely.

I leave my fear in the inky depths of his eyes and emerge clean and unafraid. Not fully healed, not quite whole, but together just enough to lend my voice to the emotions blooming in my chest.

"I love you too."

30

NADIA

Two weeks of exchanging I love yous with Sebastian have me feeling like I'm living in a fairy tale. Every day there's goodness beyond what I thought I'd find in this lifetime. Love with no boundaries and desire that doesn't wane even when we're in a room full of people at a charity event for a foundation I never heard of before tonight in a dress made by a designer whose name I can't pronounce.

Sebastian had the caviar black halter dress covered in Swarovski crystals custom made to match the fabric used to make his tuxedo, and when we saw each other dressed to the nines, looking and smelling divine, we nearly tore each other apart. I'm glad we settled for a quick and steamy session in the back of the limo on the way to the event because it's been such a lovely night I would have been sad to miss it, to lose out on a chance to watch Sebastian be honored by the New Haven Victim Assistance Network for the buildings he's converted into shelters for women and children.

I cried when he gave his speech, when he spoke about the work he's been doing long before he met me, and how he's become more passionate about it because of me. The moment he stepped off the stage, I was in his arms, crying once again, which has become something of a norm for me these days. Now we're dancing and I can still feel moisture lingering in my eyes, ready to fall at any given moment.

"Why do you look like you're going to cry again?"

Sebastian's hands are on my waist, and his lips are at my ear. We're in a room full of people, surrounded by bodies and the sound of flowing conversation, but to me it feels like it's just us. We're in a moment again. We've been in a moment for the past two weeks, but I don't run from them anymore. I let myself stay in it. I let myself stay with him, and he takes care of me.

"Because I keep getting reminded of how amazing you are, and it makes me love you a little more."

"Just a little?" he asks, a teasing lilt to his tone as he spins me around the floor. "Because I thought you'd be head over heels by now."

"I am, and every time I think I can't fall any deeper, you go and prove me wrong."

"What can I say? I'm good like that."

"Don't make me regret giving you a compliment, Mr. Adler."

"I'll do my best, Miss Hendrix."

His hand goes to my back, and the dip he lowers me into pulls a surprise but delighted gasp from me. And when he comes down too, placing a hot, wet, open mouth kiss on my neck, I let out a breathless moan that has him lifting me back up and staring at me with heated eyes.

"Let's go home, precious."

I know why he wants to leave. I know what he wants. I want it too. I've wanted it all night. With him, I want it all the time, but I don't want to cut this night short when he's the honoree.

"Sebastian, we can't go. Tonight is about you."

"And I've already fulfilled all of my duties for the night, which means—" his hands skating down my sides and around to my ass to grab an inappropriately incendiary handful "—I can take you home, get you out of this dress and make you come so many times you forget your own name."

"Which one?" I joke, hoping a shared laugh will keep us from ripping each other's clothes off in the middle of the dance floor.

" Any of them. *All* of them." We're chest to chest. His forehead resting on mine. Our eyes focused on nothing but each other. "Nadia Hendrix. Nyla Hawthorne. The future Mrs. Adler. Take your pick."

My heart skips a beat. Since we started saying 'I love you,' Sebastian has been generous with the phrase and with words that communicate his promise to put a ring on my finger. And every time he does, my heart skips a beat and my brain short circuits and I panic a little before I remember that this man knows me. He knows all my secrets and my shame, and he still loves me. He still wants to share his life with me. He still wants to marry me.

Every reminder he gives me, every hint at our future, acts as a salve on a wound I didn't think would ever heal. Quiets the voice in my head that still repeats Beau's lies sometimes, that still believes I'm worthless and undeserving of a love as good as this. Of a man as good as him.

"I love you." It's all I can say, and all I need to say.

Sebastian's eyes melt, going soft in that way they only do for me. "So you'll come home with me then?"

"Yes." I rise up on my tip toes and give him a soft kiss. "After I use the ladies room, and you say goodbye to your brother and thank Sienna for the award."

He's grimacing as I spin out of his hold and head to the bathroom, leaving him to embark on a brief farewell tour on both of our behalves. It won't take him long since his parents and Zoe have already left and Andreas wasn't able to make it. That means all he has to do is find Luca and Sienna, and, judging by the energy that's been passing between the two of them all evening, he'll probably luck up and find them somewhere together.

The line for the bathroom closest to the ballroom is packed, so I head up to the second floor of the venue to attend to my needier than usual bladder and rejoice when I get to pee in complete privacy. When I'm done, I start to head back down the stairs but pause near the top when I see what feels to me like a familiar frame in a slinky red dress heading out the door. I only catch her profile—milky skin, one high cheekbone, the tip of a button nose and a fleeting streak of blonde hair —but I know it's her.

"Bianca?"

I rush down the steps, needing to see, needing to confirm for myself that it's her, but by the time my heels hit the first floor, she's gone. Still, I push my way through the crowd of people making their way outside and stumble out onto the side walk hoping that I can catch her. Disapproving exclamations caused by my rudeness hit my back as I scan the road in front of me, and I don't care because I have to see. I have to know. Because if Bianca is in New Haven, that means Beau must be too.

"Nadia?"

I turn and see Luca standing to my left near the valet stand, looking at me like I've lost my mind. I think I probably have. My heartbeat is erratic, and the thought of Beau being in New Haven, close enough to touch me, close enough to hurt me, to hurt Sebastian, has anxiety clawing its way through my chest.

Oh, no, not again, not now.

A panic attack is the last thing I need. I place my palm over my heart and push out a breath, forcing myself to smile like I haven't just seen a ghost. "Luca, hey."

His head tilts to the side, and he moves closer to me. "You okay?"

I swallow the truth, which is that I'm not okay at all, and give him a lie. "I'm fine. I just needed some air."

"Yeah, me too." Even though I know there's no hope of me finding Bianca now, I still keep searching the street for her. I'm trying to be covert, but Luca is paying a little too much attention tonight. "You sure you're okay?" he asks, both of his brows pulled together in a mix of concern and confusion.

I force my gaze back to his face, angling my body toward him to show that I'm fully engaged in the conversation now. "I'm fine. Did you have a good evening?"

Sebastian and his siblings don't look alike to me, but right now, with Luca grimacing the way his older brother was when I left him standing in the middle of the dance floor, they look more alike than ever.

"Something like that."

Now my brows are the ones pulling together. Luca is usually the most upbeat, happy guy I know. Nothing gets to him. Hell, he even managed to smile and joke his way through the news that their father almost had a heart attack and died—information Everett was forced to reveal when it came out that there would be no deep fried turkey at Thanksgiving this year—which makes the persistent frown marring his features particularly disturbing.

"Wanna talk about it?"

Tucking his hands into his pockets, he turns away from me, focusing back on the street. It's a defense mechanism, a way to keep me from seeing that he's about to try to bullshit me. "About what?"

"Whatever is going on between you and Sienna Ryder. You two have been exchanging looks all night, and it's clear by the energy passing between you that there's history there."

Tension turns his jaw to stone. "There's nothing going on between me and Sienna Ryder."

That's a lie. It's clear from the way he says her name. And if I wasn't a person used to guarding secrets with her life, I'd push him for answers, demand details for my own selfish reasons like sating my curiosity or taking my mind off the possible Bianca sighting.

"It's okay if you don't want to talk about it, Luca."

"There's nothing to talk about, Nadia."

The valet arrives with his car, and he finally looks at me again, glancing between me and the door. "Do you want me to wait with you? I'm sure Seb won't be long."

"No, I'm going to head back inside and get him."

"You sure? Because if he finds out I left you standing on the side-walk in the middle of the night, I'm never going to hear the end of it."

"Damn right you won't."

Luca and I turn to find Sebastian walking up behind us. He looks mildly agitated, but I think that has more to do with me and my disappearing act than his little brother. When those stormy pools of champagne land on me, all censure and desire, I know that I'm right.

"I thought *you* were going to the bathroom and coming right back," he says, looping an arm around my waist and dragging me to his side.

"And I thought you were saying your goodbyes."

"You told me to say goodbye to two people, precious, one of whom is standing out here with you."

"Well I guess that should make it easy for you to complete your task. Now—" I reach up and pinch his cheek, putting on my best baby talk voice just to annoy him "—*say goodnight to Luca.*"

Sebastian hardly ever rolls his eyes, and when he does, it always makes me laugh because the act seems completely at odds with his usually serious demeanor. Tonight, I'm laughing extra hard because he's rolling his eyes at me while wearing a tuxedo and holding an award that speaks not only of his kindness but the influence that comes with his name. In my experience, men like that take themselves far too serious to indulge in an act normally attributed to teenage girls, so it makes me a weird kind of happy to know that the man I love is capable of both unwavering austerity and playful annoyance.

He pulls my hand away from his face, forcing me to release my hold on his cheek so he can bring one of the offending fingers to his mouth and bite it. It's more of a nibble, really, but it still does ridiculous things to my body. Like sending sparks down my spine and heat to my cheeks, as well as other parts of me that I should not be thinking about when we're standing in front of his little brother.

Luca huffs out a dry laugh and shakes his head. "Night, you two."

"Goodnight, Luc," Sebastian returns, a smirk pulling his lips into a devilish line that makes my thighs clench with anticipation. I know what that mouth can do. I've witnessed it. I've woken up to it and went to sleep dreaming about it too many times to count, but I still crave it like I've never had it before. The man could be licking my literal bones, and I'd still ask him to give me more. To go deeper. To lap at me until his teeth, tongue and taste buds collide with marrow, until he's consuming the very essence of me.

Amusement and desire dance in Sebastian's eyes. "Hold that thought, precious. We still have to get the car."

Thankfully, tonight the car comes with a driver, a partition and enough leg room for me to drop down to my knees in front of Sebastian the moment we're alone. My fingers are impatient as they work to undo the buttons holding his pants together, and Sebastian laughs.

"You could just ask for help," he says as he takes over undressing himself.

"I don't want help, I want your dick in my mouth."

"You can have both, baby."

Before I can respond, his dick is free. It stands at attention in front of me, proudly erect with a bead of precum emerging from the slit at the top that I scoop up with the tip of my tongue. Sebastian lets out a hiss while his hips lift in a silent demand for more. I oblige, gripping his shaft with two hands and opening wide to swallow his weeping tip.

"*Fuck.*"

His hips lift again, and his fingers go to my hair, grasping the silky strands with a force that renders me motionless for a second. I shake my head, dislodging his hold to remind him he's not in control right now. Out of the corner of my eye, I see him dig his fingers into the leather of the seat, and I smile to myself, knowing it has to be killing him to let me control the tempo.

Because of how desperate I was to have him in my mouth, I know he's expecting this to go fast, for me to take him to the back of my throat over and over again, fucking him with the wet heat of my mouth. That's actually exactly what I was planning to give him, but his impatience has earned him something else.

With both hands holding him steady, I decide to focus solely on his tip. Licking and sucking and swirling my tongue around the sensitive head with the gentlest pressure and the lightest flicks of my tongue on the bottom side where the head connects to his shaft.

"Jesus, Nadia, *please.*"

I flick my eyes up to his face and find beads of sweat on his brow and desperation etched into his features, and I'm hit, suddenly, with the thought that no one gets to see him like this but me. No one gets to unravel him, to take him apart piece by piece and put him back together again. That honor is all mine, and I won't cede it to anyone. I won't give it up for anything, not even the demons from my past.

The realization is a catalyst, urging me to go faster, to take him deeper, to push him to the brink of pleasure and then one step beyond it. When I pick up the pace, Sebastian throws his head back and his throat constricts, tightening around a guttural moan that starts to tear through him at the same time his dick begins to pulse in my mouth. Instead of pulling back, I push down, welcoming the hot spurts of his satisfaction into my throat and swallowing them down. It takes a while for him to finish, but I don't move until he's done, until I've wrung him out and licked him clean.

"God damn," he pants, eyes filled with wonder as he wipes the corner of my mouth with his thumb. "You're incredible, you know that?"

"I do."

We're both grinning like fools when the car comes to a sudden stop in front of my building. The abrupt break in movement causes my stomach to turn, and I frown, placing a hand on my belly to still the sudden wave of nausea.

"You okay?" Sebastian asks as the driver opens the door.

I can't answer him because I'm too busy scrambling to my feet, rushing out of the door and past the driver, making it to the standing potted plant next to the entrance to my floor just in time to vomit in the soil. I'm still heaving when Sebastian makes it to me, and I try to push him away, to keep him from seeing, and smelling, the contents of my stomach that are most definitely going to kill the poor snake plant inside the pot.

"No, go away." I try to swat him with the one hand that's not clutching my stomach, but he refuses to budge, so I give up. When he sees that I've surrendered, he gently lifts my hair away from my face and holds it quietly until I'm done.

Feeling disgusted and suddenly exhausted, I wipe my mouth and try to straighten only for the world to go fuzzy right in front of my face. I sway to the right, and Sebastian is right there, scooping me up into his arms.

"Are you okay?"

I close my eyes because keeping them open when the world is spinning makes me more nauseous. "Yeah, I think I just stood up too fast after..."

Ugh. Just saying the word vomit makes me dry heave. Sebastian's eyes go wide with increasing alarm when my body tenses like it's preparing for another purge, but he doesn't let me go, he just starts walking, moving to the door that the driver—a man named Lincoln, I think—is holding open.

I keep my eyes squeezed tight and try to focus on breathing while Sebastian walks gingerly to the apartment, obviously trying not to trigger my already upset stomach. Once we're inside, he carries me all the way into my bedroom, sits me down on the bed, and starts to undress me.

The heels are the first thing to go, and I moan my appreciation at being released from footwear hell.

"Nadia," Sebastian says, his tortured voice leaving me with no choice but to open my eyes and look at him. He's on his knees with my right shoe still dangling from his fingertip. "Don't make sounds like that when you're sick."

"I'm not sick."

"You just—"

I hold up a hand. "Don't! Don't say anything that even alludes to what I just did to that potted plant."

He gives me a look that calls me ridiculous but eventually gives in. "Fine. I won't say it, but we both know what happened and what it means for our night, so no moaning, okay?"

"I'll try my best, babe, but you've still got to take me out of this dress, and the strapless bra, so you might hear a sigh of pleasure or something."

He bites back the smile trying to tip up one corner of his mouth and offers me his hand. I take it, allowing him to lift me off the bed and whispering a silent prayer of thanks that being on my feet doesn't come with another wave of nausea.

"Turn around."

Moving with a world of caution, I spin in his arms, and his fingers go to the hidden zipper holding my dress together at the back. I don't moan when he finally gets me out of it, but I definitely let out a relieved breath or two. Those sounds of contentment are the soundtrack for the rest of our night, playing on repeat while Sebastian wraps my hair, washes me under the steam of water raining down on both our naked forms, and finally, after completing my seven step skin care routine, lotioning my entire body and putting me on my favorite pair of silk pajamas, puts me to bed.

"I'm sorry if me being sick ruined the end of your night," I whisper.

Sebastian lays a tender kiss to the top of my head. "You didn't ruin anything, precious. Go to sleep. You'll feel better in the morning."

I'm swaddled in the comforter and the warmth of his body, already half asleep when his words reach my ears, so I do as he says, falling into a fitful sleep that's filled with dreams of Bianca and Beau.

31

SEBASTIAN

Nadia doesn't feel better the morning after the gala. Or the morning after that. For two days, she's been sick. Throwing up off and on and sleeping when she's not hugging the toilet. I don't know what's going on with her, what stomach bug she's caught, but as I'm sitting in my office at Ludus, listening to Russ give his update on Beau Montgomery, I'm wondering if maybe I caught it too.

Because I do feel sick.

But that probably has more to do with the words that just came out of Russ' mouth.

"What do you mean he's not in LA?"

Russ is the toughest motherfucker I know. I've never seen him look so much as worried about anything in his life, but when my fists slam into my desk and my voice booms over his head, he flinches. It's a small flinch, but a flinch nonetheless, and that's how I know this conversation is going to go to shit real fucking fast.

"I mean that after Nadia disappeared, Beau left LA to find her. He went to Florida first because that's where she was supposed to be with her…" he hesitates, and that annoys me. Everything he says and does that isn't giving me a solution to the threat Beau Montgomery's existence poses to Nadia's safety annoys me. I narrow my eyes at him, and he continues, abandoning his broken sentence. "He left LA and went to Florida, and we don't know where he went or what he did after that. It's like he fell off the face of the Earth, completely abandoned his operation in LA, left several of the girls living in his house. No one has seen or heard from him in months."

"You think he's dead?"

It would be the preferred outcome, but I doubt that's what's happened. Nadia called Beau a snake, and snakes like to hide out underground when the conditions above become unfavorable. Losing his living, breathing punching bag that he holds responsible for every bad thing that's ever happened in his life, would constitute as unfavorable conditions for Beau.

Russ shakes his head. "No. There are no bodies in the morgue in Los Angles county or any of the surrounding counties matching his description."

"What about the girls that work for him?"

"What about them?"

"Have any of them heard from him? Seen him? Are they at all concerned about how they're going to make ends meet without him?"

"They've all moved on," Russ says. "Even the girls living in his house are working for someone else now or doing it on their own. As far as I can tell, the consensus is that Beau isn't coming back, so they've all figured out new ways to survive."

His words make my chest tight, and for the first time in a long time, I feel fear run a circuit through my system. I, admittedly, haven't been operating in the world of sex work for long, but I feel pretty confident in saying that Beau abandoning his only source of income is virtually unheard of. Traffickers like him put a lot of time into building their roster of girls and spend even more of that time manipulating and abusing those girls to get and keep them under their control, all in the name of money. That Beau would walk away from everything he's built, leaving no safeguards or procession plan in place, to hunt down Nadia speaks of a dangerous level of determination.

I've dealt with men who operate with single minded focus. That doesn't scare me. But that focus is normally money, and when I prove that I can give them what they want, they walk away happy, never to be heard from again. The problem with Beau is that the one thing he wants is the only thing I'll never let go of.

My phone vibrates on my desk. I pick it up and see two texts from Nadia that came in within seconds of each other.

> Nadia: Guess who ate three saltines and drank a can of ginger ale without vomiting?!

> Nadia: Me. In case you were wondering, it was me.

The smile that tugs up the corners of my mouth is impossible to resist, so I give in to it, letting it take over my whole face as I text back.

> Sebastian: Good job, precious.

"You really love her, don't you?" Russ asks, pulling my attention away from my phone.

I nod, feeling vulnerable as hell. "More than anything, which is why I need you to put together a security detail as soon as possible."

"How long do I have to get it done? The guys I'd prefer to work with will need a few days to get stateside."

"You don't know anyone local?"

"The only guy in New Haven I'd work with is Hunter Drake. He runs a self-defense gym on the outskirts of town that he started when a gig we did together went sideways. He won't get back in a suit for anyone."

I glance at my calendar. Thanksgiving is in two days, so Nadia will be by my side until she goes back to work on Friday. I tried to talk her into taking off Friday and the weekend too, but with Nic and Sloane's engagement party happening on Saturday she wasn't having it.

"Get them here by Thursday night. I don't care what it costs."

Russ nods. "Yes, sir."

"Is that everything you have for me?" I ask, eager to get back to Nadia.

"I've got one more thing, but it's not related to Beau Montgomery."

Since Beau is my top priority at the moment, I'm tempted to tell him to table it for another day, but something about his expression tells me I need to know now.

"What is it?"

* * *

WHEN I WALK through Nadia's front door a little over an hour later, I have miso soup in one hand and a dossier containing information about her paternal grandparents in the other.

Russ stumbled across it when he was doing his initial deep dive into her. Apparently, someone as good at what they do as Russ is at what he does, had Nadia's real name flagged and reached out a few days ago. Russ met with them first, vetting them before he brought any information to me, and now I have papers in my hand that won't do a damn thing for Nadia but open up old wounds.

She's curled up on the couch when I come in, looking adorable in one of my t-shirts with a haphazardly tied scarf on her head. The can of ginger ale she was so proud of drinking sits empty on the coffee table in front of her, and there are saltine crumbs on the corner of her mouth when I kiss her.

"Babe! Don't kiss me on the mouth! We still don't know what I had, and I don't want to get you sick."

"If you really think a little stomach bug is going to stop me from kissing you, you don't know me at all."

"If you think I'm going to hold your hair while you hug the toilet, you don't know *me* at all," she tosses back, all sass and good health thanks to my diligent care-taking which apparently means nothing to her.

"Damn, it's like that?" I sit down on the coffee table, blocking her view of the TV, and she giggles. "I nurse you back to health and bring you miso soup to celebrate you finally being able to keep some food down, and that's how you gone treat me?"

Upon mention of the soup, her eyes go to my hands, but they skip right over the soup and go to the folder. She sits up, looking more alert than she has in days. "What's that? Is it about Beau?"

I put the soup on the table behind me and shake my head. "No, it's not about Beau. Russ didn't have any new information on him."

It's not a lie, but it's also not quite the truth. I just don't think it's worth it to tell her what Russ said when it amounts to a whole bunch of nothing that will just make her scared.

"Then what is it, Seb? Is it about me?" Her eyes search my face, and I have no choice but to answer her, to tell her this truth if only to make up for not telling her the other one.

"Yes. It's about you and your grandparents."

"The Hawthornes? What about them?"

"They're looking for you."

Her brows knit together, forming a long line of confusion. "They're what?"

Slowly, with my eyes still on hers, I open the file Russ gave me and place it in her hands. Inside is a printed copy of Russ' email correspondence with a private investigator from Los Angeles named Jeremiah Savage. Nadia scans the documents, reading the same words I read an hour ago in my office, learning that her grandfather Timothy Hawthorne, and her grandmother, Lucy, have been trying to track her down for six months.

"Jeremiah, the Hawthorne's PI, told Russ that they want to know you. Apparently, your grandfather had a health scare at the beginning of the year that put some things in perspective for him."

She closes the folder and tosses it on the coffee table beside me. "And I'm supposed to, what? Drop everything and go running into their arms? Forgive them for hating my mom just because she was poor? Act like they didn't leave me on my own to grieve my parents when I was 16 fucking years old?"

I watch her bring her knees up to her chest and hug them. It's such a protective position, one that comes from years of having to soothe herself, of having no one else to lean on when she was in pain. She doesn't have to do that anymore though, and I remind her of that fact by moving to the couch and sitting beside her, by wrapping my arms around her shoulders and pulling her close.

"You don't have to do any of those things." My lips are at her temple, and I lay a kiss there. "I just wanted to bring this information to you in case you wanted to take advantage of the chance to have a family again."

Nadia turns to me, her eyes rippling pools of genuine emotion. "*You're* my family."

32

NADIA

"Pecan pie *cheesecake*?" Des' nose wrinkles in disgust as she sifts through the hangers on the clothing rack. We were supposed to be getting lunch and catching up before she leaves to see her family in North Carolina for Thanksgiving, but we got distracted by the opening of a new boutique and ended up shopping instead.

"Don't knock it 'til you try it, babe."

"Have *you* tried it? Because you know the rule of all Black households is that you don't experiment on Thanksgiving."

"Yes, Des, I made it a few weeks ago, and Sebastian loved it."

"Sebastian loves you, that means his opinions on your cooking can't be trusted."

"Elle also loved it," I toss back. "And she's not in love with me."

Instead of responding, she sticks her tongue out at me and saunters off toward the dressing room with several dresses looped over her arm, leaving me to ponder the wisdom of debuting a dessert at my first Thanksgiving with the Adlers. I'm trying to find jeans in my size that will also be long enough to reach my ankles when the hairs on the back of neck stand at attention and the unbidden sensation of eyes on me sends fear trickling down my spine.

Knowing my propensity for anxiety based overreactions, I push a calming breath out and turn my head slowly, glancing over my shoulder in the most casual way possible. Considering that my heart is currently slapping against my ribs, it's not the most convincing act. The woman standing beside me with her newborn strapped to her chest gives me a wary look, and I almost laugh because everything in her eyes says that the last thing she needs right now is an encounter with a crazy woman. The smile I give her is brittle, so it doesn't do much to calm her, and she tosses the shoes in her hand back on the shelf and walks away.

I'm too preoccupied with the lingering feeling of being watched to be offended, and when I swing my gaze in the other direction, I see the same shock of blonde hair from the gala heading towards the front door.

"Wait!" I shout, drawing the attention of every shopper in the boutique. They all watch as I rush through the maze of clothing racks and jewelry displays to follow the ghost from my past out the door. I catch up to her just as she's about to cross the street, my hand wraps around her elbow, and I yank her back, forcing her to face me.

Green eyes that have watched me cry, studied my bruises, crinkled with humor in the wake of a rare display of my sense of humor, and narrowed with jealousy and contempt when she thought I was getting everything she deserved, meet mine, and we both stand there staring at each other, stunned into silence.

Bianca breaks first, breaking free from my hold and tucking blonde strands, that are shorter than they were the last time I saw her, behind her ear. "Nyla, hey."

"*Hey?*" The step I take back is more of a stumble that suggests she's struck me. I guess in a way she has because 'hey' is too casual a greeting coming from a woman whose presence on this sidewalk means trouble has come to New Haven, and it's coming for me. "Is that all you have to say, Bianca?"

"What do you want me to say?"

Now I want to strike her, my hands ball into fists as if to signal the desire I'm suppressing. "I don't know. Maybe you could start with telling me how you found me and where Beau is hiding?"

"Beau?" She repeats, confusion pulling her pouty lips down into a frown. "I'm not here with Beau, Nyla."

"Don't lie to me, Bianca. Why else would you be here, in New Haven of all places? Why else would you be stalking me?"

Her head falls back, and the throaty laughter that spills from her lips takes me back to the days when she was the only bright spot in my life. My heart is still pounding, my brain screaming at me to walk away from her because Beau could appear at any moment, so I don't have time for her laughter.

"Bianca, I'm serious," I say, scanning the sidewalk for any sign of him.

"I know." She giggles, looking back at me. "That's what makes it so funny. You still think the entire world revolves around you, Nyla."

There's the contempt again. The thinly veiled dislike I've done nothing to deserve from the woman who was supposed to be my best friend.

"I don't think the world revolves around me, but I do think that it can't be a coincidence that you're here, in the place I ran to when I escaped your boyfriend."

All traces of humor leave her face, and she turns somber, crossing her arms over her chest. It's the first time I notice that she's dressed nice. Like *really* nice. Nicer than she ever did when she was with Beau. Her hair is trimmed and has been recently styled, her clothes aren't quite designer, but they're more expensive than her usual threads, and her skin is smooth and supple. She looks healthy.

"Beau is not my boyfriend anymore."

"What?"

A strong breeze sweeps down the sidewalk, bringing a snap of cold with it. Bianca shivers, rubbing at the thin fabric of her red trench coat. "Can we not have this conversation on the sidewalk?"

"I'm not going to a secondary location with you."

Her brows pull together. "A secondary location? Nyla, please. This isn't a true crime documentary." My only response is my own crossed arms and lifted brow, which makes her sigh. She looks over her shoulder and then back at me. "There's a cafe right there on the corner. We could sit down, get warm, have a cup of coffee and I can tell you all about how and why I left Beau's sorry ass in the dust."

Bianca has been known to be manipulative, so I don't completely trust that the teaser about her leaving Beau was just an innocent slip of the tongue. In fact, I know it wasn't, but it doesn't stop me from shooting Des a quick text promising to call and explain why I had to leave so suddenly and following her inside the cafe. Once we're seated at a table by the window with our coffees in hand, I sit back in my chair and cross my arms.

"Start talking."

She takes a long sip of her coffee, probably just to get on my nerves. When she finally starts talking, she looks away from me, shame clouding her eyes. "I guess I should start with an apology."

"An apology? For what?"

"For believing the lies Beau told me about you stealing clients from me. For being a bad friend to you. I never should have trusted him." Her fingers are in her lap underneath the table, but I know her well enough to know that she's picking at her cuticles. It's the one nervous tic she has.

"He started hitting you."

I don't ask because there's no need to phrase it as a question when I already know. Beau is an abuser, and that desire to exert control and impart fear doesn't die when your chosen victim leaves.

Bianca nods, finally bringing her eyes back to mine. "When you didn't come home, he lost it and started taking it out on me."

My heart splits in two, and all my apprehension falls away. I reach across the table with my palm facing up, and she takes it. "I'm sorry, B. I never wanted to leave you, but I..."

"You had to," she says, finishing for me. "I get it, Nyla. If you stayed, he probably would have killed you eventually."

A tremor runs through me, and I want to tell her that I wasn't running to avoid death, that leaving put me in more danger than staying ever could have because the only promise Beau ever made me, the one he used to keep me from running after the first time I tried to leave, is that he would kill me if I did it again. He locked me in a room for days, only coming in to beat me within an inch of my life. Every time I so much as thought about running, those beatings were in my head, a reminder of what would happen if I was caught. A reference of violence that made me think death was preferable to life.

"He got close a few times, but I'm still here. We both are."

Bianca squeezes my fingers. "Yeah, you're right. We are."

"How did you get away?"

"After you didn't come back from the job in Florida, Beau lost it. At first he got really mean and nasty, taking all of his anger and frustration out on me, and then one day I woke up and he was just...gone."

"Gone?"

She nods. "Gone. No one knew where he was or if he was coming back, and I didn't care. I grabbed all my shit and ran to my cousin in Pasadena."

"Tiffany?" I ask, recalling the name of the only family Bianca has in California. I never met her, but Bianca says she was the one who got her into sex work in the first place.

"Yeah, I hid out at her place for a while, avoiding work because I was scared I was going to end up running into Beau at a party or something. Then I just got tired of being scared and not being able to afford any of the shit I like, so I started working with Tiff. She introduced me to Omar, the client I'm here with. He paid me ten grand to come home with him for the holidays and pretend to be his long term girlfriend." She smiles and lets go of my hand so she can gesture to her outfit. "The clothes came with the gig, and I get to keep them after we're done."

The tension that was lining my shoulders melts away when I realize that this, her being here in New Haven, is just kismet. I'm not accustomed to happenstance, to random acts of fate that don't spell disaster for me.

"That's great, B." I take a sip of my coffee, willing my stomach not to rebel because this is the first time I've had anything other than water or ginger ale since the night of the gala. "Were you two at a gala the other night? I could have sworn I saw you."

"Oh, yeah. That domestic violence thing?"

"Yeah, you were wearing a red dress. I thought I caught a glimpse of you walking out the door."

"At least someone there saw me in it. Omar and I got there late. We missed dinner and everything, and then the asshole bailed on me." Her nose wrinkles in annoyance, and I'm hit with the sudden memory of her rehashing all the details of her dates with clients while I remained tight lipped about mine. "Apparently his ex-girlfriend heard about him bringing me home and wanted to have a conversation with him."

"That sounds... complicated. Where's Omar now?"

"On a work call or something?" She shrugs. "I didn't ask questions when he gave me a stack of cash and told me to make myself scarce for a few hours."

"Sounds like a good set up."

Her eyes rove over my face, and I know she's doing the same visual assessment I did of her just minutes ago. "Not as good of a set up as what you have going on here. You've got me thinking maybe I should stay in New Haven and find me a big spender to finance my life."

I bristle internally. This is what I've always hated about my relationship with Bianca. It takes all of five seconds for us to go from nice, normal conversation to verbal jabs and back handed compliments.

"No one is financing my life, Bianca. I have a job, and I make good money that allows me to take care of myself." It's not exactly the truth considering the fact that I've yet to successfully make a rent payment, but it's all I'm willing to give her because I'm damn sure not going to tell her about Sebastian, Cerros or any other good thing in my life.

"Calm down. I was just making conversation," she says finally, drumming her nails on the table. "So, tell me, what happened to you after you left for that job in Florida?"

I tell her everything I'm comfortable sharing, which is mostly information about the horror movie of a weekend that laid the foundation for my escape. She gasps when I tell her about the accident, and tears well in her eyes when I admit to praying for death.

"After the accident, I ended up here in New Haven. I met some kind people who helped me out and got a good job."

"Are you planning on staying here?" My eyes narrow into slits, and Bianca laughs. "Damn, Nyla, I'm just asking a question. It's not like I'm going to call Beau and tell him you're here. I wouldn't even know how to reach him."

"Do you think he's looking for me?"

Bianca stares at me for a long second before she answers. "You know he used to say that your life and his were linked? When you left, he'd say it all the time. He'd get drunk and beat me and mumble about how you had to come back to him because your life was his. To control. To ruin. To *take*."

The emphasis on the last word makes my heart stop. My fingers shake as I bring my cup to my lips and take a sip of coffee I can't even taste.

"What's that supposed to mean, Bianca?"

"It means I don't *think* he's looking for you, Nyla. I *know* he is. And when he finds you, which I swear I won't help him do, I hope you have more than a few kind people in your corner."

33

NADIA

Zoe's warnings about how intense Madeline gets in the kitchen during Thanksgiving has, thus far, been an exaggeration. Sebastian and I arrived a little after noon and found her playing music and drinking wine while she mixed up the cornbread needed to make the dressing. She welcomed me with open arms, ordering Sebastian to put the cheesecake I made in the fridge and exit the kitchen immediately to leave the two of us to our work. Sebastian left me with a kiss on the forehead and then ran off to find his father and siblings in another part of the house.

We've been at it for a few hours now, and the only thing left to do before dinner is served is put the rolls in the oven, which is what Madeline is doing when her sister, Adrienne, walks into the kitchen with a red velvet cake in her hand and a smile on her face.

"The party has arrived!" She does a cute little shimmy that Madeline joins in on almost immediately. With the two of them standing side by side, I can see the resemblance. Only, it's more than a resemblance. They have the same umber skin and round, deep set eyes that are filled with kindness when they settle on your face. I'm drying off a bowl from the last round of dishes I washed when I feel both sets on me.

Madeline's gaze is all motherly affection and pride, while Adrienne's is all happy curiosity.

"Sebastian didn't tell me you two are twins."

Both women cackle, and I look between them, wondering how that never came up in conversation. "We don't typically advertise it," Madeline says. "Addy, this is Nadia Hendrix. Nadia, this is my sister, Adrienne."

"Nadia!" Adrienne comes at me with her arms open wide. Her hug is as warm as her expression when she pulls back and smiles at me. "You are radiant!"

"Uh, thanks." I find myself laughing because it's such an uncommon compliment. "I'm so glad to finally meet you. Sebastian has told me so much about you."

He calls her his favorite aunt, which is why I was nervous about meeting her. Well, one of the reasons, anyway. The other reason walks through the door with a scowl on his face that only deepens when he sees me in his mother's arms.

Vince.

"Everything except the fact that I'm his mom's twin, huh?" Adrienne asks, completely unaware of the uncomfortable energy that's just taken over the kitchen. Vince is hugging his aunt, but his eyes are still on me. They're blood shot and low, which suggests that he's high. Usually, that would make me hopeful for a more mellow version of him, but Vince strikes me as the kind of person whose worst traits are exacerbated by substances, not calmed by them.

"Yes, ma'am. I guess he didn't think that was pertinent information."

"I'm surprised he thought to mention my mom at all," Vince says, his voice thick with disdain. Everyone turns to look at him, and between his mother and aunt's disapproving stares, he's forced to make the comment sound like it wasn't a sad beginning to a cheap shot. He scrubs a hand down his face, and when his hand moves over his mouth, it's pulled into a disturbing smile. "I would have thought he'd be too caught up in charming you to tell you anything about us."

My stomach turns, and I feel bile creeping up my throat but fight it back. "Not at all. Sebastian talks about his family all the time. I was really sorry to hear about you losing your job at Cerros."

Vince's smile turns into a scowl, and his lips part like he wants to say something. I don't give him the chance. "If you two would excuse me, I think I'm going to run to the restroom before dinner starts."

"Don't be long!" Madeline says, her tone sweet as sugar as it follows me down the hallway to the bathroom near the entry way. Maybe that's why I don't hear Vince's footsteps, why I don't realize that he's followed me until his hand stops the bathroom door from closing and he forces his way inside.

I open my mouth to scream, but he's on me before I can do anything. One hand over my mouth while he pins me to the wall with his body and kicks the door closed with one foot. This close I can smell the alcohol seeping out of his pores and see the remnants of fine white powder in his nose hair. I can feel his breath on my face, see the hate in his eyes and trace every inch of the scar that must be a result of the fight he had with Sebastian months ago.

"See what your boyfriend did to me?" he sneers, finally removing his hand from my face. I should scream, but I can't. It's frozen in my throat. I nod, and for some reason, maybe because I've faced much scarier men than him, I smile, which makes him angrier. He grips my jaw with outraged fingers that squeeze until it hurts. "You think it's funny?"

"I think you deserved worse."

"You know what you deserve, *Nyla*?"

My heart stutters to a stop, and I blink, shocked to hear my given name coming off his lips. Vince's face transforms into a mask of sick satisfaction. "That's right, bitch. I know exactly who you are."

"You don't know me."

That feels like such a ridiculous thing to say when he's literally just proven that he does know me. I just don't know how. I mean, I think I know how, but I'm too afraid to explore that reality.

"Yes, I do. I know you used to live in LA. I know you used to spread your legs for every man that was willing to throw a dollar and some dick your way. I know you have a scar on the inside of your right thigh."

Bile is no longer rising in my throat. It's filling my mouth, gathering on my tongue. I swallow it back down, which just makes my stomach roil more, but it doesn't matter because there's only one way Vince could know about the scar on the inside of my thigh, and that possibility has the world falling away from me in chunks of devastation and fear.

Vince is watching me closely, so he sees when it hits me. "That's right. I meant what I said when I told you that you looked familiar. Maybe I would have recognized you sooner if you were sitting on the bar with your legs spread wide for me again."

I'm going to be sick and not just because I've swallowed this morning's breakfast down for the second time today. But also because my senses are being invaded by Vince's putrid scent and my mind is spinning, flipping through the vast library of mental snapshots my brain has unwillingly stored of the men I've been forced to sleep with. I wish I could say for sure that Vince isn't among them, but the truth is I don't know. The truth is the moment Sebastian said Vince lived in LA before he came to New Haven, I knew it was possible, but LA is such a big place with no shortage of low lives, I thought that possibility would be small. Minuscule. Non-existent.

Now, I'm literally starting that possibility in the face, being held hostage by it and the past I've tried to let go of but refuses to let go of me.

Tears gather in the corners of my eyes, and I blink them away, refusing to give Vince the satisfaction of seeing me cry. "I've never spread my legs for you."

"Oh, but you have, *Nyla*," he says my name like an insult, like a slur, and I hate Beau for refusing to let me use another name when I was working because he thought it was funny to deny me the layer of protection the other girls had, to let perverts and predators call me by the name my parents gave me, to strip away the last bit of my dignity.

I didn't tell Sebastian, but that's why I chose to keep using Nadia even after he learned my real name. That name doesn't belong to me anymore. It's no longer mine. It belongs to the woman who was brutalized and exploited, to the woman who might have slept with his cousin and can't even remember.

"I'm not surprised you don't remember," Vince says, continuing his diatribe despite my devastation. "It was a Christmas party at a mansion up in the hills, and things got pretty wild. You were on more shit than I was, but we had a *good* time. I'd forgotten all about it, but the other week I met up with my boy Elliot—he's the one that took me to the party—and we got to talking. He reminded me about all the things I did to you."

I wish I could call him a liar, but I can't because I just don't remember. Waves of self-loathing and nausea roll through me, and I shove Vince away, narrowly missing his shoes as I aim for the toilet. The force of the retching makes my ribs hurt and my throat burn, but I'm thankful because the sound and smell send Vince running for the hills. Between the vomiting and the crying that follows, I don't know how long I spend in the bathroom, but when I emerge, Sebastian is coming down the hall, clearly looking for me.

He takes one look at my face, which has to be tear stained and puffy, and rushes to my side, pulling me into his arms for a quick hug before leaning back and taking my face in his hands.

"What's wrong, precious?"

"Dinner's ready," someone calls from behind us. Sebastian turns, revealing Vince standing at the end of the hallway.

"We'll be there in a second," he says, turning back to me and effectively dismissing his cousin. "Tell me what's going on. Is it Vince? Did he say something to you?"

For a moment, for the briefest of seconds, I consider telling him the truth, but then I decide against it because I know how this will play out. Sebastian won't hear anything but the fact that Vince followed me into the bathroom and put his hands on me, and he'll lose it. They'll fight, and Vince will happily tell everyone what he knows about me. Not just my name, but every shame I carry deep in my bones, including the ones I don't remember.

I can't let that happen, so I shake my head. "No, Vince hasn't said a word to me since he got here."

Relief causes Sebastian's shoulders to sag, and I know that I made the right choice. He caresses my cheek with gentle fingers I'm not sure I deserve. "Then what's going on, baby? Are you feeling sick again?"

The tenderness laced in his tone makes me want to cry. There's no question. I *don't* deserve this. I don't deserve him. A man who looks at me with reverence and handles me with care. A man who won't rest until he knows what's wrong and has done everything in his power to fix it.

Only there is no fixing this. There is no fixing me. There is no changing my past or reversing the damage it will cause to our future.

"No. I'm fine."

"Nadia." He pins me with a hard stare that implores me to be honest even though I know I can't. "You look like you've been crying, so I know that something is wrong."

My teeth sink into my lower lip, and I search my brain, knowing I have to give him something. "I was just…" I trail off, hating that I have to be dishonest with him. "I was just thinking about my parents. Thanksgiving was the last holiday I spent with them, and it's always a hard day for me."

Technically, it's not a lie. Thanksgiving *is* a hard day for me. But today was easier. It felt better. Until a few moments ago.

Sebastian's features soften, and his hand snakes around to the back of my neck, gripping my nape to pull me in close. He lays a kiss on my forehead. "I'm sorry, baby."

"It's okay. I'm used to missing them, it's just that some days are harder than others."

"Is it because we're here? Do you want to go home?"

"No!" I reply, my tone fierce and sure because my need to get away from Vince doesn't outweigh my desire to share this holiday with Sebastian and his family. "No," I repeat, a little calmer this time. "I just needed to sit with my feelings for a moment."

"And you decided to do that alone?"

"Yes, you were with your family."

"*Our* family," he says, correcting me. "And so what? No matter who I'm with, where I am or what I'm doing, I'm always available to you."

"I know that, Seb." I sigh. "But I'm not going to to interrupt your family time so we can rehash the last moments I had with my mom and dad."

"You should. I want to hear about every moment you remember having with your mom and dad. Tell me something. Tell me anything. I'm here, I'm listening, and we're not moving until you give me a piece of your sadness to hold."

God, I love this man.

My heart swells with it, my soul burns with it, my bones *ache* with it.

Raising up on my tip toes, I press a kiss to his lips, thankful in this moment that Madeline keeps mouthwash in her guest bathrooms because my mouth doesn't taste like vomit and tears. Sebastian lets the kiss intensify and then turn gentle before he breaks it.

"I'm waiting, precious," he murmurs against my lips.

With no choice but to comply, I reach for a bittersweet truth no one else knows. "I was supposed to be on the flight with my parents. I was supposed to be on that plane, but I decided at the last minute to stay home because I was mad at my mom. I don't even remember why, just that I was. I was supposed to be on the plane, Sebastian, and before I met you, I spent every day wishing that I had been."

It's such an ugly, broken truth it makes my chest ache. Sebastian's too, I think, because several emotions play over his features and each one is more heartbreaking than the next.

A sad smile pulls my lips up. "Now you see why I didn't want to share. Sometimes you have to hold your own sadness, keep your own secrets, carry your own pain."

"When you were alone in the world, that might have made sense, precious, but you're not alone anymore, which means your sadness is my sadness, your secrets are my secrets, and your pain—" he kisses me again, slow and long as if he's trying to leech the pain from my system with his lips "—your pain is my pain."

I want to feel comforted by that, but with every passing day, and near constant reminders of my past lurking around every corner, I'm scared that Sebastian's words will become more than a promise. They'll become a reality, and my pain won't just be his pain, it'll be our ruin.

34

SEBASTIAN

I can count the number of times Nadia and I have argued since we've been together on one hand, and I won't even need all five fingers. Communication isn't something we usually struggle with because, more often than not, we find ourselves on the same side of important conversations.

Foolishly, I thought that meant introducing Nadia to the security team Russ put together would go off without a hitch, but I was wrong.

"Do *you* have a security team?" Nadia asks, her arms folded over her chest as she paces in front of her desk, heedless of the fact that there are six men standing behind me. Six men with military and tactical backgrounds that have required them to see and do things they can't speak about with anyone. Six men who barely made it through the threshold before she laid into me about not needing or wanting them around.

Like I said, we rarely argue, but Nadia has been in rare form for days, and after Thanksgiving, her mood has only gotten worse. She's been distant and jumpy, agitated with everyone but especially me even though she says I haven't done anything to upset her. I guess that's just changed though.

"No, I don't need a security team. Your safety is the priority."

This conversation reminds me of the one I had with Talia when she found out about the price Cheese had put on my head. She pressed and pressed and pressed for me to give in, but I didn't because I knew I could take care of myself. Talia's concerns barely registered for me. Her fears background noise underneath the roaring of the part of me that is always looking for a fight. There's no one in this world I'd love to hurt more than Beau Montgomery, but as I look at Nadia, I can feel that desire taking a back seat to her worry. Every bone in my body preparing to yield to her, to cave, to give in ways I never would with anyone else.

She looks past me to the men who are shuffling with discomfort at my back. "Get out."

"Nadia."

"I don't want to have this conversation in front of them, Sebastian."

With a sigh, I turn to the men we're currently talking around, speaking to them directly for the first time since we met in my office an hour ago. Russ, the only man on the team I didn't meet for the first time today, presses his lips together to bite back a laugh. He told me that Nadia would get in my ass about hiring security without discussing it with her first. I barely contain the urge to flip him off, clearing my throat to give him an order instead.

"Show your men around the building and make sure they all have up to date photos of Beau Montgomery."

"Copy that," Russ says, opening the door and gesturing for the men to file out. Once they're gone, I turn my attention back to Nadia. She doesn't look any less hostile now that we're alone, and even though she's mad at me, the scowl on her lips just makes me want to kiss her. I cross the room, intending to do exactly that, but she holds out a hand to stop me.

I pause just a few feet away from her. "Are you going to tell me why you're so angry with me, precious, or am I going to have to guess?"

The use of her nickname makes her visibly deflate, and I feel a bubble of hope rise in my chest. She sighs and sits down on the edge of her desk, but she still doesn't speak.

"Do you really hate the idea of having a security team that much?" I ask, inching closer. "I mean, if I could, I would keep you with me all day, every day, but since you have a life and want some semblance of independence, I figured this was our best option."

This time, she doesn't stop my advance, and by the time the last word leaves my lips, I'm right on her, my hands on either side of her face, thumbs rubbing small circles on the soft skin of her cheeks. I watch her eyes melt right in front of me, going from raw fire agate to liquid pools of caramel that bubble with emotion.

"I don't mind the security," she admits quietly. "I just hate that I'm their only focus."

"Your safety is my top priority, precious, of course you're their only focus."

When Russ walked the men into my office, I told them they should be prepared to eat, sleep and breathe Nadia Hendrix until Beau Montgomery is no longer a threat.

Her hands go to my sides, fingers digging into the fabric of my suit jacket. "And what about your safety, Sebastian? You just keep making all these decisions focused on protecting me, but you're not doing anything to protect yourself. You could get hurt in all this."

There's a world of meaning layered in her words, and I get the feeling that she's not just talking about physical harm. My eyes rove over her features, trying to parse out what's happening underneath the mask of genuine concern. Nadia can be hard to know, hard to read, slow to reveal what's happening in that head of hers. I've had to learn how to be patient, how to give reassurance and space to work things out on her own instead of asking questions that would give me the information necessary to fix it all on my own. It's hard. Especially when I know she's spent so much of her life fending for herself.

"No one is going to get hurt, baby." Leaning down, I place a kiss on her lips. "Not me, and certainly not you."

"Certainly not me because I have a security team?" she asks, skepticism pulling her lips to the side.

I smile, kissing her again. "Precisely."

She shakes her head. "I want at least two of those men on you,

Sebastian. I know that Beau is coming for me, but I don't want you out there with no one watching your back."

"You *know* he's coming for you?" I repeat, wondering if the certainty in her tone is stemming from her being in possession of information I'm not yet privy to. "Why do you say it like it's a forgone conclusion?"

"Because it is, Sebastian." Nadia pushes me back and the pacing starts again, making me feel like we're right back where we started. She's wringing her hands together. "You know it, and I know it. Hell, even Bianca knows it."

"Bianca?" Sparks of recognition light up my brain. I know that name, but it takes me a second to place it, to realize that it's the name of Nadia's friend from California. She told me about her on the night she told me her real name. As far as I know, Nadia left everything and everyone from her old life behind. Her mentioning a former friend who had a romantic relationship with Beau is raising all kinds of red flags for me. "When did you talk to Bianca, Nadia?"

Panic causes her eyes to flare, and now I realize that she didn't intend to let that name slip past her lips. She was going to keep whatever conversation or covert meeting they had a secret from me. The thought fills me with an overwhelming sense of anger, not at her, per say, just at the situation.

"A few days ago. I ran into her at a boutique in town."

"And you didn't think to tell me she was in New Haven?"

She bites her lip, and even though I'm mad, I still can't help but acknowledge how fucking beautiful she is. "I was going to tell you, but when I saw her at the gala, I thought I was going crazy."

"Wait, wait. What?" I'm forcing a calm I don't feel into my voice because I refuse to yell at her because I know it would be triggering. "You saw her at the gala?"

"I wasn't sure. I thought it was her, but she left before I could confirm. And then when I was out with Des for lunch, I saw her again."

"So she's following you." I already have my phone out, sending Russ a text about Bianca's presence in New Haven.

"No, she's not. She's here working, but she's not with Beau. Apparently, he jumped ship when I disappeared."

I nod. "Yeah, Russ' intel turned up the same information, which is what made me decide to get a security team in the first place. So, you don't think she's a threat?"

"I don't. We parted ways on a good note. She even gave me her number, so we could stay in touch if I wanted. I told her I wasn't sure because I wanted to keep some distance between my old life and my new one, and she seemed to understand that."

Everything she says sounds good, but I can't do anything with good. I need facts. I need the certainty that comes along with a deep dive into Bianca's entire existence.

"Do you plan on using it?"

Some emotion I can't name passes behind her eyes, and she shrugs. "I don't know."

"Would you mind giving it to me?"

"So you can give it to Russ and have him look into her?"

There's no point in lying. "Yes."

"Yeah, okay, I'll text it to you."

With the conversation over, Nadia's pacing slows to a stop, and she crosses her arms again, but this time it's not a defensive posture, it's a self-soothing one. The only thing I want to do in this moment is hold her, so that's what I do. She melts into my embrace, wrapping her arms around me and wincing when I squeeze her too tight. I loosen my grip, pulling back to look at her.

"Did I hurt you?"

"No, my boobs are just a little sore. I think my period is about to start."

"Is that why you've been in such a bad mood for the past few days?"

She scowls at me. "Are you really pulling the crazy, hormonal lady card right now?"

"I didn't call you crazy or hormonal. I just asked a question."

"A stupid question." The laugh building in my chest is killed by the withering gaze she settles on my face. "Don't laugh at me, Sebastian."

"I'm not laughing at you, baby. I'm just trying to understand why you seem to hate me these days."

Mood swings are not something I'm unfamiliar with. Talia would have them all the time, even when she wasn't on her period, and when Zoe was going through puberty every family gathering was a minefield that had to be navigated with care and precision. But Nadia's mood swings are...different. Epic in a way that makes my heart wrench and my head spin because I don't know what to do to fix it. Just like I don't know what to do with the tears springing in her eyes right now.

"I don't hate you," she says, a huge tear skating down her cheek. "I love you. I've just been a little grumpy lately."

Now she's pouting, which just makes her all the more adorable and confusing and leaves me no choice but to drop a kiss on her lips. The kiss keeps me from telling her that being grumpy isn't any different from being in a bad mood. It also seems to settle the erratic energy flowing between us.

"I'm sorry I didn't tell you about Bianca," she sighs against my lips.

"And I'm sorry for keeping you in the dark about the security team."

"I'm not mad about you hiring them. I'll do whatever is necessary to stay safe, but I want you to be safe too, so can you please have at least one of them on you at all times?"

"Just one?" I murmur, my hands running down her back, over her ass and the skin tight skirt that makes it sit up higher. She's gained weight since we've been together, and while it looks good on her, it feels even better in my hands. Her breath catches when I lift her up, and she wraps her legs around my waist while I walk us back to the wall of glass that gives spectacular views of the city.

"I figured I should make a compromise," she says, already squirming against the hard press of my dick between her legs.

"Your willingness to make concessions is much appreciated, Miss Hendrix." My lips go to her neck, and I pull the delicate, citrus scented skin into my mouth, licking and sucking until she matching the rhythm I've set with my mouth with a slow churning of her hips.

We were both too tired to do anything but go home and fall into bed after we left my parents' house last night, so I'm desperate for her. Too desperate to be patient or gentle. Too desperate to preserve the integrity of her underwear when I hike up her skirt. Too desperate to do anything besides groan in her ear when I finally slip inside the silken perfection of her pussy.

"Always so wet, precious. Always so fucking ready for this dick," I murmur, driving into her with long, thorough strokes that make her whimper and grip my hair.

"Sebastian, *please*."

"I got you, baby. I always take care of you, don't I?"

"Yes," she moans, pumping her hips to meet me thrust for thrust.

We don't have a lot of time, and I don't have a lot of patience, so I'm not going slow, and Nadia isn't being quiet. Her moans mixed with the soft suctioning of her walls around my shaft fill the office, pushing us to the edge of pleasure with alarming speed. Nadia goes over first, pulsing around me while her fingers threaten to rip my locs from my scalp. I follow, coming in long, hot spurts that empty my balls and fill Nadia's pussy to the brim, making it so the evidence of our shared desire starts to leak out of her before I've even pulled out.

Both of our chests are heaving, harsh breaths tangling together as we trade tender kisses that make everything feel okay again.

"I'll have Russ assign two of the guys to me," I concede, looping back to the beginning of the conversation.

"Compromise?" she asks, a sated smile curving lips I can't stop myself from kissing.

"Compromise."

35

NADIA

I t only takes me a few hours to regret compromising with
Sebastian on the security front, and that regret is prompted by the
reality of four steel faced, gun toting men driving me to my first
appointment with Dr. Suffrant—the gynecologist Desiree recommended I see.

With everything going on at work and the stress of trying to
remember the party Vince swears we fucked at, I almost forgot that I
scheduled this appointment, and now, with two of the four security
guards standing on opposite sides of the waiting room while I fill out
my new patient paperwork, I kind of wish that I had.

"Nadia Hendrix," the nurse standing in the doorway that leads to
the patient rooms calls. I stand and Tyler and Enzo, the two imposing
figures casting shadows all over the waiting room, start to move
toward the door too.

Amanda, the nurse, frowns, and I turn around to hold up a hand.
"There's no way in hell the two of you are coming back there with me.
Sit down, read a magazine and try not to scare any pregnant women."

"Yes, ma'am," Enzo says, his tone curt as he turns around and
heads back to his unofficial post also known as the space beside the
front door.

I follow Amanda to the back, feeling relieved when she proceeds with business as usual instead of asking what the scene in the waiting room was about. It doesn't take her long to check my vitals, get my weight, height and all the other fun things nurses do before doctors come in and ask you to strip down, and before I know it, I'm sitting on an exam table waiting for Dr. Suffrant.

She comes in with a smile on her face and an air of confidence around her that makes it easy to see why Desiree likes her so much. Her sable skin is smooth, attributing a youth to her demeanor that doesn't match her years of experience or the wisdom behind her brown eyes.

"Nadia," she says, perching on the rolling stool in the middle of the floor with her eyes on my chart. "What brings you in today?"

"Well, I was hoping we could discuss birth control options."

"Sure, but not for another nine months."

"I'm sorry?"

"We can discuss birth control options after the baby is born."

Surely, I didn't hear her right. There's no way I heard her right. I open my mouth, intending to ask her to repeat herself, but nothing comes out. My voice has gotten lost somewhere in the shuffle of shock and horror. Somewhere in the maze of science I don't understand and math that doesn't add up.

After the baby is born.

I'm going to have a baby?

"That's right you are," Dr. Suffrant says, alerting me to the fact that I've spoken out loud. She slides closer to me on the stool and places a comforting hand on my leg. "I take it you and your partner weren't trying?"

Trying.

Images of Sebastian and I fucking against every available surface without a condom or lick of common sense between us flit through my mind, and I laugh. I laugh so hard, I end up doubling over and clutching my sides because of course we weren't trying. We haven't even had a conversation about whether or not we want kids. But we damn sure weren't doing a thing to prevent this. Except I thought I *was* doing something. The thought seems to sober me up, and when I straighten, Dr. Suffrant is looking at me with a sparkle of humor in her eyes that tells me I'm not the first person to burst out laughing after hearing unexpected news.

"But what about my birth control? I have the implant, the one in my arm." I gesture stupidly to the arm in question, and Dr. Suffrant nods.

"Yes, I saw on your intake questionnaire that you've had it in for almost three years, but you don't remember the exact date, so it's possible you could have had it for longer, right?"

"I guess so. My life was pretty…hectic around the time I received it."

Hectic meaning a blur of beatings I didn't deserve, parties I didn't want to go to, drugs I didn't want to take and sex I didn't want to have that made my memory unreliable. All I remember is that I went to the free clinic on my own and got it done after one of the girls had a pregnancy scare, but pregnancy scares were a dime a dozen in my world. Plus, no one from the clinic was following up with an escort with no health insurance and a made up address that might as well have been 123 Sesame Street, so I don't have any way of knowing for sure when I got it. I just know that I did, and that it was supposed to be effective and this wasn't supposed to happen.

Not yet.

"I see. Then given the very positive pregnancy test, it seems likely that your implant expired, leaving you without any form of protection."

"Oh."

It all makes sense now. The sore boobs, the vomiting, the mood swings. Everything, except the vomiting, which I'd attributed to some isolated case of food poisoning and then disgust at being in such close proximity to Vince, seemed to fit my pre-menstrual symptoms. Were they a little more intense than usual? Yes, but I thought that was just an indication of a rough period ahead.

"I can't be pregnant."

Can't doesn't feel like the right word, but it's what comes out. Dr. Suffrant nods with understanding.

"You don't have to be," she says, moving over the the counter where there are pamphlets on everything from HPV to abortion, and my heart skips several beats when her long, elegant fingers grip the edge of the latter.

I jump to my feet. *"No!"*

Dr. Suffrant spins around with a quickness. "Nadia, it's okay."

"No, it's not. I just...I don't...I can't be here right now."

Any response from my doctor is lost in the sound of the metal knob of the door slamming into the wall as I flee the exam room with the same urgency I fled the scene of the car accident that led me to New Haven and Sebastian.

"Nadia, wait!" Dr. Suffrant calls out, but I'm already moving, turning to the right toward the door with an exit sign above it that I'm sure is only supposed to be used for office staff. My chest is tight and my lungs are burning as I bend at the waist to try to catch my breath. It's so quiet outside, and when I finally get my bearings, I realize that I must have gone out of the employee exit because all of the cars in this part of the parking lot are empty.

I'm not thinking. Not really. Because if I was thinking I would have went back into the building and listened to what Dr. Suffrant had to say. I would have went back out the front instead of sneaking around the side, avoiding the other two members of my security team while also using the ride share app on my phone to order a car home.

My anxiety riddled brain tells me that's the only place I want to be, that once I'm there, inside the walls of my home, everything will make more sense, but even when I'm home staring at the eight positive pregnancy tests I bought at the grocery store downstairs, I'm still confused.

"How did this happen?"

It's a stupid question because Dr. Suffrant already told me how this happened. Expired birth control. Why is that even a thing? It shouldn't be a thing. Birth control should last forever. No, that's ridiculous, but it should at least give you a warning before it just opts out of doing its job, leaving you high and dry in your time of need.

The constant vibrating in my purse—which is beside the damning sticks with double pink lines, blue crosses, and, perhaps the most damning of all, bold letters that spell out the word in all caps—alerts me to the fact that my phone is ringing. *Again.* I've lost count of how many times I've heard it ring since I stumbled through the door, choking down vomit and wondering how often in office pregnancy tests are wrong, but I know it's a lot.

I know it's a number that indicates that the security team I abandoned at the doctor's office are now aware I've disappeared. I know it's a number that indicates that Sebastian knows I'm currently missing in action. And I also know it's a number that means I should be doing something besides staring at the pregnancy tests that confirm Dr. Suffrant's assessment of my situation.

I'm pregnant.

Holy, fuck, I'm pregnant, and I don't know what I'm going to do about it.

I'd be lying if I said I haven't been thinking about family and what it would look like to have one of my own since Sebastian told me he loved me. Those thoughts seemed to double after he revealed that my paternal grandparents were looking to have a relationship with me, but they also came grinding to a halt the moment Vince made those disgusting insinuations on Thanksgiving. It was hard to even stomach my dinner while sitting across the table from him and harder still to get back in touch with the part of myself that, for a fleeting moment, felt worthy not only of being a part of the Adler family, but adding to it.

And now, here I am, in a cloud of shame and confusion because I'm not prepared for any of this. For the conversation I'll have to have with Sebastian about what I might have given Vince before it belonged to him. For the conversation where I'll have to explain how I—a woman who has spent so much of her life actively avoiding pregnancy —wound up getting knocked up by a man like Sebastian. Everyone will think I planned it. They'll say it was a ploy for me to sink my claws into him, to tie my life and financial standing to him in a permanent way. They'll suspect that I've tried this before, and it won't matter that Sebastian is actually the first man I've never used a condom with —which is kind of surprising given my history. It won't matter that I was just so wrapped up in being happy that I forgot to think about him *actually* wrapping it up.

As I sink down into a chair, I find myself wondering if this is how my mother felt when she found out she was pregnant with me. She probably did, and when the news came out, my grandparents confirmed her worst fears. The only saving grace was the love between her and my dad. A love that was the result of a bond built over years of knowing and fighting for each other. Sebastian and I have only known each other for a few months, less if you count the fact that up until a few weeks ago he didn't even know my real name. He loves me and I love him, but men that grow up with bank accounts like his are trained to set all emotion aside when it comes to situations like this.

A small helpless whimper escapes me, and I bite my lip, forcing myself to fight back the tears that want to fall. I'm scared and over-whelmed, and that overwhelm increases ten fold when I hear a commotion outside my front door. Almost immediately, I know that Sebastian is somewhere in the mix. I feel his energy as several large and imposing frames come crashing through the door.

"NADIA!" Sebastian roars, breaking through the crowd with his face a thunderous mixture of anger and fear. When he spots me at the table—standing now because I don't want him to see the pregnancy tests resting on their individual boxes in neat lines just yet—there's momentary relief that's quickly overtaken by fury.

He stalks towards me, and I find that I can't move a muscle as he closes the distance between us. I don't flinch because I know that Sebastian won't hurt me, and I don't run because the only thing I truly want is the comfort of his arms. With one hand that's shaking with tension and the desire to be gentle, he reaches for me, snaking his hand behind my hair to grip the nape of my neck and draw me into him. His lips press into the skin of my forehead, and I feel the fear and worry radiating off of him underneath the layers of the anger. He holds me there for long seconds, and I let him because I need this closeness too.

"Four hours," he growls, letting me go. "Four hours ago you agreed to do whatever is necessary to stay safe, and yet, you take the first opportunity available to disappear into thin fucking air without so much as a word to them or me."

It's not a question but an accusation that drips with censure and love. That both makes my heart swell and break. I didn't mean to worry him.

"I'm sorry."

Sebastian shakes his head. "I don't want you to be sorry, Nadia. I want you to be *careful*. When Russ called and said you were gone, I thought…" He lets the sentence break in half, but I see the naked truth of his fear in his eyes. He shakes his head again, this time to clear the thoughts away. "Why would you just leave the doctor's office like that?"

Tears blur my vision. I don't know what to say. I don't want to tell him. I don't want him to be angry or think that I was trying to do this on purpose, that I was trying to trap him. *Oh, God.* My stomach turns as my entire body revolts at the thought of him thinking so little of me. I didn't plan this. I didn't want this, this unexpected surprise situation, but I do think I could want this baby.

"Nadia? Did you hear me? Why did you leave the doctor's office like that? What did you need that was so important you had to leave right then?"

I turn, cognizant of the fact that there are more eyes on me right now than Sebastian's. His are all I care about though. They're all that matter as I pick up the pregnancy test closest to me and turn back around to put it in his hands.

"One of these."

36

SEBASTIAN

Two pink lines.

I always thought I'd be done in by something more substantial. A bullet, a heart attack, some random act of divinity that would strike me down where I stood, leaving nothing of me but an imprint made of ash. Never did I think it would be something I would hold in my own hand, see with my own eyes.

I can't stop looking at it.

My whole world has come grinding to a halt, and it's all because of two pink lines and the woman in front of me who won't stop biting her lip. She's nervous, afraid, in shock just like I am, and my heart pounds with the demand to comfort her, to kiss her, to make love to her until she's relaxed and sated and all traces of worry and fear are gone. The desire is so strong, I almost forget the presence of the men at my back, but Russ' not so subtle clearing of his throat reminds me.

I turn to him. *"Get out."*

They file out with tense shoulders and clenched jaws, grateful that the verbal lashing I've been giving them since they let me know they lost Nadia is over. The second they're gone, I'm facing her again, and her bottom lip is trembling.

"I didn't do this on purpose, Sebastian" she gasps, tears crowding her eyes. God, she's so fucking beautiful no matter what she's doing, but I hate it when she cries. "I swear, I wasn't trying to trap you. I swear."

Now the anxiety etched into her features makes sense. She was worried I would think what most rich and powerful men think when the woman they've just started sleeping with winds up pregnant unexpectedly. Honestly, the thought never crossed my mind, but even if she had plotted to make this happen, I wouldn't be feeling anything close to what she thinks is going through my head right now.

"Oh, precious, come here." I open my arms, still holding the positive pregnancy test in one hand, and Nadia crashes into me. She squeezes me tight, but I hold her gingerly, like the precious thing she is. My lips are at her temple in a second, layering what I hope are comforting kisses on her skin. "I know you didn't. Neither of us were trying to make this happen, but it's okay. We're okay. *You're* okay."

A shudder rolls down her spine as she pulls back to look up at me. "You're not mad?"

"No, baby, I'm not mad. How could I be? We were both in this together, weren't we?"

She nods, and the motion causes the tears lingering on the rims of her beautiful, brown eyes to fall. They're hot and wet as they land on my arm, soaking into the skin exposed by my rolled up sleeves. I want to kiss her tears away, to pick her up and spin her around until she laughs instead of cries and then drop to my knees and pull up her sweater to expose her belly that's still flat because it's too early for her to be showing, right?

"How far along are you?" The question drops like a bomb between the two of us, and I don't understand the expression on Nadia's face. Not fully. Not until she steps out of my hold and starts pacing like she does when she's going to say something that breaks my heart. "Nadia?"

"I don't know, Sebastian!" She stomps her foot impatiently and spins around, showing me features that are wrought with fear and confusion. "I don't know anything except that I'm pregnant, and I shouldn't be."

My heart aches, and I can't help it, my eyes drop to her stomach, to the invisible life we unintentionally created but I want more than anything. *I want.* Those two words echo in my mind, at odds with the expression on Nadia's face that says she doesn't.

She doesn't want to have this baby.

She doesn't want to have *our* baby.

And it's her choice, of course it's her choice, but God, even thinking it sends shards of glass rushing through my veins in angry cascading waves that threaten to tear me apart.

This can't be happening.

Like Nadia, this baby is something I didn't know I wanted until the possibility of it was standing right in front of me. I fought like hell to have Nadia, to gain her trust and make her mine, but this time? This little thing inside of her that we made together? I can't fight for it. I can't ask for reasonable terms or request more time. For the first time in my life, I'm sitting in a negotiation with all my cards on the table, no leverage to speak of, and a gag order that would prevent me from utilizing either if I had them.

I take a seat in the chair closest to me and rest my elbows on my knees, letting the weight of what I've gained and lost in the span of a second press down on me.

"You don't have to be pregnant, Nadia. We can make an appointment, and—" Her hand goes to her stomach, and I stare at the protective span of her fingers as hope tries to bloom in my chest. I can't let it. I can't read too much into what's probably nothing more than instinct, so I push through, forcing myself to finish the sentence. "We can make an appointment, and get it taken care of."

"Is that what you want?" she asks quietly, her eyes still watery, her fingers still guarding her stomach. "To get rid of it?"

I have to bite back the words that will tell the truth because I don't want to influence her decision. "I want whatever you want, precious."

There's the wobbly lip again. It makes me want to go to her, but I can't because I know as soon as I touch her, I'll be on my knees, begging her to want this as badly as I do.

"That's not an answer, Sebastian."

"I can't give you an answer, Nadia. What I want doesn't matter because it's your body, so it has to be your choice."

As much as I hate it, that's the truth. There is no us in this conversation, just her. What she wants. What she needs. What she chooses. I'll still love her. I know that. I'll still love her with everything in me, but I'll also be holding my breath until the day when she's ready for us to do this again. Hopefully, that day will come soon.

I'm staring at her hand on her stomach again, and when she moves it, my gaze snaps to her face. Self-consciousness skitters across her features. "But what if I make the wrong choice?"

"That's not possible."

"Yes, it is! We've just started dating, Sebastian. We're still learning each other. There's so much you don't know about me, so much I don't know about you. Things I might need to know if I decided to have this baby, things I might need to know if I didn't."

My heart lurches, and every beat is a mix of revolt and pain at being forced to face a reality I don't want to consider. Nadia watches me, waiting for my response, and I school my features into a carefully blank mask before I reply.

"You know that I love you, and that I'll do whatever is necessary to protect you."

"Of course, I know that, Sebastian." She's pacing again. Her long legs covering more ground than usual because she's agitated and moving fast. "But what about the little things?"

"What little things?" I push to my feet and try not to crumble under the wave of emotion crashing down on me. Nadia's posture is reluctantly open as I approach. To my complete relief, she let's me take her hands. "Ask me anything, precious. I'll answer. I don't have any secrets from you."

"It's not about secrets, Seb. It's about the simplest things like when your birthday—"

"March 29th," I interject, ready to share, to give her anything she wants, anything she needs to make this work. "My birthday is March 29th. Yours is February 22nd. My favorite color is black, and yours is somewhere between yellow and cream, and your comfort shows are all some form of copaganda. You cry when Publix commercials come on—"

"Because why do they have to do all of that to sell groceries?" she asks, playfully exasperated for just a moment.

"We know the things that matter, Nadia, and what we don't know we'll learn. We have time to learn." It's as close to a persuasive statement as I'll allow myself to get because I won't force her hand. Nadia's lips quirk, which causes a dangerous bubble of hope to inflate in my chest.

"Those are all things you know about me. We're talking about the things I don't know about you."

"Like what?"

"Well, for starters, where you live. We're going to have a baby, and I've never even been to your place. To any of your places."

We're going to have a baby.

My heart alternates between pounding a million miles a minute and ceasing to beat altogether when those words grace my ears, bouncing off of every part of my skull, igniting the fire of maybe burning in my chest only for it to be extinguished moments later when I process the end of her sentence.

Any hope I had for a positive outcome for this situation disappears the moment I realize I'm going to have to tell her the truth. I don't know how long I thought I'd be able to hide this from her, but I didn't expect to be revealing information I'm certain is going to make her upset on the heels of such important news.

Pulling in a deep breath for strength, I take one of her hands in mine. "We can go to my place now if you'd like."

Nadia gawks at me, and if I wasn't so fucking scared of how this whole situation is going to turn out I would be laughing at seeing her with her mouth hanging open like her jaw has come completely unhinged.

"I'm not leaving this building until we figure this out."

"You don't have to leave the building, precious," I say. "You don't even have to leave this floor."

"Sebastian, please stop joking. You're here all the time, but this isn't your *actual* home. I'm talking about the place with the address that's listed on your license, the place where all your mail is sent, the default place in your food delivery app..."

When Nadia is in an anxiety spiral that's manifesting itself verbally, her body tends to go on autopilot. Which means that the moment I start pulling her toward the front door, she follows without a bit of resistance. As she's listing out all the things that qualify a dwelling as someone's home, I lead her out of her unit and down the hall to the one I moved into the day after she signed her lease. I'm fishing the key out of my pocket when she finally tunes in to what's happening around her.

"Why are we here?" she asks, but I can tell by the tension coating her words that she already knows the answer.

"You said you wanted to see my place," I respond, sliding the key into the lock.

"You don't live here." She drops my hand, taking a step back. "Sebastian, tell me you don't live here."

My only response is the open front door with my keys still hanging from the lock. Nadia shakes her head and steps back again. Her brows are knit together in a tight line, and her eyes are narrowed into slits.

"Are you serious right now?" she asks through clenched teeth. "You live here? All this time, you've been my neighbor, and you didn't say anything? Why?"

"Because I knew you wouldn't understand."

"Wouldn't understand what, Sebastian?" Her arms are folded over her chest now, and her nostrils are flared. All things that indicate just how badly this conversation is going to go. I place my hands in my pockets and lean against the wall beside the open door Nadia can't stop glaring at. With a sigh, I launch into an explanation, hoping my intentions will buy me a little bit of goodwill from the woman I love.

"That I've owned this building for years, but I didn't start using it as my primary residence until you chose to live in it."

"Why would you do that? We weren't even together when I chose this building."

"Because I wanted to be close to you in case your past caught up to you."

Her feature soften, but only marginally, not enough to make me breathe easy. "You could have just been honest about that, Sebastian. There was no need for all the cloak and dagger nonsense."

I could leave it here. I could just accept my lashings and tell her she's right, so we can turn our focus back to the topic I actually want to discuss, but that wouldn't be smart because there's one more thing I need to tell her.

"You're right, precious. I should have been honest with you about this." I lick my lips, preparing them to speak a truth that will likely upend the precarious peace sitting between Nadia and I. "There's something else I need to tell you."

A wariness I can only attribute to the stress of the day and this conversation settles along her features, carving out a home in the frown lines in her forehead. "What is it?"

"This unit isn't the only one I own."

"You own the whole damn building, Sebastian, you're going to have to be more specific than that."

She spits the words out, which is how I know she already knows. She can see the truth I've yet to speak on my face, and she doesn't like it.

"When I bought this building, I fell in love with it for the same reasons you did. The history in the original features mixed with the modern design elements, the proximity to Cerros, but most of all, I fell in love with the views from the top floor, from *this* floor. My plan was always to turn the two units into one. I had Nic draw up plans and everything, but things kept coming up that needed my attention more than the renovation, so I put it off. At first, I was annoyed about having to keep putting it on the back burner, but then you came along, and you needed somewhere safe to be, and I needed to be able to be close to you, and I was grateful that it worked out the way it did because other-wise I wouldn't have been able to—"

"Lie to me for weeks," she says, injecting venom into the words she's just used to cut my sentence short. "You wouldn't have been able to strong arm me into unknowingly moving into a place that you own or pretend to be just as confused as I was about why my rent payments kept getting reversed. Otherwise, you wouldn't have been able to spend every night in my bed knowing you had your own on the other side of the fucking wall. Otherwise, you wouldn't have been able to turn me into an unwitting charity case!"

This isn't the first time she's used those words to refer to herself, to suggest that that's the way I see her, but today they cut deeper than they ever have before because today she's not just the woman I love, but also the woman carrying my child.

"Nadia, you are not a charity case."

I push off the wall and reach for her, but she backs away.

"That's how it feels, Sebastian. I don't want to be some kept woman who has everything handed to her by a man and hasn't earned anything on her own. I can take care of myself."

"I know you can take care of yourself, Nadia. You've been doing that since you were 16 years old, but you don't have to do it by yourself anymore. All I wanted to do was give you a break from doing it all on your own, and I'm sorry for not being honest about how I planned to achieve that, but I'm not sorry for any of the rest of it because it's not charity, it's love. And I'll always love you like that, Nadia, because I don't know any other way, and my heart won't allow me to learn one."

To emphasize my point, I cover the heart in question with my hand, turning my next words into a pledge I know by the look on her face she won't accept today.

"The way I love you demands everything from me, Nadia. My time, my energy, every free moment and the claimed ones too. It dictates that I deplete every resource at my disposal and not only do I honor that edict, I do so without ever thinking about how I'm going to replenish them because as long as I'm in possession of your smile then the things I don't have don't matter. You mean more to me than any job I could give you, any roof I could put over your head or any amount of money I could put in your bank account. None of it matters to me. *You* are what matters."

Nadia shakes her head. "And the truth matters to me, Sebastian. That's all I'm asking you for. I don't need any of the rest of it." Her shoulders, which, just seconds ago were up around her ears, begin to slump at the same time wariness takes over her features. She turns on her heels and heads back to her door, leaving me to follow on uncertain feet.

"Nadia, wait." I pause on the other side of her threshold. Not because I don't want to go inside, but because she won't let me. She's standing on the inside of her place, her hands gripping the door. "What are you doing?"

"I'm going to bed. Today has been—" Tears turn the brown of her eyes into glittering pools of caramel. "—today has been a lot, and I just want to go to take a shower, go to sleep and forget the last few hours even happened."

I wonder if she knows. If she's aware that those words, followed by the prompt closing of her door in my face, have relegated me to my own private hell. Have sent me tumbling into a hole so dark, so desolate, that nearly twenty four hours later, when I'm standing on the rooftop at Nic and Sloane's engagement party, I still haven't found my way out of it.

What I have found is Nic who is using his rare moment of solitude to check on his friend, Chris who seems to be in as somber a mood as I am. He's doing a worse job of hiding it though, lingering at the bar with a drink in his hand and his eyes focused on someone on the other side of the roof before he settles them on Nic and me. As soon as we're close enough, Nic claps him on the shoulder and asks if he plans to pout in his drink all night.

"Maybe," Chris says, taking a long pull from the glass in his hand and emptying it. Something about his outward expression of the turmoil I'm feeling inside but have had to tuck away in order to carry out my duties as Nic's friend, the owner of the venue and hopeful best man, pulls the corners of my mouth up into a reluctant smile.

"Woman troubles will do that to you, Nic. Don't tell me you've forgotten so quickly."

The annoying smile on his face as Chris and I toast to our shared misery tells me that he has, in fact, forgotten. Chris notices too.

"Happiness tends to be a catalyst for amnesia," he says, which just makes Nic's smile grow wider. He stretches out his long arms in a 'what can I say' type gesture that makes me want to punch him.

"Listen, I spent twelve years in misery, so forgive me if I'm ready to leave all that shit behind me."

"That shit being where Chris and I are currently living?" I don't know how long Chris has been an unwilling resident in this town called Misery, but I've only been here for a day, and I'm ready to fill out a change of address form. I haven't seen or heard from Nadia since she closed the door in my face. When I went to her place this morning, she was gone, and when I called, she sent me straight to voicemail. She's also been ignoring all of my texts. The only reason I'm standing here with Nic and Chris right now and not leading a damn search party through my own building is because Russ has provided regular updates that let me know she's okay.

"Exactly," Nic says. "And I'm hoping you two will be willing to take a vacation from your misery for the wedding."

"Of course man," Chris says, placing a reassuring hand on Nic's shoulder. "Can't have your best man scowling in your wedding pictures."

I laugh my first genuine laugh since yesterday because the thought of Nadia and I still being at odds by the time Nic and Sloane's wedding comes around is preposterous. And even if we were, I wouldn't let my personal issues ruin my friend's big day.

"You don't have to worry about that, Chris. I know how to turn it on for the camera."

"You?" Chris asks, his eyes on Nic's face. We both watch the smile he's been sporting all night dissolve. "Sebastian's gonna be your best man?"

"Absolutely," I respond with confidence, but Nic shakes his head.

"No." He clears his throat, splitting an uncomfortable look between the two of us. "I haven't chosen a best man yet."

"But you know who the obvious choice is."

I'm about to bring up the whole canceling reservations to give him and Sloane privacy for their first real date when Chris chimes in. "Maybe the man who invited him to the party where he met the love of his life?"

"*Well, shit.* I might not be able to beat that."

But I'm damn sure going to try. I'm rubbing my chin, trying to figure out exactly how when Sloane summons Nic from the other side of the rooftop. He leaves Chris and I to our best man standoff with a fake ass apologetic look neither of us is buying.

"You might as well give it up," Chris tells me, his eyes focused on the direction Nic is walking in. Judging by the look on his face, the woman who has him all wrapped up in knots is over there too. "The best man spot is going to me."

I want to argue, but I don't because if anyone should be standing beside Nic on the day he marries Sloane it should be the man who introduced him to her, especially because from what I can tell, the woman he's in love with will be standing next to the bride.

"Fine. Just promise you'll let me plan the bachelor party."

Surprise colors his features, but he accepts my terms with an extension of his hand, which I take happily.

"Sounds good," he says. "That way you'll be the one Sloane puts a hit out on."

"She wouldn't be the first."

Chris gives me a look that tells me he's trying to discern whether I'm serious or not. I open my mouth to tell him it, in fact, is not a joke, when Sarah, one of the servers working tonight, interrupts.

"Mr. Adler, Miss Hendrix needs to see you."

Instantly, my mind is filled with thoughts that tell me something is wrong. Nadia has been avoiding me all day, and she's working, so the only reason why she would be calling for me right now is if something is wrong.

"Excuse me, Chris, as you can see, I'm needed elsewhere. I'll call you with the details for the bachelor party."

It's an abrupt ending to an otherwise pleasant conversation, and I can't bring myself to care whether it seemed rude or not. All I can think about is Nadia and whether the problem is with her or the baby.

Please, God, don't let it be her.

Please, God, don't let it be the baby.

Please, God, just let everything be okay.

37

NADIA

Sebastian storms into my office and makes a beeline for me. Everything about his posture and expression suggests that his intention is to pull me into his arms and demand to know what happened, who did it and how he can fix it after he confirms for himself that I'm okay. I move around my desk, ready to assure him that everything is fine, but when his eyes drop to my hand on my stomach, we both stop short.

I've been doing it all day, rubbing my belly, trying to get a feel for the life growing inside of me. It's like the moment I accepted that I was pregnant, I haven't been able to keep my hands off of it. Last night, I went to sleep on my back—because I was scared sleeping on my stomach would hurt the baby—with my fingers splayed over the slight pudge I'm sure only exists in my mind, wishing that Sebastian was there to feel it, to tell me if it's real or not. He knows my body so well. He has every inch of me memorized, so he'd be able to tell me for sure. I wish I could ask him now, but he's too busy trying to force his eyes to stay on my face.

In an attempt to make it easier for him, I tuck both of my hands inside the pockets of my dress. That seems to do the trick. Sebastian crosses his arms, and I run appreciative eyes over his imposing frame and the black suit he's wearing.

"Are you okay?" he asks, his voice strained because he wants to ask about the baby and he doesn't know how. I hate that we're in this weird position, that he doesn't know what he's allowed to ask, and I don't know what to say. And while I meant what I said yesterday about not appreciating his dishonesty, I don't like the spot we're in right now.

"I'm fine, and so is the baby."

His shoulders sag with relief, and he runs a hand over his hair, down to the nape of his neck, which he grips tightly. "Thank God."

"I'm sorry for shutting you out yesterday," I offer quietly, stepping towards him because I just want to be in his space. "That wasn't fair. We were both still reeling from the news of the pregnancy, and emotions were high. You didn't deserve that."

"You don't have to apologize for needing time, precious, but I do need to apologize for not being upfront with you about our living situation. You deserved to know the truth, so you could make an informed decision."

"I forgive you. Can you forgive me?"

I'm right in front of him now, and when he reaches for me, fingers skating over my waist to come to rest at my back, I lean into him. He pulls me closer, but he doesn't squeeze me as tight as he normally does.

"I'd forgive you anything, Nadia."

The solemnity of his words makes my heart ache. I know what he's trying to say. He said it in my apartment last night even though there was hope in his eyes when he uttered the words. I don't have to be pregnant, and if I choose not to be, we'll be fine. He'll still love me and want me. We might not have a baby, but we'll have each other. That knowledge makes it easy for me to lend my voice to thought that's been running through my mind since Dr. Suffrant told me I was pregnant.

"I want to keep the baby."

I speak the words into his chest, laying them over his heart, hoping they'll seal whatever fracture our exchange last night caused. Sebastian pushes out a harsh breath, and his arms go slack as he sinks to his knees in front of me.

"Sebastian?" I take his face in my hands. "Is that okay with you?"

"Of course that's okay with me, precious," he murmurs, shaking his head to dislodge my hands so he can bury his face in my stomach. Reverent lips press soft kisses to my skin through the fabric of my dress, and I giggle because the hair from his beard makes it tickle. Sebastian looks up at me, love and adoration shining in his eyes. "We're going to have a baby."

"We are."

There are tears in my eyes as I gaze down at him, at this man who has given me more than I could have ever hoped to have in this world. At this person who's gone from being a stranger, to a friend, to a lover and now the father of my child in mere months. Everything good in my life, which now includes this baby, *our baby*, is possible because I decided to trust him, because he decided to love me, and that's just so fucking beautiful I can't help but cry.

Well, I guess it's more of a sob really, but it doesn't matter because it comes from this place deep down inside of me that's filled with happiness. With joy. With love.

Sebastian rises to his feet, but he keeps his hands on my waist and both of his thumbs on my stomach rubbing small, comforting circles. I know now that he'll be just as obsessed with my stomach as I am. That he'll note every change, every stretch mark and centimeter of growth. Hell, he'll probably be one of those men who want to make a cast of my belly before I give birth, and I'll let him because I love him.

"Happy tears?" he asks, a grin curving his lips.

I nod, smiling through the tears in question. "The happiest."

"I love you, precious. I love you so much."

"I love you too, Sebastian. Thank you for the flowers."

That's originally what I called him up here to say, but the moment I laid eyes on him I forgot all about the bouquet I saw getting delivered through the doorbell camera app.

"What flowers?" The smile on his face falters, and mine does too.

"The ones you had delivered to my place."

Sebastian shakes his head. "I didn't send you flowers, Nadia."

"Yes, you did," I insist, stepping back and moving over to my desk where I left my phone. "I watched the guy deliver them just a few minutes ago." As I'm talking, I open the app up again and find the bouquet still sitting in front of my door. Sebastian is at my side now, and I push the phone in his hand. "See? They're white lilies. Like you sent me the first time."

I'd thought it an odd choice, but I figured he was once again trying to ease me into celebrating another new beginning. Now, judging by the look on his face, I see that I was wrong. My heart starts to pound.

"You did send them right, babe?" I ask the question even though I already know the answer. Even though I know that if Sebastian didn't send them then there's only one other person in this world who would have.

My stomach turns, and the small meal I forced myself to eat before I came into work today starts to work its way up my throat. I slap my hand to my mouth and rush around Sebastian to get to the bathroom. He's right behind me as I bend over the toilet and retch until my ribs ache and my throat burns, rubbing small circles on my back with one hand while the other holds my hair away from my face.

When I'm upright again, he steps back, giving me room to go to the sink and rid my mouth of the taste of despair clinging to my tongue with the toothbrush I've taken to keeping in here. Thankfully, he waits until I've finished pulling myself together to request an explanation with a silent stretching of his eyes through the mirror. I train my eyes on the reflection of his.

"The first time you sent me flowers, you sent white lilies." He nods but remains quiet. I swallow around the lump in my throat that's blocking the rest of my explanation. Why can't we just be happy? Why does every good thing in my life have to be accompanied by a devastating reminder of the bad. "When I saw them waiting for me in front of my room at the motel, I froze because I thought they were from Beau."

Sebastian tries to keep his cool, but I see his protective side flaring up, more lethal and potent now than it was even a day ago because he's not just protecting me now, he's protecting the life we created together.

"The first time he beat me, he gave me flowers. White lilies because they were his mother's favorite. It became a routine. Choke Nyla until she passes out and can't swallow for weeks, and then buy her flowers to remind her that you think she deserves this because your mother died in the same plane crash she lost both of her parents in. Throw Nyla down a flight of steps and fracture her sternum then make her leave the hospital before she can actually get medical attention. Punch Nyla so hard the ring you always wear leaves imprints of the letter M in her skin and buy her white lilies to remind her that she deserve the pain."

My eyes fall shut, and images of every beating, every bruise and cut play behind my eyelids. My voice is nothing more than a fearful shudder when I continue.

"Crack a vase of those same flowers across Nyla's head when she refuses to accept them after you break her arm and then use the biggest shard to slice up the inside of her thigh while you give her a lesson on anatomy and how long it takes to bleed out when your femoral artery has been severed. He didn't buy me flowers after that."

Sebastian curses, and I feel the rage coming off of him seeping into my skin as he pulls out his phone and starts typing, presumably sending a message to Russ and the rest of the team. I allow the heat of it to soak into me, to warm me from the outside in, but it's still not enough to ward off the shiver from the fear that's lodged itself into my bones.

"If you didn't send those flowers, Sebastian, that means Beau did. That means he's found me, and I'm not—" my hand goes to my stomach as I turn around to face him "*we're* not safe."

Just moments ago, I was happy. Hopeful. Excited for the days ahead, for a life with the good kind of uncertainty for once. Now I'm just afraid. Now I'm just sad. Now I'm just angry because how dare Beau try to touch my happiness with his bullshit? How dare he try to poison the life I built here with my own two hands?

Sebastian sees the shift in my eyes, and his glitter with the same kind of determination, allowing him to shift gears. To exchange the words of comfort I'm sure were lingering on his tongue for other, more informative ones.

"Tyler and Enzo were the closest to the building," he says, glancing at his phone where the report must have just come through. "They said there's no note, so we don't have any way of knowing for sure that they're from Beau."

"They're from him, Sebastian. I know it."

"I believe you, precious." He runs a soothing hand down my back, trying to calm me. "That's why we won't be going home tonight. Russ is already scrubbing through security footage while Tyler and Enzo try to find out if the person who left them works for a local florist shop."

Something about the way he phrases that statement sparks an image of Beau in my building and at my doorstep leaving those flowers for me. Just the thought sends a fresh wave of fear through me. It sweeps away every bit of the anger, leaving nothing but crippling terror. "You think it was him at the door? You think he left the flowers?"

I watched the man approach with the bouquet, but nothing about him seemed familiar through the lens and distance provided by the camera. He was tall, average height and weight. Just like Beau. He was also wearing a hoodie with the hood pulled up and around his face. That didn't strike me as odd since it's been so cool outside, but now that I think about it, it could have easily been an attempt to obscure his features from the camera.

"His picture has been given to every security person and staff member in our building, so that's not likely, but we still have to explore the possibility."

"Right." I nod, wishing any of those words were comforting.

Sebastian steps in close, and his fingers go under my chin, lifting until my eyes are on his. "You're safe, okay? I got you. I'm right here, and I'm not going to let anything happen to you." His hand goes to my stomach. "To either of you. We'll stay here tonight. I'll have Russ and the entire team post up outside, and I'll watch over you as you sleep. Whatever it takes to make you feel safe."

"I'll feel safest in your arms."

He reaches out his hand to me, and I take it, allowing him to haul me into his orbit. He drops a kiss on my temple. "Then you'll sleep in my arms, and once we know what's what, then we'll go home."

"Tomorrow. We'll go home tomorrow."

"Nadia, I don't know if—"

"Promise me, Sebastian. Tomorrow we go home."

It's not fair of me to ask him to promise me an outcome that's so far out of his control. I know that, but I also know that I need the certainty, the confidence I don't have and can only get from him.

"I promise. We'll have all of this figured out by tomorrow."

38

SEBASTIAN

I hate breaking promises.

Especially to Nadia.

I promised her we'd be back home by Sunday night, but on Monday morning, we, once again, woke up in the Presidential suite at Cerros with the heavy weight of worry and frustration pressing down on us because no one can tell me with absolute certainty that Beau Montgomery is not in New Haven.

It hasn't even been a full forty-eight hours, and she's already grown impatient.

She wants to go back home, and I want her safe, so I can't let her. There are too many unknowns. Deep down, I know that she gets that, but it doesn't stop her from being mad at me when I explain it again. We've had the same conversation five different times, and every time, she gives me the cold shoulder at the end of it.

"You can't ignore me forever." I reach over and take her hand, linking our fingers together before pulling them into my lap. She doesn't pull away, and I'd like to attribute that to her softening a little, but I know it probably has more to do with her not wanting to make another scene in the doctors office she apparently sprinted out of the day she found out she was pregnant.

"I'm not ignoring you, Sebastian. I'm just not talking to you."

"What's the difference, precious?"

The daggers she shoots me with her eyes are sharp enough to cut through bone, so I press my lips together and resign myself to a life of silence. At least until we get out of here. Once we're alone again, I'm going to eat her pussy and talk her through every orgasm I ring from her body.

"Stop thinking so loud," she hisses, a slight red tint taking over her cheeks as desire battles annoyance for the primary spot in her eyes. When she's not angry with me, she's desperate and needy, begging me to fuck her. Just the thought of how she begged last night makes my dick throb. Nadia slaps my thigh with her free hand. "Sebastian, I'm serious."

"I'm just sitting here, Nadia, what do you want me to do? Not be attracted to you?" Leaning over the arms of both of our seats, I place my lips at her ear. "Not think you're the most beautiful woman in this room? Not think about how unfair it is that your pussy tastes sweeter these days? Not wonder if I'm going to get a chance to taste you today?"

I definitely am. I know it. She knows it.

"Hendrix!" A voice calls, forcing us to jump away from each other. Several pairs of eyes swing in our direction, watching as I stand and help Nadia out of her seat. The nurse standing at the door smiles broadly at us as we approach.

"Nadia! So nice to see you back." She glances at me and then back at Nadia. "More security?"

"No." Nadia laughs. "This is my boyfriend, Sebastian. Sebastian, this is Amanda."

"Oh, so you're Dad?"

My chest swells with pride at being called Dad even as I bristle internally at the fact that the title of boyfriend doesn't come close to capturing what I want to be to Nadia.

"That's right," I say, finally. "I'm Dad."

"Well let's hope you do a better job of keeping this little lady in the office than those other guys did," Amanda quips, holding the door to the back open for us to pass through. Nadia doesn't appreciate her humor, I can tell by the way she turns stiff as Amanda takes her vitals. And when we're settled in the exam room, waiting for the doctor, she rolls her eyes long and hard.

"Am I going to have to hear jokes about that throughout this entire pregnancy?" she asks, her tone sharp and defensive. "I was in shock. I'm sure I'm not the first person to run out of here."

If I say what I'm thinking—which is that the staff in this building can probably count on one hand the number of times they've had a patient flee, leaving a confused security team in their wake—we'll end up fighting, so I opt for silence and a supportive nod. Nadia sees right through it, and her eyes turn into thin slits just as the door to the exam room opens. My savior is a Black woman in a white coat with laughing brown eyes that answer Nadia's question about whether or not constant jokes are going to be a part of her experience here.

To her credit, Dr. Suffrant tries to hold it together. She really does, but the moment Nadia shakes her head and says, "Not you too," she falls apart. Her laughter erupts inside the room, bouncing off of all four walls and infecting Nadia. Within seconds, she's joining in, cracking up at the expense of her former self.

"I was in shock," she repeats, giving the doctor an explanation she didn't ask for as she sits down on the stool across from us.

"I know, darling, and I'm so sorry for laughing. I've just never seen anything like that in all my years of practicing medicine. Thank you so much for coming back in."

"Thank you for being able to see me again so quickly," Nadia says, sobering up.

"Of course, I was happy that you called. We have so much to discuss, but first, please introduce me to your partner."

Both women turn their attention to me, and Nadia makes quick work of the introductions. Once again, that word, boyfriend, grates against my skin when she says it, and the pain of it makes it hard to be pleasant. Hard, but not impossible. I take Dr. Suffrant's hand when she offers it to me, giving her a genuine smile because I've read great things about her and the work she does to keep Black women from dying while giving birth. When she hears my last name, her eyes spark with recognition.

"Adler, as in the Adler wing at the New Haven Regional Medical Center?"

I nod. "Yes, ma'am, although, I believe it was my mother who made the donation that resulted in the wing being given the family name."

"I see." Dr. Suffrant nods politely before turning her attention back to Nadia. "I assume you're here to discuss your options, correct?"

"Yes," Nadia says, and for some odd reason I find myself holding my breath, afraid that in the last five seconds she's changed her mind and decided she doesn't want to keep the baby after all. When my head starts to feel all fuzzy inside, I force myself to release that thought and tune into the conversation. "Sebastian and I have decided that we want to keep the baby."

Dr. Suffrant looks at me for confirmation, and I feel my head begin to bob up and down without any instruction from my brain. Thankfully, it's good enough for the doctor. For the rest of the appointment, all of her attention is on Nadia and the baby. She gives Nadia a full work up, which includes some early scans of the little person growing inside of her, and writes her a prescription for some anti-nausea medicine as well as prenatal vitamins.

We leave the appointment feeling lighter and more hopeful than we have since the flowers arrived on our doorstep, and when we get to my parents' house for lunch, I'm barely containing the desire to share the news with everyone who will listen.

And by barely, I mean not at all.

Nadia and I standing in the entry way when I finally burst.

"I think we should tell them about the baby," I say, taking her coat and hanging it up in the closet by the door. There's a picture of our baby in the pocket of her coat. Right now, at almost eleven weeks gestation, they're only the size of a strawberry, but to me, they're huge. This large and looming figure that rests in the clouds above my head, shining light and hope down on me.

"What?" Nadia asks, and her expression tells me that she heard me, she's just asking me to repeat myself to make sure she heard me correctly.

"I think we should tell them about the baby."

She shakes her head. "No, Sebastian, we can't. It's too early. I'm not even out of my first trimester."

"I know, but Dr. Suffrant said you and the baby are both healthy and that everything is looking good."

"And she also said that the risk of miscarriage is significant until I get through the twelfth week of pregnancy."

I almost open my mouth to tell her not to think like that, to remind her that just because bad things *can* happen doesn't mean they will, but then I remember who I'm talking to. I remember that the woman in front of me is an orphan and a survivor of abuse. I remember that one day her life was good. She had parents and a home full of love and happiness, and then, in the blink of an eye, it was all taken away from her.

Of course, she's afraid. Of course, she's thinking about the things that could go wrong instead of the things that could go right. Of course, she'd want to hold this secret close to her chest until the risk is minimized, until the likelihood of tragedy lies within an acceptable boundary that's nowhere near her or our child.

"You're right," I concede. "We can wait to tell them."

Nadia bites her lip, and she's so adorable I want to kiss her. "Just for a few more weeks, okay?"

Her compromise is appreciated but unnecessary. I put my hands on her waist and lean down to plant a kiss on her lips. "A few weeks. Forever. Whatever you want, precious."

"We can't wait forever, Sebastian," she murmurs, breathless as I kiss a line down her neck. "Eventually someone is going to notice that I'm not drinking wine, and I'm going to start showing soon."

The promise of her growing belly elicits a groan from deep in my chest, and the sound of it vibrates against the delicate skin of Nadia's neck. She squirms her way out of my hold, laughing at my reaction.

"Do you have a thing for pregnant women, Mr. Adler?"

"I have a thing for you, Miss Hendrix." I reach for her again, but she dances her way out of my touch, forcing me to follow her as she runs down the hall toward the kitchen. I cross the threshold mere moments after Nadia does, but she's already sought asylum on the barstool between my father and Luca who both give me questioning looks when I enter the room.

"Everything okay, son?" Dad's question does very little to cover the snicker Nadia tries to hide behind her hand. I give her a look that communicates exactly how I intend to punish her later before turning my gaze on my father.

"Yeah, Dad, everything is fine."

"Great, now we can eat," Mom says, taking the lid off of the pot of chili on the stove. She's already set out bowls with freshly shredded cheese and sliced jalapeños on the counter next to a pan of sweet potato cornbread and a host of other fixings we never manage to eat.

"We're not waiting for Dre and Zoe?"

"Zoe has a client and Dre has some important meeting at the school he apparently can't miss," Luca says, hopping up to grab a stack of empty bowls from the cabinet for us to eat out of.

"It's not just any meeting, Luc," Dad replies. "The board has offered him a new position at the university."

I take two of the bowls Luca just sat on the counter. One for me and the other for Nadia who is still seated because for some reason scooping food out of pots makes her less likely to eat it. "What's the position?"

"President of the University." This comes from Mom who is smiling wider than she did the day Dre won that spelling bee with no front teeth. "They want him to replace Dr. Daniels. He told me everyone on the board said he's the best man for the job."

"What happened to Dr. Daniels?" Nadia asks.

"Sex scandal," Luca replies. "Apparently he was harassing female professors, offering them promotions in exchange for sexual favors and retaliating when they turned him down. The board gave him the boot immediately, and now they want Dre to take over because he's as straight laced and boring as they come."

"Your brother is not boring, Luca," Dad shoots back, his voice a clap of thunder and strike of lightening all in one. "He's responsible and level headed, which is exactly what the school needs right now."

"President Adler," Mom muses, and the pride shining in her eyes turns the conversation to more positive topics that we float through with ease as we eat and drink the bottle of Rioja Riserva from 2008 that Mom bought specifically for Nadia to try with the chili. She was so excited about the pairing, things got a bit awkward when Nadia refused, saying she was planning on sticking to water because she didn't want the wine to interfere with a new medicine she was taking. Dad and Luca bought the excuse without so much as a second thought, but Mom didn't. And I spent the rest of lunch trading panicked looks with Nadia and warning looks at my mom that, by some miracle, she chose to honor up until now.

Now being after lunch when Nadia is already in the car, and I'm standing on the porch on my own because Dad is in his office and Luca has already left.

Her eyes stretch wide with an unspoken question, and I shake my head.

"Just leave it alone, Mom."

It's not a confirmation or even a denial, but somehow she's still bouncing on her toes with excitement. "You don't have to say anything, Sebby. Just tell me what color I need to paint the nursery."

"Bye, Mom." I lean in and give her a kiss on the forehead, appreciating her excitement even though I've given her nothing. "I love you."

"I love you too, son. Tell Nadia I love her too," she calls as I jog to the car. I throw up a hand in acknowledgment before dropping down in my seat and slamming the door shut. Nadia's eyes bore into the side of my face.

"Did you tell her?"

"No, precious. I didn't say a word to her about anything."

"But she knows, doesn't she?"

"She suspects, but I didn't confirm."

Nadia leans back against the head rest and closes her eyes. "Good. Thank you for waiting. I know that must have been hard for you."

"Not really, especially since the next time we see them for lunch, you'll be far enough along for us to share if you feel comfortable."

She cracks one eye open, squinting her confusion. "I won't be through my twelfth week when we see them next Monday."

"Right." I glance at her as I switch lanes, wondering how she forgot about this trip to California to check on the progress Andre, Nic's right hand man who did end up taking on the job, is making on the resort. It's been on my calendar for weeks now, which means it's been on hers too. "But we won't see them next Monday because we'll be in Los Angeles."

"We?" Both of her eyes are open now. "Who's we?"

"You and me." I'm tempted to pull over and conduct some kind of neurological exam to ensure she didn't bump her head at some point during the day when I wasn't looking. "Do you seriously not remember me telling you about this trip?"

"I remember you telling me that you were going to Los Angeles, but we never talked about me going."

"Of course you're going, precious. I'm not leaving you in New Haven alone."

"But I won't be alone, I'll be with the security team you hired to keep me safe."

With one hand on the wheel, I use the other to pinch the bridge of my nose. "Nadia."

"Sebastian," she says, mimicking my serious tone to hide the way her voice is shaking. "I'm not going to Los Angeles. I have a job to do and a baby to prepare for."

"You have plenty of vacation days, Nadia, and you can buy baby clothes anywhere."

"Exactly." She snaps her fingers in a manner that can only be described as sarcastic. "Which means I can buy them right here in New Haven where you, me, and this baby will live."

"Nadia, I can't leave you in New Haven."

Just the thought unsettles me. I wouldn't be able to get anything done because I'd be worried sick about her. I'll be worried in Los

Angeles too, especially because that's an area Beau is familiar with, but at least I'll be close if something happens.

"And I can't go to Los Angeles, Sebastian."

I catch it again, that note of fear lacing itself around the name of the city she used to reside in, and as I stop at a red light, I stare at the hard line of her jaw.

"Are you scared to go there?" I ask, softly.

"No," she says, refusing to admit the truth we both know, leaving me no choice but to voice my own fears.

"Well, I am," I admit, and Nadia's eyes snap to my face. "I'm scared of losing you, of losing our baby. I'm scared of having to go back to navigating this world alone. I'm scared that the realest, deepest love I've ever known is going to be snatched away from me, and there's nothing I can do about it. I'm scared, precious, and I need you with me because I don't know how long I'm going to be gone, and I don't know how to be without you."

39

NADIA

Sebastian leaves me with no choice but to go with him.

I mean, how do you say no to a man who is as powerful as he is passionate, as handsome as he is kind, and as ruthless as he is vulnerable?

Don't even waste your time trying to come up with a reasonable response because the answer is you don't.

You put in a request to HR for time off that's already been approved because your boss is in love with you.

You pack nothing but your anti-nausea medicine and prenatal vitamins because he's already got clothes and everything else you could possibly need waiting for you in the penthouse he has in the heart of Los Angeles with views you never got to appreciate when you were a resident.

And you stay in that penthouse every day going stir crazy while he splits his time between his office in downtown LA, a construction site in Santa Monica, and you, which leaves you lonely, bored and more susceptible than usual to making bad decisions like going out to eat with your ex-best friend who may or may not have told the man hunting you like a dog where he could find you.

"You're not meeting up with Bianca," Sebastian growls into the

phone. The unfortunate thing about pregnancy hormones is that everything this man does lately either infuriates me or turns me on. Both
things make it hard for me to focus long enough to make a valid
argument.

"Yes, I am, Sebastian."

It's all I've got, and it sounds as juvenile to my ears as it must
sound to his, but the thing is I don't care because I'm already dressed,
and this outfit is too cute to be wasted on the four walls of this house.

"Look," I say, sitting the phone down and putting him on speaker,
so I can put on my shoes. "I've already let Russ know where we're
meeting. He sent Enzo and Tyler down to the restaurant to check it out
beforehand, which means him and Josh? Jason? I can't remember the
other guy's name, but you know who I'm talking about."

"Jared," Sebastian offers, a bit of humor coloring his tone. He
thinks it's cute that I'm suffering from pregnancy brain already.

"Jared," I huff. "Jared and Russ will drive me to the restaurant, and
I promise I won't leave their sight. I just have to get out of this house. I
feel like I'm going crazy sitting here alone all the time."

"I'm sorry I've been so busy, precious. I'm going to be home early
tonight."

"Babe, I wasn't trying to make you feel bad. I know you have to
work. It's fine. I just want to share a meal with someone that isn't the
demon spawn you put inside of me that wants to eat everything but
doesn't like anything."

This kid isn't even here yet, and they're already running my life.
Dictating what I eat and when I eat it. Revolting every five seconds by
sending the food I just ate to satisfy a craving back up the way it came.

"Demon spawn, huh? Just this morning you were gushing about
how cute they're going to be and telling me you love them more than I
ever could."

I shrug even though he can't see me. "All of those things can be
true at once."

"If you say so, precious."

"I do."

The line goes quiet, and I know that we're both sitting in the quiet of the happiness talk of our child has infused into the conversation. Every time we talk about the baby this happens. We allow for a moment of silence to fully soak in the appreciation of the goodness that is coming our way in the form of a little person that, with any luck, will be the perfect blend of the two of us.

"Where are you and Bianca going for lunch?" Sebastian asks when the moment is done. I do a little victory dance, glad he's on board because I was going either way, and give him the details he needs. Once he has the information he needs, we hang up, and I head out the door with Russ and Jared.

The restaurant Bianca chose is a family owned Italian spot twenty minutes away from Sebastian's place. I use the ride to calm my nerves and gather my thoughts, so I can be fully prepared to discuss the real reason I reached out to Bianca in the first place. I was content to let our chance meeting in New Haven be the last time I saw my ex-best friend because in my mind there was no point in dragging old, and not so healthy, relationships from my past into my new life. But then the conversation with Vince at Thanksgiving happened, and I was forced to reconsider.

Bianca is the only semi-safe tie I have to my old life, and we worked every single party together, which means she's the only person who can tell me if what Vince said is the truth.

When I arrive at the restaurant, she's already seated at a table near the front. She waves me down when I enter, and I leave Russ and Jared at the hostess stand talking to Tyler and Enzo.

"You have a security team now?" Bianca asks, by way of greeting.

"Yeah, I do."

My curt answer signals my lack of interest in following that thread of conversation, but Bianca refuses to acknowledge it.

"Because of Beau?" Her brows pull together in a tight line. "Is that really necessary?"

I pick up my menu and pray for patience even though I know it's not something I have a lot of lately. "The last time we saw each other, you told me he was planning to kill me, so yeah, I think it's necessary."

"Nyla, no one even knows where he is. What are you going to do? Have security follow you around until the end of your days."

The last thing I want is to live out the rest of my life with Russ, Jared, Enzo and Tyler watching my every move, but if I need to do so to keep myself and my family safe then that's what I'll do.

"If I need to."

"Must be nice to have money to blow like that."

I slam my menu down a bit more forcefully than I intended, causing the glasses on the table to shake. Bianca's eyes stretch wide, and I remind myself to play nice, to be patient, so I can get the information I need from her and get the hell on.

"You look good, B," I say, the smile on my face as fake as the compliment. "I'm so glad we were able to get together."

"Me too. Although, I was surprised when you texted and let me know you were in LA."

My response is interrupted by the appearance of our server, and we pause the conversation just long enough to order food and drinks. Once we're alone again, Bianca turns expectant eyes on me. She's waiting for an explanation, for a reason why I've had her number for weeks now, but only just chose to use it today. Since she already knows I have an ulterior motive, I don't see the point in dancing around it.

"I had a question to ask you."

"That couldn't be asked over the phone?"

"I wanted to look you in your eyes when you answered it."

She crosses her arms and sits back in her seat. "Okay, shoot."

I study her defensive posture and immediately decide that there's another, more pressing, question I need to ask her now. "Well, actually, I have two questions."

Bianca arches a brow, and I can tell she knows exactly what I'm going to ask her first. "Go ahead and ask, Nyla."

"Have you told anyone about me being in New Haven?"

Only a few seconds pass by between my question and her answer, but it feels like longer. It feels like an eternity to wait to find out if my safety and my new life have been compromised by a woman I used to trust.

"No. I haven't told anyone, but what you really meant to ask if is if I've told Beau, right?" Again, there's no point in lying, so I nod. Bianca's eyes narrow like she's offended that I don't trust her. "I told you I don't know where Beau is. I haven't seen or spoken to him in months about anything, but especially not about you."

Relief washes over me, reminding me that I still care about Bianca. That it still means something to know that I can count on her to keep my secrets and, sometimes, tell me the truth, which she's doing right now. I know it. Just like I know that the flowers that led to me being exiled from my home came from Beau even though no one can prove it. Bianca's honesty should be comforting, but it unsettles me even more because it adds another layer of confusion to the Beau in New Haven situation.

Because it makes me wonder who could have given him the information that resulted in the taunting floral arrangement and why sending them is all he's done to make his reemergence in my life known.

"What's your other question?" Bianca asks, pulling me out of my reverie just as our server arrives with our food. I don't have an appetite anymore, and I don't know whether to contribute it to the baby, the confusion around Beau or the fact that I'm about to have to repeat the horrific allegations Vince launched at me during Thanksgiving.

I push my plate away from me and pick up my glass to take a sip of water. "Do you remember us ever working a Christmas party at a mansion in Hidden Hills?"

She squints into the bowl of pasta in front of her, and I see the wheels spinning in her brain. Bianca has an excellent memory, so it doesn't take long for the flicker of recognition to show in her eyes.

"Yeah, it was this huge place on Round Meadow Road a few years ago, right?"

"I don't know. I don't remember."

Bianca studies my face as the details of the night that have alluded me for days come to her easily. "Oh, yeah, that makes sense considering how high you were."

You were on more shit than I was, but we had a good time.

Vince's words echo in my head, and I shudder, taking Bianca's assessment of my condition as confirmation of what he said. I never got high willingly. Beau always drugged me to force me to cooperate when we were going to parties, which means I never knew what I was taking or how much. The fact that I can't remember this night at all, means I must have been really bad off.

"Do you remember any of the guys?" My stomach turns, and I take another sip of my water, hoping it will settle. "Do you remember any of the guys I was with that night?"

"No." She twirls her fork around in the bowl, picking up a spiral of angel hair pasta covered in a white sauce. I stare at her with tears of frustration threatening to fall from my eyes, but then she continues. "There weren't any guys, Nyla. You were so out of it, you couldn't stand. The guy who paid Beau to bring us as entertainment refused to let you in, so I stayed with you in the car while you slept it off."

The moment my brain processes those words, every doubt, every worry, every shame, every fear about not being worthy of this new life I've created for myself, dissolve into a puddle of nothingness at my feet, leaving me ready and open to walk into a bright and loving future with Sebastian.

The one he's been hinting at since we first kissed.

The one I dream about every night when I fall asleep in his arms.

The one the ring I found in his sock drawer this morning tells me is going to be made a reality sooner rather than later.

* * *

AFTER I LEAVE BIANCA, I don't feel like going home, so I have Jared and Russ take me to the nearest mall where I spend a good bit of Sebastian's money on baby clothes and random items I'm not sure we'll need. Now that we're closing in on week twelve of pregnancy, and inching further and further away from the threat of miscarriage, I'm starting to get excited.

To feel more hopeful and less afraid.

Somewhere between buying onesies and purchasing a stroller the sales lady kept referring to as the Rolls Royce of infant transportation, I decide that tonight is the night Sebastian and I make the pending arrival of a new Adler known to the world. Once I have the thought in my mind, I run with it, grabbing all kinds of stuff that can be used to make a pregnancy announcement, and hoping that when Sebastian gets home, he'll be able to help me sort through them all to find the best one.

When it's all said and done, I leave the mall with enough bags to take up the trunk and cover half of the backseat. I end up needing all four of my security guards to get everything into the penthouse.

"You can leave it all right here," I say, gesturing to the large dining table in the center of the living area. "Sebastian and I will wade through it all when he gets home."

"Sounds good," Russ replies as he rolls the stroller through the door and parks it by the table. Just seeing it in our space makes flutters of excitement roll through me.

"Thanks for your help, guys." I split an appreciative smile between the four of them. "Why don't you guys take off? I'm in for the rest of the night, so I don't need you."

Tyler glances at Russ, and I see the silent plea in his eyes. "What do you think, boss?"

Russ rubs at the back of his neck with one hand. "I don't know, Nadia, we're not supposed to—"

"Leave me alone in my own home?" I ask, a teasing smile tilting my lips. "You know as well as I do that there's no where safer for me than inside these walls, so take your men and go. You guys deserve a night off."

Before any of them can protest again, I start shooing them out of the door. They leave me in a mixed cloud of reluctance and excitement, and when I close the door after them, soaking up the first true silence I've experienced in a while, I breathe a sigh of relief and head over to the table to start unpacking things.

I'm halfway through the first bag when my energy starts to wane, and my brain starts flirting with the idea of a bubble bath. Never one to pass up an opportunity to spend time in the giant soaker tub, I drop a onesie that says 'First grandchild coming soon' onto the table and head for the bathroom.

The moment I enter our bedroom, something feels off, and I pause just inside the threshold and look around the room, finding, to my great relief, that there's nothing out of place.

"You're just being paranoid, Nadia," I murmur to myself as I move into the bathroom. Even though I'm sure that's true, I still check behind the door before I close it and turn the faucet on. When the water starts to steam, I shed my clothes, leaving them in a heap on the floor that I'm trying to muster up the energy to bend over and pick up when the bathroom door creaks open.

"Hey, you're home early." I turn, expecting to see Sebastian, to fall head first into those familiar twin pools of champagne. What I see instead, shocks me to my core, sends tremors of fear down my spine and forces my heart into a free fall that ends in my stomach.

"What are you doing here?" I ask Vince, shrinking under the sickening weight of his gaze as it runs over my naked frame. The instinct to cover myself is strong, but I find that I can't move, that I can't do anything except stare at him, taking in the hate in his eyes, noting how it's etched itself into his features.

"I brought you a present," he says. His eyes are wild and unfocused as they run greedy passes over my body. Over my breasts and nipples, skating down my belly to the apex of my thighs and lingering on a scar he lied about having seen in person. It doesn't seem to matter now, knowing that he lied before, because the conversation I had with Bianca feels like it happened in another life, and in this life, in this ugly reality, I'm alone with a man who hates me, with a man who has already decided that he's going to hurt me.

"You need to leave, Vince. Sebastian will kill you if he finds you here. You need to go. Now."

To my surprise, he does start moving. And for a second, I think the stumble to the right he does is voluntary. The beginning of him doing the smart thing for once and running for his life. But then I realize that the stumble wasn't intentional on Vince's part, that it was caused by a rough hand on his shoulder, shoving him out of the way to make room for a more terrifying figure in the door frame.

When Vince was standing in front of me, I was too scared to move, but now that Beau is standing in front of me, I'm terrified by what will happen to me and my baby if I stay still. I stumble backwards, tripping over my clothes and landing on the floor with a strangled gasp. Beau's razor thin lips pull into a tight, triumphant smile as he stands over me. I gaze up the long line of his body, at his clenched fist and the gold signet ring with an M in the center, and eyes that sparkle with delight and destruction, and I know.

I know that he's come to make good on his promise to kill me.

40

SEBASTIAN

The first thing I notice when I walk through the door is how quiet it is. Nadia usually always has some form of noise going, whether it's Desiree on speaker phone while she prepares a snack in the kitchen, music playing while she's folding clothes or the TV on while she lays on the couch, there's always something happening, so it strikes me as odd that when I come home, I'm greeted by nothing but silence.

The second thing I notice is the shopping bags on the dining table and the stroller parked beside it. It's enough to distract me from the silence, to pull me over to the table, where I look through several of the bags and see baby clothes as well as a wide range of items meant to announce a pregnancy to family members. My favorite thing is the onesie Nadia left sitting on the table because I know she bought it with my parents in mind. I clutch it between my fingers as I move toward the bedrooms to find her and ask if this means that we can finally tell people.

Our room is empty, but the bathroom door is cracked and there's water running, which means she's probably about to take a bath. I push the door open with a smile on my face that dies a quick and painful death when I see her on the floor, curled into a ball with her arms around her stomach. The onesie falls from my hand, and I watch in horror as the white cotton flutters to the ground, landing in a puddle of water tinged red with Nadia's blood.

"*Oh, baby*," I sink to my knees and crawl over to her, afraid to touch her because she's so still and I'm scared she might be cold to the touch, because I don't know where the blood is coming from and I don't want to make it worse.

God, could it get any worse?

Her lip is swollen and bleeding, her face is bruised. Everything is bruised. I ghost fingers over her side, noting the angry flares of blue and purple under her skin, and I don't even realize that I'm crying until I taste the salt of my tears on my lips. I don't even realize I'm screaming for help until the bathroom is filled with the voices of my two security guards—Bruce and Kendall—coming from behind me. I throw myself over Nadia's bloody and broken form, shielding her from their eyes.

"What the fuck happened?" Bruce asks, holstering his gun.

I can't answer him even though I know exactly what happened: I failed her. I told Nadia she would be safe, I told her I would protect her, and I failed her because Beau got to her. He came into our home, and he hurt her again because I wasn't here.

Kendall drops to his haunches beside me and reaches for Nadia, presumably to check for her pulse because she's so still, but I shove him way. "Get the fuck away from her!"

His eyes go wide as he hits the side of the tub. "We need to know if she's alive."

"Don't fucking touch her," I growl through clenched teeth.

"Sebastian." Bruce runs a hand over his head, everything about his tone and posture indicating that he's about to try to reason with a mad man. "We won't touch her, but we need to know if she's alive. We need to get her some help, okay?"

Kendall pulls out his phone. "I'm going to call 911."

The mention of the police, in even the vaguest of terms, brings me back to myself, back to the part of me that looks at situations like these and thinks several steps ahead. My priority is getting Nadia help, but I won't take her back to the same hospitals that failed her over and over again. I won't let this attempt on her life, on our baby's life, be written off by cops that might still owe the perpetrator a favor or two.

Nadia's health and well being is a private matter that will be handled with care and discretion by a team I trust. And the justice that needs to be exacted on her behalf won't be found in a courtroom, or handed out by some judge who'll take one look at Beau's pale skin and blonde hair and say he's a good boy who made a mistake. It'll be doled out by me, and I won't be fair, diplomatic or judicial.

"No." I shake my head, digging my phone out and unlocking it before tossing it to him. "Chantel McCarthy. You call her and only her, tell her to get here *now*."

The firmness in my tone sets Kendall in motion because he pushes to his feet and starts dialing, walking out of the room to handle the call and tracking water everywhere. Bruce is still behind me, waiting for an order.

"Bruce, grab the robe on the door and hand it to me." He does what I say, averting his eyes from Nadia's body when I sit up to take it from his hand. "And please turn that fucking water off."

"You can't move her," he says, leaning over the tub to shut off the faucet. "Not even to put that robe on her. She could have a spinal injury and moving her will make it worse."

He's right. God, I fucking hate that he's right. I fucking hate that the love of my life is lying here like this, hurt and vulnerable and there's nothing I can do to fix it except drape a fucking robe over her and pray Chantel and her team—a group of doctors with varying areas of expertise that all specialize in concierge care people like me pay an arm and a leg for—get here soon.

A moan that's all pain and sorrow pulls me out of my head and back to Nadia. To her bruised face, to her swollen lips and her rasp of a voice that says my name over and over again.

"I'm here, precious." My hands cradle her head gingerly, and she looks at me with eyes that struggle to focus. "I'm right here."

"*Sebastian.*" Her face crumples as tears skate through the dried blood under her right eye. "It hurts. Everything hurts."

Despite the pain, she still tries to move when I lift off of her, still tries to use her hands to conduct her own examination of her stomach. "I tried to protect the baby. I tried."

Between the tears and her shaking fingers, I'm already in the midst of unraveling. Coming apart in a way that there's no coming back from, but when I look down and realize for the first time that the blood on the floor, the blood mixing with the water from the overflowing tub, the blood soaking into the fabric of my pants, is coming from between her legs, I'm no longer coming apart. I'm completely undone.

And still, I have to hold it together because she doesn't know. She can't know that the life we created is in jeopardy, she can't know that I failed them both so fucking spectacularly.

"I know, baby. I know." I cover her body with mine, careful not to put any of my weight on her when I press a ghost of a kiss to her forehead. "Please don't move, help will be here soon."

"I was so stupid. I sent everyone home, and I was alone." More tears gather in her eyes, and her bottom lip trembles. "I didn't even hear them come in."

"Them?" Any answer she planned to give me is stolen by an interruption in her consciousness and panic winds itself around my ribs. "Nadia? Baby, can you hear me?"

Her eyes flutter open and then close again, but she doesn't answer me. I don't think she can.

"They're in here!"

Kendall's announcement is followed closely by the pounding of several sets of footsteps, and suddenly the bathroom is full of people. Chantel and her team swoop in immediately and someone tries to pull me away from Nadia, but I resist.

"I'm not leaving her."

Chantel places a gloved hand on my shoulder, and I meet her eyes. She's not my doctor, but she is an old friend. We met in middle school and stayed in touch over the years. She's the person I went to when I needed to create the network of doctors I use to provide medical services to the girls at Ludus.

"Sebastian," she says, her voice soft but firm. "You have to give us room to work. You have to give us space to help Nadia, do you understand?"

"And the baby," I mutter as I rise to my feet, backing away slowly even though every muscle in my body is demanding that I stay close. "She's almost twelve weeks pregnant." My voice breaks over the words. I spot the onesie on the floor and bend down to pick it up. The white fabric is now pink, tinged with sorrow and all my regrets.

* * *

HOURS LATER, the onesie is still in my hand, and with every second that passes without Chantel or someone from her team coming to the waiting room of the private hospital they moved Nadia to after they did their initial assessment at home, I grip it tighter.

It's a lifeline. The only tangible thing I have left of the reality I existed in before I walked into that bathroom and everything changed. I can't unsee it. I can't unlearn the harsh truth of my failure, so I just sit with it, letting it crush me.

"You couldn't have known, Seb," Russ says from the chair beside me. Him and the rest of the team were at the hospital when we arrived. I didn't even have the energy to be mad at them for leaving Nadia because I was too busy blaming myself.

I still am.

Which is why instead of responding to Russ, I just grip the onesie tighter and pray. For Nadia. For the baby. For myself because if I lose them, it will destroy what's left of me.

"I know how Beau got in," Russ offers, which piques my interest. I turn my attention to the computer screen he's just aimed in my direction. The footage is from just a few hours ago, somewhere around the time when Nadia was out shopping for baby clothes, and in it Beau is being guided down the hallway that leads to our front door by...

"Is that Vince?" I squint at the footage even though I know I'm seeing it correctly. Even though I know it's my cousin using the key I gave him when I let him stay at my place years ago when his was being fumigated to let the man who abused and exploited Nadia into our home.

"How the fuck do they know each other?"

"They share a drug dealer," Russ says, grimacing as he turns the computer back around. "It didn't come up in my earlier searches for Beau, but I have footage of them arriving and leaving the building together. The plates belong to a low level dealer from Culver City named Amari Paul."

Anger pulses through me in forceful jolts that make it impossible for me to stay seated. Russ watches me pace, his jaw as tense as my shoulders. He's almost as angry as I am, which is good because it means he won't ask any questions when he hears what I'm about to say next.

I pause in front of him. "I need you to do something for me."

"Anything."

"Get me a gun, something efficient and powerful that can't be traced back to me."

His expression shifts from open and willing to hesitant in a matter of seconds. I guess I read him wrong. "Why do you need a gun, Sebastian?"

"Because when you find whatever rock my cousin and Beau are hiding under, I'm going to drag them out by their feet and put a bullet in each of their heads."

It should feel odd, swearing an oath to take two lives while I pray that two others will be saved, but it doesn't. It only feels right. It only feels like the solution to a problem I should have taken care of a long time ago. It only feels like the beginning of penance that I'll be paying to Nadia for the rest of my life.

"Sebastian?"

All thoughts of my lethal promise and the disturbed look on Russ' face cease to matter when I hear Chantel's voice behind me. I rush over to her, desperate for information, for knowledge that won't change Vince and Beau's fate, but will change mine.

"How is she? Is she okay?"

To my absolute joy, Chantel nods. "She's doing great. All of her scans are clear. We just got her settled in her room, and she's sleeping, but I know you want to be back there with her."

She starts to walk down the hall, and I follow, eager to lay eyes on Nadia, to see her face and hear her voice. We're standing outside the door when Chantel pauses and places a hand on my forearm.

"I have to warn you, there's a lot of bruising and her lip is pretty badly swollen."

I bite the inside of my cheek to keep the scream building in my throat from piercing the quiet in the hallway. "I understand."

The courage to ask about the baby eludes me, and it takes me a second to realize that I don't ask because I don't want to know. In just a moment, I'll walk into this hospital room and Nadia's face with tell me everything, her eyes will tell me what we've lost, her lips will utter words that are laced with blame. But right now, outside in the hallway, I can imagine that there are two miracles waiting for me on the other side of this door, not one who might hate me, who might send me away the second she sees me.

"Ready?" Chantel asks, her long fingers gripping the handle on the door.

I'm not ready, but I nod anyway. The door swings open, revealing Nadia's prone form in an oversized hospital bed that swallows her whole. Chantel didn't lie when she said the bruises were bad. They're everywhere. On her face, her neck, her arms. And there are so many wires. An IV in her hand, a blood pressure cuff wrapped around her bicep and a blue, elastic band wrapped around her midsection with a small white clip attached to it.

It's only as I'm looking at that strap that I hear it.

The thump, thump, thump of our baby's heartbeat filling the room.

41

NADIA

God started answering my prayers again.

I don't know when He decided to tune back in to my life, but I'm glad He did because otherwise I wouldn't be alive and neither would my baby. Beau came there to kill us. I saw the determination in his eyes when he stood over me, felt it in the force of his fist the first time it collided with my face and in every punch and kick that followed. By some miracle, and for reasons I'll never understand, he didn't follow through with his plan. Maybe he thought I was dead. Vince certainly seemed to think so because when he dragged Beau out of the bathroom, and back to whatever circle of hell they both somehow reside in, he kept saying it.

You killed her. Fuck, Beau, you fucking killed her.

I didn't think I was dead, but I did think I was dying, and for the first time since my parents died, I shunned death. Ran from it. Hid from it. Sought out life and found it inside me, nestled in my womb. I curled myself around it and waited, praying to be found, to be saved, praying to *live*.

Almost two weeks later, and I'm still healing, still hurting, still grateful for the pain that means I'm alive and the man who got me to the people that made sure it stayed that way. Sebastian hasn't left my side since the day of the incident, which is as adorable as it is annoying. Adorable because he cares so much. Annoying because I can't so much as change the channel on the TV without him asking why I'm holding the remote.

I know that he's concerned, but I'm feeling smothered, which is why I'm currently shuffling down the hallway towards our bedroom on my own while he's in his office having some top secret meeting with Russ that apparently couldn't wait until after the shower Sebastian promised to help me with when we got home from the hospital this evening.

Common sense says I should wait for Sebastian because I haven't done this much physical activity in weeks, but the itching and the smell coming from my scalp says going another moment without hot water and a ton of shampoo might finish the attempt Beau made on my life. I find myself wishing for Zoe's skillful hands and gentle laughter as the full scope of what I'm about to do hits me. Winded just from walking down the hall, I pause just outside the closed door of the room Sebastian and I share and try to catch my breath, realizing that I don't just miss Zoe's hands, I miss Zoe. And Madeline, and Luca. I miss Andreas and Everett and Desiree.

I miss everyone and everything that makes my life in New Haven feel whole.

When they learned about the attack, and the dialed back version of the secrets from my past that led to it, everyone reached out, sending flowers and well wishes, offering to get on the next flight to Los Angeles to sit at my bedside and give Sebastian a break. He shut those offers down, knowing I wouldn't want anyone to see me all bruised and banged up, and that it would be hard to keep the news about the baby under wraps with everyone hovering inside my hospital room.

After all the bleeding, which led to me being diagnosed with placenta previa, Sebastian and I both agreed to wait a little longer to share the news of the pregnancy with our family and friends. With all of my other business out in the open, it feels nice to have at least one secret between us.

"What are you doing back here?" Sebastian asks from behind me, causing me to nearly jump out of my skin. I turn toward him with wide eyes and a repentant smile that does nothing to dislodge the disapproving frown pulling the corners of his mouth down.

"Looking for you?"

He cocks a brow. "Did you suddenly forget where the office is?"

"No." I cross my arms and lean against the wall, trying to look casual even though Sebastian is seeing right through me and it suddenly hurts to breathe and stand at the same time. "Why would you ask that?"

"Because you walked right past it, precious."

"Oh."

Sebastian shakes his head, closing the space between us just in time to catch me when the pain in my ribs makes me light headed. He scoops me up in his arms, cradling me gently against his chest.

"You were supposed to wait for me to help you shower, baby. You promised you would."

I let my head rest in the crook of his neck and sigh. "I know, but I couldn't take the itching any longer."

"Itching?" he asks, turning around and heading away from our bedroom.

"Yes, my scalp is itchy, Sebastian, I need to wash my hair."

"I'm going to wash your hair for you, precious."

"Then why are you carrying me away from our room?"

We're passing through the living area now, heading to the other side of the penthouse where the guest bedrooms are. I haven't spent any time back here, and as far as I can tell, Sebastian doesn't either.

"Because I had all of our stuff moved over here," he says, kicking the door to a bedroom that's similar and size and layout to ours open. "I couldn't go back in that room," he continues as he carries me into the bathroom and carefully lowers me onto the counter between the dual sinks. "And I figured you wouldn't want to either."

"I didn't," I admit, watching him move over to the bathtub and turn on the faucet. I stare at the stream of water as it starts to steam, and my brain shifts between the present in the past in rapid flashes that steal my breath.

"Hey," Sebastian murmurs, suddenly standing in front of me. "You okay?"

I swallow hard, pushing down the lump of emotion in my throat. "I think so."

"You don't have to be," he reminds me, reaching up to remove the hair tie holding my dirty tresses in a sad ponytail. I tilt my head back, leaning into his touch as he massages my scalp. "You can be sad and scared and angry. You can be whatever you need to be with me."

The deep timbre of his voice and the gentleness of his hands makes me feel safe enough to surrender to the memories I've been pushing away for days.

"I was running a bath when they came. At first it was just Vince, and I was naked, and the way he looked at me just made me feel... dirty."

"He won't ever lay eyes on you again. He'll never make you feel that way again."

His breath is a warm caress over my face, and I revel in it, allowing it to make me feel brave enough to tell Sebastian about the conversation Vince and I had on Thanksgiving. I open my eyes and settle a solemn gaze on Sebastian's face.

"The way he made me feel that day paled in comparison to how he made me feel on Thanksgiving."

Sebastian's brows pull together. "What do you mean? I thought you two didn't talk."

"I lied."

"Why?"

"Because Vince knew my real name, and he knew about my past. He used that information to make me believe that we slept together at a party I couldn't remember going to, let alone working at."

I know now that the information Vince used to manipulate me, including the details about my scar, were given to him by Beau. Sebastian explained their connection to me a few days after the incident, telling me all about how a chance meeting at a party thrown by their shared drug dealer led to them discovering the link between Vince and Sebastian and Beau and me.

The sigh Sebastian lets out is heavy, world weary, and I feel bad for dropping this bomb on him when he's been living in an extended state of stress for weeks now.

"That fucking bastard. Why didn't you tell me?"

"I was ashamed, Sebastian. I felt like my past was closing in on all sides and it was going to cost me everything, that it was going to cost me you."

Rain clouds descend over his face, turning his eyes stormy as he caresses my cheek with gentle fingertips. "When I fell in love with you, I chose to love all of you. Your past. Your present. Your future. All of it. I don't care what you've done or who you've been with. Who's hurt you or who you've hurt. You're mine, Nadia, and there's nothing in this world you could do or have done that would make me stop loving you."

I'm so sick of crying. It feels like it's all I do these days, but there's no stopping the happy tears that slip out of the corner of my eyes because of Sebastian's words. He brushes each one away with the pads of his thumbs and leans in to take my mouth in a kiss that wants to turn deeper even though we both know we can't let it. Sebastian breaks first, pulling away with a regretful smile.

"Let's get your hair washed, precious."

The offer is too tempting for me to delay it any further, so I slide off the counter gingerly and lift my arms in a silent request for Sebastian to remove my t-shirt. He obliges, making quick work of my clothes and then stripping down himself. Moments later, we're both soaking in the warm water of the bath. My back to Sebastian's front as he lathers shampoo in his hands and scrubs my scalp clean.

"Mhmmm," I hum, leaning back into his touch. "That feels so good."

Sebastian's dick pulses against my thigh, and I laugh, which makes it pulse again. "Nadia," he growls, his voice a mix of admonishment and desire. "Behave, please."

"I'm not doing anything!"

"You're moaning and squirming around in my lap. You know that shit makes my dick hard."

"Me breathing makes your dick hard, Sebastian."

He kisses my shoulder. "That's how it's supposed to be."

"I miss sex," I murmur breathlessly. "Being on pelvic rest sucks."

"It does." His hands trail down my body until they come to rest on my stomach. "But it'll all be worth it when this little one comes into the world safe and sound, right?"

"Right," I agree, resting my head against his shoulder and closing my eyes.

"Tired?"

"Exhausted."

"Sit up, precious, I need to finish with your hair."

I try to keep my head upright. Really, I do, but as he works, my head lolls and my eyes struggle to stay open. Sebastian doesn't complain, probably because he knows there's no point. He just keeps moving from one step to the next, rinsing out the shampoo, adding in conditioner, detangling my matted tresses and rinsing again. Then he stands us up and starts the shower, washing us both off with quick and efficient strokes of his large hands over both of our bodies.

After the shower, he carries me to bed and rubs me down with lotion before pulling a loose night gown over my head and brushing my hair back into a loose bun. The tender way he cares for me brings tears to my eyes once again, and I sink back into the pillows of the bed with a full heart and a scalp that is finally itch free.

Sebastian stands at the edge of the bed, pulling on his own clothes. I watch him get dressed between heavy blinks that get longer with each passing second, noticing that the clothes he's chosen aren't meant for sleeping.

"Where are you going?" I ask, slightly alarmed because he hasn't left my side in days.

"I have some work to do," he says, leaning down to press a kiss to my forehead.

I reach up, wrapping my arms around his neck to attempt to pull him down onto the bed. "Will you stay with me until I fall asleep?"

"Of course I will, precious." He sinks into the mattress next to me, and I roll over, turning my back to him and resting my hand on my stomach. Sebastian's hand covers mine, and I smile, sighing contentedly before slipping off into a peaceful sleep.

42

SEBASTIAN

I hold Nadia for close to an hour just to make sure she's fully asleep, and then I slip out of bed. I told her I had work to do, but what I didn't tell her is that the work has nothing to do with any of my businesses and everything to do with the two lives it's my responsibility to end.

When I got Nadia home from the hospital this evening, Russ pulled me into my office and gave me an address to a run down apartment building where Beau and Vince have apparently been holed up, hiding from me. As I walk down the dark alley behind the building that smells faintly of piss, I smile to myself, wondering how the two of them could be this dumb. Beau doesn't know me, not yet at least, but Vince does. He knows how single minded I am. He knows that once I decide to do something, I won't stop until the task is complete. That once someone or something has my attention, there's no corner of this Earth dark or remote enough to hide them from me.

This building is both dark and remote, and judging by the silence in the hallways, it's also probably abandoned, which is good for me. It means there won't be any witnesses, no one to remember a man dressed in all black with a glock in his hand and murderous intent on his face as he stalked the halls alone. Russ insisted on coming with me, but I needed him with Nadia, watching over her while I wipe Beau Montgomery and the threat he poses to her life off of the face of the planet.

I find him exactly where Russ said he'd be, in the apartment at the end of the hall on the third floor. He jumps to his feet when I bust through the door, the gun in my hand already aimed at his head. Most people would go for center mass, riddle his torso with bullets until they emptied the clip, but I'm aiming for efficiency and that many shots would be loud and leave an even bigger mess for the cleaning crew I have coming in behind me.

"I was wondering when you'd come," Beau says, blue eyes glittering with excitement because idiots like him thrive on chaos. He tilts his head to the side, sizing me up as his greasy blonde strands fall into his eyes. "You're shorter than I thought you'd be."

"And you're exactly what I thought you'd be."

"Nyla's told you a lot about me then?" He licks his lips when he says her name, and the finger I have on the trigger twitches.

"Don't say her name."

"Why not? All she could do when I was beating her ass was scream yours. She thought you were going to save her." The laugh that passes through his lips turns my vision red. "Vince and I both got a kick out of that. We laughed about it for days. We probably would have still been laughing when you got here, but as you can see—" he gestures grandly at the couch in the corner of the room where my cousin is passed out with a needle in his arm "—he's not really in the laughing mood right now."

It takes me all of five seconds to realize that Vince isn't breathing.

"He's dead."

Beau glances at Vince and then back at me, blowing what's supposed to be a regretful breath out between his thin lips. "Damn, sorry for your loss."

He's getting a kick out of this. I can tell by the gleeful crinkle of the corners of his eyes. By the way he's barely containing a laugh as he searches my face for any trace of pain. He wants me to be hurt, to be broken up by the death of a man I came here to kill.

I take great pleasure in showing him how truly indifferent I am. I shrug, my features still and stoic. "It's not my loss. Vince was a waste of skin, and the only person in this world who will miss him is his mother, but even she will get over it eventually."

"Still, that's gotta suck, huh? Only being able to turn one of us in to the cops."

"Cops?" I laugh, and it's a dark and lethal sound. "Who said anything about the cops?"

For the first time since we've come face to face, I see a flicker of fear pass over Beau's haggard features, and now I'm smiling because he's finally realized that I'm not the man he thought I was.

That I didn't come here to make a citizen's arrest and haul him off to jail.

That I'm not some misguided soul seeking justice through the judicial system.

He looks into my eyes, and he sees that the only things I believe in are the bullets in this gun and the ease with which I'll pull the trigger.

I step closer, and his hands go up as he backs into the wall. The way he stumbles backwards makes me think of Nadia doing the same thing, of her backing away, running from violence he was so intent to bestow upon her.

"Hey, man, you don't want to do this," Beau's voice shakes, and I laugh again because he has no idea, does he? He doesn't know that I've been dreaming of this moment since before I even knew his name or the sorry story of his life. He doesn't know that the moment I laid eyes on Nadia, the threads of our fates intertwined, and I became her justice and his reckoning.

"Yes, I *really* do."

43

NADIA

I wake with a start, sore and disoriented because for the first few seconds of consciousness, my brain forgets that I'm no longer in the hospital room. I lie still, allowing the details of the day to wash over me. Coming home from the hospital in the early evening. Trying to sneak and take a shower on my own. Bathing with Sebastian while he washed my hair and then falling asleep in bed beside him.

Before he got into bed, he said he had some work to do, so I slip out from in between the covers and pad through the halls of the penthouse toward his office, trying not to be triggered by the eerie quiet that reminds me of the day of the attack. Pushing out steadying breaths, I open Sebastian's office door, expecting to find him sitting behind the large oak desk working on some time sensitive problem only he can solve and letting out a sharp gasp when I find the room empty.

"Babe?" I call out, leaving the office to check the kitchen even though I know from the first time I passed through it, that it's empty.

"Nadia?" The sound of Russ' voice causes me to nearly jump out of my skin, and I spin around to find him walking through the front door. "Everything okay?"

"Yeah, I was just looking for Sebastian. What are you doing here?"

Russ shifts on his feet, looking uncomfortable. "Seb had to step out for a minute."

"Oh." There's something odd about his expression, about the deliberate vagueness that answers my question but not really. I walk around to the fridge and pull out two bottles of water, keeping one for myself and sliding the other over to Russ who's now standing on the opposite side of the island. "Did he say how long he'd be?"

"No, but he should be back any minute now." He takes the water bottle between his large palms and holds it there without opening it. "You feeling okay?"

"Yeah, I'm good."

"And the baby?"

I take a small sip of my water and run a hand over my stomach. "Doing great as far as I know."

"Listen—" Russ starts, but I shake my head, already knowing what he's about to say. I've gotten the same speech, in some form or another, from every member of my security detail over the last few weeks. Tyler was the first to make it, lamenting over eager he was to leave that day because he was hungover and needed the rest. Then came Enzo and Jared, who expressed his regrets over not clearing the penthouse before they left me. Russ is last, and as the team leader and the only member of the detail who knew me before, I know the situation is weighing heavily on him, so I waste no time absolving him of his guilt.

"You don't have to apologize. At the end of the day the only people responsible for what happened to me are Vince and Beau, and one day, they'll get what's coming to them. I don't know when or how, but I have to believe that. I have to believe that I'm not bringing a child into a world where the karmic scales always balance out in the favor of low lives like those two."

Russ rubs at his chin, another strange look on his face. "I appreciate you saying that, but I still want you to know that I won't ever forgive myself for the way things went down. It won't ever happen again."

Any response I might have given him is blocked by the lump of emotion forming in my throat. It's always there these days, when I'm reminded that I have so many people in my life who love and care for me. People who know my past and have literally seen my bruises and still want me around.

And the man leading the pack, the one who started the trend of goodness in my life, just walked through the door.

Russ and I look up when we hear the front door close, but I only I seem to be surprised by the gun he's just pulled out of his waistband. Russ just walks over and takes it from him, removing the magazine and examining the remaining rounds inside it.

"Sixteen." Russ looks at Sebastian's hard features. "You only fired once?"

Sebastian's eyes land on me, and he must see the horror on my face because he hesitates before responding, averting his gaze from me as he says, "Once was all I needed."

I lose my grip on the water bottle in my hand, and it lands on the counter with a heavy thud, the cold liquid splashes up, wetting my night gown and sending a chill through my entire body.

"You shot someone?"

Sebastian and Russ share a look, and I watch the silent communication with frustration clawing at my chest. I need answers, and I need them now because there's a gun in Russ' hand that Sebastian fired, and they're both so calm it makes me feel like I'm losing my mind.

"What's going on, Sebastian?" I ask, my shrill voice laced with panic and confusion as I step around the island and go to him. He reaches for me with the same hand he was just holding the gun in, and I know that I'm crazy, that I'm past the point of common sense, because I'm almost certain he just killed someone and I don't even attempt to back away. I take his hand and let him lead me into the office. Russ doesn't follow, so when the door to the office closes, it's just Sebastian and me in the room with my fear.

"Sit down, precious," he urges, his hand on my shoulder to encourage me to lower myself into the seat. I do as he says, though I'm moving slowly, my eyes on his face.

"Sebastian. You have to tell me what's going on because I'm freaking the fuck out here."

He drops down onto his haunches between my legs and takes my trembling hands in his. "Everything is okay, Nadia. You don't have to freak out."

Why is he so calm?

How is he so calm?

I don't get it. I don't get anything right now.

"Of course I have to freak out," I hiss. "You came home with a gun in your hand. I've never even heard you talk about a gun and now you know how to fire them? And you *shot someone?*"

"Beau, I shot Beau."

Now things make even less sense.

"When did you…how did you find Beau?"

"Russ found him."

"Did he also give you the gun?"

Sebastian nods, his eyes trailing over my face, cataloging every reaction to the information he's giving me. "Yes, Russ gave me the gun."

"And you used it to shoot Beau."

This is the part that makes the least sense to me. The gun I can wrap my head around. Russ helping with procuring the gun tracks. Sebastian coming face to face with Beau is where it all falls apart. I can't picture the two of them in the same room, but I should have known this would happen. I should have known that after the attack Sebastian wouldn't let it rest.

"I used it to *kill* Beau," he says, countering one hard to accept statement with another. I shake my head, tears of disbelief and fear cascading down my cheeks.

"No," I whimper. "Sebastian, no. You didn't. Tell me you're joking."

His brows pull together, and I read confusion and maybe even a bit of anger in his eyes. He doesn't understand why I'm upset, why I would shed tears for a man who spent the last decade abusing me. The tears aren't for Beau, though.

They're for Sebastian.

They're for me.

They're for the child I'll have to raise on my own because their father squandered his life and freedom on erasing a man who wasn't worth the time or effort.

"You didn't kill him, right? Please tell me you didn't kill him."

Instead of answering me, Sebastian lets go of my hand and reaches into his pocket, pulling out a small piece of gold jewelry that he places in the palm of my hand. With quivering breaths and a pounding heart, I look down and find a signet ring with a M in the middle.

It's Beau's ring.

"Oh, God," I wail, dropping it on the ground. "Sebastian. Do you understand what you've done? Do you know what this means?"

"Yes, Nadia, it means that he won't ever hurt you again."

He's right. Beau is dead, and the cloud of darkness his life has cast over my head for almost half of my life has disappeared. But that doesn't matter to me right now.

"That's true, Sebastian, but it also means you're going to prison. That you won't get to be there when our baby is born. That you'll spend the rest of your life behind bars, away from the family you've risked everything to protect. Did you even consider that when you tracked him down and *murdered* him in cold blood?"

Both of his hands come up, and he cradles my face between warm palms. "Of course, I considered it, precious. I considered everything. I had a plan in place before I stepped foot inside the building where he and Vince were hiding out."

"Vince?" I swallow the bile rising up in my throat, picturing Sebastian's aunt's face and the features she shares with his mother seconds before images of Vince's corpse fill my mind. "Vince was there too?"

"Yes, but he was dead when I arrived. A drug overdose."

But the look in his eyes tells me that if he wasn't, there would have been two bullets missing from that gun. Two life sentences waiting to come crashing down on Sebastian's head, upending his life, tarnishing his legacy, leaving me alone to raise our child and navigate the fractured remnants of his family.

It should bother me that the potential jail time is all that's bothering me. Everything else— the gun, the body he dropped, the signet ring on the floor by my feet—ranks low on my list of concerns. I don't care about any of it. I just care about him, about losing yet another good thing in my life because of Beau fucking Montgomery.

"I can't lose you, Sebastian." I push to my feet, biting my bottom lip as I start to pace the length of the office. "I don't want to lose you."

"You won't lose me, precious," he says, standing as well.

"You don't know that! You can't know that! After they find his body, all it will take is one witness, one person to say they saw your car or your face at the scene of the crime, and then it's all over."

There's no fear on his face. No concern. No regret. He folds his arms across his chest, and it's then that I notice that his clothes are different. He must have changed before he came home.

"They won't find a body because there's no body to find," Sebastian says, and the calm in his tone settles my nerves a bit.

"What does that mean?"

"It means that after I killed Beau, I had his body taken to a funeral home and cremated. He's nothing more than ash now, precious."

I pause, and the last of the anxiety making my muscles tight melts away. "So, he's gone?"

Sebastian nods, and tears well in my eyes. "He's gone, precious. He can't hurt you anymore. And nothing is going to take me away from you or the baby. We're going to have a long, beautiful life together, Nadia."

A world without Beau in it.

It feels unreal.

I've spent so much of my life afraid of Beau, locked in the prison of fear he built around me. All this time I thought he was the only one who had a key, the only one with the power to free me, but as I look at Sebastian, at the sincerity in his eyes and soak up the certainty in his tone, I realize that was never true.

After the accident, I ran towards freedom, towards life even when I wasn't sure I wanted to live, and then I collided with Sebastian and he did the rest. He saw the shroud of shame and the painful, hopeless cocoon I'd built around myself and used gentle hands and patient fingers to massage it open, to coax me out.

He watched with eager eyes as I took leaps of faith that taught me things I thought could never be true about me again. And when I took flight—eyes alight with fear and wonder because I forgot what it felt like to soar—he rejoiced along with me.

And when Beau came back, snatching me from the sky with violent hands to try and shove me back into that prison, Sebastian took a sledgehammer to every cinder block wall. He demolished the threat.

He set me free.

He released me, once and for all.

I go to him, crossing the room on shaky legs and wobbly knees that give out the moment I'm within his reach. He opens his arms, catching me by the waist and pull me into him, welcoming me into the solace of his embrace, into the salvation of his love, into a life full of peace and absent of fear.

44

SEBASTIAN

Four months later

"**S**ebastian, I can't drink wine for another three months, so why do you insist on torturing me by making me pick out bottles for everyone else to enjoy at my baby shower?" Nadia asks from the center of the cellar I started building after her first visit to my parent's house where she fell in love with theirs.

It was my intention to show it to her when I came clean about living in the unit down the hall from hers, but we never made it through the door. I would have been more upset about the delay if it didn't work out so well. My initial plan was to bring her into the converted pantry space and tell her all about how I tracked down the bottles left in circulation from Thornehill Vineyards, so we could start our joint wine collection with her parents' legacy at the forefront.

Having to wait weeks to get her back to New Haven and back to my place, meant I didn't have to tell her about my plan, I got to show her it in action. I got to watch happy tears swell in her eyes and reap the benefits of her gratitude right then and there.

We haven't spent much time in the cellar since then, but tonight, while our home—which is finally the beautiful meshing of our two units—is being over run with our family and friends, I'm eager to have her in here.

Not because I need her help selecting a wine for everyone to drink.

But because here, in our home, among the only tangible representation of Corrine and Maxwell Hawthorne's life and legacy, aside from their beautiful daughter, is the one place that felt right to me when I pictured getting down on one knee and asking Nadia to be my wife.

"I'm not trying to torture you, precious, I just wanted an expert opinion."

"And a view of my ass," she huffs, glancing over her shoulder to pin me with a knowing look. I'm leaning against the counter closest to the door where she keeps all her decanting and wine filtering gadgets, trying to act casual even though the ring box in my pocket is burning a hole in my pants.

"That's just an added bonus." I grin at her, and she rolls her eyes, turning her attention back to the shelves surrounding us.

"Why don't you just do this rosé?" She gestures to the clear bottle with pale pink liquid inside of it on the shelf closest to her, not even bothering to look at the label or ask what exactly I'm trying to pair the wine with. It's a tell tale sign that she's agitated, and I need to hurry up before she storms out of here and finds the nearest chair to sit down.

"Hmmm." I tap my lips. "What about the '93 Thornehill Pinot Noir?"

She turns to glare at me, moving so fast I'm surprised she didn't crack her neck. "You seriously think I'm going to let you open that bottle today when I can't even drink it?"

"You could probably have a small sip."

Her eyes narrow. "You're joking right?"

"Nope. I think we've let it sit long enough."

I push off the counter, pretending to head toward the shelf that holds the bottle in question because I know it will make her move over to it too.

"Don't even think about it, Adler." She snatches it off the shelf, and her expression goes from surly to startled when she sees the envelope taped to bottle. It's thick and white and it has her name written on it in my handwriting. "What is this?"

I shrug. "Open it and see, precious."

The room is quiet as she remove the envelope from the bottle and puts it back in its coveted place on the shelf. As she pulls the paper out, pools of caramel rushing over the deed for the house and land in Sonoma her parents raised her on, I lower myself to the ground, kneeling in front of her with an open ring box in my hand.

"Oh, my God," she whispers, still looking at the paper. When she moves it away from her face and finds me down on one knee, the whisper becomes a scream that she quiets with a hand over her mouth. "Sebastian, what are you doing?"

"Finding out if you've had enough time to prepare your heart for what mine wants to ask of it," I say, transporting us back to that first day in Zoe's office, to that first time we trusted the moment to hold us instead of letting it break.

Tears slips down her cheeks, and she nods. It's all the confirmation I need to continue.

"I wanted to be able to give you more than a ring today. I wanted to be able to promise you more than a life of financial stability and unconditional love. I'll give you all of those things too, but more than anything, I wanted to give you back your home as a way to thank you for being mine. You're my safe place, Nadia. My sanctuary. This ring is a promise that I'll always be those things for you too. That as long as I'm alive, you'll never have to face another day, another battle, another obstacle, another choice on your own because I will always be there to protect you, to support you, to love you. Do you believe that?"

"Yeah," she gasps, the sound mixing with a joyful laugh. "I believe that."

"Then will you please do me the honor of being my wife?"

Her answer is a crush of her lips against mine. It's a deposit of salt and moisture and the sweet taste of her mouth. And while it's lovely, I need more. I pull back, breaking the kiss to gaze up into her beautiful face.

"Is that a yes, Miss Hendrix?"
"That's a hell yes, Mr. Adler."

The End

ALSO BY J.L. SEEGARS

Restore Me: The New Haven Series (Book #1)

Again: A Marriage Redemption Novella

Revive Me Part One: The New Haven Series (Book #2)

Revive Me Part Two: The New Haven Series (Book #2)

Revive Me Part Three: The New Haven Series (Book #2)

ABOUT THE AUTHOR

J.L. Seegars is a dedicated smut peddler and lifelong nerd who's always had a love of words, storytelling and drama. When she isn't writing messy and emotionally complex characters like the ones she grew up around, she's watching reality TV, supporting her fellow authors by devouring their work or spending time with her husband and son.